Rory's Promise

MICHAELA MACCOLL · ROSEMARY NICHOLS

CALKINS CREEK
AN IMPRINT OF HIGHLIGHTS
Honesdale, Pennsylvania

For *"Auntie Sis"*
Sister Norine Estelle Nichols
1916–2013

Calkins Creek
An Imprint of Highlights
815 Church Street
Honesdale, Pennsylvania 18431
Printed in the United States of America
ISBN: 978-1-62091-623-0
Library of Congress Control Number: 2014935295
First edition

10 9 8 7 6 5 4 3 2 1

Design by Barbara Grzeslo
Production by Margaret Mosomillo
The text of this book is set in Garamond 3.

To the Sisters of the House,
Necessity compels me to part with my darling
boy. I leave him, hoping and trusting that you
will take good care of him. Will you let some
good nurse take charge of him and will you try
to find some kind hearted lady to adopt him
and love him as her own. . . . It would break
my heart to have him grow up without a mother
to love and care for him.

A letter to the Foundling Hospital, July 1870

PART ONE

New York

CHAPTER ONE

A CHILD'S CRY, SHARP AND FEARFUL, STARTLED RORY AWAKE. Her eyes darted about the shadowy dormitory. It was still dark outside; dawn was some hours away. Was it the new boy, Harry? He'd been found under a railroad bridge living on what the rats left, and he often woke with nightmares. But he usually howled. More likely it was Violet, Rory's own sister.

After three years of minding the little kids, Rory didn't throw back the warm covers just yet. Often the orphans would cry once then fall back asleep. She'd wait for a second cry—and then try to silence that one before the other children woke. Rory pulled the covers up around her chin, enjoying the bite of chill on her face. The Sisters of Charity believed a child needed fresh air at night so until All Saints' Day, otherwise known as the first of November, the windows stayed open.

A hand tugged at Rory's blanket. Holding back a sigh, Rory propped herself up on one elbow and looked into Violet's eyes, bright blue even in the dim light.

"Rory, are you awake?" Violet asked in a lisping whisper. She was five years old to Rory's twelve.

"I am now, you little pest," Rory answered. Her words might be harsh but she had no worries that Violet's feelings would be hurt. To outsiders, Violet might seem sweet and biddable, but Rory knew how tough she could be.

"I have to pee."

"Violet, you're five now. You are old enough to pee without my help," Rory said.

"I'm afraid of the water closet. It's so noisy and I'm scared it will swallow me up!"

"You can pee in the pot and I'll flush it in the morning. That way we won't wake everyone else." Rory swung her feet off the bed onto the tiled floor. She led Violet by the hand to the brand-new water closet down the hall. It was loud, louder even than the new elevated trains on Third Avenue. Violet squatted on the little pot next to the porcelain toilet. Afterward, Rory dumped the contents into the toilet bowl. Violet slipped her hand into Rory's and the two sisters walked together down the long hall.

When they returned, Rory wasn't surprised to find two other children curled up together on her narrow bed.

"What are you lot doing here?" she demanded, pretending to be fierce. "You're supposed to stay in your own beds."

There was no answer from the children. They kept their eyes tightly closed and snored impossibly loudly and with a suspicious regularity.

With a sigh, Rory said, "Hop in, Violet." She shoved the kids this way and that to make room. On the strength of being Rory's real sister, Violet used her sharp elbows to make sure she had the best spot, curled up in the small of Rory's back. Within a few minutes, Rory had been lulled back to sleep by the genuine snores and quick breaths of the three younger children.

"Rory!" A stern voice woke Rory a second time. "The children are supposed to sleep alone." Rory opened her eyes and had to put her hand over her eyes to block the sunlight pouring in. Sister Maureen stood at the foot of her bed. Short and plump, she resembled a dumpling in her white working uniform.

"What children?" Rory asked, rubbing her eyes with her fists. In her experience, this made her look younger, less likely to be scolded. She patted the bed. "What are these rascals doing here?" She began to shake the kids awake. "Honest, Sister Maureen, they weren't here when I went to bed last night."

Sister Maureen shook her head and lifted young Harry out of the bed. "Rory, this is precisely why the older children are moved out of the nursery and into the dormitory. How old are you now?"

The dormitory that Sister Maureen was threatening wasn't too bad. Rory knew the other girls from school and liked them well enough. But the dormitory wouldn't have Violet, and as far as Rory was concerned, that was the end of the argument. Rory leapt out of bed, dislodging Violet, who almost rolled off the bed onto the spotless tiled floor. Catching Violet just in time, Rory stared at Sister Maureen over her sister's head. "I have to stay with Violet. I promised my Ma."

The stern look on Sister Maureen's face began to soften. "Besides," Rory said, pursuing her advantage, "however would you get them all washed and dressed for breakfast if I wasn't here to help?"

Sister Maureen glanced around the long narrow nursery where eighteen beds lined the whitewashed walls. Rory knew exactly what the nun was thinking. Eighteen boys and girls, ages three, four, and five, took a lot of caring for. Usually a Sister and two nurses would be responsible. For the past three years Rory had deliberately carved out a place for herself as an extra caregiver, washer, wiper-upper, hair comber, clothes darner, and the first person the children called in the night. Her position at the Foundling was unique and she fought to keep it every day.

In a cajoling voice, Rory asked, "Please let me help, just a little longer?" She tensed, waiting for an answer. Rory had never once spent a night away from Violet.

"Well . . ."

"Thanks, Sister," Rory said happily, shepherding the sleepy children into a line to use the water closet. As she led them out of the nursery, she heard Sister Maureen's exasperated voice.

"But, Rory, I didn't agree to anything!"

Rory hurried the kids into the hallway. Out of sight was out of Sister Maureen's mind. At least for today, Rory could stay put.

CHAPTER Two

Rory sat down gratefully, already exhausted, and it wasn't even breakfast yet. The children were clean and dressed and off to the dining room on the first floor of the main building. Despite all the morning hurry, Rory had found a few extra seconds to make sure that the purple bow in Violet's curly red hair was placed just so. The time it took was repaid by the sweet kiss Violet gave her as she joined the long queue of children hurrying downstairs to their first meal of the day.

Now Rory finally had some time to herself. Moments alone were rare and to be cherished. Another reason to avoid the dormitory! She braided her long red hair into a neat plait; her fingers had grown nimble taking care of so many small children. Rory slipped into a clean pinafore skirt she had pulled from the dresser she shared with Violet. The skirt fell only a few inches below the knee—too short to be quite respectable. As she tugged on her leather boots, she could see where her big toes had stretched the leather. No wonder her toes always hurt.

What she wouldn't give for a new dress! Or shoes that had never been worn before. There was a scarcity of donated clothing in the nursery box to fit a girl as tall as she, and shoes for her size feet were always in short supply. Rory dared not draw attention to her constantly increasing height because it always led to questions about her age. Girls in the dormitory had clothing that fit—the shoes too. But once Rory admitted that she was growing, the Sisters would insist that she move in with the older kids. The Sisters hated anything that interfered with their rules and sense of order. That was Rory Fitzpatrick in a nutshell. So Rory kept her head down and did what was best for her and Vi.

The street noises grew louder, full of the voices of women and the cries of babies. Tugging at the hem of her skirt, Rory braced herself. Every other day Rory would go to the Foundling school, but not on the first Wednesday of the month. Today was payday for the one thousand wet nurses employed by the Foundling Hospital. The wet nurses had babies of their own at home but they provided mother's milk to orphaned babies for a substantial fee each month. Rory had assumed the duty of ensuring that no one cheated the Sisters. It was just one more way to show the Sisters how much they needed her.

The line of women and babies snaked from the main entrance of the Foundling on East Sixty-Ninth around the corner to Third Avenue. The sight of so many women and babies was remarkable enough that drivers of private cars and carriages slowed down to stare.

Rory began with the women at the front of the line, waiting to enter the building. The first was a woman in her thirties, with a broad face and pale eyes, holding a swaddled baby against her breast.

"Mrs. Healy," she scolded, "little Brian looks pale. Is he getting enough fresh air? The Sisters say that's important."

"Look at you, little miss bossy." Mrs. Healy laughed. "For all you're only thirteen, you talk like one of the nuns."

"I'm just twelve," Rory corrected her.

"You look older."

Rory glanced about to make sure none of the nuns had overheard Mrs. Healy. "Just mind that Brian gets out at least once a day. Your eldest can take him—he's nine now, isn't he?"

"When my eldest gets home from the shoe factory, he's too tired to mind a baby, especially a stranger."

"This stranger," Rory stressed the word, "is worth ten dollars hard cash a month to your family. Remind him of that."

She moved on. The Sisters had never asked her to play policeman to the wet nurses, but Rory knew firsthand how deceitful people could be. It made Rory angry to think of the Sisters being taken advantage of. Babes in the wood, they were. Besides, Rory was the closest person these children had to family. She would take care of them as well as she took care of Violet, as long as she was able.

No trickery caught her eye until she reached Mrs.

O'Flanagan, who had worked with Rory's Ma in the shirt factory before she started taking babies for the Foundling. Mrs. O'Flanagan was an old hand at wet nursing. She always had a baby of her own, so she was happy to take in orphans for the stipend. When she saw Rory, she quickly turned her tall, straight body away from Rory's view.

"Hello, Mrs. O'Flanagan," Rory said loudly. Reluctantly, the wet nurse turned round. "How is Danny?" she asked.

"Just fine," Mrs. O'Flanagan said, in the thick brogue of Ireland. "He's a little love."

"Let me hold him, he's a favorite of mine." Rory planted herself in front of Mrs. O'Flanagan and waited.

"Look at you, grown so tall," Mrs. O'Flanagan said. "You're the spitting image of your mother."

"Thanks, Mrs. O'Flanagan." Now Rory knew something was wrong. Mrs. O'Flanagan and her mother had never gotten along. "But we were talking about Danny."

"Are the Sisters taking good care of you? They promised they would."

"The Sisters don't lie," Rory said. As firmly as she could manage, she said, "Let me see him." She held out her arms.

Mrs. O'Flanagan held tight to the baby. "He's just fallen asleep," she said, looking down severely at Rory.

"I won't wake him," Rory assured her.

Slowly, Mrs. O'Flanagan handed the baby over. Rory snuggled the baby and gave him a kiss on the cheek.

"A lovely babe," Rory said, very quietly so only Mrs. O'Flanagan could hear. "But he's not Danny. He looks like your own boy. Brendan, isn't it? Where's Danny?"

Mrs. O'Flanagan's eyes took on a shifty look.

"Mrs. O'Flanagan, don't lie to me. I know Danny and that's not him." Rory braced herself; so many things could happen to these defenseless babies.

Finally Mrs. O'Flanagan slumped, as though Rory had pricked her and let all the air out. "The babe is just fine, Rory. He's at home. But he's got a rash. A bad one—it fair turns your stomach to look at. The nuns are so fussy they might take him away and I can't afford to lose the money."

"Where's the rash? In the diaper?"

Mrs. O'Flanagan nodded. "And on his back."

"I'm sure it's nothing that an ointment won't cure," Rory said. "Go get Danny and I'll make sure Sister Kathleen is fair with you."

"But I don't want to lose my place!"

"I'll wait in the line for you," Rory said. "But bring Danny right now or else I'll have to tell the Sisters and then you'll lose any chance of working for them again."

"You're fiercer than the nuns, you are. I won't be long," Mrs. O'Flanagan said, but she was already edging past the other mothers. Rory leaned against the wall, knowing she wouldn't have long to wait. Mrs. O'Flanagan lived in a tenement a short horsecar ride away, decent lodging for her family paid for with the money from the Foundling. She knew she had done the right thing. Mrs. O'Flanagan would be back soon with the correct baby.

"Well done." A familiar voice at her back startled Rory.

"I couldn't have handled it better." Rory whirled around to see Sister Anna, the nun in charge of all the children. She had a nose for a lie; all the kids, including Rory, were wary of her.

"Truly?" Rory kept her eyes fixed on Sister Anna's folded hands.

"Tell me, how did you know that baby wasn't Danny? We see so many."

Rory looked up, eager to explain. "Danny has a birthmark here." Rory indicated under her left ear. "But I'm sure the baby is fine. You'll see."

"I believe you, my dear. You've an instinct for the good in people." In a sadder tone, she added, "And the evil."

"After all the Foundling has done for me and Violet, the least I can do is make sure you don't get swindled."

"I don't know what we would do without you, Rory." A slight smile played on Sister Anna's lips. "But shouldn't you be in class?"

"Sister, anyone can do arithmetic, but I'm the only one who knows the difference between Danny and Brendan."

"Just for today, then," Sister Anna conceded. "But I think it's high time we had a talk about your future."

"Now?" Rory gulped.

"Soon." In the way all the nuns had, Sister Anna glided away, almost as if she was skating on ice.

Rory narrowed her eyes as she watched Sister Anna leave. Had Sister Anna finally decided that she was too old to stay in the nursery with Violet? Rory trembled; tomorrow was the time to worry about the future.

CHAPTER Three

Rory only had to hold Mrs. O'Flanagan's place for a few minutes before she returned with a plump and bright-eyed Danny. They quickly reached the head of the line, at an alcove off the main entrance of the Foundling, where Sister Kathleen looked like a giant seated at her small desk. Rory whispered to Mrs. O'Flanagan, "Let me do the talking."

Rory stepped in front of the desk. "Good morning, Sister Kathleen!" she said cheerily.

Sister Kathleen was a tall, thin woman who rarely smiled. Her eyes darted past Rory to the baby. "Who do we have here?" she asked.

Rory marveled that the Sisters saw these women and babies every month but couldn't tell them apart. Rory knew everyone's name and history. She could no more mistake one child for another than she could switch her own head with Sister Anna's. Little Willie had the longest eyelashes, and tiny Mary Dolan had been born too early and still wasn't a proper size. "This is Mrs. O'Flanagan, Sister. And the baby is Danny. Mrs. O'Flanagan is a bit concerned about his rash and wonders if you could take a look."

Sister Kathleen was the Foundling's expert on childhood ailments, in charge of ensuring that each baby was being well cared for by his wet nurse. She removed her ledger from the desk, whipped out a clean cloth to cover the wooden surface, and indicated the baby should be placed there. The chubby little boy gurgled and threw out his fists. Sister Kathleen undid the large pin holding the cloth diaper together. "What do we have here? Oh my . . ." Her voice trailed off. She looked sharply at Mrs. O'Flanagan. "Have you been changing his diaper regularly?"

"Of course she has," Rory said quickly, holding up the clean diaper. "I know it looks awful, Sister Kathleen, but you know that Mrs. O'Flanagan has always done right by the Foundling." Rory turned to the older woman. "This is the fourth babe you've taken?" Mrs. O'Flanagan nodded. "And as soon as she saw the baby was ailing, she asked for help. Why, a babe's own ma couldn't do more!"

Sister Kathleen pursed her lips and considered. She examined the babe's clothes, grudgingly admitting they were clean. "When did the rash start?"

"Just a few days ago," Mrs. O'Flanagan hurried to get the words out of her mouth.

"Is there anything new in the house? A different kind of food, perhaps?"

"No." Mrs. O'Flanagan was regretful, as if she wished she

19

could say the family had started to eat nettles. Anything to protect the family's income.

Rory was peering over Sister Kathleen's shoulder. She reached in and rubbed the unsoiled diaper between her fingers. "Sister, look." Rory held out her fingers covered with fine white powder.

Sister Kathleen's mournful face brightened. "Have you tried a new soap?"

"That I did!" Mrs. O'Flanagan said. "I ran out and my neighbor gave me some of that Ivory soap. It smelled ever so nice."

Sister Kathleen's head bobbed, certain of her diagnosis. "The baby—"

"Danny," prompted Rory.

"Danny's skin is reacting to the new soap," Sister Kathleen went on. "Try your old soap and see if the rash goes away. If it doesn't, then be sure you come back. Don't wait until next month." She gave Danny back to Mrs. O'Flanagan, made an entry in her ledger, and handed over ten one-dollar bills.

"I will," Mrs. O'Flanagan promised, clutching her money. The Foundling had discovered long ago that a decent wage ensured that the wet nurses took good care of the babies.

Rory continued her watchful patrol of the line. The last woman didn't collect her money for several more hours. By the time the bells began to toll for the afternoon Mass, Rory was dead on her feet in her too-small boots. She groaned; she'd never get any rest in the chapel. The priest was sure to have them jumping up and down with every prayer. She glanced to the side of the imposing entrance at Sister Kathleen's cozy nook. Rory imagined herself napping comfortably in that quiet place. She smiled to herself and sidled up to Sister Kathleen. "Sister, did you hear that the Archbishop of New York is saying Mass today?"

"I had heard that," Sister Kathleen said wistfully. "I would love to hear him but I'm scheduled to sit at the intake desk this afternoon."

"You shouldn't miss it, Sister," Rory said earnestly. "I'd be happy to mind the desk for you."

"Would you?" Sister Kathleen's solemn face looked hopeful. "I couldn't ask . . ."

"Go, Sister," Rory insisted. "I'll wait here until after Mass."

"Bless you, child." Sister Kathleen hurried away just as the bells fell silent.

The formerly busy entry hall was deserted; everyone except Rory was at Mass. Rory sat at Sister Kathleen's desk and watched the dust motes drift in the light from the tall windows. It wasn't long before she put her head on her forearms and dozed.

A touch on her arm startled her awake.

"Miss," asked a timid voice. "Is this where I leave my baby?"

CHAPTER Four

RORY LIFTED HER HEAD. BLINKING, SHE REMEMBERED WHERE she was. A young woman stood in front of the desk, a baby in her arms. Down-and-out by the look of her with much-mended clothes and a pinched face with sunken cheeks. With a sinking heart, Rory realized the woman was here to abandon a baby.

"You're in the right place," Rory said.

"Why, you're just a child yourself," the woman exclaimed. She peered around the empty hall. "Who's in charge here?"

"I am, but if you wait a little time the nuns will be back," Rory said, hoping she would stay. Rory had never had to deal with a mother giving up her baby. Usually she only saw the babies after the mothers were gone.

"I can't wait," the woman said. "If I do I might lose my nerve."

Rory gave her a searching glance: the mother wasn't very old, maybe eighteen or nineteen.

"You can leave him in the cradle and the Sisters will take care of him." She gestured toward the white wicker cradle by the door. A representative of the Foundling was always at the desk to receive a baby, day or night. Until Mass was over, that representative was Rory.

The mother stared down at the baby, who was carefully swaddled in a blanket cleaner than her skirt. She glanced up and met Rory's eyes. "What's your name?" she asked.

"I'm Rory."

"My name's Patricia, but everyone calls me Patty. Are you a foundling?"

Rory shook her head hard. "I'm an orphan. Foundlings are abandoned," Rory explained. "My Ma and Da are dead. I may not have any parents but I know where I came from."

"So if I leave my baby here, he's a foundling . . ." Patty's voice caught.

Rory's heart sank. She hadn't meant to make Patty feel even worse; she just hated being mistaken for a foundling. The distinction might not matter, but to her it was the difference between being loved, even for a short time, or being discarded, handed over to strangers.

"Tell me, Rory, are they kind in this place? Will they take care of my baby boy? Raise him up in the Church?" She held her baby under Rory's nose. His eyes were tightly shut and he had a tuft of black hair that sprang from his head like a patch of grass.

"The Sisters are very kind," Rory answered. "You know how Jesus said suffer the little children to come unto him?

The Sisters practice that here. He'll be safe. They'll give him clothes, food, church, everything he needs."

Patty's eyes devoured Rory, taking in every detail, from her red braids to the worn boots that peeked out from under the desk. "You don't look as though you've missed any meals lately."

Rory winced at the hunger in Patty's voice. "Your boy will get fed three times a day. And real food too. Even meat sometimes," Rory assured her.

Patty's lips started to quiver. "I don't want to leave him, but I can't care for him." She began to cry, silent sobs that racked her body. Clutching the baby to her chest, she leaned against the desk. "I have a cousin in Utica who says she can get me a job. But I can't bring him. I've been at my wits' end."

Rory stood, uncertain what to do. Finally she imitated the kindness of the Sisters and came from behind the desk to put her arms around Patty and the baby. She held both of them until Patty stopped sobbing. "You can trust the Sisters to take good care of him," Rory said.

The woman touched the babe's mouth with her fingertip. Even fast asleep, his tiny lips sucked as though he was hungry. "Joseph's not weaned yet. How will he eat?"

"They'll bring in a wet nurse."

Patty's face asked the question.

"Another woman who's just had a baby," Rory explained. "So he'll get good milk." Rory put her hand to her heart. "I promise."

"As soon as I'm on my feet again, I'll come back and get him," Patty said, a resolute tilt to her jaw. "They'll give him to me, won't they?"

"You have three years from today to claim him," Rory assured her. "But after that, they'll place him with a family."

"I'll be back before then," Patty vowed.

Rory said nothing. She knew only too well how few mothers returned. She straightened up and helped Patty back to her feet. "Do you want to leave a note?"

"A note?" Patty shook her head.

"Write down your name and anything you want the Sisters to know about the baby." Rory reached into her pocket and pulled out a notebook and sharpened pencil.

In a hoarse voice, she said, "I can't write nor read."

"All right," Rory said as kindly as she could. "I'll write what you tell me." A moment later the note was written.

My boy, Joseph, was born on March 1, 1904. Do not be afraid of the sore on his stomach. It is nothing but ringworm. He has been baptized by Father Reilly at Our Lady of the Holy Rosary Church. I would like his name to stay the same. Please take care of him until I can come back.

Patricia O'Halloran

Patty watched Rory's hand moving across the paper with admiration. "Can you read too?"

Rory bit her lip to keep from smiling; the last thing she

wanted to do was embarrass Patty. "Yes," she said. "And do arithmetic too. The Sisters think education, cleanliness, and godliness are the path out of poverty." She paused. "Not in that order."

"Will my Joseph learn all that too?"

Rory nodded. "Well, once the babies are old enough, they receive some schooling until they are placed with a family. The older kids go to school to learn a trade."

Patty started to protest but Rory interrupted. "They don't make us go to work—but they teach us skills so we can get a job. If I weren't needed to help with the babies, I'd probably learn how to typewrite. Or sew. But I'm a rotten seamstress."

Patty took a deep breath. "Then I'm doing the right thing for Joseph," she said. She gently placed the baby in the wicker cradle, smoothing the blanket across his small body. The baby didn't peep. Rory wondered if Patty might have given Joseph a dose of spirits to keep him quiet but she didn't want to ask.

As Patty kissed the baby on his forehead, Rory got a lump in her throat. Carefully not looking at the cradle, Patty said, "Can you watch over him? I know it's asking a lot, but . . ."

"I will," Rory promised. "As long as I can."

Patty grabbed Rory's right hand and brought it to her lips. "Thank you." Without another word, Patty ran out the door.

The Sisters always said it was wrong to judge, but Rory couldn't help comparing Patty to her own mother. Even when they didn't have enough to eat, those last days when Ma was dying, she never once thought of getting rid of her and Vi. A real mother never gave up her children. It was that simple. On the other hand, that parting had cost Patty dearly.

Rory rocked baby Joseph. She rubbed her fingers across his wrist, frowning at its thinness. But otherwise he seemed in good health. He opened his eyes and stared up at Rory, his slate-blue eyes unfocused. Joseph's fist opened and he grabbed her finger.

"Hello, little one," she said. "If you were my little brother, I'd never let you go."

The baby gurgled as if to defend his ma.

"Maybe she'll come back, Joe," Rory agreed. "But even if she doesn't, we'll take good care of you."

Suddenly Rory had an urgent need to see her sister and give her a big hug. Children were abandoned here all the time—but not Rory and Violet. As long as they were together, they were a family. Rory had known her Ma and even had a few memories of her Da before he fell to his death from the elevated train track he was building. She knew where she had come from and she'd make sure Violet knew too. It was just one more reason she and Vi had to stay together.

CHAPTER Five

Rory waited with Joseph until Sister Kathleen returned from Mass. The Sister stopped short when she saw the baby.

"Another one?" Sister Kathleen said with a *tsk-tsk*ing noise on her tongue.

Rory nodded.

"At least this one came in during the day." Sister Kathleen picked up the baby and inspected him, especially examining his shock of black hair for lice eggs. "I always feel sorry for the mothers who are so desperate they leave the babies in the middle of the night."

"They're all desperate," Rory said, the haunted expression of Joseph's mother still fresh in her mind. She felt guilty for judging Patty so harshly.

Whirling around to avoid the Sister's eyes, Rory fetched the ledger. She watched as Sister Kathleen recorded all the details they knew about little Joseph. In the final column Sister Kathleen entered a date three years from the day. That was the date his mother would lose all her rights to Joseph and the Foundling Sisters could do with him what they wished.

"Poor little one," Rory whispered, kissing him on the forehead. "But you will be looked after here."

"Of course he will," Sister Kathleen said, gathering up the baby in her arms to take him to the nursery.

As Rory watched them go, she remembered when she had first arrived, on a cold, rainy September night, carrying two-year-old Violet on one hip and a small satchel with their few clothes on the other. Those last days that Ma had been dying, she'd made Rory promise to go to Sister Anna. The burial arrangements were all made with their neighbor, Mrs. O'Malley. She had helped nurse Ma and she had kept Ma's things, "as payment," she said. The only thing Rory had been able to salvage was Ma's necklace. Her hand went to the saint's medal hanging around her neck. The Virgin Mary. Ma's patron saint. *Fat lot of good the saint had done for Ma*, Rory thought. Immediately she felt guilty. Ma would be so angry at Rory for thinking such a thing, not to mention what Sister Anna would say.

Relieved of her responsibilities for the moment, Rory didn't want to go to class. She made her way to the chapel, carefully avoiding any nuns who might ask where she was going or, more specifically, why she wasn't going where she was supposed to be. Funny how she hated having to go to chapel for services every day but it was her first choice whenever she wanted to be alone. Every room in the huge Foundling complex of buildings, schools, and hospitals was plain and serviceable, except for the chapel. It was beautiful, not huge, each side of the square room perhaps sixty feet long. The decorations in the chapel were gifts from the powerful and wealthy donors who supported the Foundling.

A large circular window over the entrance faced south and the afternoon sun streamed in. The domed ceiling made Rory feel as though she was in heaven. Best of all, the room was empty. Here she could think. But first she had to pay her respects to her favorite statue. The Virgin Mary, dressed all in blue and white with gold trim, stood in her own alcove.

First she said her own Hail Mary. That was only proper. Then Rory settled in for a nice chat. "Hi, Lady Mary," she said, craning her neck to see the beautiful face. "We've got a new baby. You should keep an eye on him. His name is Joseph—like your husband—so you won't forget. I know there are a lot of us to look after." She described how Violet was still up to her old tricks in the middle of the night. And about the wet nurses in line with the babies. "Please, Lady Mary, take care of them, especially the babies."

Rory made the sign of the cross and turned away. The pulpit to one side of the white marble altar beckoned to her. Making sure she was unobserved, she climbed up to where Father Robert usually stood to deliver his homily. Rory put her shoulders back, took a deep breath, and pronounced, "And on the eighth day God decided that all the children get to go to the park and play." The words rolled off her tongue and filled the corners of the chapel. Emboldened, Rory added,

"And they should have ice cream every night. And no more strengthening gruel. Ever. Amen."

"Rory!"

Rory stepped back, startled. She fell off the pulpit platform and skinned her knee.

Sister Anna glided down the aisle, her expression stern. "Rory Fitzpatrick! This is the house of Our Lord, not a theatrical stage!"

Rory scrambled to her feet, trying not to wince at the sharp pain in her knee. "Sister, I was just . . . just wondering how Father Robert manages to be heard in every corner of the chapel."

Cheeks flaming with color, Sister Anna said, "The excellent acoustics in the chapel are no excuse for your disrespectful behavior. And I take offense at your suggestion that you aren't fed properly."

"I'm sorry, ma'am." Rory bobbed a short curtsy and started to make her exit. *That could have been worse*, she thought.

"Wait," Sister Anna said.

Rory stopped and slowly turned around. "Yes, Sister?"

"I need to talk to you." Sister Anna glanced around the ornate chapel. "But not here. In my office." Without waiting for Rory's response, Sister Anna led the way out a side door.

Rory reluctantly followed. No good news was ever delivered in Sister Anna's office.

CHAPTER Six

"You LIED TO ME!" THE WORDS FLEW OUT OF RORY'S MOUTH.
She clapped her hands over her mouth; after three years at the
Foundling she knew there are certain things you never say to
a nun.

Sister Anna stared at Rory, her gray eyes flinty and hard.
"That is quite enough, young lady." She was seated at her
desk. Sister Anna and the desk suited each other: square and
imposing. There were two wooden armchairs in front of Sister
Anna's desk and a small leather-covered sofa against the wall
under the high windows. There were cracks in the leather but
the room was spotlessly clean.

"But you promised that Violet and I would stay together.
You promised!" Rory's body shook with anger, and she had
to clasp her hands tight to keep from trembling. She had
declined Sister Anna's invitation to sit down, preferring to
face trouble on her feet.

"You and she have been sheltered at the Foundling for

three years," Sister Anna said. "You know our mission, to find our foundlings a suitable family. We have found a good family for Violet."

"Violet has a family. Me! Ma sent us here so we wouldn't be separated." Rory began to pace around the room, remembering her first night at the Foundling. The Sisters had tried to separate Rory from her sister. Rory had screamed and held on to Violet as though their lives depended on staying together. Finally Sister Anna had agreed that Rory could stay with Violet for the time being. Rory had stretched that brief reprieve into three years.

Sister Anna glanced down at a piece of paper on the desk. Rory recognized it as the form for every new orphan at the Foundling Hospital. The ink on little Joseph's paper was still wet. But it was the first time Rory had ever seen Violet's or her own.

"We need to make room for new orphans," Sister Anna said. "Violet will have a very good home."

"But where are you sending her, Sister?" Rory asked, stunned. She had just explained the rules to Joseph's mother but somehow she had never dreamed they would affect her and Violet. How could she have been so shortsighted? Her mother had expected more of her.

"It doesn't matter. Just know that it is a good home," Sister Anna replied.

"It's the *only* thing that matters. Where are you sending her?"

"Watch your tone, young lady." Sister Anna's voice was

icy. "I'm trying to make allowances because I know you are upset, but I won't tolerate rudeness."

It took an effort—the habit of obeying Sister Anna was bone-deep—but Rory put her hands on the back of the chair in front of the desk and looked her squarely in the eyes. "Will she be close? Will I still be able to see her?"

Sister Anna's gaze dropped.

"Where is Violet going?" Rory could be as stubborn as she needed to be.

"Out west."

"How far west?" Rory's voice was small. The only thing she knew about the West was her favorite issue of *Wild West Weekly*. A visitor to the Foundling had left it behind and Rory had claimed it for her own. She'd read it a dozen times and she had serious doubts that a suitable home for Violet lay between those pages. There were Indians, coyotes, and rattlesnakes in the West.

"A week's journey by train."

"A week away!" Rory shoved the chair aside and clenched her fists at her side. "I'll never see her again!"

Sister Anna stood up from behind her desk and came around to Rory. She stooped to put her arm around Rory's shoulders. Rory could feel the nun's crucifix pressing into her back.

"No, Rory," she said. Her manner was matter-of-fact, but Rory thought she heard a little bit of pity in Sister Anna's voice. "You won't see her again. She'll have a new family. We have found it best for the children we place to sever all ties

with their former lives. It is easier for them. And for you."
She fell silent, as if waiting for Rory to speak, but Rory was
staring straight ahead, thinking more quickly than she ever
had in her life.

"Violet's new parents are good Catholics," Sister Anna
went on. "And they are eager to have her; they especially
asked for a redheaded girl."

Rory grabbed the end of her own red braid and shoved it
toward Sister Anna's face. "If that's what they want, let's give
them two!"

"They only asked for one girl, I'm afraid. And you're
twelve. We want them to have a younger girl." Sister Anna's
voice was resolute and Rory had to fight to keep down the
panic in her stomach. "You know our policy—we send
younger children so we're sure they will be loved and part of
a family, not put to work."

"Send another orphan! Lord knows you have plenty!"

"The Lord's name is not to be used lightly, Rory."

"Then He should take better care of his children!" She
grabbed at Sister Anna's hand. "I told my mother I would
look after Violet. *I promised.*"

Sister Anna stroked Rory's palm. "Rory, you've done
exceptionally well with Violet. She's healthy and bright as
a new button. But at five years old, she's the ideal age to be
placed. She needs parents. You should make this easier for
her, not harder."

Sister Anna's gentle voice washed over her while her
calloused hands tried to soothe Rory's. Rory kept her eyes on

Sister Anna's hands. How strange that the nun in charge of so much at the Foundling had calluses. But that was Sister Anna—she wasn't afraid of hard work.

"Rory, you know it would be best for Violet if you let her go," Sister Anna said smoothly. "If you love her . . ."

"No!" Rory shouted, shoving herself away from Sister Anna. "You're a nun. What do you know about love?"

"Rory!" Sister Anna stepped back as if she had been slapped. Her thin face had red spots high on her cheeks.

"No, I'm not listening to you anymore. You're trying to trick me." Rory reached for the door and threw it open. Pausing in the doorway, she cried, "You're a liar and a baby thief! I won't let you take Violet away from me!" She slammed the door before Sister Anna could say another word.

Standing in the hall was a younger orphan, staring at Rory, her mouth open like a hole in the middle of a doughnut.

"What are you looking at?" Rory demanded.

"No one talks to Sister Anna that way," the girl whispered with a panicked look at the door. She pulled out a rosary and ran it through her fingers as though she could rub away Rory's sins.

"It's about time someone told the Sisters what's what!" Rory said, defiance in her voice. But as she got her breath back, she began to wonder how much trouble she was in. What would happen if Sister Anna turned against her? Rory might lose any chance to be with Violet.

Sister Anna's doorknob began to turn. Rory couldn't face her. She flew down the hallway, ran down two flights of stairs to the main hall. It was suppertime and the entryway was deserted.

The wide double doors to the outdoors beckoned. Rory had never gone out by herself—the Sisters frightened the orphans with stories of truants being snatched off the street by the police. With a toss of her head, Rory pushed open the door. If something terrible happened, it would serve Sister Anna right.

CHAPTER Seven

Rory PAUSED AT THE TOP OF THE STEPS. THE LATE-AFTERNOON sun was bright and for a moment she stopped, blinded. Sixty-Ninth Street in front of the Foundling was busy with people walking home after work. Shaking off caution, Rory marched out alone, leaving the Foundling behind.

Two Sisters in their outdoor habits were coming up the wide steps. Rory pushed her way past them. One of them, Rory wasn't sure who, called, "Rory! Where are you going? You can't go out now. The truancy police . . ."

Rory ran down to the corner and then up Third Avenue as fast as she could, leaving the Sisters' rules and warnings far behind. Dodging walkers as the sun went down, she hardly knew where her feet were going. The homes along Third Avenue passed in a blur. The low setting sun cast shadows from the houses on the west side of the street and from the trees in Central Park. Tears streaming down her face, Rory turned down Seventy-First Street until she reached Fifth Avenue.

She hesitated for a scant second to be sure she could dodge the carriages traveling down Fifth Avenue, and then ducked across the sidewalk into Central Park through the Children's Gate. It was a familiar walk from many Sunday excursions with other children from the Foundling, and the park was where she was always happiest. Even though it was in the center of New York City, Central Park felt like a different world. A place where grass and trees grew and buildings didn't shut out the sky. But now the park was quiet, with no screaming children's voices or nannies scolding their charges.

A stitch in her side stole her breath away and she slowed to a walk, pressing her hand to her waist. She could feel the leather in her boots splitting at the toes. She crossed the park toward the lake and stopped only when she reached her most favorite place, the fountain on the water's edge. Half panting, half sobbing, Rory couldn't stop railing at the Sisters. It was so unfair. Rory had mostly followed their rules. She'd worked hard to take care of the children and kept up her studies. And how did Sister Anna reward her? She took away the only thing Rory cared about!

The bronze angel atop the fountain held a lily in one hand as she blessed the water flowing beneath her with the other. Rory scooped water to cool her face and neck. At this hour, the park was almost empty and she had the angel to herself. Rory craned her neck to look up at the angel's beautiful face. Sister Anna had told her that a woman designed it and Rory liked it all the more for that. One bronze foot stepped forward and her wings unfurled as though she was about to take flight. Never had Rory envied her so much.

"I wish I could just fly into the sky," she told the angel. "What should I do? I have to save Violet before they take her so far away I can't find her. But how? The Foundling has been our home for three years."

The angel's eyes were fixed on the distant horizon.

"Well?" Rory asked impatiently. "I haven't asked you for much—at least you could help me now that I'm really in trouble."

Was it her imagination or did the angel's wings ruffle as though she was irritated by Rory's demands?

"So you want me to figure it out for myself?" Rory put her damp fist under her chin and considered. The Foundling hadn't always been their home. Why not return to Hell's Kitchen, where she had lived with her parents? She hadn't been back since Ma died, but maybe she could find some of her mother's old friends. Other girls her age got jobs and supported their family. Rory could do the same. She dried her face with her skirt and straightened up. With a spring in her step from having made a decision for herself, she headed across the park to Columbus Avenue. An omnibus came lumbering down from the north. Rory ran alongside. When it slowed for a carriage turning right, she hopped onto the back. There were two boys, very dirty, perched on the rear fender too.

"Hello," she said.

They scowled at her and gestured to the driver in the front of the omnibus. "Shhh."

Rory pressed her lips in a tight line and kept her eyes looking straight ahead. There were unspoken rules to catching rides on the taxis and buses. Never, ever draw attention to yourself or your fellow illegal passengers.

As soon as she reached Fifty-Fifth Street she hopped off. Her companions didn't flicker an eyelash at her departure. Where the avenue intersected with Fifty-Fifth Street there was a saloon on every corner. In three years Rory had managed to forget the sound of poor men and women drinking their cares away; the loud laughter always had a cutting edge. Violence was never far away in Hell's Kitchen.

She quickly moved past the saloons into the street crowded with vendors selling goods from carts or trays suspended from their necks. Boys were hawking newspapers or offering to shine shoes. The smallest children scoured the street for bits of wood or coal, fallen from a passing cart—anything to feed the stove tonight. Rory had done the same in her time. She watched a little boy steal an apple from a fruit stand. She had done that too. She remembered so clearly her reasoning— how could it be wrong when she was so hungry? And she had always shared the loot with Vi.

She passed a man selling roast chestnuts, a smell Rory loved. She took a deep sniff and started to cough, her eyes watering. Rory covered her mouth with the clean handkerchief from her pinafore pocket. How could she have forgotten the smells of the street? The stench of sewage from the privies in the courtyard behind every building or the fresh horse manure steaming on the street? Had her neighborhood always been

41

this bad? Or had it gotten worse while she was away?

She reached her old building. She stared at it for a moment trying to decide if it was smaller now. It seemed impossibly narrow, wedged between two larger tenements. The door was propped open. Rory took a deep breath and walked in. The wail of a child's crying filled the hallway. The smell of coal fires, cabbage, and burned potatoes hit her senses like a policeman's nightstick thumping a drunk's skull. Unmistakable. Unforgettable.

The stairs were rickety and uneven. Nor had they seen the business end of a broom in years. The scents of vinegar and borax of the Foundling, not to mention the spick-and-span tiled floors, seemed from another world. As she began to climb, a boy dressed in knickerbockers and a shirt that was too small for him came rushing down the stairs. Rory pressed herself against the wall, recalling clearly how she used to race down the same steps, despite Ma's warnings.

Their room had been on the third floor in the back. There was no running water and the single privy was in the tiny back courtyard. At the time, Rory knew they were lucky not to have to share their room with another family. She caught a glimpse of the fire escape outside. It was strung with clotheslines and lined with trash and rags. Rory remembered she couldn't see the sky from the alley. Memories of the past washed over her in waves, threatening to drown her if she wasn't careful.

The baby was still crying and Rory thought that baby's ma might be out working. For the last three years she hadn't heard a baby cry so long without being comforted. She wanted to find the child and hold him close, but she knew better than to knock on any strange doors. Her mother had always tried to keep her away from the other kids in the building. "The likes of them are not for you, Rory," Ma had said. Back in Ireland, Ma had gone to school for a few years. It was always her dream that Rory and Violet would go to school and get a proper education. Even when Da had died, Ma worked her fingers down to the bone to keep her children decent. They had been all right, even if Rory had gotten tired of eating potatoes all the time.

When the cough came, Rory tried to tell herself Ma was just tired from her job at the shirt factory. It was the chill in the air. Anything but the truth. But Ma would have none of that. "There's no use fooling yourself," she had said. "Just promise me you'll take care of your little sister."

Rory stared at her old door. "I swear, Ma." The three-year-old promise still lingered in the air.

The door swung open and a voice bellowed, "Mavis! Are you finally home? Where's my supper?"

A large, gaunt man wearing a dirty pair of pants and a grimy undershirt stood in the doorway. Unsteady on his feet, he grabbed the doorjamb to stay upright. Even from ten feet away his breath stank of liquor. His bleary eyes spied her and his lips curled in a grin. Rory backed up as he stumbled in her direction. He lunged for her. Rory turned on her heel and bolted toward the stairs.

Down two flights and she paused in the tiny hall to catch

her breath. Hell's Kitchen was horrible. What was she doing here? There was nothing here for her and Violet. She had to return to the Foundling and somehow convince Sister Anna there was another way. She slammed through the door and burst into the street, colliding with a large man dressed in blue. She fell to the ground, the wind knocked out of her.

A beefy hand grabbed hers and hauled her to her feet.

"Got you!"

CHAPTER Eight

Rory STARED UP THE LONG ARM IN A BLUE COAT TO A LARGE
policeman with a wicked smile on his face.

"Thought ya could double back and get away, did ya?"
he asked in a thick Irish brogue. "Outsmarted yerself this
time!" With his free hand, he adjusted his round cap with
the insignia of the police on the front. Rory had jarred him
as she fell.

Writhing under his grip, Rory glared up at him. "I wasn't
running from you. You've got the wrong kid."

"Do I now? And I suppose you aren't part of that gang of
thieves?"

"I'm no thief," Rory retorted. "I live at the Foundling.
Ask them and they'll tell you."

He burst out laughing. "That's a new one. First street
kid I ever heard who wanted to be a foundling! If you're at
the Foundling then why aren't you there? The nuns don't let

45

their kids run the neighborhoods. You're a dirty scamp like all the rest of the street kids."

"Honest, I live with the nuns at the Foundling," Rory explained patiently. If she told him enough times he would have to check.

"Honest? Ha!" With his free hand he tweaked her nose. "I used to walk that beat and I know a bit about it. Why don't you tell me which building you live in?"

"St. Irene's Residence," Rory shot back.

"Ha! That's where the babies live!" he crowed. "I knew you were lying." He pushed her forward. "Let's go."

"No, wait!" Rory cried. "I do live there. Ask Sister Anna Michaella. She lets me stay with the babies because my sister is there."

He kept shoving her forward. "I've met Sister Anna before." He tugged at his collar with his free hand as if the memory was not a pleasant one. "Sister usually dresses her kids a bit more respectable." He glanced down at her too-short skirt and leather boots where her big toe had finally split the leather.

"I keep growing," Rory said with an edge of desperation. "Just last week the ward Sister was saying she was at her wits' end trying to find me shoes." She plucked at the hand on her arm. "You must believe me! Please?"

"You're good." The officer grinned. "I almost believe you!"

"Just take me there. Any of the Sisters will tell you . . ."

He laughed. "Think I have time to be parading across the park, do you? Not a chance." He marched her a few steps down the street to a black paddy wagon. Somehow all the vendors and shoppers had melted away. Rory wasn't surprised; it had always been like that when the cops were on the street. The policeman unlocked the back door of the wagon. Inside was a metal cell on wheels. A bench lined both sides and there were iron rings bolted to the walls. There was already a prisoner inside. His face was bruised and bloody, and one eye was swollen shut. He was in handcuffs that were threaded through the iron rings. His body was slumped and twisted against the wall, almost unconscious.

Rory's feet dragged on the sidewalk. She began breathing faster. Her heart beat too quickly in her chest. She didn't belong in there. "Don't make me go in there," she begged. "Not with him." He must be dangerous to be handcuffed. Rory couldn't afford to take chances—what would happen to Vi without her? "Please, sir?"

"You've changed your tune now, I see," the officer said, his grip relaxing slightly.

This was her chance. Rory kicked him hard in the shin. He let go and shouted in pain. But no sooner did she turn to run than he grabbed her long braid and hauled her back.

"Ow!" Tears escaped down her cheeks. "Let go of me!"

"If you really are at the Foundling," the policeman said angrily, "they'll be glad to be rid of you." Limping, the policeman shoved her into the wagon. "Not so bold now, are you?" he grumbled, rubbing his knee. "You'll stay in there until we get back to the precinct." He slammed the metal door and Rory was trapped.

The narrow metal wagon was dark except for thin lines of light rimming the edges of the door. The light told her there was air, but still Rory couldn't breathe. She huddled in the corner, as far from the other prisoner as possible. His breathing was ragged and Rory wondered if his insides were hurt. When her Da had fallen from the elevated train tracks, he had lived for a few days, wheezing just like that. The doctor said his ribs were broken. Rory sat for hours at his bedside those last days while Ma was at work, just listening and praying he would live—and keeping Violet quiet so he could get his rest.

Rory wanted to kick herself. The children at the Foundling never went outside without the nuns. Rory had been warned time and time again. The police were always looking for poor kids to pull off the streets. What happened to the children afterward had never been specified, like the threat in a fairy tale. Don't go outside alone or else. But Rory had not listened. Now she would find out the ending firsthand.

The wagon lurched forward and Rory cried out. There was nothing to cushion the jarring of the wagon over the cobblestone streets. Her companion groaned. Rory bounced from one surface to another. Her elbow hit the wall with an impact that made her whole arm numb. When the wagon stopped, she rubbed the sore spot and wished she had kicked the policeman harder. Outside, she could hear traffic noises and the voices of lots of men. The door swung open and Rory blinked in the bright streetlight. She was at the Eighteenth Police Precinct. No one could mistake that pink granite building with the telltale pillars holding up the green police lamps. She'd been here with Ma when Da had died. Not a day she cared to recall.

Another policeman joined hers. "Well, O'Rourke, get much of a haul?"

"An idiot who got himself knocked out at McAllister's tavern and a kid." Rory's policeman, Officer O'Rourke, scowled. "A little hellion. She tried to tell me she's with the Foundling Hospital but she didn't know the name of the right dormitory."

"These kids will lie as soon as look at you," the other officer agreed.

"I am not lying!" Rory protested. "Just ask Sister Anna if I am telling the truth."

"I don't know about you, O'Rourke, but I don't have time to go interrogating nuns."

"Me neither. In fact, they scare me a bit. Always have since I was a wee lad in Dublin."

Rory stared at them, disbelieving. "You won't send for her? But then how will I get home?"

"Lass, that's not my concern," O'Rourke said. Taking a firm hold of her arm, he escorted her up the short flight of stairs into the precinct house.

"You can't do this to me!" Rory protested. "It's not right. The nuns will miss me."

O'Rourke snorted. "The likes of you ain't missed by nobody."

Rory's jaw dropped. Was it possible? Wasn't she important

to somebody? Well, Violet, of course. But Violet couldn't help her. Rory's heart ached when she thought of how frightened Violet would be when Rory wasn't sitting beside her at supper. This was what happened when she disobeyed the Sisters and didn't respect authority. The nuns had warned her. And before that, Ma had warned her too. When would she learn?

O'Rourke led her past a wooden counter where a line of people were shouting at the duty officer. Rory tried to dawdle so she could listen, but O'Rourke propelled her into a large room that seemed to be occupied by enormous men in blue uniforms. The noise was deafening. He led her to a hard bench against a wall then sat down at a desk across from her. "You'll wait here until the matron comes to collect you," he said. "Don't move; I've got my eye on you."

Rory felt tiny on the bench. Even her legs weren't long enough to touch the floor; the back of her thighs ached as her feet dangled. She leaned back against the wall and looked around. The room was filled with policemen, criminals, and victims, all talking at the top of their voices. Sometimes Rory had to look twice to tell the difference between the criminals and the victims. A policeman escorted an old lady, clutching a stole around her shoulders, to stand in front of Rory.

"Do you recognize the miscreant who stole your purse?" he asked.

"Maybe her . . ." the old woman said, peering through thick spectacles at Rory.

Rory eyes widened. "I didn't steal anything! Ma'am, truly

I didn't!" She sat up straight and tried to look innocent.

"Not her, Mrs. Montgomery," the policeman said. "I meant the pictures."

Rory looked over her shoulder and noticed the wall was covered with hundreds of cards. Each card had a hand-drawn portrait of a criminal with a description beneath of his or her criminal record and unusual habits. She slumped against the wall in relief. As Mrs. Montgomery nearsightedly looked at the cards, Rory idly read the card at the end of her nose about "Gentleman Joe Dapper." That couldn't be his real name, Rory thought. She read on. Gentleman Joe dressed like a gentleman and talked his way into society weddings and made off with the gifts. He was partial to presents from Tiffany's. Looking at his posh face, Rory would never have pegged him for a criminal. Even Sister Anna could have been fooled by him. But on consideration, Rory decided her Ma would have seen right through Gentleman Joe.

"Do you like the rogues' gallery?" O'Rourke said in her ear, startling Rory. "Just be thankful I'm getting you off the streets so your picture will never be up here. I don't suppose you can read, but each of these men and women are desperate criminals."

"I can read, Officer O'Rourke. The nuns taught me." She added pointedly, "Because I live with them!"

He scowled. "You are a stubborn one." He stepped aside and revealed an older woman with a narrow face and dark beady eyes staring down a pointed nose. She wore a black uniform and a sour expression.

"Matron, here's the one I told you about. Watch her, she likes to kick."

"After a few days staying with me, she'll be as biddable as a lamb," the matron said. She held out a hand that was red and cracked.

Rory's eyes burned from the smell of lye.

"C'mon, girl," the matron beckoned.

Rory shrank against the wall. "What about Sister Anna? Won't you tell her I'm here?" She winced to hear how scared she sounded.

"See what I mean?" O'Rourke said to the matron.

The matron grabbed Rory's shoulder and shook her. "Liars don't prosper here," she said. "You'd better remember that."

CHAPTER Nine

"I'M NOT LYING!" RORY CRIED. "I BELONG TO THE FOUNDLING."
Rory felt as if she were sinking beneath the surface of a lake.
If she didn't find someone to listen to her, the waters would
close over her head and she would die.

"Lying or truthful—it don't matter," the matron said
to O'Rourke, as though Rory hadn't said a word. "All the
children end up on the trains in the end. Such an economical
solution to the problem."

"What problem? What trains?" Could the matron's trains
and Sister Anna's be the same? That seemed unlikely.

"Don't be afraid," the matron said, although Rory could
see clear as day that the matron relished Rory's fear. "After
you're unclaimed for a few days—"

"Days!" Rory squawked.

"Hush, don't interrupt me. After a few days, we'll send
you to Children's Aid. They take all the poor children who

have some work in them and send them west. It's a fresh start you'll have." The matron's smile didn't reach her eyes.

"Please, just tell Sister Anna I'm here," Rory begged. "My name is Rory Fitzpatrick. She'll come for me, I know she will."

"If she comes, she comes. Now I don't want to hear another whine out of you or you'll find out what it's like to miss a few meals." With a sharp gesture, she indicated that Rory should precede her down a long hallway. Swallowing hard, Rory forced her feet to move. The matron took her up three flights of stairs to the top floor and unlocked a door that opened into a large cell. A window was set high in the wall. Now that the sun was down the only light came from a dim electric bulb high overhead. A girl lay on a bench bolted to the wall. In the corner was a chamber pot with an ill-fitting lid. Rory could tell by the smell it hadn't been cleaned today. The matron shoved her inside.

"No fighting or you'll feel the back of my hand." The door clanged shut behind her and Rory heard the squeak of the key closing the lock. She turned slowly to face her companion. The other girl looked a little older than Rory. She had dark black hair and pale green eyes. Her dress was filthy, as if she had fallen in the mud, and the hem badly needed mending. Her bare feet had a calloused look as though she rarely wore shoes.

Rory gave her a tentative smile and met with a cold stare. "Hello," Rory said finally.

"What do you want, Red?" the other girl answered.

"My name's not Red. It's Rory."

The girl burst out in cruel laughter. "That's a boy's name."

"It's my name." Rory shrugged. "Do you have a problem with that?" That was how kids on the street talked in Hell's Kitchen.

With a nod, as though Rory had passed a test, the girl said, "I'm Brigid." Rory could hear the Irish in her voice. "What are you in for?"

"The policeman thought I was a thief," Rory said, blushing. "But he was wrong."

"That's what everybody says," Brigid said. "It's never true."

Rory started to protest but then wondered what possible difference it could make what Brigid thought. "So what did you do?" Rory asked.

Brigid shrugged. "The coppers caught me picking a gent's pocket."

"Oh," Rory said, making sure to keep her voice neutral. In the old days she'd stolen food to eat, but never money. She had always known in a pinch she could explain food thievery to her mother, but never cash. But who knew what would have happened if she hadn't found sanctuary at the Foundling for her and Violet after Ma died. Rory might have become a thief too. She couldn't judge Brigid without living her life. "What will happen to you now?"

"I'll pay for my crimes," Brigid said, her expression as gloomy as the single light bulb in the ceiling.

In a tiny voice, Rory asked, "How?"

"With my very life," Brigid said, hiding her face in her hands.

Rory could feel the blood draining from her head and, without willing it, took a step backward. Brigid peeked from between her fingers and burst out laughing. "Look at you, Red. You shouldn't be let out on the streets without a minder. I'm only joking. I got no family so it's the orphan train for me. But it'll be the end of me too. Kids never come back."

"From where?" Rory asked.

"Don't you know nothin'?" Brigid said. Without waiting for an answer she said, "Poor kids get put on trains to the West like farm animals."

"But sometimes they go to specially chosen homes and they get to be part of new families," Rory said, parroting Sister Anna. But was she sure about that? Sister Anna had let Rory believe that she and Vi could stay together. What else had she lied about?

Brigid snorted and looked pityingly at Rory. "Not likely. The people out there need workers, so they meet the trains and pick out the strongest and best. Then they put them to work. To those farmers you're no better than a beast."

Rory's breath caught in her chest. "That's . . . that's . . . why, that's slavery!"

"It gets worse," Brigid said, leaning forward to whisper in Rory's ear. "Some of those men want wives and don't care how young they are."

Rory's knees buckled and she sank down to the bench.

"Still, it might be better than thieving or begging on the streets." Brigid looked her over. "You must do pretty well to keep so clean."

"I'm not a beggar," Rory explained. "I live at the Foundling."

"What's that?"

"An orphanage on the East Side. The nuns there have been good to me. I get room and board and school."

"Do they make you work for it?" Brigid asked.

"No, of course not," Rory said with indignation. "I help with the babies, but that's because I want to stay with my little sister. They want me to learn a trade and get apprenticed out. But I make myself useful so they keep me with Violet."

"It sounds too good to be true," Brigid said flatly.

Rory sighed. "From here, it looks like heaven."

"Why'd you leave if it's so good?" Brigid shot back.

"I ran away even though I should've known better." Rory rested her chin on her hand and sighed again. "Sister Anna is going to kill me."

"You think you're ever going to see her again?" Brigid laughed, then she started to cough. Rory smacked her on the back until she recovered her breath.

"Of course I'll see Sister Anna again," Rory said, willing it to be true. "She'd never abandon me here." But there was doubt in her voice where there had never been any before. After the cruel things Rory had said, what if Sister Anna didn't ever want to see her again?

"If that's true, I'd like to meet this nun of yours." She closed her eyes and shortly began snoring, leaving Rory alone with her fears.

What if Sister Anna left Rory to rot here? Sister Anna had hundreds of children to look out for; what if she decided she could do with one less? Violet would be sent off to the Wild West and Rory might never see her sister again. Loaded on a train like cattle, Rory would be claimed by a family more interested in her strength of body than her strength of mind. She would never finish her education. Worse yet, she might be taken in by a cruel family who would beat her and never give her anything more than scraps to eat. They would chain her to a post and make her turn a spit like a dog. Or maybe she would have to sleep with the cows. She might get scalped like the settlers in the *Wild West Weekly* magazine. Rory pinched herself hard before she worked herself up to hysterics. Of course, Sister Anna would come.

But what if Sister Anna couldn't find her? It was a big city and Rory had gone all the way to Hell's Kitchen, miles away from the Foundling. A tear rolled down her face, followed by another one. Rory rarely cried unless she was hurt, but she had really ruined things for herself this time. She had thrown away everything in a fit of temper. Her eyes felt heavy and she closed them just for a moment.

When she opened her eyes again, the harsh electric light hurt her eyes. Brigid was still sleeping. As Rory wondered what had awoken her, she heard voices in the hall, muffled and indistinct. She rushed to the door and put her ear to the crack in the jamb.

"Officer, if Rory told you she was with the Foundling I am confused why you did not send for me at once. We have been searching for her for hours. This is the third precinct I have visited." It was Sister Anna! She was speaking in what Rory thought of as her most nunnish voice.

O'Rourke sounded like a whipped dog, all his bravado and bullying gone. "Sister Anna, we thought she was lying and didn't want to disturb you."

"Nonsense, O'Rourke. Rory is honest to a fault." There was a brief silence; Rory pressed her ear against the door. She didn't want to miss a word.

"This is not the first time you've mistreated one of my children," Sister Anna went on, implacable. "I think I shall ask His Excellency the Archbishop to write a letter to the chief of police. Again."

Rory almost giggled when she heard O'Rourke wheedling, "Ah, ma'am, I mean Sister, there's no call to do anything like that, is there? I'll just unlock this door and you can take your lass with you. No harm done!"

The door lock squeaked and Rory jumped back. No sooner had the door swung open than Sister Anna stepped inside, filling the doorway with her tall frame. Her dark nun's bonnet shadowed her face. "Rory, it's time to go."

Rory wanted to run and hug Sister Anna, but that would never do. She contented herself with waking up Brigid to say goodbye. "This is the nun I told you about. She came. I knew she would!"

CHAPTER Ten

Rory followed Sister Anna toward a waiting horse cab.
She hung back to rub the horse's nose, postponing the trouble
she knew was coming. His coat was rough and his eyes were
dull; the horse looked like he needed as much help as she did.

"Rory!" Sister Anna's voice made her start.

"Yes, Sister." Rory climbed in. Sister Anna settled back in
the seat as the cab lurched forward. Silence filled the cab and
Rory wasn't interested in breaking it. She leaned away and
pressed her ear into a leather seat that smelled of mold, her
eyes fixed on the shadowy city passing by. She'd forgotten how
loud the taverns could get, although she well remembered
not being able to fall asleep at night. A woman in a scanty
dress stumbled out of a tavern and hit the side of the cab. The
cabbie shouted at her, using such language that Sister Anna
covered Rory's ears.

"I've heard worse, you know," Rory said.

"I know," Sister Anna said sadly. "But no child should

hear such things." She took Rory's hand and didn't let it go until they reached the Foundling.

Back home, Sister Anna brought Rory to the kitchen. Rory loved the Foundling kitchen. There was an enormous cast-iron stove in one corner and shiny copper pots hanging from the ceiling. Rory knew the cook's secret; there was a fat black cat that liked to sleep on the floor under the stove. Cook doted on the animal but Sister Anna would never allow her to keep it. As they walked in, Rory saw the tip of a black tail disappearing into the pantry.

The cook had kept a bowl of stew and fresh bread for her. Rory wolfed it down, all the while waiting for the axe to fall. Sister watched her eat, still silent.

Finally Rory could not stand to wait another moment. Stumbling over her words, she said in a rush, "Sister, I'll take any punishment you have for me if only you'll let me stay with Violet!"

"Rory . . ." Sister Anna sounded tired. "I don't want to punish you, but you have to face the facts. Violet is going."

"I thought you cared about us," Rory said, keeping her voice quiet. Sister Anna had rescued her and deserved a chance to explain. "After all we've been through, how can you split us apart?"

Sister Anna sighed and sank into a chair next to Rory. "Someday you'll see that I'm doing the right thing by Violet. I understand why you were upset. To someone your age, three years with your sister seems like an eternity. But we must move forward, and Violet needs a home." She removed her bonnet and placed it on the table then ran her hands through her short hair. "That's better. It's been a very long day."

Rory stared, distracted by Sister Anna's never-before-seen hair. "You've got red hair too," she said, wonder in her voice.

Sister Anna smiled. "Perhaps that's why I understand you so well." She reached over and tucked a stray strand of hair behind Rory's ear. "Today when you left my office . . ."

Heat flushed Rory's face to the tips of her ears.

"I was furious," Sister Anna said. "And frightened. I am very glad that we found you and brought you back to where you belong. We see so many children. It doesn't do to get attached. But you, Rory, have managed to find a special place at the Foundling."

Rory wiped the bowl with a bit of soft bread and waited. There had to be more.

"Rory, you have many good qualities. But you have just as many faults. The worst is how you tend to leap first and ask for permission afterwards. It shows that you don't respect authority. Orphans don't have that luxury." Sister Anna sighed. "I wish they did."

Relieved, Rory glanced up at Sister Anna. She was startled by the remnants of worry in Sister Anna's expression. How exhausting it must be, Rory thought, to be responsible for all of the children. Loving them but having to send them away all the same. Knowing some would succeed but many wouldn't. How could she do it?

Sister Anna folded her bonnet neatly over once, then twice, staring down at her hands. "We'll find something for you to do here. You'll find it easier to say goodbye to Violet then." She put her hands flat on the table and pushed herself up. "It's late and we've talked about this incident enough."

"Sister, may I take a bath?" Rory scratched her head. "I'm afraid of what I might have picked up in jail."

Clearing her throat, Sister Anna agreed. "Exactly what I was going to suggest."

Rory gathered her courage. "Sister, what about Violet?"

"Come to my office after breakfast. We'll talk then," Sister Anna insisted. "Now go get clean."

The bathhouse was in another building but there was a long underground passage so the children and nuns didn't need to brace themselves against the outdoor weather in the colder months. Rory walked down the long, familiar tunnel, lit by electric light bulbs installed in the old iron gaslight fixtures. After visiting her old home, she couldn't believe how much she took for granted here at the Foundling. In Hell's Kitchen she'd never even seen a bathtub. Water had to be carried up the stairs from the one pump and then heated on the small stove and poured in a basin. But here she could just turn on the oversized metal bath knobs and hot steaming water cascaded into the porcelain tub with its clawed feet.

She took twice as long in the bath as she usually did, scrubbing hard to make sure she left the filth and lice of the jail behind. She wondered about the girl Brigid and if she had ever taken a long hot bath like this. There were definite advantages to living at the Foundling. What else would she miss if she ever had to leave? Central heating. The plentiful food. The library. Even her little chats with Sister Anna.

She walked back through the tunnel, the concrete floor cold to her damp feet, and the electric bulbs flickering like lightning bugs. Sometimes, Rory thought, her place at the Foundling felt like one of these new bulbs in an old gas fitting. It shouldn't work, but somehow it did. A light bulb burst and died in a shower of sparks, leaving Rory to walk the last ten yards in near darkness. So much for staying at the Foundling. Maybe it was a sign. If Violet had to leave the Foundling, then Rory had to go too.

Clean and dry, she crept into the dormitory. Rory made a beeline past the other seventeen beds straight to Violet's. Her sister's hair, as red as Rory's, was splayed across the white pillow. She lay on her back, arms extended, snuffling as she slept. The marks of dried tears and snot streaked her face. Rory put her head in her hands and rubbed her scalp so hard it hurt. Her sister had cried herself to sleep and it was all Rory's fault. She pulled the blanket up to Violet's neck and for a moment rested her hand against her sister's forehead. She let Vi's steady breathing calm her. After a time, Rory felt the knots in her neck and shoulders dissolve. "Violet," she whispered as she kissed her precious sister. "I'll never leave you again."

CHAPTER Eleven

THE NEXT MORNING RORY KNOCKED GINGERLY AT SISTER Anna's office door. The nun was sitting behind her desk examining a file. She closed it when she beckoned Rory to come in. Before Rory could get a word in, Sister Anna began speaking. "Our decision about Violet is final. I'm very sorry, Rory, but she leaves next week on the train out west."

Rory took a deep breath and spoke rapidly. "Sister, they threatened to put me on an orphan train at the jail. The matron and the police officer thought it was just the thing for a delinquent girl like me."

Sister Anna's mouth tightened. "That Officer O'Rourke! You are not going on a Children's Aid Society orphan train, and neither is Violet."

"But she's taking a train—"

"The orphan trains you heard about are despicable. The Children's Aid Society doesn't select good Catholic homes for the children before they get on the train." Almost as if she was thinking aloud, Sister Anna went on, "Sometimes I wonder if that is their true purpose—to remove young Irish children from the streets and take them far away from the Church."

"But what happens to the children?" Rory asked.

"The children can be claimed by almost anyone. The Society's recordkeeping is sloppy and sometimes they lose track of the children altogether. The children just vanish."

"Will that happen to Brigid?" Rory asked.

"Was that your . . . cellmate?" Sister Anna asked.

Rory nodded.

"No doubt some find good homes, but not all. Not nearly all." Sister Anna's eyes were bleak.

"How are your trains any different?" Rory asked.

"The agent and I write to parishes all over the country to find good Catholic homes. No one gets a child without a reference from the parish priest. I match the child to the family. We inspect the homes before they can keep the children."

Rory considered Sister Anna's words. It sounded good, but who knew what happened in the world outside the Foundling.

"We don't ever forget them either," Sister Anna continued. "We write to the families to see how the child is. And most important, the Foundling has the legal right to take the child back if the home is unsuitable in any way." A shadow crossed her face. Rory wondered if she was remembering a child in trouble. "Sometimes we make mistakes, but we try to correct them. Violet will be safe and happy. I guarantee it."

Rory was going to have to think quickly to stay one step ahead of Sister Anna. "I know, Sister," Rory said, staring at her feet. "If you've found the perfect family, you can't afford to lose this chance for Vi." Behind her back, she crossed her fingers.

"Really?" Sister Anna sounded surprised. She examined Rory's face, her eyebrows raised. Rory steeled herself to meet the nun's searching look without flinching.

"Of course, Sister. But I wonder . . . Do you think I could write to her? She's the only family I have." Without much effort, Rory let her voice tremble. "Even if we aren't together, I can't lose her completely."

"Perhaps," Sister Anna said slowly. "It's irregular, but not unheard of."

"Thank you." Her initial purpose was achieved. Now Sister Anna would tell her where Vi was going. Time to distract her further. Rory asked, "Sister, what about me?"

"You've been very helpful with the babies," Sister Anna began.

Rory grimaced. She had quite enough of changing diapers and braiding hair. "But you don't really need me for that."

"Your schoolwork is good. Especially your writing and reading. You could study to become a nun," Sister Anna spoke persuasively.

"Become a nun?" Rory took a step back. "I want a life. No offense intended."

"None taken, Rory." Sister Anna's lips twitched. "Well,

we could apprentice you. Perhaps as a typewriter, although your training class with Sister Mary Alice did not go well."

"Who knew all those keys could get so tangled?" Rory said.

"You could learn a skill like glove making or sewing."

Rory shook her head. "Have you seen my stitches? Sister Barbara says they will be the death of her. And when I tried to make gloves, I was all thumbs." She held up her hands in a helpless gesture.

Sister Anna laughed. "Perhaps not sewing. What about studying to be a teacher? Or a governess?"

Rory shook her head. She wanted a future that didn't require taking care of small children. Except for Violet, of course.

"Do you have any suggestions?" Sister Anna asked.

After a moment's hesitation, Rory, staring at the floor, said, "I like to tell people what to do. Maybe I should be a boss of something."

Sister Anna didn't say anything. Rory peeked and saw that Sister Anna had pressed her hand against her mouth and was quivering with pent-up laughter.

"Sister! Are you laughing at me?"

"No, of course not." But Sister Anna's voice was strangled. "A boss sounds excellent. Do you have any ideas of what kind of boss?"

"Not yet," Rory said, glaring at Sister Anna suspiciously.

"Before you can be a boss, you might have to learn to take orders," Sister Anna said helpfully.

"Oh." Rory thought for a bit. "If being a boss doesn't work out, maybe I should write stories."

"That's no way for a young lady to make a living," Sister Anna said.

"I could write for a magazine." Rory grew more excited. "How hard could it be to write a *Wild West Weekly* story? All I need are cowboys, Injuns, six-shooters, and mustangs."

Sister Anna's face appeared so tightly pinched her ears seemed to move together. "I see I shall have to keep a closer eye on your reading habits." She pressed her palms together. "I'll have a good think about your future and we'll talk later. But for now, we have to arrange the sewing."

"Sister, perhaps you misunderstood about my stitches? All thumbs!"

"Dear, we have fifty-seven children to take west. They'll each need a new outfit. And we sew colored labels into their collars to make sure that each child goes to the location I've chosen for him or her."

"Can Violet's be violet-colored?" Rory asked, making her voice wistful, as though Violet was already gone. "She would like that."

Sister Anna reached across the desk and patted Rory's hand. "I think that can be arranged. And don't worry, Rory. Violet will be happy."

"I know." Rory's voice sounded convincing. Violet would be happy because Rory was going to be with her. Even if she had to go as far west as the Pacific Ocean to make that happen.

CHAPTER Twelve

"Rory, you're tying my bow too tight. My hair hurts." Violet scowled at her sister.

"Hush, don't be foolish. Your hair can't hurt. Your scalp can hurt like the dickens, but not your hair," Rory said. She finished fixing Violet's hair and tugged the little girl's dress to make the hem even. "There you are. Pretty as a picture. Your new family is going to love you."

Violet shot Rory a startled glance. "But I thought . . ."

"Shhh!" Rory warned, jerking her head to indicate Sister Anna, who was moving about the dormitory trying to catch little Jimmy Harris. He scuttled under the first of the cribs lined up against the wall. Wise to his five-year-old ways, Sister Anna waited at the last crib and when he emerged, she scooped him up with one arm. With her other hand she checked his collar. "Number fifty-four," she said and then let him go. Her assistant, Sister Eileen, a sixteen-year-old novice who had just come to the Foundling, consulted a list clipped to a board. Sister Eileen, with her sweet face, sparkling black eyes, and dimples, was going on the train to help Sister Anna manage all the paperwork with so many adoptions.

"Fifty-four. Jimmy Harris. He is going to Clifton, Arizona, to the Flores family. His ribbon should be purple."

"Violet, Sister Eileen," Sister Anna corrected with a quick glance over at Rory and Violet.

Every child's assigned number had been painstakingly sewn into his or her clothes. The ones that Rory had done might have included a few specks of blood for her pains. The number was matched to the adoptive family Sister Anna had chosen for him or her. The color ribbon said which city the children were going to. Rory marveled at Sister Anna's power to organize fifty-seven adoptions all at once. Rory had been trying to catch a look at the list all week. She still didn't know anything about Violet's family. She only knew that Violet's number was twenty-two and her ribbon was also violet. But now Rory knew that a violet ribbon meant Clifton, Arizona.

"Vi," she whispered. "You're going to Arizona." She stumbled on the unfamiliar word.

"What's Arizona?" Violet asked.

"It's a nice place," Rory lied. In fact, she knew nothing at all about Arizona except that it was a territory. What was Sister Anna thinking—sending Vi into a place that wasn't even grown up enough to be a state?

Rory glanced outside the window. The carriages were lined up, waiting to take the children to the train station. The youngest children were running around the dormitory, overexcited by all the commotion. The Sisters bustled in and out, picking up the small case for each of the children chosen to go west. Each child had a brand-new dress or set of boys' dress clothes. The rest of their clothes had been mended and made as presentable as possible. Violet's small case was a little fuller than the others because Rory had stashed an extra bundle of clothes and treasures inside, including her copy of *Wild West Weekly*. Where they were going, she might find it useful.

Violet stared into Rory's blue eyes, identical to her own. "Rory, tell me again that we'll be all right."

"Yes, as long as you do what I say." She bent in and whispered into Violet's ear, "Remember what I told you. You are going to get in the taxi without me. I'm going to say goodbye and you have to look sad."

"But I will see you again?" Violet had asked this question a dozen times and her anxiousness broke Rory's heart.

"Yes. I'll find you," Rory assured her. "But you have to be convincing when you leave. Cry if you can. Sister Anna has been watching me like a hawk ever since . . . Never mind. She's been watching me lately." Rory had no intention of telling Vi that a cop had hauled her off to jail. That unfortunate episode was a secret known only to Rory and Sister Anna.

"Rory, I'm scared." Violet grabbed Rory's hand and squeezed hard enough to leave marks. "I don't want to go on a train." Her lovely blue eyes started to tear.

"It's going to be a grand adventure, Vi," Rory said enthusiastically, to ward off the crying storm. "And remember, you won't be alone. The other kids will be there and Sister

Anna. Sister Eileen is coming too—stick close to her. And I'll be there as soon as I can."

"What if you don't come?" Vi whispered.

"I'll come," Rory said in a voice that should end the matter. But she didn't reckon on Vi, who could be as stubborn as Rory herself.

"How can I be sure?"

With an impatient sigh, Rory pulled a silver chain from around her neck. Hanging from the chain was a tarnished saint's medal. "See this?" she asked.

"It was Mama's," Violet said, staring at the medal swaying from Rory's hand. "And you got it because you are the oldest." Rory had had to reinforce that lesson several times because Violet wanted the medal for herself.

"You know I'd never risk losing this, right?" Rory said.

"Right."

"I'm going to lend it to you." She lifted up Violet's thick red hair and clasped the necklace around her neck.

Violet stroked the medal, her lips in a round 0 of pleasure.

Rory pointed at the necklace. "This is my promise that we'll be together soon." She hugged Violet. "So you have to give it back when we *both* get to Arizona."

Vi fixed her eyes on Rory's face and nodded slowly. The medal was more convincing than Rory's reassurances.

"Rory!" The girls sprung apart at the sound of Sister Anna's voice. She stood behind them, like a great bird of prey watching over its dinner.

"Sister Anna!" Rory said. How much had she overheard?

"You're needed to help the rest of the children too, not just Violet."

Violet hid her face in Rory's skirt.

"Violet," Sister Anna said in a kind voice. "Let me see your collar."

"She's number twenty-two," Rory said, speaking quickly, hoping that Sister Anna wouldn't notice the necklace and begin asking questions.

"Twenty-two," Sister Anna repeated for Sister Eileen's sake. Sister Eileen looked up from the list. "Violet Fitzpatrick. She's going to Ramon and Elena Martinez in Clifton, Arizona."

Rory mouthed the name. Elena Martinez. What kind of name was that? What would she be like? Would she be kind to Violet? Would she understand that Violet was very brave except when it came to hairy spiders? Would she notice that Violet might not talk much but that was because she was thinking so hard? Would she love Violet? And most important of all, would she welcome a second red-haired daughter who was good with children and knew her letters and multiplication tables?

"Rory!" Sister Anna's voice broke through her troubled thoughts. "The other children . . ." she prompted.

Turning to Violet and giving her a last hug, Rory said, "I'll see you outside, Vi." Hurrying to assist the other Sisters, Rory carefully did not look back at Sister Anna but she imagined she could feel the Sister's eyes watching her even as she supervised all the other children.

CHAPTER Thirteen

THE GREAT BELL RANG IN THE MAIN HALL OF THE FOUNDLING. Rory squared her shoulders and took a deep breath. It was time. She helped the nuns shepherd fifty-seven children, the youngest only three years old and the eldest just six. Outside a line of horse-drawn taxicabs waited for the children. The nuns kept the smallest children from wandering under the hooves of the horses. Older boys from the school hoisted the trunks high onto the roofs of the taxicabs. The trunks were full of the children's suitcases, as well as ample supplies of foodstuffs, medicines, and linens for the journey. Rory kept Violet close by her side. At first Violet tried to pull away but the moment she saw the hubbub, she pressed herself into Rory's skirt.

Sister Anna seemed to be everywhere: overseeing the luggage, directing the drivers, counting the children. The other nuns who cared for the babies on a daily basis watched from the top step, like a line of stone-faced bowling pins. If they were affected by so many of their charges departing for the Wild West, Rory could not tell from their faces. Except for Sister Maureen, who dashed the tears from her eyes, only to have to do it again seconds later.

"Sister Maureen, if you cannot control yourself, return to the dormitory." Sister Anna's stern voice instantly dried Sister Maureen's tears. "I won't have you upsetting the children."

Sister Maureen inclined her head. "I'm sorry, Sister Anna; it's just that they are so small. And they are going so very far."

"They are going to proper families who will give them a home and raise them as good Catholics," Sister Anna said loudly. "They are very lucky."

Rory overheard and snorted. "Some home, on the other side of the country." Rory's impudence was carefully planned; she didn't want Sister Anna to wonder why she was being so docile.

Sister Anna fixed Rory with a stern glare. "Rory, that's enough. Now say your farewells to Violet; we'll be leaving soon." Raising her voice, she scolded one of the boys for letting a trunk drop to the ground.

Rory knelt down so she could be at Violet's level. "It's time for you to go."

Violet glanced at Sister Anna. "All right, Rory."

"I won't see you for a very long time," Rory said deliberately, conscious of Sister Anna's listening ear.

Nodding, Violet said, "I know."

"You're being very brave," Rory said, watching Sister Anna from the corner of her eye. As soon as the nun's attention was diverted, she whispered sharply to Violet, "Too brave! You've got to look upset! Like this." Rory made a sad and anxious face. As though Rory was looking into a mirror, Violet's face contorted to match Rory's. Violet blinked so many times that her bright blue eyes filled with tears and she stuck out her lower lip so it could tremble in a pitiful manner.

"Good girl," Rory said approvingly. "Now, a last hug."

Pressed tightly against Rory's body, Violet whispered, "This is a game, right? You're coming to rescue me?"

"Sooner than you think." She unwrapped Violet's arms from around her waist. "I promise." She touched the medal hanging around Violet's throat with the tip of her finger. "Take care of Mama's necklace. I want it back and it had better be in perfect condition."

Squeezing her lips together, Violet nodded. Rory buried her face in Violet's neck and inhaled everything she loved about her little sister. Then she lifted Violet up and into the waiting seat in the taxi. Each cab would carry half a dozen children and at least one minder. Now, it was time to make sure she wasn't left behind. She turned and stopped dead, almost running into Sister Anna's dark skirts.

Her voice unusually tender, Sister Anna said, "I'll watch over her on the journey."

Rory nodded. The tears she brushed away were not as pretend as she would have liked. What if something went wrong? What if this really was the last time she saw Violet?

"Sister, it's too hard to watch Vi leave," Rory said. "I'm going inside."

Sister Anna looked as if she was about to say something

when a trunk crashed from the top of a carriage to the pavement. She rushed over to make certain there was no damage.

This was her chance. Rory slipped between the cabs to the street side. Shielded from the Sisters' view, she ran to the last of the carriages. Catching hold of the lowest rung on the ladder on the back of the cab, she pulled herself up as quickly as she could. This was one of the most dangerous moments of her plan. Could she hide on top of the cab amidst the luggage without being seen? She squeezed between two trunks, tucking her skirt close to her body. The only way to see below was to slither to the front of the cab and prop herself up on the rail to peek at the street.

Then one child realized he was leaving the only home he had ever known. The wailing started with him and spread to the other children, from cab to cab, like a tenement fire leaping from building to building. Peeking over the railing, Rory saw the nuns were crying too. Even Sister Anna had tears in her eyes. As though Sister Anna had a sixth sense, she glanced up at the top of the carriages. Rory pushed her body into the cab roof and closed her eyes tight. With relief she heard Sister Anna announce it was time to go to the ferry that would take the group to the train. Sister Anna stepped briskly into the first cab in line without a backward glance at the Foundling. Why should she, Rory asked herself. Sister Anna would be coming back.

The first cab lurched into motion, followed by the rest. Rory's driver shook his reins and the taxi moved forward in line.

Rory propped herself up on one elbow and watched the bulk of the Foundling disappear down the street. Then it hit her. She would never see any of this again. No New York. No Foundling. No Sister Anna.

Rory shook herself. Enough of self-pity. Hadn't Rory always known exactly what she wanted? If Rory had to abandon every familiar person, place, and thing to stay with Violet she would do it. Just before the cab turned a corner, Rory waved and whispered, "So long, Foundling."

PART TWO

The Journey

CHAPTER Fourteen

WEDGED BETWEEN THE TRUNKS, RORY TWISTED HER BODY SO
she could kneel and watch the city fly by. Ahead of her, she
could see the line of eight other cabs, like a funeral procession
making its serpentine way across Sixty-Ninth Street to Fifth
Avenue. Underneath her, the sniffling and moaning of six
little kids and the exasperated tones of the nurse floated up
to her. Rory smothered a giggle; fifty-seven children would
overwhelm the nurses and nuns in no time at all.

It was forty blocks from the Foundling to the ferry. Rory
got to see a new Manhattan, as different from Hell's Kitchen
and the Foundling as chalk was from cheese. She forgot the
trunk poking her in the back as posh hotels towered over
the streets. But they were nothing compared to St. Patrick's
Cathedral. She'd been inside once before when the Sisters
took the orphans at Easter, but she hadn't had the chance
to admire the soaring spires. She lay flat and imagined her

soul floating up into the sky, as though this cathedral was the entryway to the kingdom of heaven.

As the cab traveled south, the women on the sidewalks became more fashionable. Rory forgot herself in the thrill of gawking at the latest styles—the women here wore elaborately flowered hats and dresses with barely a bustle. One young woman was riding a bicycle. The front wheel was almost as high as Rory's taxicab. Rory let go of her grip on the railing to wave gaily. The young woman looked surprised for a moment, then smiled and waved back.

The cabs turning at Thirty-Fourth Street shook Rory out of her reverie—she didn't have much time to figure a way off this cab roof, onto the ferry, and on board the Sisters' train—all without being seen. One glimpse of her and Sister Anna would send her back to the Foundling. And that would be the end of Rory and Violet together. She could not fail. She pulled a kerchief she had borrowed from the clothes bin in the older girls' dormitory out of her pocket and tied it around her head to disguise her flaming red hair.

The cab turned into the Ferry Terminal. After a short wait it rumbled onto the Pennsylvania Railroad ferry, jostling for its place among other cabs, wagons, and even a few automobiles. Rory crept to the edge of the carriage, watching and waiting. Everywhere Rory looked she saw travelers in vehicles and on foot, all much too busy to notice one girl on top of a cab. To her surprise, the Sisters didn't leave the cabs. The surest way to stay with Violet was to remain where she was, so Rory waited and enjoyed the fresh breeze off the river.

From her high perch, she had a perfect view of the far-off shore of New Jersey. Other than a little cluster of buildings right in front of the ferry, New Jersey seemed to be mostly trees.

The ferry blew its horn three times and began its journey across the Hudson River. Beneath her, Rory heard the renewed sobbing of small children who had never been on a boat before. It took all of Rory's determination not to climb down and check on Violet. But she had to think of the plan. Violet needed Rory to stay hidden until it was too late for the Sisters to send her back.

The river was choppy and the wind was cold out on the water. Rory wondered if she would ever see New York and the Foundling again. She tore her eyes away from the shrinking city. There was no use in looking back, she thought; time to worry about the future. Especially the next hour or so.

The ferry bumped against the dock on the New Jersey side. A large sign proclaimed it was Exchange Place. Workers pulled the ferry to the dock with ropes slick with the gray river water. After a wait that seemed endless, Rory's cab moved forward to dry land. It lined up next to the other eight cabs. As soon as Sister Anna got out of the first cab and began supervising a small army of porters to collect the luggage from the tops of the cabs, Rory clutched the railing on the cab roof, ready to spring to the ground.

But she hesitated. Was it better to get off before the porters reached her cab? Or wait, hoping to remain unseen and then make her escape when the carriages were unloaded?

An authoritative voice said, "Hurry up, we have to get these kids to their train."

Before she had made up her mind, the children beneath her had been helped out—some with tearstained faces—and were gathering in a tight knot near Sister Anna.

The carriage shook as a porter scurried up the ladder. Rory nearly screamed when the porter's bald head and then his face popped up over the top rung. The porter took one look at Rory, recoiled, and fell back to the ground with a loud cry.

"Stop fooling about. We don't have any time for your jokes," the authoritative voice said.

"There's someone up here," the porter exclaimed. "Scared the bejabbers out of me."

"Let me see." A heavier body started clambering up the ladder.

Holding on to the railing at the top of the cab, Rory swung her body off the carriage away from the ladder. She dropped four feet to the ground, hitting with an impact that took her breath away. Then she scurried under the carriage.

"I don't see anyone." The authoritative voice was exasperated.

"'Twas a girl! She was there, I swear!"

"Have you been drinking again? I warned you last time . . ."

"I haven't touched a drop!" The porter's bald head shone with sweat.

Through the carriage wheel's spokes, Rory shifted her view from the porter's boots to the other side of the carriage where she could keep her eye on Sister Anna. She was counting the children in pairs, directing the frightened children into a neat line. The children huddled together, clasping each other's hands tightly. Violet clutched Sister Eileen's hand.

Several of the children looked green; the motion of the ferry on the water had not agreed with their delicate tummies. Violet didn't appear sick; she looked furious, her lower lip between her teeth. Violet's eyes crisscrossed the terminal looking for Rory. Rory knew that Violet would have something sharp to say when they were finally together again.

The chief porter, the one with the authoritative voice, approached the Sisters. "Sisters, we have all the baggage. We'd best hurry," he said. "The train leaves in a few minutes."

"They won't leave without us," Sister Anna said confidently.

"They would and they will, Sister!"

While Sister Anna argued with the porter, Rory slipped out from under the carriage. She circled wide away from the Foundling group to blend in with the other passengers crowding into the station. She looked back to see Sister Anna leading the way to the train, her back straight and her black cape floating out behind her. She looked like one of the carved wooden ladies on the front of sailing ships, cutting through the waves of people. The passage of almost sixty orphans through the chaos in the station caused a murmur of comments and smiles from the other passengers. Even Rory had to admit they looked adorable. There was Violet staring about the busy station with a wide-open mouth.

"Hold on, Vi. Just get on the train and I'll be with you

soon," Rory muttered. She gave herself a shake. She had to forget about Vi for a minute and get going. First, to find the St. Louis train and get aboard before the Sisters did. Rory spotted a chalk-written sign listing the departures. She scanned it impatiently until she saw "St. Louis Express. Track 3." Taking off at a run, she headed for the tracks.

A steam engine waited at the end of the platform, belching out little puffs of smoke as though it was getting ready for a major effort. Travelers were already boarding. Although there were dozens of passengers on the platform, she felt suddenly alone, as though the sun only shone on her, inviting everyone to notice the unaccompanied orphan. Her scalp started to sweat under her kerchief.

"All aboard!" A man in uniform was bellowing his message up and down the platform. Rory took care not to attract his attention.

She didn't have much time. A large man in a brown checked suit stood at the rear of the train, pacing and looking at his watch every few seconds. He was arguing with an official from the train.

"They'll be here. The Sisters never miss a train," the man in the suit said. "Have you any idea how difficult it is to move fifty-seven small children? And their luggage? And food and bedding for a week?"

"No," the official answered. "And Mr. Swayne, I don't care. This train has a schedule to meet. As a courtesy we permitted your group to add a car to the train . . ."

"Half of your company's Board of Directors are patrons of

the Foundling Hospital," Mr. Swayne retorted. "I assure you, your train will wait if need be. But I think I see them."

Hiding her face, Rory hurried past the two men as though she were a paying passenger. She made her way past the engine car, followed by the coal car, the baggage car, and several passenger cars where men in uniforms directed passengers. The farther down the platform she went, the more worried she became. Her heart was pounding and her palms were moist. How was she to find the Sisters' car without asking anyone? Thinking of Mr. Swayne's conversation she wondered how you added a car to the train anyway. Maybe it was better to just sneak onto the train and find the Sisters after the train left the station. How hard could it be to find almost sixty orphans, escorted by nuns in full black habits and nurses wearing their working white uniforms?

Taking a deep breath, Rory climbed into the nearest car. Unluckily, a conductor was making his way down the rows of bench seats. Rory ducked behind the last bench and the wall and tried to make her lanky body small and unnoticeable.

"What do we have here?" A mincing voice accompanied a strong grip on her arm. Rory squealed as he hauled her from her hiding place.

"Where's your ticket, miss?" The conductor was a small man whose uniform seemed a tad too big.

Rory straightened up and met his eyes squarely. Her only chance was to brazen it out. "I'm with the Foundling," Rory muttered. "Do you know where they are?"

The conductor frowned. "If you really were with the

Foundling, you'd know they have their own car at the rear of the train. And the Children's Aid Society kids already boarded." He nudged her back to the doorway. With every step Rory knew she was closer to losing everything. She didn't move and he would have to shove her to get her to leave.

"No ticket, no ride, little girl," he said. "Now move, before I call the police."

Rory slowly let him push her. She was halfway out the door when she saw Sister Anna not twenty feet away.

The man in the brown suit walked backward in front of Sister Anna. "The train won't wait for you, Sister."

"Of course it will, Mr. Swayne," Sister Anna said, but her step quickened. The little children were practically running and the porters with all the trunks were red-faced and panting.

Rory whirled around, her back to the platform and Sister Anna. "Mister, I really am an orphan. My little sister is with the Foundling. If you throw me off then my family is wrecked forever. Please let me stay!" She locked her hands around the door handle and held on for her life.

"If you haven't paid, you don't ride my train." He began to pry her fingers off the handle. Out on the platform, Sister Anna passed by, too intent on her argument with Mr. Swayne, the Foundling's agent, to notice Rory.

"But mister, just give me a chance!" Rory said desperately.

"OFF!" he shouted and pushed her from the train. Rory landed on the platform, falling on one knee and tearing her dress. He closed the door behind her with a slam. Her kerchief fell to the ground and through the tears in her eyes Rory groped to get it back.

At that moment the train whistle blew twice. Rory looked up and down the platform. There were no more passengers. The train jerked as the steam engine began pulling out of the station. Unstoppable.

It was too late. She had lost Violet. Her stomach contracted and she retched. Her head in her hands, she felt for the first time what it was like to be alone.

"Hey, Red!" A voice from above startled her. Rory jumped to her feet, looking up. "Remember me? From jail!"

Brigid was hanging from a window just barely wider than her frame. She was grinning. The train moved slowly, taking her closer to Rory and then away.

A jolt of hope through her body felt like lightning. Rory ran alongside Brigid's window. "I have to get on this train!"

"Why should I help you?" Brigid's broad smile had more than a little malice in it. Rory didn't care. She had a second chance and she wasn't going to waste it.

"'Cause I'll owe you one!" Rory panted.

"How do I know you're good for it?"

"I never break a promise!" Rory shouted.

"It's a deal!" She leaned from the window and stuck both her hands out toward Rory. "Jump!" she commanded.

Rory stretched out her arms and leapt for the moving train.

CHAPTER Fifteen

Rory's hands caught hold of Brigid's. Her knees and feet banged hard against the side of the train. The clicking of the wheels against the rails sped up and the passing air pushed against her body, blowing her skirt up over her head. Luckily there was no one to notice. Rory saw the train had cleared the platform. If she fell now she'd drop to sharp stones.

"Pull yourself up," Brigid ordered.

"I'm trying," Rory gasped. "Don't let go!"

Rory struggled to climb up, the toes of her worn boots sliding against the side of the train. Rory could see the top of the window was cutting into Brigid's arms, but the girl's grip didn't loosen. Rory kicked at the side but her feet couldn't find any purchase.

"Hurry!" Rory cried.

With a huge yank, Brigid hauled Rory up. Rory let go with her right hand and took hold of the window sash. Brigid grabbed Rory's shoulders and Rory tumbled through the window to the wooden bench beneath.

"Thanks," Rory managed to say, panting for air.

Brigid collapsed in the corner between the bench and the window. "I couldn't believe it when I saw you there on the platform," she wheezed. "I wasn't sure until I saw that hair, then I knew."

"My hair?" Rory patted at her head but her kerchief was gone.

"What are you doing here?" Brigid asked. "I thought your nuns would never let you get shipped out."

Rory sighed. "They shipped my baby sister instead. They took her from me and are sending her to a family in Arizona."

"Ah, Red, that's rough," Brigid said. Her voice was husky and she seemed to have trouble catching her breath. Rory remembered Brigid had had a bad cough in jail too.

"I'm stowing away so we don't get separated," Rory said.

Brigid grinned appreciatively. "Red, I didn't know you had it in you."

With a shrug, Rory said, "I'm just doing what I have to. What about you?"

"I told you I was doomed to head west," said Brigid. "The Society put me on the first train."

"You were right," Rory agreed. "Where are you heading?"

"St. Louis, I think. So where are your precious nuns and sister?" Brigid asked.

"They have a private car at the end of the train."

"A private car? Ooh-la-la." Brigid whistled. "It has to be a lot nicer than this."

Rory examined her surroundings. There were wooden benches, the seats covered with a thin fabric. Every bench had three or four kids her age or older crammed into it like sardines in a tin. At the end of the car, there was a partition with a curtained door. That must be where the toilet was. There was nothing else in the car.

"I'd just about given up when you called to me," Rory confessed. "I'd still be on that platform without your quick thinking." It was a miracle, she thought but didn't say. "I owe you."

"They called me Fast Fingers Brigid on the street," she said ruefully. "I'm glad I could be useful for something other than thieving."

"Of course you are!" Rory exclaimed. "Sister Anna always says we're on this earth for a purpose. We might not know what it is, but God has a plan for everyone."

"That's nice to hear," Brigid said. "Usually people just tell me I'm worthless. When I got this cough my uncle threw me out. He didn't want to get sick too."

Rory gazed at her for a long time. Brigid's tough exterior showed some signs of cracking. She reached over and touched Brigid's hand. "At the Foundling, the nuns say no one is worthless." Rory spoke from her heart. "And they take care of anyone who asks for help."

"They sound nice," Brigid said.

"Yeah, they were. But I won't be going back," Rory said.

She felt a spasm in her chest. This wasn't a game she was playing. If she were separated from Violet, if she lost track of the nuns, if she got stuck on this train . . . so many ifs. And no backup plan at all.

"I hope it works out for you," Brigid said.

The girls were silent. At the front of the carriage, the curtain moved aside. A tall boy about Rory's age swaggered out and headed for Rory and Brigid. He had black hair and his face was disfigured by pockmarks. His large hands had cuts across the knuckles. She recognized the type from her days in Hell's Kitchen. He might be a kid like them, but he was in charge and he'd beat up anyone who disagreed. He stared at Rory, taking in every detail, from her sweaty face to her torn dress.

"Brigid, who's this?" he asked.

"This is Red," Brigid answered, not meeting his eyes.

"She's in my seat."

Rory stood up and stumbled at the unfamiliar movement of the train. "I'll change seats." Brigid had helped her out; Rory didn't want to get her into any trouble.

"Jack, there's room. She's one of us," Brigid said, pulling Rory back to the seat.

"Then why didn't she come with Miss Worthington?" he accused. "She ain't on the list."

"Half the names on the list are wrong," Brigid shot back with more courage than Rory would have had. But then Rory's life at the Foundling had been so occupied with small children, she didn't have much experience with older kids.

"Worthington said there's just enough food to get us to St. Louis. We can't be feeding strays. How'd she even get in here anyway?"

"I came through the window," Rory said.

He glanced at her, then back to Brigid. "How do you know her?"

"We met in jail."

His ugly face lightened with a smile. "I met some of my best friends when I was enjoying the hospitality of the New York cops."

Rory moved to make room for him. "I won't be here long," she said. "And I promise not to eat anything."

"Why are you here? No one wants to go out west."

"I do." She explained the situation with Violet. "The Sisters won't take older kids, so they left me behind."

"Nuns stole your sister? That's bad news."

Rory felt she had to explain why the nuns were good people. "The Sisters aren't like your Children's Aid Society. They're kind and they want to do the right thing by Violet. They've got a nice family all lined up for her. For every one of the orphans."

"And you believe that?" Jack sneered. "All grown-ups lie."

"Not Sister Anna." Rory's certainty stopped Jack in his tracks.

Picking at one of the scabs on his knuckle, he asked, "So what are you going to do? Take her off the train?"

Rory shook her head. "Nah, a good family is worth a

look. If I like what I see, I'm going to try and convince them to take me too."

"What if they won't?" Brigid asked.

"Then I'll take her away. We'll make our own life in the Wild West." Rory wished this part of her scheme was better planned. She could see the doubts in her companions' faces.

"It don't matter," Jack said. "The nuns'll send you back as soon as they find you."

"Not if I time it just right," Rory argued. "There are fifty-seven kids in that train car with only seven grown-ups."

"So?" Jack asked. "We've got fifty with only three minders."

With a grin Rory said, "The oldest is six. Most are three and four years old."

Brigid burst out laughing. "By the time you show your mug, they'll be desperate."

"I don't get it," Jack said with a scowl. "What's so funny?"

"You've never taken care of little kids, have you?" Brigid asked, still chuckling. "They're a lot of work. And as soon as you get one to sleep, another one wakes up."

"Exactly!" Rory said. "Plus at the Foundling I took care of lots of kids anyway, not just my sister. They'll be so happy to see me, they'll forget about sending me home."

With the wiliness learned on the street, Jack put his finger on the weakness in her plan. "But the nuns will be coming back to New York. They'll just bring you with them."

Rory caught her bottom lip between her teeth. "I'll climb

that mountain when I get there. But for now, I need to hide for a day or so."

"You can stay with us," Brigid offered.

The train began to go slower. After a moment, Rory heard the brakes stopping the train.

"What's happening?" she cried, pressing her face against the window, trying to see why the train wasn't moving. "Do you think they know I'm here?"

Jack's voice from behind her made fun of her fears. "You think they'd stop the train just for you? With all the rich people who'll cut up something fierce if their trip is delayed? We're just letting some other train go by."

"Are you sure?" Rory asked.

"Course I'm sure," he said. "Girls don't know anything about trains."

Brigid shoved him. "Like you know anything about trains. You're just guessing."

"Stands to reason," he muttered. He got up and crossed the aisle to join the other boys peering out the window.

Rory leaned back against the bench and let out a long breath. Brigid was staring behind Rory as though she'd seen a ghost or, worse, a conductor. Rory sensed movement from the other kids behind them. "Brigid, what's wrong?"

"Quick, get down, Red!" Brigid whispered. "It's Miss Worthington."

As Rory ducked down onto the floor underneath the bench, she caught a glimpse of a tall woman wearing a shabby traveling dress. She was moving along the corridor counting off the kids. She came closer, close enough that Rory could see her boots were as worn as Rory's. She added Brigid to the tally and moved on.

The lady stopped at the front of the carriage and raised her voice so she could be heard. "There are sandwiches here. One for each child. And there's a bucket of drinking water and a cup. Take turns and don't spill anything. There's nothing else until dinner." With that she moved to the next car.

Rory stayed hidden, watching the feet of the kids scramble to line up for their sandwiches. The kids had clothes that looked new. Some of them even had new shoes. She wished she did.

After a time, Brigid came back. "Come out, Red, it's safe."

Rory rolled out from under the bench and tried to dust off the dirt on the creases of her skirt.

"Don't worry about it," Brigid said. "You're still cleaner than most of us. They gave us new clothes but the only baths we've had were ice cold." She had a thick sandwich between her hands. She pulled it into two pieces and handed one of them to Rory.

Rory realized she was starving. Breakfast at the Foundling was a long time ago. "Thanks!" She took a large bite. "Ugh!" she said, grimacing. "It's mustard." She chewed gingerly and forced herself to swallow it. She looked between the slices. Sure enough, it was mustard and mustard only. No cheese. No meat. She had seen Sister Anna supervising the food for the journey. Not only were the Foundling kids going to get fresh bread, meat, and cheese; there was fruit for dessert.

Brigid was bolting it down as though she had not eaten in days.

"Here," said Rory, handing the mustard sandwich back to Brigid. If she thought this was good, she must be far hungrier than Rory.

Brigid shrugged. "Are you sure?"

"I am."

Brigid devoured Rory's half sandwich in two bites.

Rory had thought to wait a day or two before finding Sister Anna and Violet. Her stomach rumbled. If she didn't want to starve, she might have to make her move sooner than she had planned.

CHAPTER Sixteen

As THE TRAIN MADE ITS WAY ACROSS AND DOWN NEW JERSEY, Rory stared out the window watching the backside of buildings. The train whistled every time they came to a road. She had never traveled so quickly, changing from open countryside to small town and back again. No sooner had she noticed they were passing through a town than they were speeding out of it. How could she get her bearings when the train never stopped moving? After hours of traveling, Rory faced the facts. The world was much bigger than she had thought. Who would care about a twelve-year-old girl and her baby sister? Rory sighed. She knew who. The farther west the train went just hastened the moment when Rory would have to face Sister Anna.

Brigid came back from the curtained toilet. "Red, you have to try it."

Rory raised her eyebrows. "Why?"

"When you pee it goes straight onto the tracks—you can see the ground from the toilet."

"Later, maybe." Rory smiled. "Are you sure that no one will ask any questions about me?"

"Miss Worthington counted us once already—and I don't think she's the type to do any more work than she has to."

Rory gave a sharp nod. "Then that's all right."

"When are you going to tell the nuns you're here?" Brigid asked. "Then you won't need to worry anymore."

"The first stop is Philadelphia, right?" Rory asked. "I'll wait until after then. The last thing I want is for the nuns to find some Good Samaritan who'll escort me back to New York."

"I saw the Foundling car being loaded with lots of trunks," Brigid said. "What's in all those trunks anyway?"

Rory had seen Brigid's small bundle of a few mended clean clothes. "Just some clothes," she said, making it seem like each child didn't have a new outfit. "And food for the trip. Medicines. And Sister Anna's paperwork."

"Oh." Brigid wiped her mouth with the back of her hand. "And what about you? You don't have any clothes but the ones on your back—and you made a right mess of those."

Rory glanced down at the rip in her skirt and the streaks of tar and dirt. "I hid some clothes with Violet's things."

Brigid's green eyes were admiring. "You thought of everything."

"Not everything, or else I wouldn't have needed your help." Rory grabbed Brigid's hand. "When I go back I can't ever tell Sister Anna how I got on the train. She'd kill me."

"You ran away. How can you be so sure of your welcome?" Brigid asked, her head tilted toward Rory.

A dozen images of Sister Anna flashed through Rory's mind. Some stern and angry and others stern but kind. "She'll be mad. But she won't be surprised. She knows I'd never leave Violet." She leaned forward, her voice dropping to a whisper. "It's my secret weapon, really. I think she likes how I stick to Violet, no matter what." She nodded sharply, convincing herself. "She'll let me stay."

Brigid looked down at her feet, not meeting Rory's eyes. "I wouldn't mind having a sister like you."

"Really?" Rory felt a warmth start in her chest and radiate through her whole body. "Thanks, Brigid. You'd be a good sister. I love Violet, but she'll never be as quick-witted as you. She's never had to survive by herself like you and me." Rory chewed on a torn fingernail. "I wish you could meet her though. We could all be friends."

"We won't get the chance, will we?" Brigid said with a curled lip. "In a few days, some stranger'll pick me off the auction block to do who knows what."

"They don't actually sell you, do they?" Rory felt faint. Brigid couldn't be sold like a piece of meat. Slavery was a thing of the past.

"Naw," Brigid said. "But it feels like it. Miss Worthington said we have to clean up. As if we could with a bucket of cold water and no soap. And mind our manners something sharp. She said the sooner we're picked, the sooner she can go home."

Rory squeezed Brigid's hand without saying a word. How awful, she thought. No matter how angry she was with Sister Anna, no matter what terrible accusations Rory had hurled at her, she knew that Sister Anna would do her best for the children. And Rory had no doubt that Sister Anna would act out of love. Not just because it was her job.

CHAPTER Seventeen

THE CONDUCTOR CAME INTO THEIR CAR TWICE. MISS Worthington made her rounds too, clutching a handful of tickets and counting the kids in a halfhearted manner. Every time there was any danger of Rory's discovery, Brigid was able to warn her in time and she hid on the floor under Brigid's feet.

Rory passed the long hours watching the scenery change outside the window. Fields as far as the eye could see were planted with . . . Rory wasn't sure what. Workers in some of the fields were gathering large golden stalks. Could that be corn? When there weren't fields or small towns, there were trees turning all shades of gold and red and orange. She had thought Central Park was big, but now she knew that her eyes hadn't been wide enough or tall enough to see a real forest. The world kept getting bigger. Rory pinched her arm to remind herself that she was still exactly the same size.

Sometimes another train would come rushing toward them, faster and faster as though it was going to smash into them. But at the last minute, Rory saw the train was always on another track altogether.

Once, Brigid shook Rory awake to see an outcropping that had words painted on it. "They've even got wall writing out here," she said.

Rubbing her eyes, Rory said, "You didn't have to wake me up." But she understood. It was reassuring to find similarities between here and home: rotten kids everywhere were painting their thoughts in places carefully chosen to irritate grown-ups.

"Look at that!" Rory said as they slowed to pass through a station. Another train was there, its engine stopped under a water tank. A sluice was pouring water into the engine. "It's like feeding a baby," Rory said with a giggle.

Brigid gave Rory a sidelong glance. "If you say so. You're the expert on babies."

Big clouds of steam billowed out, hiding the train's engineer in his little compartment. The girls burst out laughing. "This baby expert never saw a kid do that!" Rory said.

As the sky began to darken, Miss Worthington had Jack and another boy distribute sandwiches. Brigid tore hers in half and handed it to Rory. This time Rory was hungry enough to accept.

"Thanks," Rory said, tucking into it. "It's not that bad."

"Anything is good when you're hungry," Brigid said.

"When I go back to the nuns I'll bring you some food," Rory promised, talking around the stale bread and mustard in her mouth.

Rory was half asleep when the conductor announced, "Philadelphia is the next stop! Philadelphia is next."

Rory and Brigid peered through the window. The train clicked slowly through block after block of city.

"It's big," whispered Brigid.

Rory spoke past the nervous lump in her throat. "Yeah, it's almost as big as New York. But remember, New York is the greatest city on earth."

"And so far, the only city either of us has ever been to," Brigid answered back.

At Philadelphia's station the train stopped inside a great glass-roofed building alongside many other trains. Rory pulled the window down and winced at all the noise outside. There were more horses and carriages than cars, but just as many people as in Exchange Place. Philadelphia was the final destination for many passengers and there were whistles for porters. Passengers got on and off the train, some because it was journey's end, but others just to stretch their legs.

Rory's fingers gripped the window's edges tightly. What was she thinking, throwing Vi and herself into the huge world? She was an idiot to think she could control anything out here. She should have stayed at the Foundling and hid Violet until Sister Anna left with the others. Yes, that would have worked. How was it that she only thought of this now when it was too late?

"I'm going out," Jack said, interrupting her thoughts.

"We're not supposed to," Brigid warned.

"Nobody tells me what to do!" Jack said. But he didn't make it as far as the door before Miss Worthington stopped him.

"All of you are supposed to stay on the train at all times," she said. "It's more than my job is worth if I let you leave, even for a minute."

Rory ducked down under the window sash when she saw Sister Eileen walk toward her car with a change purse. Giving Sister Eileen enough time to pass by, Rory poked her head up. She watched Sister Eileen bargain with a vendor to buy fresh fruit from a cart. She also called to another vendor with cans of fresh milk to follow her back to the last car. Fresh fruit and milk. Rory had to speak sternly to her stomach to keep it from growling. When she did return to the Sisters, she would eat well. All at once, Rory felt better. Her plan had gotten them this far; she and Violet would be fine. Better than fine.

"Does Sister Eileen look tired to you?" she asked Brigid.

Brigid nodded. "Exhausted." They both giggled.

Suddenly Sister Eileen began yelling. Rory stuck her head out the window to see what had attracted the young novice's attention. A flock of women, nuns in black habits and nurses in white, were running across the platform. She leaned out farther to see what they were chasing. It was a child. A child with red hair and a determined expression.

"Rory, you can't let them see you!" Brigid urged.

"It's Violet!" Rory said to Brigid over her shoulder. "She got off the train somehow."

"Rory! I want Rory!" Violet screamed. Sister Eileen dropped her groceries and ran after her. Violet dodged the Sister's arms, darting under a stopped wagon. "Rory!"

Sister Eileen didn't hesitate. She fell to her hands and knees and crawled after Violet while the other adults surrounded the wagon.

Without thinking, Rory started to head for the door. "I'm coming, Vi!"

Brigid hauled her back to the seat. "Are you nuts?" Brigid asked. "Have you come this far to give yourself away now?"

Rory stopped struggling. Brigid was right. She held up her hands and Brigid let her go, watching her with suspicion. Rory returned to the window and peeked out. The nuns had managed to corral Violet. A vision of a wild bronco being captured popped into Rory's mind. She'd read Violet a story in *Wild West Weekly* where a horse had to be cornered like this. Violet had apparently taken it to heart.

The nuns passed her window carrying Vi, who kicked and writhed in their arms. In a voice grown hoarse from screaming, she called, "I want my sister!"

"What's happening?" Brigid asked, watching Rory warily.

"She's back in the train," Rory said, slowly closing the window and sinking back down to the seat. She pinned her arms against her stomach trying to stop shaking. "She was scared. I should never have left her alone for so long. She thinks I abandoned her."

"You didn't have a choice, did you?" Brigid asked. "She's a kid. She'll get over it."

"No!" Rory sat up and glared at Brigid. "Violet never has to suffer. I'm here to make certain she doesn't. I have to go to her." Rory calculated how far they were from New York and how difficult it would be to send her home. Too difficult, she decided. "As soon as the train leaves the station, I'm finding Sister Anna."

It took Rory a moment before she noticed the disappointment on Brigid's face. "What's wrong?"

"Nothing," Brigid said. Tears glistened in her eyes and she rubbed them with the back of her hand. "I got something in my eye." She got up and stomped off to the water bucket. While she was gone, Rory figured it out.

Brigid didn't return until the train had left the city and entered the dark countryside. She slouched in her seat, not meeting Rory's eyes.

"I'll miss you too," Rory said, staring straight ahead.

"Who said anything about missing anybody?" Brigid said. "I've never needed anybody and I don't need you."

Rory punched Brigid in the shoulder. "Don't be maudlin. I'm only going to the end of the train. This isn't goodbye."

With a deep sniff, Brigid said, "Maybe it is, maybe it isn't."

"I'll see you later. I promise," Rory said, getting up and walking toward the end of the car. She glanced back and saw Brigid staring out the window.

Rory entered the first-class car and then a car filled with

stout men smoking cigars and drinking strong spirits. Rory held her nose and tried to open the far door to get to the Foundling car, but it didn't budge.

Rory leaned against the door and thought hard. The only thing between her and Violet was a single locked door. Now that she was so close, Rory couldn't let another minute pass without holding Violet. Maybe Jack knew how to pick a lock? Some street kids did pick locks. Maybe she should just knock? But then she might lose the element of surprise, which she thought would be to her advantage. Rory was afraid she would need every advantage she could get when she faced Sister Anna.

The conductor, the same one who had thrown her off the train, entered the car from the other door. Without thinking, she ducked behind a seat. But as she cowered on the floor, she thought better of hiding. Why not let him help her? He owed her for the humiliating way he had treated her. She stood up, dusted off her skirt, and planted herself in front of him.

He stared at her in surprise. "You!" he said. "How did you get here?"

"I snuck on," Rory told him, without a trace of apology.

"You won't stay on for long," he threatened. "At the next stop . . ."

"Thank goodness," Rory said. "I was afraid you were going to bring me back to the Foundling Sisters. They'd punish me something fierce for hitching a ride on the train."

The conductor smiled, but not a nice smile. "On second thought," he said, "perhaps I was too hasty. You're the Foundling's problem; they should take care of you."

Rory blinked to force tears to her eyes and let her lower lip tremble. "Oh please, mister, not the nuns!"

The conductor twisted her arm behind her back and frog-marched her to the locked door. He pulled a keychain from his belt and opened it. They had to cross the narrow gap between cars and Rory made the mistake of looking down at the tracks rushing beneath her feet. Her stomach heaved. The train went over an iron bridge and Rory could see a river running below. She froze, her eyes fixed on the river's sharp rocks. The conductor laughed.

"I don't think you have the stomach for train travel, little girl, if this scares you. Wait until your car gets all the way to Arizona. There's only one track out there. High in the mountains, the train goes up a track that a goat'd be afraid of. You won't be so bold then!" He pushed her toward the final car.

For a moment, Rory could see the Foundling group before they were aware of her. Sister Anna was standing in the aisle between the cushioned seats, her back to Rory. Her bonnet was askew, something Rory had never seen in all her time at the Foundling. Beyond Sister Anna was a sight that made Rory laugh: fifty-seven children were climbing over the seats and rolling on the floor. The nurses and Sister Eileen were slumped onto seats as though they didn't have the strength to stand. When the conductor opened the door, a loud whoosh echoed through the car. It almost, but not quite, was louder than the sound of Sister Anna shouting at the children to sit still.

Violet came running and hurled her body into Rory's arms. "It's about time!"

CHAPTER Eighteen

Sister Anna turned slowly. Her eyes bulged ever so slightly when she saw Rory.

Rory stepped into the middle of the car, her eyes fixed on Sister Anna's face. Violet slid out of Rory's arms and wrapped herself around Rory's leg like a vine choking a tree. Resting one hand on Violet's shoulder, Rory gently dragged Violet as if Vi were a wooden leg.

Suddenly the din in the train car faded away, as the rest of the children sensed something important was happening. The only sound was the train wheels rattling and spinning on the tracks. Sixty-three pairs of eyes were focused on her as she moved forward. Rory only walked fifteen feet, but the journey felt far longer than the distance she had already traveled from the Foundling.

Little William shouted, "Hey, it's Rory!"

Sister Eileen shushed him and watched Sister Anna nervously.

Sister Anna looked almost like her usual self, except for the set jaw. Step by step, Rory waited for some sort of sign, a clue as to what Sister Anna might say or do. Finally she stopped in front of Sister Anna and waited. After a long moment of silence, Rory realized that Sister Anna was waiting for her to speak.

"Hello, Sister Anna."

Her eyes dark with an emotion Rory couldn't quite identify, Sister Anna said, "Rory."

"I couldn't let Violet go alone. So I came too." There it was. Her confession and her explanation. It was up to Sister Anna now.

"And what about the children you were responsible for back at the Foundling?" Sister Anna asked. "Did you just abandon them?"

Rory pinned her arms against her stomach. Sister Anna was right: Rory had thought only of Violet and left the little ones without so much as a goodbye. What kind of person could do that?

"You lied to me!" Sister Anna said suddenly, as though the words couldn't stay inside her any longer. Now Rory recognized the look. It was betrayal. Her own face had looked the same when Sister Anna had disclosed her plans for Violet.

Rory sucked her cheeks in to keep from crying. Had Rory pushed Sister Anna away for good? "Violet's my family. It was wrong of you to take her away," Rory cried. "And it was wrong of you to try and make me like it!"

Sister Anna spoke past lips tight with anger, "You have to

go back to New York."

Violet lifted her face from Rory's skirt and shrieked. "No! Rory can't go away again!" Violet clung even tighter to Rory's legs and began to sob.

Rory's heart was thudding louder than the steel wheels on the train tracks. She had come too far to be sent back now. Somehow she had to convince Sister Anna to let her stay. She said, "I'll just run away again. And then I'd have to get to Arizona on my own." Rory didn't want to sound like she was threatening Sister Anna; she was just saying the truth.

"Nevertheless, you don't belong on this train," Sister Anna said. "At the next city we stop at, I'll make arrangements to send you home."

"I don't have a home. I'm an orphan!"

"You always have a home at the Foundling," Sister Anna said in a clipped voice that discouraged argument.

Rory ignored the warning signs and barged ahead. "Like Violet does? How about the other fifty-six?" Before Rory could say anything else, she saw Mr. Swayne coming up the aisle. His suit had tiny, dirty handprints all over the trouser legs. He coughed to get Sister Anna's attention.

She turned around. "Yes, Mr. Swayne?"

"With all due respect, Sister, it won't be easy to send her back. I don't have money in my budget to be buying extra tickets. And how will I find someone reliable in a strange city to escort her?"

Sister Anna stepped backward so she could see both Rory and Mr. Swayne. "We pay you to make the traveling arrangements. It's absolutely necessary that she returns to New York. Immediately." Her voice was granite hard.

"Sister?" Sister Eileen stood up from the seat where she had collapsed. Her face looked exhausted. Her complexion was pale. "Excuse me for interrupting. But as you know, Rory has a wonderful way with the little ones. They listen to her. And goodness knows we could use an extra pair of hands."

Rory schooled her face not to show satisfaction. She knew she'd been right from the start—none of these grown-ups had ever tried to take care of so many kids for so long. They needed her help. If only Sister Anna's anger and injured pride wouldn't keep her from doing the sensible thing.

"Sister, if we let Rory stay, we're rewarding her disobedience." Sister Anna was implacable. "It would be a terrible example to the other children at the Foundling."

Sister Eileen took a deep breath. It was no easy thing to challenge Sister Anna. "Sister Anna," she said, "I don't wish to speak out of turn, but those other children aren't here. Rory can help us take care of these little ones, and isn't that our first concern?" After a moment, the words burst from her throat, "Six more days with fifty-seven children—I don't know if we can survive it!"

Mr. Swayne added, "We'll bring the girl back from Arizona. If she travels with us, there's no need to buy her a ticket."

Sister Anna's severe look traveled from Sister Eileen, over the exhausted nurses, and rested on Rory. There was a long pause. Finally she spoke: "You think you've won a battle, but if I let you stay, Rory, you'll have to work harder than you ever have in your life."

Rory nodded, though not too eagerly. "I will, Sister, gladly."

Someone in the car sighed loudly in relief.

Violet looked up at Rory. "You're staying?" she asked.

Rory nodded. Violet bounced on her toes, grinning. She glanced at the other kids. "I got my sister back!"

Sister Anna waited until Violet had calmed down. Then she said for Rory's ears only, "You can accompany us to Arizona and settle Violet with her new family. Then you return to the Foundling with us." She grabbed Rory's chin to make certain that she understood.

"Yes, Sister," Rory said dutifully.

As soon as Sister Anna's back was turned, Rory knelt on the floor to give Violet all the love she'd missed for the past two days. To her surprise, Violet held her at arm's length. Looking older than her five years, Violet whispered, "Are you going back to New York without me?"

Rory's slow smile was reflected on Violet's face. "Fat chance, Vi! You can't get rid of me that easily!"

CHAPTER Nineteen

THE FOUNDLING'S CAR WAS DELUXE ACCOMMODATIONS COMPARED to the Children's Aid Society car. The seats had leather cushions and the fittings were made of brass. Even if Rory had to share with fifty-seven runabouts, this was traveling in style.

Rory had barely gotten her bearings when Sister Eileen warned her that there was illness aboard. "Several of the children have bad stomachaches. I'm worried it's the start of an epidemic. In a tight space like this, it won't be any time at all before they all have it." She paused. "Violet too."

Rory knew all too well about disease. Her skin went cold at the thought of Violet sickening. "I'll look after her, Sister Eileen," she promised.

As soon as she had a quiet moment, she sat down with Violet on the last seat nearest the door that led to the rest of the train. She sniffed and understood why the seat was empty. It was next to the toilet, a small separate room. Placing her hands on Vi's shoulders, she said, "What's wrong?"

"I've got an ache in my tummy." Violet curled up and held her stomach.

"Did you eat something bad?" Rory asked.

Violet shook her head.

Rory put the back of her hand on Violet's forehead. "You don't have a fever."

There was a whooshing sound from the toilet room. Little William Norris scurried out of the toilet, his trousers around his ankles. "Violet," he cried. "You were right. The little door opens up and the ground is moving so fast. You could fall right in!"

Violet's eyes were as wide as William's. "I know. I lost my favorite violet-colored hair ribbon. I won't ever go in there again."

Rory considered the two children as she helped William pull up his trousers. "Violet, have you been to the bathroom since you got on the train?"

In a whisper, Violet answered, "I peed. But I couldn't do the other. I was too scared."

"No wonder your stomach hurts! If I hold on to you so you can't possibly fall in, will you be able to go?"

Violet nodded meekly.

"You're a little fool," Rory said as she led Violet to the toilet. "You could have made yourself sick."

Violet stared down at her feet. "After you help me, can you hold William? And Katie? And Mary?"

Rolling her eyes, Rory nodded. So much for the epidemic.

These nuns really had no business venturing outside the Foundling.

After a long evening escorting the children to the toilet, Rory was dead on her feet. Fortunately so were the little ones. The conductor came in and helped the nuns and Rory transform the leather seats into cozy Pullman beds. What an improvement over sharing a hard bench with Brigid. As soon as she had the children in their nightclothes, Rory took the opportunity to stretch out and rest her feet. Violet snored gently as she snuggled, content, against Rory's back.

Rory couldn't sleep. She stared out the window at a world that was darker than Rory believed possible. The moon hadn't risen yet. The only light Rory saw was from the windows of scattered houses as the train chugged past them. She was drifting off to sleep when a sharp rap on the door between cars startled her awake. Her eyes darted toward the nuns and nurses, but they were sleeping soundly. Rory eased away from Violet's warm body and went to the door. For a moment she was surprised that it opened so easily. Then she saw that the door could not lock on the inside, probably for safety's sake. She opened the door just wide enough to peek out and saw Brigid, her black hair whipping in the wind. She pulled the door a bit toward her so Brigid could step in and then closed it quickly. It seemed they had been lucky. No grown-up demanded to know who was visiting at such an hour.

"What are you doing here?" Rory whispered.

"I came to see how you are faring." Brigid looked around

the luxurious car and whistled. "This is nice! I wish I was one of your orphans!"

"Shhhh!" Rory hissed. "Scoot into my bed so if they wake they won't see you." Rory shifted Violet to one side to make room.

"A bed? You're living in style," Brigid said. "We've got boys sleeping on the floor." She glanced down at Violet. "Is this the famous Violet?"

Rory nodded.

"She's cute," Brigid said. "Were the nuns very mad at you?"

Rory shrugged. "Mad enough. But they needed me too much to send me back."

"Your plan worked." Brigid fanned herself. "It's so hot in here. Why don't you open the windows?"

Rory explained that an ember from the engine had blown in and landed on one of the nurses' skirts. It started to smolder and the nurse had just escaped being burned. Since then, Sister Anna had ordered the windows shut.

"Golly," Brigid said simply. "And I thought it would be dull back here."

Rory guessed why Brigid was there. "I saved some food for you, so I'm glad to see you."

Brigid stiffened. "That's not why I came."

"I know," Rory said. "But you shared your food with me. I was hoping to do the same." She pulled out a thick sandwich made with fresh bread and a generous helping of beef.

Brigid sniffed and licked her lips.

"Also a couple of apples and some cheese," Rory said.

"Maybe these will help you get through a few of those mustard sandwiches!"

"I thought nuns were poor," Brigid said, stuffing the apples and cheese into her pockets.

"Not these nuns. They have generous friends. That's how they got this car."

"Thank you for the food," Brigid said, her mouth forming the words around a healthy bite of her sandwich. "Miss Worthington just told us that we don't have any more food until we arrive in St. Louis tomorrow afternoon."

Rory stared. "But you'll all be starving by then!"

Brigid shrugged and tore off another bite of her sandwich. "Jack's so hungry that he's sworn he'll run away if he doesn't get a family that gives him a proper meal."

"St. Louis . . . that's where you . . ." Rory trailed off.

Brigid nodded.

"It won't be so bad," Rory continued. "You know the World's Fair is there?"

Brigid shrugged. "So?"

"Look at this." Rory pulled out a booklet that Mr. Swayne had picked up in Philadelphia. "There's fountains and fireworks and exhibits from all over the world."

Brigid wouldn't take the booklet. "I won't be seeing the fair. It's off to the block with me."

"You don't know that," Rory said. "Sister Anna said that sometimes the Children's Aid kids end up in really good homes. That'll be you."

"Those Sisters sure do teach you to hope for the best,

don't they?" Brigid said.

In the darkness, Rory couldn't see her face, but Brigid sounded as though someone was choking her.

"But we know better. I've never had any luck before; why should I get a family now?"

"Because you deserve one," Rory said simply. "I don't often do this, mind you, but I'm going to pray for you and the others to have enough food to eat, then I'm going to ask for you to get a good family."

Brigid snorted and then almost giggled. "Do you think that'll work?"

Rory held out her hands. "Sister Anna always says that the Lord will provide."

"Rory? Who are you talking to?" Sister Eileen appeared in the aisle, yawning. Brigid started as though she was about to bolt, but where could she go? Rory put her hand on Brigid's forearm and she went still.

"Sister Eileen," Rory whispered. "This is my friend Brigid."

Sister Eileen wrinkled her nose. "She isn't from the Foundling, is she? Did she stow away too?"

Rory weighed the dangers of telling the truth to Sister Eileen. She was only a few years older than Rory. And she wasn't really a nun yet. She was training to be one. But since Sister Eileen had kept her promise to look after Violet, Rory decided to trust the novice. "She's traveling with the other orphans."

"The Children's Aid Society children?" Sister Eileen was horrified. "Rory, she doesn't belong with us. She has to go back immediately before she is missed."

Brigid spoke up. "No one will miss me. Our minder, Miss Worthington, couldn't care less."

"Still, you don't belong here." Sister Eileen might be the newest Sister, but she could be as strict as Sister Anna.

"Sister Eileen, the Society children are starving. They didn't bring enough food for the journey." Rory was certain if anything would sway Sister Eileen to their side it would be the thought of hungry children.

Sister Eileen's face clouded over. "Brigid, is that true?"

Brigid nodded. "We ran out of mustard sandwiches late this afternoon. There's nothing else but water."

"Mustard sandwiches," Rory said with emphasis on mustard. "No meat, no cheese. And now they don't even have that."

"That's appalling!" Sister Eileen looked back into the car and reassured herself that they were unobserved. "Rory, get that box of bread and cheese. Throw some fruit in too."

Rory was careful not to wake Violet. "What about Sister Anna?"

"I'll explain in the morning. But our Savior told us to care for the little children, not just the ones in our railroad car. She won't begrudge our charity."

Rory packed the box, including some sweets that she knew Brigid would love. When she returned, Brigid got up to leave.

"I don't want to meet your Sister Anna. Good luck, Red," Brigid said, holding out her hand.

"It's not goodbye," Rory said. "I'll see you tomorrow."

Brigid's face was hidden in the shadows but her shoulders were slumped. Rory set down the box and hugged her friend.

For a moment, Brigid hugged her back then pushed Rory away as though she couldn't bear to be touched by someone who cared about her.

Sister Eileen held open the door and Rory handed Brigid the box of food. She leaned in and whispered, "See, ask and you shall receive! If God could answer the food prayer this fast, who knows what will happen tomorrow? He has all night to work on it."

"Bye, Red." With a nod, Brigid disappeared into the windy darkness between the cars.

Sister Eileen pulled the door closed. Crossing her arms, she faced Rory. "You shouldn't have let her come in," she said sternly. "The door is locked for a reason."

"Brigid was a good friend to me. She helped me sneak onto the train and hid me from the conductor."

"I'm not sure that's how I would describe a 'good' friend," Sister Eileen said, but a whisper of a smile crossed her lips. "In any case, Rory, you mustn't trust the Children's Aid Society children. They're street kids. Criminals as often as not. I wouldn't be surprised if Brigid was a thief or a beggar in New York."

"All of us," Rory gestured to the rest of the sleeping children, "would be on the streets if it weren't for the Foundling."

"All the more reason not to associate with the Children's Aid kids. We'll make sure you stay on a proper, decent path."

Sister Eileen checked that the door was firmly closed. "Good night, Rory."

If the likes of Brigid aren't decent, Rory thought, *then the nuns don't know what they're talking about.* She'd never questioned the infallibility of nuns before, except where Violet's and Rory's futures were concerned. For a moment, she wondered if she'd be struck down for such disrespect.

Nothing happened.

"I guess they're wrong about that too," Rory said to herself.

CHAPTER Twenty

MR. SWAYNE MARCHED UP AND DOWN THE CAR LIKE A CAGED animal. Whenever Sister Anna was occupied, he tried to slip off to the smoking car, but Sister Anna caught him every time. Mr. Swayne had worked with Sister Anna for several years. It made Rory laugh to see the two arguing like an old married couple. Rory knew Mr. Swayne was a father. She thought he would have gotten accustomed to the noise of the children by now, but he tugged at his earlobes, as though he had an earache.

"Mr. Swayne," Rory asked quietly.

"What is it, Red?" he asked.

Rory narrowed her eyes—she had grown to accept Brigid's calling her that, but she didn't like Mr. Swayne doing it. Even though he had argued with Sister Anna to let Rory stay, Mr. Swayne was not her friend.

After a moment she asked, "When do we get to St. Louis?"

"It's the next stop. In," he consulted a silver pocket watch,

"fifty-eight minutes. It's a shame we don't have time to get off and see the fair."

"Will we be able to see it from the train?" Rory asked.

He nodded. "Better than nothing, I suppose."

Sister Anna had approached silently and Mr. Swayne jumped when she touched his elbow. "Mr. Swayne."

Rory tried to catch her eye, but Sister Anna purposefully avoided her. In fact, since Rory had talked her way onto the train, Sister Anna had barely spoken to her.

"We'll be delivering ten children in St. Louis."

Ten! Rory wondered which children would be going. She'd miss each and every one of them.

"We'll have them ready," Sister Anna continued. "I'll expect you to find the new families and verify their identities."

"Sister, don't I always?" Mr. Swayne grinned.

"Which children?" Rory seized the moment to try and mend her fences. "Sister Anna, I can help."

Her lips slightly pursed, Sister Anna considered and said, "Sister Eileen has their names."

"Of course." Rory gave her a big smile, but did not receive one in return. With a sigh, she said, "I'll start right away."

Violet trailing at her heels, Rory made her way down the swaying car to find Sister Eileen, who was trying to grab one of the children to check his color ribbon against her list.

"Rory!" she cried with relief in her voice. "Can you tell me which one is Brendan Burns?" She checked the list. "He's number eight."

Brendan was a mischievous four-year-old who was rolling

on the floor, his arms wrapped about himself, giggling at Sister Eileen's predicament. He stopped laughing when Rory pointed at him. "That's Brendan." Under her breath she muttered, "He's not a number—he's a person."

"Aw, Rory," he complained. "She never would have guessed!"

"Sister Anna said I should help you," Rory said to Sister Eileen.

Sister Eileen pressed her palm to her heart. "Thank you," she said. "Can you get Brendan ready?"

Rory and Violet took Brendan down to the buckets of fresh water that were loaded on the train each day to keep the children clean and decent. "Violet, you scrub his face. You'll have to use soap."

A gleam in her blue eyes, Violet nodded. Rory went to the trunks of clothes and looked for the bundle marked with the number eight. She pulled out Brendan's brand-new sailor suit. Between Violet and Rory, they managed to wash Brendan, brush his mop of curly, sandy-colored hair, and wrestle him into his new outfit.

By the time Rory delivered Brendan, Sister Eileen and the nurses had managed to get the other nine children, mostly girls, presentable. Rory glanced around the train car and noticed more little girls than boys. She'd never thought about it before and asked Sister Eileen about this.

"Sister Anna told me that most families ask for girls. Perhaps they think that girls are easier to bring into a house."

"Maybe," Rory said, hoping it was good news for her and Violet. If a family wanted one little girl, they might want two, especially when the older girl was expert at making herself indispensable. She thought back to her time with the Children's Aid Society kids. "But with Brigid's group, there were more boys than girls."

"There's always a need for strong boys on the farms, so the Children's Aid Society brings more boys on the trains knowing they'll get chosen."

"What about the girls?"

"They find homes too." Sister Eileen patted Rory's arm. "I'm sure your friend will be fine."

Rory wasn't so sure. Brigid wasn't strong enough to work on a farm. Every time she exerted herself, it took her ten minutes to get her breath back. And that cough didn't sound too good. What if no one wanted her? Brigid was tough and loyal—but those weren't qualities that a grown-up might notice at first. Rory would bet that families wanted girls to be sweet and cute, like Violet.

Rory could hear the whistle of the train and the sound of brakes being applied. Not enough to stop the train, but enough to slow it down.

Standing by the window, Mr. Swayne shouted out to the car, "We're crossing the Mississippi!"

All the children, nurses, and nuns rushed to the right side of the train. For a moment Sister Eileen cried out as though the train might tip over. Rory thought Sister Eileen was being silly; the train was stable, wasn't it? She nudged another child over so she could be next to Violet at the window. The train was traveling over a wide river on a high steel bridge. Rory pointed to a boat passing beneath the bridge to Violet.

The *oohs* and *aahs* of the others made her look up toward the city. Mr. Swayne was right; they could see the World's Fair grounds.

"Rory, it's just like the book!" Violet said. Rory had been reading and rereading aloud the booklet about the World's Fair to keep the children occupied. The Sisters had packed all the necessaries for a long journey, but hadn't thought much about entertainment.

"It's beautiful," Rory whispered. She could see an enormous bright wheel turning slowly on the horizon. She wondered if it might spin off and roll across the prairies. If it raced the train, Rory bet it would win.

"How do they fit the whole world there?" Violet asked.

Rory smiled. "It's not really the whole world. But fifty countries and forty-three of the forty-five states have pavilions where they tell everybody about the best stuff they have." She caught a glimpse of a rainbow of water. "Look, Vi, those must be the colored fountains we read about."

When the train took a curve and the grand spectacle was lost from view, Rory and Vi sank into the seat.

"I want to see more," Vi said. "Can we go inside that big wheel?"

"No, honey," Rory said. "We won't be leaving the train."

"I hate the fair," Violet muttered.

Rory sighed. How silly to feel like she had lost something precious when she'd only glimpsed it from a train. But maybe Vi was right—if they couldn't go to the fair, maybe it was better to not even catch a glimpse of it. "Vi, love, life is full of beautiful things we can't keep. But there's plenty of things we can hold on to."

"Like Ma's necklace?" Vi asked slyly.

"You're a little scamp," Rory said. "Just for that, the tickling monsters are going to get you!"

"Not the tickling monsters!" Vi shrieked with laughter as Rory pounced on her sister, tickling her under her knee and in the ribs.

A hand tugged on Rory's skirt. She stopped playing with Vi to see Brendan. His usual cheeky grin was gone. "Rory," he asked, "what's going to happen to me?"

She knelt down to look him straight in the eye. "You are going home. A family has asked just for you and they're going to love you and take care of you forever." At that moment, for Brendan's sake, she made herself believe it.

"Really?" His eyes were wide. "How do you know?"

She nodded. "Because if they don't, they'll have to answer to Sister Anna!" She lightly punched his arm. "And to me."

Slowly a broad smile appeared on his lips. "All right."

It seemed no time at all before the train pulled into St. Louis. The station looked like a fairy-tale castle, with turrets and a stone clock tower. As soon as the train hissed and whined to a halt, Mr. Swayne leapt down to the platform. Inside the car, Sister Anna collected the children who were being placed with St. Louis families. The little girls had their hair curled and wore the special pinafore dresses that made them look like china dolls. Brendan in his sailor suit completed the angelic scene. Mr. Swayne hopped back into the train. "I've found them," he said. "Father McMartin has them inside the depot."

Sister Anna frowned. "Isn't there someplace more private for us to meet the parents?"

"Maybe when the World's Fair isn't in town." Mr. Swayne's grin was crooked. When Sister Anna started to protest, he held up his hand. "But the stationmaster owes me a favor. He's letting us meet in his office."

Sister Anna drummed her fingers on her list. After a moment, she said, "Very well. Lead the way."

Mr. Swayne held open the door and helped Sister Anna to the platform, followed by each child accompanied by a nurse or a nun. Sister Eileen tried to take Brendan's hand. But he ran to Rory, hugging her so hard he almost knocked her over.

"Come with us, Rory," Sister Eileen said sharply. She looked to the station to see Sister Anna and the others disappearing through a wide door. "Just so he doesn't make a fuss. Hurry!"

CHAPTER Twenty-One

Rory and Sister Eileen walked quickly to catch up, swinging Brendan by his arms so his feet barely touched the ground. He laughed with delight. They slipped through the doors and stopped, staring at the enormous space with a high domed ceiling made of brick and a glittering chandelier lit with thousands of electric lights. Mr. Swayne was talking with a priest next to a door marked STATIONMASTER. Behind the priest were women, staring hopefully at the little ones. The door to the office opened and Rory caught a glimpse of Sister Anna sitting at the desk, her files spread out in front of her. One of the hopeful mothers came out with little Frances, a quiet girl Rory didn't know very well. The mother was beaming and Frances clutched a new doll under her arm.

Sister Anna called to Mr. Swayne and another mother was led in with a child. Rory knew Sister Anna was making her final judgment: was this woman worthy of taking one of Sister Anna's foundlings? Brendan was next.

Rory smoothed his hair and kissed his cheek. "It will be all right," she said. "I promise. Just be a good boy and your new mother can't help but love you."

His solemn eyes stared at her. "Bye, Rory."

"Goodbye, sweet pea."

Rory watched the adoption closely. Brendan's new mother couldn't take her eyes off him. At first Brendan was shy, but she soon won him over with a carved wooden toy shaped like a locomotive. He was going to be all right. The other meetings were the same. A few tears, but on the whole the excitement of the new mothers seemed to reassure the children. Rory was reassured too.

Satisfied that the children were in good hands, Rory took the opportunity to step into the main depot and look around. Underneath the chandelier, a large crowd had gathered in the center of the room. At first Rory thought they were waiting for a train. But then the main door to the trains opened and Miss Worthington appeared, leading the Children's Aid Society kids in a ragged line. The crowd stirred and began to murmur. They were waiting for them, Rory realized. Brigid was near the front of the line. She looked freshly scrubbed and Rory could tell she was standing up very straight. Rory drifted closer to watch. If only Brigid could be adopted by a kind family too!

Miss Worthington spoke with a man in a black suit straining to contain his wide belly. She called him Mr. Singer. He had a neatly trimmed beard and a pince-nez perched on his nose. He reminded Rory of the worthy donors of the Foundling. They gave their money generously and expected to be treated like kings when they came to inspect how their money was being spent.

Mr. Singer said, "I hope you don't mind if we do the placing out here. Normally, we go to the union hall down the street, but every space has been taken by the World's Fair."

Miss Worthington looked flustered, but she tried to be polite. "I'm sure it will be fine, but how unfortunate that the fair is taking place right now."

"Nonsense, good lady! The fair is quite marvelous. I hope you will take the opportunity to see it while you are here. Of course, you could be our guest. My wife would gladly have you stay with us."

Miss Worthington shrugged. "It will depend. If we get rid of all the children here, then I can stay a few days to make sure they are settled."

Rory bristled. Miss Worthington made the orphans sound like extra kittens, a burden to be gotten rid of.

Miss Worthington went on: "If we can't place all the children, I'll have to get on the train and find homes for them in the next town." She glanced at the waiting crowd. "You've made inquiries about everyone?"

Mr. Singer nodded hard, setting his stomach to jiggling. "I know all these fine folks, or else they've been vouched for by someone I do know."

"Very well, shall we get started?"

Mr. Singer spoke loudly to attract the attention of the waiting crowd. "On behalf of the St. Louis Children's Committee, I'd like to thank you for what you are about to do. These poor children have never known a good home. Your kindness will be repaid a hundredfold!"

Rory was standing behind a well-dressed couple. The lady's face was just shy of beautiful and she wore a purple hat that set off her pale blond hair. She turned to her husband, her eyes shining. She said, "Darling, I knew we were right to come. We can do so much good here!"

Mr. Singer went on, "The Children's Aid Society appreciates the sacrifice you are making to offer these poor children a home. Let's begin!" He gestured to the first boy that Rory now recognized as Jack.

Jack swaggered to the empty space between the line of orphans and the would-be parents. Mr. Singer said, "What's your name, son?"

"Jack," he muttered.

"Ladies and gentlemen, this is Jack. He's a fine-looking boy. Who wants him?"

A short man dressed in plain clothing—he looked like Rory's idea of a farmer—stepped forward. "I might take him. But he looks too thin. Can he work?" Without so much as a by-your-leave, he took hold of Jack's arm and squeezed it. Jack pulled away.

Mr. Singer laughed. Rory frowned; his laughter had a sinister sound to it. "He's stronger than he looks. And you can see that he's got spirit. He'll be able to earn his keep. Do you want him?"

"Does he have any experience on a farm?" the farmer asked.

"These are all city kids. But that doesn't mean he can't learn!" Mr. Singer said.

"I suppose he'll do as well as any of them," the farmer said. "Do I have to send him to school?"

"Until he's fourteen," Mr. Singer said with a glance at Miss Worthington. "But the Society understands that schooling might have to take a back seat when your crops need tending."

"Come, boy," the farmer said.

Jack glared at him, his eyebrows drawn together like a thick caterpillar across his forehead. It broke Rory's heart to see how hurt he looked. Couldn't these grown-ups see how being treated rudely made Jack rude in return?

Miss Worthington stepped forward. "I'll need your name and address, of course. The CAS will visit once a year to make sure the boy is healthy and attending school."

The man scowled. Miss Worthington hastened to add, "Depending on the harvest, of course."

Jack was led away without even the chance to say goodbye to the others. Now it was Brigid's turn.

"Take a look at this one. A bright young thing, and pretty too." Mr. Singer turned to Brigid and asked her name. "Her name is Brigid, ladies and gentlemen. She'd be a fine parlormaid or minder for your children."

Rory overheard the well-dressed woman talking to her husband. "She might do, dear. I like the look of her. She could help me with my charity work."

The husband replied, "Are you sure? She looks a little sickly."

"I don't think so. She looks like she's missed a mother's care. We could give her that."

The man still wasn't sure. "With that dark hair, she looks a bit wild."

Rory stepped forward. The couple looked kind enough and rich enough to take care of Brigid. "Excuse me," she said, tugging at the woman's sleeve. "But I know the young lady and I can attest to her good character."

The couple exchanged amused glances. "That's very sweet, my dear," began the woman. "But you're a child yourself."

"Sister Eileen of the New York Foundling can speak for her, too!" Rory pointed over to where the nuns stood with Mr. Swayne. Sister Anna was there too. Rory didn't feel it necessary to mention that Sister Eileen was the young novice standing behind them. If they assumed she was indicating Sister Anna, always an impressive figure, so much the better for Brigid.

"Really?" The husband seemed inclined to be impressed. "We aren't Catholic . . ."

"Neither is Brigid," Rory assured them, not caring for the moment if it was true. Right now a good home was more important than religion. "But Brigid's fine qualities were apparent to the Sisters on the train journey."

"Hurry, dear, before someone else claims her!" The lady

grasped her husband's arm.

The husband nodded and spoke loudly enough to be heard. "We'll take her!"

Brigid looked up and searched the crowd to see who had spoken. Her eyes lit on Rory, who pointed to the couple and gestured with her thumb up. Brigid nodded to show she understood Rory's message.

The man led his wife over to Miss Worthington to sign some papers. Brigid rushed over to Rory.

"What did you do?" she asked wonderingly. "Why did they choose me?"

"Why wouldn't they choose you? You're going to be the best daughter ever." Rory leaned in and whispered, "But you might not want to mention your old nickname."

"You said something to make them want me," Brigid said, smiling. "I know you did."

Rory confided, "I didn't have to say much. They're good people. I wouldn't be surprised if they take you to the World's Fair."

Sister Eileen waved at Rory, gesturing for her to return to the group.

"I have to go, Brigid," she said. "Be well."

Brigid gave Rory a warm kiss on the cheek. "You kept your promise. I hope you and Violet are as lucky as me."

———————

That night Rory snuggled with Violet in their bed, listening to the sound of the train hurtling through the night. She

141

stroked Vi's hair, wondering where Brigid was now. Was her new mother tucking her in? "Good luck, Brigid," she whispered.

As she closed her eyes, she felt that just possibly she had repaid Brigid for her kindness.

CHAPTER Twenty-Two

AFTER ST. LOUIS, THE FOUNDLING CAR WAS DISCONNECTED FROM the Pennsylvania Railroad train. They waited on a sidetrack for a few hours and then the car was attached to a new, slightly shorter train that headed south. They rode for hours through forests and over rivers. The little towns by the railroad looked raw and unfinished. The distances between stops grew wider and the land more desolate. The only sign that anyone had ever been on this land before them was the reliable twin ribbons of railroad track stretching for miles. There were no animals, no houses or roads, only tall trees and swamps. The only colors out here were straw, brown, and the faint tinge of blue green in the distance under an expanse of vast blue sky. The journey began to seem like a never-ending dream.

The next stop was Little Rock. Seven children were made irresistible to their new parents. After the stop, the train was strangely quiet—not just because there were fewer children, but because the abrupt departures frightened the ones who remained. The children fell asleep easily enough, lulled by the evening prayers of the Sisters, but each night Rory was wakened more than once by a child sobbing in his or her Pullman bed.

After she settled the child, Rory would lay awake staring at the ornate ceiling with its bronze light fixtures. She'd roll over and put her arms around Vi, who would kick Rory in her sleep and throw off the blankets. "Am I doing the right thing?" she would whisper. Soon the train ride would end for Vi and Rory and they would have to go out into the world. Rory had nothing except Violet. But the more happy families she saw, the more she wondered if Vi had a future that might not include Rory. If Vi had a chance for parents and a home, could Rory stand in the way of that? But when morning came, Rory would put her doubts aside. The only thing that mattered was staying together.

As they pulled out of El Paso and chugged through New Mexico, forty children remained. Violet ribbons were sewn in their collars, indicating they were destined for Clifton in Arizona Territory. Rory was glad that so many of the kids would be in the same town. No matter what happened, they would have one another. And if Rory had her way, they would still have her. Surely with so many parents wanting children, room could be found for just one more.

Tempers were short in the stuffy car that never stopped moving. The air outside was stifling, hot and dusty. And inside the car was worse. The nuns and nurses never removed their heavy habits or uniforms. At least the children wore playclothes. With no way to wash their clothes or thoroughly cleanse their bodies, all the children were beginning to smell. Rory longed above all to be clean. She dreamed of the *drip drip* of the cistern back at the Foundling Hospital, filling an enormous tub. After a long bath, she imagined, she would slip into a clean set of clothes, smelling of starch. She still wore her too-small dress, now torn and stained. Her only nice dress was hidden away with Violet's things. Like the little ones, she would save her finery to impress a new family.

Soon, Rory thought, the journey will end. *We'll wake up from this dream and be in our new home.* She walked to the front of the car where there were two barrels of fresh water. One was for washing, the other for drinking. At every stop, Sister Eileen arranged for the barrels to be refilled, just like the locomotive getting fresh water for its steam engine. Rory dipped a tin cup in the drinking water and drank it gratefully.

She felt the back of her neck prickle. Someone was watching her. Slowly she turned around. The children were too dazed by the heat to be bothered with her. The steady rocking of the train and the monotonous click of the wheels on the track had the nuns and nurses dozing too. Swayne was in the first-class passenger car. That left only Sister Anna awake and staring at Rory.

Their eyes met. For the first time since New Jersey, Sister Anna didn't look away. Dipping the cup in the water, Rory carefully brought it to Sister Anna. Another peace offering. This time, Sister Anna accepted. She took the cup and drank deeply, draining it in a few moments. She glanced up at Rory and a faint smile appeared on her lips. "Thank you, Rory."

"You are very welcome, Sister," Rory said with emphasis.

"This has been a difficult journey," Sister Anna said. "I've accompanied the children before but never farther than Louisiana. I didn't know how hard it would be to care for so many."

"They're good kids," Rory said. "It's just tough for them to be stuck in a small space for so long."

"Rory, I always knew you were good with the children— but you've outdone yourself on this trip."

"I'm trying to make amends," Rory said simply.

Sister Anna tilted her head and waited.

Rory took a deep breath. "I lied to you. I disobeyed you. I ran away from the only home I had. I had a good reason, but . . ."

"A reason is not an excuse for deceit," Sister Anna said. "You should have trusted me."

Rory thought for a moment, then fired a question at Sister Anna: "How many orphans have you placed in new families?"

Sister Anna looked surprised. "I don't know. Several hundred at least, perhaps a thousand."

"See, there are so many, Sister Anna, you dare not love them all. If you did, your heart would be split a thousand ways when they left. But I only have the one sister."

Sister Anna stared out into the desert beyond the window. "You're wrong about that," she said quietly.

"I have another sister?" Rory asked mischievously.

A tiny bark of laughter escaped Sister Anna's mouth, lightening her mood. "No, I love each and every child. God placed them all in my care. I hate leaving them with strangers. But I have no choice."

Thinking of Brigid and the Children's Aid Society, Rory said, "At least you try to find them good homes."

"I do. And Rory, I promise you, if Violet's family isn't suitable in every way, I won't leave her there."

"I know, Sister."

Sister Anna patted the seat beside her. "Sit down, my dear. I've been thinking about your future."

Warily, Rory slid into the seat.

"You are resourceful and intelligent. And you are good with the children. What if you became my assistant?"

Rory's jaw dropped. "Your assistant?"

"Well, not right away. You'll have to finish school. But you could help me place the children and accompany me on these trips. Who better to look out for all the children of the Foundling than you? And I know that you'd never let a foster family take advantage of the Foundling or the children."

Rory rubbed the back of her neck without meeting Sister Anna's eyes. In a way, Rory had been training for this job for the past three years. But . . . "What about Violet?" she said.

Sister Anna let a small smile appear on her lips. "We inspect the foster homes at least once a year. You could see her for yourself."

Sister Anna was always so convincing that Rory had to close her eyes to think clearly. Once a year wasn't good enough. But it was a pretty good offer. "Sister," she began, "may I think about it?"

"Of course." Sister Anna looked at the watch pendant she wore pinned to her habit. "After lunch, we'll be heading into the mountains to Clifton. We'll have to get the children ready. All of them."

"Clifton must be a big town to take so many children."

She pursed her lips, considering. "I'm not certain it is. It's a mining town, I know that much. Father Mandin's letter insisted that the parents are devout Catholics and are eager to take the children." Sister Anna's voice was as confident as usual but Rory detected a shadow of doubt in her eyes.

"You're worried about something!" Rory said accusingly.

Sister Anna glanced around the car to ensure that their conversation was private. "Not worried exactly. It's just that Father Mandin didn't write his own letters. A woman in his parish did."

"Maybe he was busy?" Rory offered.

Sister Anna rubbed the bridge of her nose, which just made the crinkle on her forehead worse. "Probably. Usually Mr. Swayne would have inspected the homes in advance. But Arizona was so far we didn't do it this time."

Rory felt the same turmoil in her stomach she had when that matron had tossed her in a cell. Still, that had worked out because Sister Anna had appeared at just the right moment. Sister Anna, a force to be reckoned with, was equal to any problems in Clifton.

After they passed through a dusty little town called Las Cruces, the train began to climb. Everyone welcomed the cooler temperatures and some of the children began to revive and look curiously out the windows. The vegetation was still sparse but not so scarce as it had been in Texas. In the distance, they could see tall, blue mountains. Rory liked the look of them. Maybe Arizona wouldn't be so bad.

In Lordsville, New Mexico Territory, their car was transferred to the smallest train Rory had yet seen. There were only three pieces to their train—the engine, the coal car, and the Foundling car. Rory thought she should feel a weight lifted with the loss of the other cars, but instead their car seemed lonely and defenseless.

Sister Eileen stood with Rory under a wooden awning watching as their car was connected to the new engine.

"What kind of place are we going to?" Rory asked quietly. "Did you know that it was so far into the mountains?"

"Sister Anna knows what she's doing," Sister Eileen said reprovingly. But Rory could hear an anxious tremor in her voice.

As they slowly climbed out of Lordsville into the blue mountains, Rory was disappointed to see that up close the mountains were a dullish gray-brown in color. She noticed few houses and not one person. Rory couldn't blame the missing people; who would want to live here?

At about six p.m. they entered a narrow valley with the tracks squeezed in between a small river and steep cliffs. Rory remembered her *Wild West Weekly* reading. This was a perfect spot for an ambush. Maybe the Indians were waiting to kidnap the orphans. Although why the Indians would want forty New York City orphans was beyond her imagination. The children were here because no one wanted them back home.

She didn't see any Indians, but she soon saw something worse. The train passed an enormous building that was belching smoke, darker and more dense than the smoke from the train's engine. Behind and beside the building were heaps of what looked like coal. One hill was glowing red. Rory looked closer and realized that there was molten rock oozing down the hill. Everything stunk of sulfur. Violet started to cough and Rory put her handkerchief over her sister's mouth. "Just breathe through this, Vi," she said.

"Hellish," Mr. Swayne said to Sister Anna. She raised an eyebrow and didn't answer.

Sister Eileen crossed herself. "Virgin Mary, preserve us from the devil who must live in this land."

Rory was too distracted to pray since she was busy keeping her charges from ruining their new clothes. It was six thirty by Sister Anna's watch when the train pulled into the smallest station they had stopped at yet. It looked brand new with clean brick and a clay roof that hadn't been stained by the smoke.

A crowd of people was waiting on the platform. This wasn't unusual. In most of the towns they had visited, people had heard about the baby train and come to stare. Suddenly, a face was pressed against the glass. Then every window was full of flattened faces with bulging eyes, tapping on the windows, calling for the children to answer them. Rory realized they were all women. She stood on a seat to see over their heads. Behind the women who were trying to rush onto the train was a group of dark-skinned women who hung back because of better manners or fear.

Sister Eileen shrank from the window. "Who are these people?" she whispered.

"Perhaps these are the mothers, eager to claim their children," Sister Anna said. "Close the blinds."

Sister Eileen did as she was told. "Everywhere else the parents have been eager." As the blinds blocked the women's view there was a howl of disappointment. The tapping became a pounding and the train rocked on its narrow track. Sister Eileen said, "But these women sound—"

"Desperate," Rory said. She had a bad feeling about Clifton.

Sister Anna conferred with Mr. Swayne. She wanted to step outside and ask the crowd not to frighten the children. Mr. Swayne dissuaded her.

"Sister, that crowd sounds ugly. You shouldn't go out there. I'll ask for Father Mandin and I'll explain that we'll be handing out the children at the church."

Sister Anna frowned. "They aren't packages, Mr. Swayne. Nevertheless, I see your point."

"For safety's sake, you might want to lock the door behind me," he said.

Mr. Swayne shrugged into his coat and opened the door. The noise was deafening. Sister Anna gestured to Rory, who sprang forward, closed the door, and slid the bolt. Rory stood with Sister Eileen watching Mr. Swayne calm the crowd. With wide gestures and a raised voice he promised that there were plenty of children to be placed, but only later at the church. Slowly, the crowd backed away from the train.

Violet reached for Rory's hand and squeezed harder than she ever had.

Rory squeezed back. "Violet, everything will be fine. Sister Anna won't let anything happen to us." She glanced over at Sister Anna hoping for reassurance. Sister Anna leaned against the wall, her hands clasped together, her lips soundlessly moving. Her complexion was ashen. Standing in the center of the car, Violet clinging to her, surrounded by thirty-nine frightened children, Rory fought hard not to panic. They were in hell and the one person Rory had ever relied upon was praying.

"Everything will be fine," Rory lied.

PART THREE

Clifton, Arizona Territory

CHAPTER Twenty-Three

"LET ME IN!" MR. SWAYNE POUNDED ON THE DOOR.

"Sister?" Rory asked Sister Anna, who hesitated.

"Now!" Mr. Swayne's voice was angry.

Sister Anna gave Rory a sharp nod and Rory slid back the bolt. As Mr. Swayne shoved the door open, Rory had to jump aside.

Following Mr. Swayne was a tall, bald man, who wore plain black robes that brushed the ground. A stout woman tried to come in too. As if they had practiced it, Mr. Swayne slammed the door shut and Rory slid the bolt with a bang.

The pounding of many fists pummeled the now-locked door. Mr. Swayne opened a window and yelled, "If you don't stop right this minute, there will be no orphans for anyone!"

Rory wasn't the only one who breathed a sigh of relief when the pounding stopped and she saw the women retreat. The quiet women waiting at the back of the crowd were already gone. She hadn't noticed them leave.

"Mr. Swayne, sir," she asked. "Who are they?"

The bald man behind Mr. Swayne was the first to speak, but his answer was not in English.

"What did he say?" Rory asked. She stared at his mouth, a circle on a head as round as a baseball, spouting out nonsense syllables.

"What is happening?" Sister Anna said impatiently.

Mr. Swayne held up his hand to quell all conversation. "Those women insist that Father Mandin here"—he pointed to the man who had begun speaking—"give them orphans."

"But I don't understand," said Sister Anna. She turned to Father Mandin. "The families have already been chosen."

Mr. Swayne nodded. "Of course, Sister. The priest has the lists you made in New York."

"Then why? Why did they attack our train?" Sister Anna said, her voice rising with each question.

"Comment? Pardonnez-moi, je ne parle pas anglais."

Rory pulled on Mr. Swayne's sleeve. "Doesn't Father Mandin speak English?"

"It appears not," Mr. Swayne said. "Now hush, Red."

Rory gathered Violet close—this didn't bode well for the orphans.

Sister Anna stared at Father Mandin with dismay. "But all of our arrangements are with him! How can he not speak English?"

Mr. Swayne shrugged. "Someone at the church speaks—or at least writes—English. We've seen the letters."

"Pardon me, Mr. Swayne, if I don't find that reassuring," Sister Anna said.

There was a gentle knock on the door. Father Mandin hurried to usher in an efficient-looking woman dressed in black. Her dark hair was gathered in a tight bun and she wore a bright blue shawl over her shoulders.

Father Mandin spoke to her. "*Madame Chacon, j'ai besoin de vos compétences en traduction.*"

Mrs. Chacon spoke to Father Mandin. "*Je suis ici pour vous aider, mon Père.*" Then she turned to Mr. Swayne and offered her hand. "My name is Mrs. Chacon. I help the good Father in the church. Our regular priest is visiting family in Belgium and Father Mandin is his replacement. This is his very first posting. He came all the way from France."

"You speak French?" Sister Anna asked, relief in her voice.

She nodded. "Spanish is my first language, and the most important in our parish, but I also speak French and English."

Sister Anna extended her hand. "It is nice to meet you, madame. I am Sister Anna Michaella Bowen. I'm in charge here."

"At least you hope you are," Rory muttered under her breath.

Sister Anna continued, "Mrs. Chacon, please ask the Father about that mob. Who were those women who attacked our train?"

He responded in rapid French. "They are not ladies of our parish," Mrs. Chacon translated. "They don't concern us."

Rory snorted. "They should."

"Rory, your tone!" Sister Anna darted a scolding look at Rory, then she turned to Father Mandin and Mrs. Chacon. "Nevertheless, the child makes a good point. I've never seen such a thing in all my years of placing children."

Father Mandin was speaking again. "Forget them," Mrs. Chacon translated. "Our parish families—good Catholics all—are very eager to meet their new children. They will join us at the church in one hour." Mrs. Chacon added, apparently on her own, "I've also arranged a meal for all of you."

"An hour?" Sister Anna asked, incredulous. "But we only just arrived."

Rory spoke quickly and urgently for Sister Anna's ears. "Sister, the children aren't ready. Nothing is ready."

"I agree," Sister Anna said. "We should wait until tomorrow to prepare the children's things."

Father Mandin hastened to reassure Sister Anna. "Every family agreed to provide clothing for each child, so the children will be fine tonight," Mrs. Chacon said. "You can deliver their things when you visit the families."

Mr. Swayne clapped Father Mandin on the back and said, "Let's just get the job finished. Sister, I'm starved and I'm sure the kids are too. We've been on this train too long."

Rory silently chanted a prayer for Sister Anna to refuse. All her plans to rescue Violet, vague as they were, had been formed by her experience at the previous stops. Clifton was different, from the barren hills that glowed to the pack of wild women on the platform. To figure out how she was going to stay with Violet, she needed to know much more.

Father Mandin scowled at Sister Anna and barked a few words in French, translated by Mrs. Chacon. "I've made the decision, Sister. We distribute the children tonight."

Her lips pressed together, Sister Anna nodded obediently.

"But Sister." Rory tugged on Sister Anna's sleeve. "You're the one in charge . . . you're . . ."

Sister Anna shook her head ever so slightly. Rory stepped back, drew Violet close, and tried to accept the inevitable.

Father Mandin spat out more French. Mrs. Chacon said, "Father Mandin has asked that I go ahead now to make sure the dinner is ready. We only have a few wagons to transport you all. Can some of the children come with me now?"

Sister Anna shook her head. "No, no one is ready . . ."

If they had to go, Rory preferred to arrive first, like a scout in *Wild West Weekly*. She could go ahead to gather information and make things safer for Violet. "Sister, I could go," she said. "And a few others. That makes three less for you to manage."

"Not without an adult," Sister Anna said automatically.

"Sister, I'll be with her." Rory pointed to Mrs. Chacon. And she whispered for Sister Anna's ears only, "I'll keep my eyes open so you know where we stand."

Sister Anna hesitated. Rory could see the conflict in her face. Sister Anna didn't want to encourage Rory's independence but then again, she needed Rory's help. "Very well," she relented. Then she whispered, "Tell me right away if you see anything that worries you. And don't wander off on your own!"

Rory nodded solemnly.

The Sister consulted her list and said, "Take Violet, William, and Josephine with you."

As Rory buttoned coats on the three children, Mr. Swayne unbolted the door and swung it wide open. The train had been so stifling, Rory welcomed the cold air. Mr. Swayne jumped out of the train and then turned to help Rory. As she stepped to the platform they were both startled by a woman's deep voice.

"They're such lovely children." It was the stout woman, the ringleader of the mob emerging from the shadows next to the small station. "Wait until I tell my husband. Mr. Gatti is the best butcher in town and wants a boy . . . exactly like him." She pointed at William with her thick fingers that looked like sausages. William took a step back, behind Rory's legs. Rory looked to Mr. Swayne; for once she had no idea what to say or do.

Then Mrs. Gatti spied Violet. "Ah, there's the redheaded one. She's just like a little doll. I'll also take her."

Rory opened her mouth to protest but Mr. Swayne forestalled her. "Ma'am, as I said before, we'll be doing the adoptions at the church," he said. He lifted Violet off the train and deposited her in front of Rory. Suddenly, Mrs. Gatti pushed past them to grab hold of Violet. Before Rory could stop her, she had snatched Violet away.

"Rory!" Violet cried. "Help me!"

"I got you!" Mrs. Gatti cried. "First come, first served!"

"Give her back!" Rory yelled, putting up her fists. A man's hand closed over her shoulder, his fingers digging into her skin.

"Rory, behave yourself," Mr. Swayne said. "I'll handle this." Still holding Rory back, he said to Mrs. Gatti, "Ma'am. That child belongs with us."

Mrs. Gatti squeezed Violet tighter and she glared at Mr. Swayne. "She's mine."

"Oww!" shrieked Violet. "She's hurting me."

"Let her go!" shouted Rory.

Mrs. Gatti did not loosen her grip. "I saw her first, I get to keep her!"

"Rory!" Violet screamed, reaching for Rory.

Rory twisted her body loose from Mr. Swayne's hold and wrenched Violet away. Mrs. Gatti lost her grip on Violet except for one bit of her skirt.

"But I want her!" Mrs. Gatti said.

"You can't have her!" Rory cried, tugging Vi's skirt out of Mrs. Gatti's hands. Violet sobbed and held on to Rory as though she was drowning and Rory was her lifeline. Rory wrapped her arms around Violet, whispering that it was all right.

Mr. Swayne took Mrs. Gatti's arm and forcibly led her away, explaining that the Sisters would be here for several days.

Violet held tight to Rory's neck, her tears soaking the front of Rory's dress. Rory trembled as she rubbed Violet's back to soothe her. "Hush, Vi, the bad lady is gone."

"I hate this place!" Vi sobbed.

"Me too," Rory said grimly as they hurried toward the horse-drawn wagon, followed by Mrs. Chacon and the other children. She hesitated before climbing up. Sister Anna had made it clear that Violet would go to a family this very night. She had promised that Rory would approve, but Sister Anna wasn't in charge any longer. So what were her options? Rory couldn't stay on the train; Sister Anna wouldn't permit it. They didn't know the town and Rory didn't like what she had seen of it so far. Once they arrived at the church, Violet's fate was out of her hands. In her arms, Violet shuddered and sighed, reminding Rory that the most important thing was Violet's happiness. When she weighed the unknown family against the likes of that Mrs. Gatti, maybe the family would be the safer choice. And as for Rory, if she couldn't wheedle her way into Vi's new home, then she could get a job and stay nearby. Violet wouldn't be alone. Rory exhaled sharply and lifted Violet up to the wagon seat. Although her plan was full of holes, Rory felt better now that she had settled on it.

She followed Vi onto the hard wooden bench next to the driver. Mrs. Chacon, William, and Josephine sat behind them.

"Name's Jake," the driver said, settling in his seat and holding the reins casually in one hand. He had a face like dried leather. "Are you one of the orphans?"

"Not exactly," Rory said. "My sister is, though."

The driver gave her a quizzical look. "Then aren't you an orphan too?"

"I'm not an orphan because I can take care of myself," she said. "I don't need a family like my little sister does."

"OK," he said with a shrug. He clicked at his horse and shook the reins. The wagon lurched forward. The horse kicked up clouds of dust that hung in the air, coating clothes and hair with a thin layer of dirt. Rory shivered in the cool breeze. She wished she had a shawl like Mrs. Chacon's.

Rory looked back over her shoulder to see the train car, lit up against the twilight. She could see Sister Anna giving orders and the nurses scurrying to obey. With a snort, Rory thought that it was only the nuns and children who would listen to Sister Anna now. The priest was the boss. And Rory didn't know how to manage him at all. She couldn't even talk to him. At the Foundling Rory was sure of her footing, but here she might as well be standing on quicksand. She gave herself a little shake, reminding herself that she had a plan.

The wagon turned the corner and the train car was gone. Rory stifled a small cry, surprised at how bereft she felt. The moment she had left the safety of the train car, a crazy person had tried to steal her sister. That train car was the closest thing she had to a home right now. As the wagon rumbled down the narrow dirt road, it occurred to Rory that she had traveled on a taxicab roof, a ferry, a train, and a wagon. But she'd never been as scared as she was now.

Life at the Foundling in New York City seemed far away. She had thought the West would be like it was in *Wild West Weekly*: wide-open spaces, majestic mountains, and frontier outposts. Nothing in the magazine had prepared her for this dirty little town. Rory had to face the fact that *Wild West Weekly* wasn't a reliable guide, which meant she knew exactly nothing. Never mind. She would learn quickly, as she always had. Wasn't she here, with Violet at her side? To keep Violet safe she would do whatever she had to. She squeezed Violet tight.

"Ow, Rory, lemme go," mumbled Vi.

Rory's eyes roamed from one side of the road to the other, trying to take in as much of Clifton as she could from her perch. The road was hemmed in by wooden sidewalks and rows of closed shops. She caught a glimpse of a few people, but otherwise the street was oddly deserted. Although the street was quiet, a grating noise hovered at the edge of her hearing, something mechanical and insistent.

"Where are all the people?" she asked.

Jake laughed and pointed down an intersection with another halfhearted excuse of a road. Rory heard the saloon before she saw it. "It's Saturday night," he said.

The men are drinking their wages, Rory thought. *But that's not the noise I hear.* Then she saw a man leaving the saloon, a pair of pistols attached to his belt, just like in the *Wild West Weekly*. A real-life cowboy. At least the magazine got that right. The man lurched in front of the wagon. Jake pulled up the horse sharply.

"Watch out!" Jake yelled.

The cowboy mumbled something and shambled off in the opposite direction.

Jake grinned at Rory. "I'd have given him a piece of my mind, but there are ladies and children present." He tipped his hat.

"Don't mind me," Rory said.

But from behind her, Mrs. Chacon's voice said, "Thank you, Jake, for your restraint. We wouldn't want to give our visitors a bad impression of Clifton."

"Too late," muttered Rory under her breath.

The road was rutted and Rory lurched in her seat. Violet groaned at the bouncing, holding her tummy as though she might be sick. The buildings were wedged between the road and the bulk of the hill behind. When the sun finally set, it happened fast; in a matter of minutes it was night. Her eyes darting about the shadowy street, Rory found the sudden darkness bewildering; she lost her bearings.

"It's dark," Violet said. Her hand found Rory's and they held on to each other tightly.

"I'm here, Vi."

There were no streetlights and the lantern Jake had attached to a pole on the wagon didn't offer enough light for Rory to see any landmarks. Jake made another turn and Rory was certain she didn't know how to get back to the station by herself. She couldn't go back—only forward. And she had no idea what awaited them at the church. For Violet's sake, she willed herself not to be afraid, but Rory couldn't keep her left leg from shaking uncontrollably.

"Are you all right?" Jake asked, staring down at her leg.

She avoided answering him by asking about the eerie glow coming from a large ugly building up ahead. As they approached she realized that the building was the source of that terrible clanking noise.

"That's the smelter," he said. "Hear that? That's the belts bringing tons of ore to the fire to be melted for the copper."

A loud piercing whistle blew, making the bones behind Rory's ears ache. "What was that?" she asked.

"Shift change. The smelter burns all day and all night." As Jake explained, a door opened and a line of men, tired and dirty, filed out. They were sweaty, which Rory found odd on a chilly night.

"It's always hot at the smelter," Jake said. "The heat makes a nice change on a night like tonight."

The clanking grew louder as they approached. Violet, who disliked loud noises, buried her face in the space between Rory's arm and her waist. Jake was right; it was like standing in front of an oven. The air was gray and burned her eyes. As soon as they passed, the chill returned and they could breathe freely again. Rory shivered but not just from the cold.

"How many people live here?" she asked. Maybe the streets were empty because there weren't many people.

"Enough to run the mine and support the miners," Jake said. "Two, maybe three thousand people. It's easy enough to count the whites. They live in this area and up on the high ground. But the Mexicans are always coming and leaving. You can't count them."

"What's the high ground?" Rory asked with suspicion.

"It's the best place to live. Away from the flooding."

"Flooding?" Rory asked, gripping the wooden seat with her free hand. Now that they were away from the smelter, she heard the faint sound of water flowing in a riverbed.

Jake nodded. "We're in a canyon. The water comes rushing down from the mountains." He gestured to the hills. "The mining company cut down all the trees to feed the smelter, so there's nothing to keep the water from flooding the town. The company doesn't care—the managers live on the hill. The rest of us take our chances." His voice sounded bitter. "Last year we lost a dozen or more to the water."

"You couldn't find them again?" Violet asked.

"Hush, Vi," Rory said. There was simply no way she could leave Violet in a place filled with madwomen, armed men, and floods! Her plan, such as it was, had already fallen apart before she had even started. But what could she do? Any moment they would arrive at the church and suddenly there would be the priest and his translator to deal with, as well as a new family who expected to take Vi home.

Behind her, she heard little Josephine whimpering. She was cold and hungry. Mrs. Chacon tried to comfort her, but Jo was a determined crier when she chose to be. She wouldn't like it here either. If this place was wrong for Violet, it was wrong for all the orphans. Rory had a responsibility to them, as surely as she did to Vi. Even returning to New York and starting over would be better than remaining in this town.

Sister Anna was bound by her vows of obedience. Mr. Swayne just wanted to finish his job and go home. There was no one to think for all the orphans but Rory. Unfortunately Rory had no idea how to save even Violet, much less all forty of them.

The wagon pulled up in front of a small nondescript building made of mud and stones, wedged between the road and the steep hill behind it. The train station had been situated on an open piece of land but this church looked as though space had been made for it only grudgingly.

"Here's the church!" Jake said.

CHAPTER Twenty-Four

Rory only knew the building was a church because Jake said so. There was no stained glass, nothing familiar. She thought of the beautiful chapel at the Foundling and the soaring grandeur of St. Patrick's. How could the people of Clifton pray in a mud hut?

Mrs. Chacon helped William and Josephine out of the carriage, while Rory and Violet clambered down. She smiled at Rory and Violet. "What are your names?"

"My name is Rory Fitzpatrick, ma'am. And this is my sister, Violet."

"Ah," Mrs. Chacon said. "Violet Fitzpatrick. Aged five."

Rory gently pushed Violet behind her. "How do you know about Vi?"

"I wrote out all the lists."

"Oh, you're the one who wrote to Sister Anna," Rory said. It made sense, as she seemed to be Father Mandin's right-hand person, and the only one who understood what he said.

Mrs. Chacon stroked Violet's hair. "Such a beautiful color." She paused. "But the Sisters said nothing about a sister."

Rory tightened her grip on Violet. "I'm here to make sure she gets a good family."

"Of course she will." Mrs. Chacon was slightly offended. "Every family on the list was carefully selected by Father Mandin."

"What about Mrs. Gatti?" asked Rory, holding her breath for the answer.

"She is not on the list," Mrs. Chacon said firmly.

"That's a relief!" Rory said.

Mrs. Chacon opened the door for Rory. The sound of two dozen chattering women struck her as though she had walked into a wall. Steeling herself, Rory moved inside. The odor of cheap candles hung in the room, along with a spicy scent. If it was incense, it was a kind that Rory had never smelled before. She walked to the middle of the chapel, turning in a circle, trying to find anything that was recognizable. The cross on the wall was plain, no gilt at all. And it didn't even have the Lord Jesus on it. There were few windows. The pews were rough benches that had been pushed up against the walls. The floor was the same hardened mud as the walls. How could this be a church?

In the corner a large group of dark-skinned women waited. Rory recognized some of them from the station but others were new to her.

"Are you hungry?" Mrs. Chacon asked.

"I'm starving!" Violet cried. At the same time, Rory said, "Not now."

Mrs. Chacon chuckled. "Perhaps some water for you, Rory? The road is so dusty." She gave Rory a tin cup of water and put a small cake in Violet's hand and led her to a wooden pew. "Rory, don't worry," Mrs. Chacon said when she returned. "Elena will be a wonderful mother."

"Elena?" Rory stared at Mrs. Chacon over the rim of her cup. "Elena Martinez?" It felt like years ago, but it was only a week since she had heard that name in the Foundling dormitory.

"My good friend. We've assigned Violet to her."

"Is Elena here?" Rory asked. She didn't plan to leave Vi in this awful place, but it wouldn't do any harm to meet the woman who was supposed to get Violet.

"Of course, everyone is. They've waited so long," Mrs. Chacon answered. "She's over there in the corner." She pointed to a tall woman standing apart from the others. She was perfectly still and her long face reminded Rory of her favorite statue of the Virgin Mary. Like the other women, she wore a black dress, but her shawl was emerald green. Green had been Rory's mother's favorite color; she said it reminded her of Ireland. A good omen, Rory reluctantly decided.

"She wants a family so badly." Mrs. Chacon was solemn. "She's lost four babies already."

Rory blinked. "Four?" Maybe this Elena didn't deserve Vi. What mother loses four children?

Mrs. Chacon shook her head sadly. "This place is bad for

making babies. The air is thick with fumes and the water is full of metals from the mines. Nothing grows here. No trees. No babies." Rory wondered if Mrs. Chacon had also lost a child.

No babies. Rory blinked. She was accustomed to there being more babies than anyone could need or want. The first Wednesday of the month at the Foundling was proof of that. The Sisters of Charity had to pay hundreds of wet nurses to care for them. She began to understand the scene at the train station. In Clifton babies were precious and rare. What would these women do to get a healthy child?

Waiting until Mrs. Chacon's attention was elsewhere, Rory slipped through the crowd of women. She made a beeline for Elena Martinez, whose black eyes were fixed on the children. Her light brown hair was braided around her head like a crown. To Rory she seemed sad, but that might be because she knew Elena's history.

"Hello," Rory said.

"Hello," Mrs. Martinez said. "Are you one of the orphans?" Her voice was like a soft summer rain.

"I help the Sisters," Rory said. "You are taking one of the children?"

Mrs. Martinez's long face transformed into a smile. "I'm taking two," she said shyly.

For a moment Rory's hopes soared like the hot-air balloon she had once seen in Central Park. Maybe, somehow, Sister Anna had arranged for Rory to be taken too. It would be just like Sister Anna not to tell Rory and let it be a surprise.

Rory might have to reconsider her plan to spirit Violet back to New York.

"A boy named William and a girl named Violet," Mrs. Martinez said.

The balloon crashed to the ground. Two children, but not the right two.

"My name is Rory Fitzpatrick," Rory said abruptly. "Violet's my sister."

Mrs. Martinez looked startled, but then she held out her hand. "I'm Elena. It is a pleasure to meet you." She glanced over to where Mrs. Chacon was arranging a table in the center of the room. "No one told me that Violet had a sister."

"I'm not on any lists," Rory admitted. "I wasn't supposed to come."

"But you did anyway?" A glint of mischief appeared in Elena's eyes. "How did you do it? New York is so far away."

"I climbed onto the roof of their taxi and then I stowed away on the train."

Elena burst out laughing. "The Sisters must have been furious!" she said. "I was educated in a convent school, so I know how strict they are. But it sounds like something I might have done when I was young."

Rory permitted herself to grin back. "They were pretty mad. But Sister Anna—she's in charge—knew that I would never let Violet go to just anyone." She fixed Elena with a stern stare. "You see, I have to approve her new parents."

"Of course. You are her family." Elena nodded thoughtfully. "What would you like to know?"

Rory decided to start with an easy question. "What kind of mother will you be?"

Elena stared off into the distance as though she could see something Rory could not. "I don't know. I've never been a mother, not for more than a few days," she said. "But I know what I hope to be. Kind. Wise. Gentle."

Rory wrinkled her nose. Of course Elena had a good answer to that question. She'd say anything to get a baby. Time for something tougher. "Violet can sometimes be a little stubborn, especially about keeping her clothes clean. How would you punish her?"

Elena's mouth formed a small *o*. "Of course every child needs discipline, but I would never strike a child. And Ramon, my husband, doesn't believe in hitting either."

So far, so good. Next question. "What would you do if she couldn't sleep at night?"

"That is easy," Elena answered in a soft voice. "I would sing her a lullaby." She hummed a gentle tune that Rory did not recognize.

Rory herself was tone-deaf. "That's not a bad answer," she said, a little reluctantly. "But she likes her back stroked when she can't sleep."

"I'll remember," Elena promised.

"And what about school?" Rory asked. "Vi is smart. Will she go to school?"

"There isn't a school for the children of the mine workers," Elena admitted. "But I have an education. I will teach her. And what I don't know, we can learn together."

Rory opened her mouth to ask the most important question: would Elena consider taking Rory too?—but she was interrupted by the arrival of Sister Anna and the other children. A swelling of noise poured through the door like storm water through a gutter. The chapel, for all its bareness, carried sound beautifully. Across the room, Rory saw Vi and little Josephine putting their hands over their ears.

The would-be mothers were polite—but they stared at the children just as hungrily as Mrs. Gatti had. Mrs. Chacon spoke sharply to them in a strange language and they hurried to direct the newcomers toward the food-laden tables in the back of the room. Sister Anna was trailed by Father Mandin. Neither of them seemed as if they had enjoyed the ride together. Sister Anna beckoned to Mrs. Chacon for translations.

Sister Eileen came up behind Rory and whispered, "They are speaking Spanish. Sister Anna told me that many of the families come from Spain."

"From Spain?" Elena chuckled. "No, most of us are from Mexico." She paused, taking in the confused looks on their faces. "The copper company pays better wages than the men can earn in Mexico, so many come here to work. My husband brought us here three years ago."

"What language do you speak in Mexico?" Rory asked.

"Spanish." Elena's nose crinkled when she smiled. "That must be the mistake. We speak Spanish, but we are not Spanish at all."

"Did Father Mandin come from Mexico too?" Sister Eileen asked.

"No, he's from France. He has been here less than a year and doesn't know much English or Spanish yet."

"Then how does he talk to anyone?" Rory asked.

"*Señora* Chacon is here every day to translate. I too can speak both English and Spanish, and now, by necessity, French. Would you like a tortilla?"

"Tortilla?" Sister Eileen couldn't get her mouth around the strange word.

Rory decided she was hungry after all. "If it's something to eat, then yes," Rory said.

Elena offered them a flat, round piece of bread. She showed Rory and Sister Eileen how to add beans and meat to the bread and then roll it up. Rory sniffed at the tube of food and smelled the spicy aroma she had noticed before. She asked Elena what it was.

"It's called chili," Elena explained. "Don't you have this in New York?"

Rory took a bite. Like an explosion on her tongue, it was different from any food served at the Foundling. It burned her mouth. Waving her hand in front of her lips, trying to cool them, she asked for some water. Elena's face fell. As Rory gulped down an entire cup of water, Father Mandin clapped his hands to get everyone's attention. Mrs. Chacon translated, "The Sisters will hand out the babies now."

The chili churned in Rory's stomach. She was out of time.

CHAPTER Twenty-Five

"SISTER, HERE IS THE LIST OF PARENTS AND CHILDREN," MRS.
Chacon said to Sister Anna, who sat behind a small table. Rory
tried to get close enough to see the paper, but the spiky hand-
writing was too difficult to read from a distance.

Sister Anna surveyed the room, her eyes resting longest on
the dark-skinned Mexican women. "Where are the parents?"
she asked.

Mrs. Chacon looked puzzled. "They are all here. No one
wanted to wait another day."

"But . . ." Sister Anna began.

Mrs. Chacon interrupted her. "Father Mandin chose each
family with care, Sister. Over sixty people applied, but he
only accepted thirty."

Sister Anna took another look at the Mexican women.
"Very well, let us begin." Rory tensed as she waited for the
first name. "Gabriela Welsh, number twenty." Rory relaxed.
Not Violet. Not yet. Rory liked Elena and knew that Vi would

too, but how could Rory be absolutely sure that Elena was the mother for Vi? Rory wouldn't get a second chance at this.

"Tomasa Alvidrez," Sister Anna stumbled over the unfamiliar name. "Gabby is going to her."

Gabriela looked darling in her Sunday-best dress, her golden curls falling down her back. A tall, gaunt woman stepped forward to meet her. Sister Anna stared at the fair little girl and then at Mrs. Alvidrez, whose skin was darker than the aged oak beams that held up the mud roof.

"Is this right?" Sister Anna asked. Turning to Father Mandin, she spoke quickly. "I prefer to match each child to a family that resembles her. I find it helps the parents bond with the child."

Mrs. Chacon translated, her voice flat. Father Mandin replied, "The important thing is that Mrs. Alvidrez is a good Catholic."

"But . . . ," Sister Anna began.

With a sharp gesture of his hand, the priest cut her off. "You are too choosy, Sister. Give her the child."

Sister Anna opened her mouth to protest but closed it again. Rory couldn't help feeling a little smug that Sister Anna was getting a taste of her own medicine. By the look on her face, Sister Anna was no better at being biddable than Rory was. But nuns were bound by an oath of obedience. Another reason, in case Rory needed one, not to become a nun.

"Of course, Father, but please remember the Foundling has the final word on the adoptions," Sister Anna said respectfully, but there was a hint of warning buried in her voice too. She turned to Mrs. Chacon and said, "Does she speak English?"

"Some," Mrs. Chacon said. "We thought it best if every family spoke a little."

"Quite," Sister Anna said curtly. "Make sure she understands that in the next few days I will come to her house. If I am not satisfied, I will take the child back."

Mrs. Alvidrez said, "*Sí, sí.*" Glancing at Mrs. Chacon, she pulled some coins out of her pocket and placed them on the table. Then she took Gabriela by the hand and led her away. Gabriela glanced back at the others but went willingly enough.

Sister Anna stared down at the coins then asked Mrs. Chacon in a sharp voice, "What is this money for?"

"Father Mandin asked the families to contribute to the cost of the wagons from the train since we are a poor parish."

Sister Anna said, "If you had asked, the Foundling would have paid the cost."

At Rory's side, Elena was chewing on her knuckle, her eyes fixed on Sister Anna's list.

"Are you all right?" Rory asked.

"We are so close to having a family, I don't want anything to ruin it now," Elena said. "Would that Sister keep Violet and William from us?"

Rory's eyes found Violet across the room and then focused on Elena again. She had known the moment she had seen

Elena that she might be kind enough to make up for the awfulness of Clifton.

Rory reached out and touched Elena's hand. "I think you might be the mother for Violet. I'll tell Sister Anna so."

"Thank you, Rory. Family means everything to me. If Violet's own sister did not approve, I don't know what we would do." Elena abruptly hugged Rory. Startled, Rory froze then let herself enjoy the embrace. Now how could Rory convince Elena that two Fitzpatrick sisters were better than one?

"Next on the list," Sister Anna said. She hesitated and looked around the room until she caught Rory's eye. "Is Elena Martinez here? She is assigned William Norris and Violet Fitzpatrick."

Elena came forward. She was fairer than the other women and Sister Anna looked at her with approval. Sister Eileen brought Violet and William to stand in front of the desk. Rory made sure that she was in Violet's line of sight. Sister Anna always made the small children a little nervous. Vi's eyes sought Rory, and Rory winked.

"Mrs. Martinez," Sister Anna said, "this list says you are to receive a boy and a girl."

"Yes, Sister." Elena stared at Violet and little William. She started to chew again on her knuckle but stopped herself.

"What does your husband do?" Sister Anna asked Mrs. Martinez.

"He works at the smelter."

Mrs. Chacon stepped up to Sister Anna's elbow. "It is a very good job. Aboveground," Mrs. Chacon interjected. "He spoke for the miners against the Anglos during last year's strike."

"Anglos?" Sister Anna asked.

"The white mine workers. We call them Anglos."

"Oh." Sister Anna was taken aback.

"And Elena is educated. She will teach the children well."

Sister Anna's pen scratched on the list. "Do you have clothes for the children?"

"*Sí*!" Mrs. Martinez nodded eagerly. "I brought them— and also these toys for the *niños*." She reached in her bag and pulled out a cloth doll in a purple dress. "This is for Violet. I thought she would like this color."

Violet looked to Rory for permission. Rory nodded and Violet clutched the doll to her chest. Rory mouthed the words "thank you," and Violet remembered to whisper, "Thank you."

"And for William." Mrs. Martinez gave him a wooden horse. "My husband is skilled with his hands. He made this." William wasn't afraid to step forward and take the toy.

"William . . . ," prompted Sister Anna.

"Thank you very much," he said, eager to start playing.

Father Mandin, who had been watching the proceedings with a broad smile on his round face, spoke rapidly to Mrs. Chacon. She nodded and translated for Sister Anna's benefit. "Elena is one of the Father's most devout parishioners. She helps to clean the church and decorate it for every holiday."

Sister Anna searched around the room until she met Rory's gaze. She raised her eyebrows as if to ask Rory's opinion. Rory nodded slowly.

"Very well, you may take the children. But I will be visiting you in the next few days. The Foundling reserves the right to take the children back if everything is not satisfactory."

Elena said, "You will be satisfied, I promise." She started to move off with the two children.

Violet broke away and darted to Rory. Burying her face in Rory's skirt, she whispered, "I don't want to leave you!"

Elena's eyes appealed to Rory for help.

"Trust me, Vi. She's really nice. Just do what the Sisters want for now—it's part of my plan." Rory swallowed hard. "Remember how well my last plan worked?"

"We'll be together?" Violet asked with a sidelong look at Elena.

"Always," Rory said, praying she could keep her word. And if she failed, at least Vi was going to a good place.

"I'm keeping Mama's necklace just to make sure you keep your promise," Vi said.

"Fine," Rory said impatiently. "Now will you go with Elena?"

"Yes," Violet said.

"Good," Elena said, her words floating on a long sigh. "Here is the money Father Mandin asked for." She reached into her pocket and slid a small stack of coins across the table.

As Elena turned back to Rory and the children, the door to the church slammed open. The breeze blew out half the candles in the room. A group of angry women stormed the building, led by Mrs. Gatti. Her booming voice followed the wind like thunder after lightning.

"No! Stop! Those are *my* babies!" Mrs. Gatti cried. One of the women tried vainly to hold Mrs. Gatti back as she strode through the crowd. Shoving Elena to one side, Mrs. Gatti stood in front of Sister Anna, her hands on her hips. "The children can't go off with that . . . person. She'll poison them with her tacos, burritos, and spicy food. They should go to me. I'd give them a good home with lots of good American food." Without warning she reached for Violet.

Violet flinched and scurried under the table, near Sister Anna's feet. Elena pulled William to her side. Sister Anna rose to her full imposing height.

To Rory's surprise, Elena spoke first, loudly and clearly. "Father Mandin chose me to have these children!"

Rory was impressed. She wouldn't have thought the gentle Elena had so much fight in her.

Mrs. Gatti cried, "I saw them first. If it's a question of money, I'll pay more!"

Sister Anna looked down her long nose and said, "Mrs. Gatti, you are out of order. There is no question of the Foundling accepting money for children."

"There's money on the table," Mrs. Gatti insisted. "Something crooked is going on here!"

"Why should I have to buy the children when they are rightfully mine?" Elena asked scornfully.

Father Mandin hovered at the edge of the group of women,

chattering in French. No one paid him any attention. The Mexican women were talking excitedly among themselves in Spanish. And Mrs. Gatti was shouting in English. Rory finally understood the point of the story about the Tower of Babel; she could only hope things in Clifton would end better.

"Louisa!" Everyone turned to the open doorway and to an enormous man wearing a bloodstained apron under his coat.

"Jacques," she cried. "What are you doing here?"

"I'm looking for you and my dinner," he bellowed.

Mrs. Gatti hurried toward him, speaking softly as though she hoped he would follow her example. "Make it yourself. I'm not leaving here until I get a baby."

"A baby?" He raised his bushy eyebrows and didn't lower his voice in the slightest.

"I told you about the baby train," she said. "It's here. The children are beautiful and I don't want to miss my chance."

Mr. Gatti peered around the gloomy room, noting the nuns and the remaining children. "I'll handle this," he said, striding over to Father Mandin. They began speaking rapidly in French.

"My husband is part French. He'll soon get me my babies," Mrs. Gatti announced proudly.

The conversation between the men ended and Mr. Gatti said goodbye to Father Mandin and returned to his wife. "Come, Louisa," he said, taking her arm and leading her to the door. "There's nothing for us here and I want my dinner."

"But my babies!" She jerked her arm away from him. "I won't leave without them."

"Just go," Rory said under her breath. "You're not welcome here."

"The priest told me they are out of children." Gatti said it the same way he might tell a customer that he had no more bacon to sell.

"But there are so many."

"They're already spoken for, Louisa," he said impatiently, tugging vainly on her arm. "You're making a scene. Can we go home now? I'm hungry." He glanced at her friend. "Mrs. Abraham, help me get her out of here."

Mrs. Abraham spoke up for the first time. "Who gets to have the children? Not these women." She pointed scornfully to the remaining Mexican women. "I won't permit it."

"Who does that woman think she is?" Rory whispered to Elena.

"Mrs. Abraham's husband runs the hotel. He is very important in town. But even she cannot tell Father Mandin what to do."

Mrs. Abraham spoke loudly, not caring if her words offended. "The little darlings are as white as snow. They can't go with Mexicans! They belong with people who look like them!"

Rory's eyes flew to Sister Anna. Sister had expressed the exact same concern.

Even though Sister Anna had repeatedly told Rory it

was rude to point at people, she leveled her index finger at Mrs. Abraham. "You have no authority here. Take your friend and go."

"Not without a baby," Mrs. Gatti said stubbornly.

Mr. Gatti looked to Father Mandin and again tried to usher his wife outside. "Louisa, I know how much this means to you, but there will be other children. You've made enough trouble. Let's go."

Mrs. Abraham gestured to the remaining white women to follow her. "You haven't heard the last of this," Mrs. Abraham said with determination. "Those babies don't belong with drunks and savages."

"To keep them safe, I'm willing to take the little boy and the redheaded girl," Mrs. Gatti called from the doorway.

"Louisa, be quiet," her husband said as he closed the door behind them.

"You'll never get Violet," whispered Rory as she crawled under the table to coax Violet back into the room.

Sister Anna beckoned to Mrs. Chacon to come translate for her as she confronted the priest. "Father Mandin, we must stop for tonight. You and I have to talk about what just happened."

The Mexican women began to whisper among themselves. Sister Eileen and the nurses gathered the children close and waited anxiously for Father Mandin's answer.

"Continue with the adoptions," he commanded.

"But Father . . ."

"These arrangements have been made months ago. I asked

my parishioners to take the children and they agreed out of the kindness of their hearts. It would insult them to delay."

Sister Anna started to read the next name, but her voice caught in her throat. She took a small sip of water and tried again. "Josephine Ryan."

Elena took a deep breath and beckoned to the children. "I'm going to get the children home before there are any more scenes," she said.

"Where do you live?" Rory asked quickly.

"Quite close to here."

William went to her willingly, but Violet hung back. "It's all right, Vi," Rory whispered, nudging her forward.

Clinging to Rory's hand, Violet spoke directly to Elena, "Rory's promised not to leave me. Can she come too?"

"Of course, if she wants to," Elena said.

Rory wasn't sure if Elena was only being polite, but she didn't care. "I do." Rory made sure Sister Anna was fully occupied with the next placement. "Let's go."

Elena glanced at Sister Anna. "You won't be missed?"

"They won't even notice I've left."

CHAPTER Twenty-Six

HUGGING HER ARMS TO HER BODY, RORY LOOKED UP, BUT THE smoke from the smelter blocked out the sky. Having spent her whole life in a city, it was disappointing to still not see a full sky of stars. In *Wild West Weekly* the cowboys always talked about the stars when they sat around the campfire.

"Rory, I'm cold."

"I'll warm you up." Rory scooped Violet up in her arms and followed Elena, who was moving quickly along the street as fast as William's legs could take him. Most of the windows of the buildings were dark. The only light was the lamp in Elena's hand. How could people live without streetlights?

William began to whine about the walk, the cold, and how hungry he still was.

"You just ate," Rory chided him.

"It's not far," Elena told him. She glanced back and saw Rory carrying Violet. "William, why don't I pick you up? And when we get home, I have a special sweet dessert."

"Really sweet?" William asked, holding out his arms.

"Did you hear that?" Rory whispered, Violet's ear close to her lips. "Elena has dessert for you."

"I do like dessert," Violet said. "But Rory, you'll stay, won't you?"

Rory wanted to stop the quiver she saw in Violet's lower lip. Frankly, if she didn't have Violet to look after, Rory would have been tempted to cry too. "I have to go back with the Sisters tonight. But I like Elena and I think you will too. If you don't, we'll have a long talk with Sister Anna. All right, Vi?" She nuzzled her little sister's neck.

"You promised we'd stay together," said Violet.

Rory put Violet down and arched her sore back. When did Violet get so heavy? "I know, Vi," Rory said. "Let's see how tonight goes, all right?"

Violet shook her head. "No. I want you."

"Oh, Vi," Rory groaned.

"We're home," said Elena, stopping in front of a small house with narrow windows. She put William on the ground and felt in her pocket for the key. A large figure emerged from the shadows on the porch. Rory pulled Violet behind her and tensed to meet the new threat.

"Children, it's all right!" Elena reassured them. "It's my husband, Ramon."

The figure moved into the light spilled by her lantern. Ramon had a mustache and wore the clothes and hat of a workingman. Darker than Elena, he looked exactly like one of the cowboys in Rory's *Wild West Weekly*. Rory wasn't sure if he was one of the good guys or not, until he swept his hat off his head and gave Elena a big kiss.

"These are our children?" he asked.

Elena nodded, smiling, and gestured. "Violet and William."

Ramon jerked his head toward Rory.

"This is Rory," Elena said.

Ramon raised his eyebrows, but he was more interested in meeting Violet and William than an explanation. He knelt in the dirt so he would be face-to-face with them. He offered his hand. "Hello, little ones. My name is Ramon."

Violet pressed her body against Rory's legs, watching Ramon with huge eyes, but William took the outstretched hand and shook it.

"Ramon, I thought you were working tonight," Elena said.

"And miss the children's arrival?" he asked simply. His accent was heavier than Elena's, but Rory could understand him if she listened hard.

"Why didn't you just come to the church?" Elena asked.

He pressed his fingers to his temples. "That Father Mandin gives me a headache. Eight months he's been in Clifton and he still can't speak a language anyone understands?"

"I thought the same thing!" Rory said, unable to keep quiet any longer. "How can he do his job if he can't talk to anyone?"

Ramon twisted his neck to look up at Rory. "And who are you, young lady?"

Elena said, "This is Violet's sister. She came to make sure Violet has a good home."

He smiled slowly and nodded. "Then we should show

Rory around." He unlocked the thick door. Inside, the room was completely dark. He took the lantern from his wife and hung it from a large nail in the rafter in the center of the room. It cast wild shadows on the walls, illuminating in turn a plain crucifix on one wall and a colorful rug on another.

Violet tugged on Rory's sleeve. "Where are the lights?" she asked in a tiny voice.

Rory pointed. "That is the light. They don't have gas or electricity here."

Violet began to whimper. "Look, Vi, you can reach the ceiling," Rory said, to distract her. She lifted Violet until her fingers touched the rough plaster.

"I want to try too," William said.

"Come on, little man," Ramon said, swinging William onto his shoulders. William squealed and slapped his hands on the ceiling.

"Ramon, be careful, he'll hit his head," Elena scolded, but she couldn't help laughing.

Rory noticed that there wasn't much furniture in the room, only a small table with a bench along the wall and two stools. In the corner was a tall wardrobe for storage. Curtains separated two smaller rooms from the main one. The bright colors in the tablecloth shone even in the lantern light. It wasn't fancy but it was spotless. There was a shelf with plates and bowls. Exactly four of them. Well, Rory could share Violet's.

High on the wall behind the table was a painting of the Virgin Mary. Rory glanced from the picture to Elena—no, she hadn't mistaken the resemblance. Maybe Father Mandin was right. If everyone was a good Catholic, then they had that in common, no matter what.

"Why don't you girls sit down on the bench," Elena said lightly. "William's a big boy. He can sit on the stool here." Ramon swung William to the floor and William happily clambered up onto the stool closest to the stove.

Rory sat down on the bench and pulled Violet onto her lap. There was a small plate on the table, covered in a white cloth.

"Here are the sweets I promised. *Cochinitos*—little pigs." Elena took the cloth off the plate to reveal white pig-shaped cookies. William laughed and bit off a curly tail. Violet ate her cookie with one hand, mouthing the word *cochinito*. With the other she traced the embroidered flowers on the cloth.

"Have as many as you like." Rory rather liked how Elena's smile reached her eyes. "We don't usually have treats just before bedtime, but tonight is special."

Ramon shook the fire in the iron stove to life with a poker. The stove was small, but it warmed the room quickly. Rory watched and approved. She had few memories of her father, but one was of him carrying firewood for her mother.

As the chill left Rory's body, she noticed that the uneven wood floors in the rooms were brightened with rugs unlike any she had ever seen before.

"What are the rugs made of?" Rory asked.

"I made them by weaving colored rags together," Elena said. "Violet, if you like, I can teach you how."

Violet nodded, but her eyelids were growing heavy. William yawned and put his head on the table.

"Let's get them to bed," Elena said. "They'll sleep here." She brushed aside a curtain to reveal an alcove with two small beds made of rough wood, but cozy with thick cotton blankets. "We have our own privy out back if they need to relieve themselves."

Ramon carried William into the alcove bedroom, but as soon as Elena tried to pick up Violet, she cried for Rory.

"Hush, Vi. It's all right. I'm here." Rory undressed her sister and put her in the nightgown Elena provided.

"She's just tired," Rory offered. "Vi didn't mean anything by it."

"She'll get used to me," Elena said as if she was trying to reassure herself.

"Of course she will," Rory said.

They returned to the main room and sat at the table. Ramon was drinking a glass of beer. "Sit down, Rory," he said. "I would have known you were Violet's sister anywhere. You have the same wonderful hair."

"You don't mind red hair?" Rory asked. "Some people think it means we have a bad temper, but we don't . . . not usually."

Ramon threw back his head and laughed.

"Ramon, the children are sleeping!" Elena hushed him with a smile, then she explained, "My grandmother was from Scotland, Rory. She had hair like yours. And a temper . . . but not usually." Rory and Elena smiled at each other. "That is why I asked for a little girl with red hair."

Rory touched her own red braids. "So it's all right with you if your children don't look like you?"

Elena and Ramon exchanged looks. "In America," Ramon said, "it will be better for our children to look less Mexican and more like you."

Elena was clearing the plates from the table; when Rory caught her eye, she nodded in agreement.

Rory nibbled on the last cookie and considered. Sister Anna thought parents and children had to look alike to be a family. Rory had never heard Ramon's point of view before.

She started to speak but went silent when Ramon held up his hand and moved toward the door. Although Rory had not heard anyone climb the steps, there was a soft knocking at the door. Unconcerned, Elena continued to wipe the table. Ramon opened the door just a crack and whispered, then shut the door and turned to face his wife, his expression solemn.

"What's wrong?" Rory asked.

Ramon kept his eyes fixed on Elena. "There's a problem." He paused. "The Anglos want the babies."

Elena scrubbed the table so hard Rory thought she might wear a hole in it. "They cannot have them!" she said in a low growl. "The Father has assigned them all to us. Because we are good Catholics." She looked to the Virgin Mary on the wall and crossed herself.

Ramon said, "The Anglos don't think the white babies belong with people like us."

"Why shouldn't the children be with you?" Rory asked.

Elena and Ramon exchanged a knowing look. "There's bad feeling between the Anglos and Mexicans in Clifton," Ramon said. "Last year we went on strike for better wages and decent working conditions. It almost came to violence. And now there is no trust between us and them."

"Did the strike work?" Rory asked. "Did conditions improve?"

"Not enough," Ramon said, and the bleakness in his voice was reflected in his face.

"Why did you stay then?" Rory asked.

"We would have left long ago," Elena said. "But Father Mandin offered us the chance to have a family."

"So you waited for us," Rory said. "Well, for them." She looked toward the alcove where William and Violet were fast asleep.

Ramon reached out and took his wife's hand.

"It's that Mrs. Gatti," Rory said. "She's causing all the trouble."

Elena agreed. "She's getting the women all riled up."

Rory mouthed the words "riled up." She recognized that expression from the *Wild West Weekly*. "Like a den of rattlesnakes?"

"Yes, exactly like snakes," Ramon said with a quick smile that soon disappeared. "The Anglos want to know why they weren't aware of the children."

"Because they don't go to church!" Elena spoke sharply. "Father Mandin asked only the faithful. He said the most important thing is that the children be raised in the Church."

"Do you believe that?" Ramon looked at Rory. "I mean, do the Sisters?"

"They did when we got here," Rory said, staring down at her hands in her lap. "But I'm not sure now. Sister Anna is worried that the children don't look anything like their new families."

"In a family where there is love and God, nothing else matters," Elena said.

His mouth set in a tight line, Ramon said, "The Anglos won't see it that way. They'll see only filthy Mexicanos stealing white children." He spat the word *Mexicano* like it was a curse.

"What will you do?" Rory asked, inching her bottom to the edge of her seat.

"Trust in God and the Virgin Mother," Elena said, her eyes fixed on the picture on the wall.

Ramon dragged a chair over to the wardrobe in the corner of the room. He climbed up and pulled a rifle down from the top of the wardrobe. "I'd rather put my trust in this."

Twenty-Seven

"RAMON, PUT THAT AWAY," ELENA SAID. "YOU ARE SCARING RORY."

"I'm not scared," Rory said. "But I've never seen a gun before."

"And with the protection of Father Mandin and the Sisters you never will again," Elena said. "Let's not speak of unpleasant things. Rory, you are our guest and a child. I don't want you to worry about anything."

"But . . . ," Rory began.

A clock high on a shelf chimed the hour. "Ramon, you must bring Rory back to the church." Elena handed him his coat. "And ask the head Sister . . ."

"Sister Anna," Rory prompted.

"Ask her if Rory can come back tomorrow to meet our friends. She should be here."

"I'd love to come." Not only should she be here, Rory meant to stay. She only had to convince Violet to like it here.

And Ramon and Elena to ask her to be part of their family. And then persuade Sister Anna to agree. How difficult could it be?

Elena kissed Rory's cheek as Ramon held the door.

"I can find my own way back," Rory said, although the street was so dark she was happy to have Ramon's company.

"It's not safe here at night," Ramon said, leading the way down the street. "Not like my hometown in Mexico. There, everyone knows everybody else. And the streets are safe." He took Rory's arm to guide her around a hole in the wooden sidewalk.

"Is your family still there?" Rory asked.

"My brother and three sisters. And too many nieces and nephews to count."

"Violet and I have just each other," Rory said, managing to keep longing out of her voice. With all those children in his family, she thought, there must be room for one more. She saw the church looming in front of them; she had to ask now. "Ramon . . ." she began to say when a voice called out of the darkness.

"Rory! Is that you?"

Rory closed her eyes and sighed. "Yes, Sister Eileen, it's me." She'd have to talk to Ramon tomorrow.

"Thank the Lord," Sister Eileen said. "I've been worried about you." She stopped talking abruptly when she caught sight of Ramon. The golden light of the lantern in his hand cast eerie, elongated shadows across his face.

"Sister Eileen, this is Ramon Martinez." Rory hastened to introduce them. "He and his wife took Violet and William."

198

Sister Eileen nodded. "It was kind of you to walk Rory back." Frowning at Rory, she said, "We didn't realize she had left until just a few minutes ago."

"It was my pleasure," Ramon said. "But I also want to invite Rory to a party tomorrow."

"We'll have to ask Sister Anna," Sister Eileen said, leading the way inside. The scene hadn't changed much since Rory had left an hour earlier. Two dozen children were sleeping on the pews. The would-be mothers were waiting, slumped against the wall.

Rory whispered to Sister Eileen, "Why are they all still here?"

Sister Eileen pressed her lips together and shook her head.

Sister Anna was arguing with Mrs. Chacon. "No, Mrs. Chacon, it is *not* the same if Gwen goes to the Gonzalez family or the Lopez family. The assignments were carefully made in New York."

Mrs. Chacon spoke respectfully, but Rory could hear the irritation in her voice. "The Lopez family doesn't live here anymore. They moved away last month. The Gonzalez family is just as good. Father Mandin has said so."

Sister Eileen murmured close to Rory's ear, "It's been like this all night. Sister Anna's careful records are ruined and Mrs. Chacon doesn't understand why it matters. We've only done thirteen children so far!"

Sister Anna hit the table with the palms of her hands, startling Mrs. Chacon into silence. "That is enough," Sister Anna said. "We're finished for tonight."

"But the mothers! They have been waiting for hours," Mrs. Chacon protested.

"I am exhausted," Sister Anna said firmly. "I won't deliver any more children until I'm sure the first are well placed!"

Her face pinched, Mrs. Chacon went to speak with the remaining mothers. Rory seized her chance to introduce Ramon.

"Mr. Martinez, it is a pleasure to meet you," Sister Anna said, hiding a yawn behind her hand.

"And I you," he said. "Violet and William are lovely children, a credit to you and the other Sisters."

"Thank you," Sister Anna said. She looked at Rory expectantly, as if waiting for her report. Rory hesitated, glancing at Mrs. Chacon and the dozing priest. She leaned over Sister Anna's desk and whispered, "Sister, Ramon can answer your questions. He knows what's what in town."

"Is he trustworthy?" Sister Anna asked quietly.

"I think so," Rory answered. "Judge for yourself."

Sister Anna gestured for Ramon to sit. "May I ask you a question, Mr. Martinez?"

"I am at your service," he said.

"Usually placing orphans in a new family is a joyful event for the whole town," Sister Anna said slowly. "But today an angry mob met us at the station. Women threatened us here at the church. I don't understand what's happening."

"Clifton is not an easy place to bear children," Ramon explained. "All the women in town—the Anglo and the Mexicano women—they all have trouble having babies. And you roll in on your fancy train with forty! You might as well have brought a trainload of apples to the Garden of Eden."

Sister Anna, tired as she was, had to smile at his comparison. "But then why are they so angry?" she asked. "Father Mandin offered everyone a baby, didn't he?"

"He asked his congregation only," Ramon said. "And the Anglo women don't attend Father Mandin's church."

"Ah." Sister Anna's exhalation was full of her understanding. "So that is what Mrs. Gatti was upset about. Only the Mexican women got to ask for children."

Ramon nodded. "And the Anglos do not care for the Mexicanos."

"Why not?"

"How do the rich and powerful in New York City see the Irish?" He held out his hands and let her make her own connection between the Irish and the Mexicans.

"I see." Sister Anna sighed. "But the faith of the families is the most important thing. Father Mandin did exactly as we asked. We cannot let the babies go to Protestants!"

Ramon made a steeple of his hands and peered over his fingertips. "How many are still with you?"

"Twenty-seven," Sister Anna said. "Although my records are ruined now." She cast a baleful look at Mrs. Chacon. "It may be twenty-six or twenty-eight. I need to carefully review all the paperwork."

"Sister, you must keep a close watch on the children you have left." His gaze traveled over to the children asleep on the pews.

Rory interrupted, ignoring Sister Anna's quelling look. "Ramon, do you think they're in danger?"

"The women would never hurt them." He paused. "But try to take them, yes," he said.

"It's like that, is it?" Sister Anna shuffled through papers in front of her, taking her time to square them together. "Mr. Martinez, thank you for your insight."

Ramon smiled slightly. "Now I'd like to ask a favor from you." He explained about the party, and Sister Anna agreed to let Rory go the next day at four o'clock. "Good night, Rory, Sister."

After he had left, Sister Anna turned to Rory. "I like Mr. Martinez. But I hope he's wrong about the situation here."

"What if he isn't?" Rory asked, but Sister Anna did not have an answer.

On the ride back to the station, Rory didn't try to memorize the route as she had intended. Ramon's warning echoed too loudly in her ears. It was clear that Father Mandin would be of no help to them. That left Sister Anna. If she refused to see the danger, then it was up to Rory to find a way to keep everyone safe. Unfortunately, she thought, she had no idea how to do it.

The children and adults were all exhausted by the time they returned to the station. The engine that had pulled their train car into Clifton was gone. Rory thought about her well-thumbed copy of *Wild West Weekly*. There had been a drawing of a secluded fort, closed up tight, surrounded by attacking

Indians. In her mind she could clearly hear Ramon's warnings. Whenever Sister Anna wasn't looking, Rory cupped her hands around her eyes and pressed her nose to the window, trying to see if there were marauders in the darkness.

Once the lights were turned down, the car was silent except for the snuffling of small children and the occasional snore. *How nice to sleep alone for once*, she thought. *No Violet to kick me in the stomach or wake me every time she needs to pee.* Rory stretched in every direction, enjoying the luxury of an empty bed.

The lie lasted only a few minutes. What if Violet woke up at Elena's house, calling for Rory? Would she be afraid? Would she be able to use the old-fashioned privy? A sob escaped Rory's throat. She stuffed her fist in her mouth to keep from waking the others. She didn't need anyone's pity. Tomorrow Rory would convince Elena and Ramon to adopt her too. She and Violet would have a home together.

She pounded her pillow with her fist and curled up in the cold spot where Violet should be. It was the loneliest place in the world.

CHAPTER Twenty-Eight

THE NUNS ROUSED THE REMAINING CHILDREN EARLY THE NEXT morning. The temperature had dropped in the night and everyone woke cold and stiff. Rory helped the others dress the children in their Sunday best, again. Then off by wagon to the service at the mud church.

"Rory!" Violet came running up to her, dragging Ramon behind her. "I missed you so much!"

"Don't be silly," Rory said, chucking Violet's chin. "You knew you'd see me today." She flashed a tentative smile at Ramon. "Where's Elena?"

"She's in the back, preparing the food for after the service," Ramon said. "She'll be here in a minute. Can you believe she trusted me with the children?"

"Ramon," Rory began, taking her courage in both hands, "do you think that maybe . . ."

Father Mandin emerged from the vestry and stepped up to the pulpit. Everyone not already seated scurried for a pew.

"Ramon," Rory tried again.

"We'll talk afterwards," Ramon said.

Rory felt that everything and everyone in this town was conspiring to keep her from asking the only question that mattered. Ramon took a seat with Violet and William while Rory went to sit with the Sisters. She saw Elena hurrying to her seat just as Mass started.

The Mass was long, and without any stained glass or gilded statues there wasn't much to look at. Father Mandin spoke in Latin—that at least was familiar. Rory distracted herself by watching the worshippers. It was obvious to Rory that the Mexican women were only interested in the children. But the husbands exchanged serious glances over their wives' heads. On the surface, everything seemed fine, but to Rory the air felt charged the way it did before a summer storm. Anything might happen. Only Father Mandin seemed unaware of the electricity in the room.

After the service, Elena and the other women served fruit drinks and small cakes. The Foundling children ate greedily—no one more so than Violet. Rory tried to pull her away from her fourth cake.

"Let her eat," Ramon said, slipping Vi the cake. "This is a day to celebrate." He passed a cake to William.

"She'll get sick," Rory protested.

"Ramon!" Elena scolded. "And I was afraid you would be too strict with them."

Sister Anna and Father Mandin approached the table. Mrs. Chacon, as always, was translating.

"I'll have the families stay after church," Father Mandin said. "We'll distribute the children immediately."

Sister Anna bristled. "I told you I want to wait and see how the first group settles into their new homes."

Mr. Swayne, who had reappeared much cleaner and close-shaved after a night in a hotel, offered his opinion. "Sister Anna is right, Father. We should go slowly. This morning I had some unwelcome visitors."

"Who?" Father Mandin asked.

"A man named Mills and a Sheriff Simpson. They got me out of my bath to tell me how to do my job."

"Mills represents the copper company," Ramon explained quietly to Rory. "The most powerful man in town."

"What did they want?" Sister Anna asked.

"They want us to take back the children," Swayne said.

Elena gathered William and Violet into her arms. Rory flipped her braid over her shoulder and cast a wary eye toward the door as if an attack might come any minute.

"For what reason?" asked Sister Anna indignantly.

"They had crazy stories about the new parents being drunks and prostitutes." Mr. Swayne tipped his hat to Mrs. Chacon and Elena. "Begging your pardon, ladies."

"That is a lie!" spat Mrs. Chacon.

Elena was calmer. "The Anglos do not know us or our ways."

"They have no right to say such things," Ramon said with an ugly edge to his tone.

Sister Anna held up her hand to call for quiet. "Mr. Swayne, what did you say to these men?"

"I told them I knew my business and it was none of theirs."

"Did they accept that?" asked Sister Anna.

"They weren't happy, I can tell you," Swayne answered. "And Sister, they were armed."

"Armed?" Sister Anna asked faintly.

"With guns?" Sister Eileen whispered.

Rory shot her a look. What else would they be armed with in the Wild West? Nightsticks? Perhaps she should lend Sister Eileen her *Wild West Weekly* so she could recognize what was going on under her nose. But she felt as scared as Sister Eileen sounded. She had found a good family for Violet. And possibly for herself too. And nobody, least of all a greedy woman with fingers the size of sausages, could take that away from them. Not if Rory Fitzpatrick had anything to say about it.

———

After consulting with Mr. Swayne and Father Mandin, Sister Anna decided it was too cold for the children to remain another night on the train. Everyone was to move to the Clifton Hotel. After Ramon's warnings, Rory was inclined to believe that waking with a cold nose was preferable to what the townspeople might do if they could get to the children. But Sister Anna wasn't listening. And Sister Eileen and the nurses wanted a hotel with baths and better beds.

The Clifton Hotel was not far from the church. A large adobe building of three stories, it was the biggest place Rory had seen so far in Clifton. And the fanciest balconies on the second floor overlooked the hills beyond the town. When they entered the lobby, Rory saw not only the registration desk but also entrances to a saloon and a barbershop and a sign for a pool hall. It was as if a visitor would never have to leave the hotel.

Mrs. Abraham waited for them in the lobby. Rory watched her with suspicion, remembering the night before. But today Mrs. Abraham wasn't shouting threats; she was playing innkeeper. She showed them to their rooms on the third floor.

"You have four rooms," Mrs. Abraham said. "And they all connect." She handed Sister Anna the keys. "The bathroom and water closet are in the hall. I arranged for cots for the little ones. I can send up some food at six."

"Thank you," Sister Anna said with chilly politeness. Rory saw that Sister Anna had not forgiven Mrs. Abraham for the scene in the church.

Mrs. Abraham hesitated. "Sister, about last night . . ."

"Yes?" Sister Anna said in that nun's voice that Rory knew only too well.

"I only want what is best for the children," Mrs. Abraham said.

"As do I," Sister Anna replied. "But I decide what is best. No one else."

"Of course." Mrs. Abraham backed out of the room, her face cold and angry, her mouth set in a thin, flat line.

Sister Anna had the children's cots placed in the middle

rooms. The adults were given the rooms on the ends. Sister Anna bolted the doors in the children's rooms that connected to the hall so no one could come in without her knowledge.

"Not that I believe the children are in any danger," Sister Anna explained to Rory and Sister Eileen.

"Of course not," Sister Eileen said.

"But we are in a strange town and an ounce of prevention is worth a pound of cure," Sister Anna finished.

But Rory couldn't forget the desperate women at the station. Rory knew that if Mrs. Gatti wanted a baby, ten deadbolts wouldn't keep her out.

CHAPTER Twenty-Nine

THE CHILDREN HAD BATHED AND WERE NAPPING. AN EXHAUSTED Sister Anna dozed in a plush armchair while Rory got ready for the party. She put on her only other dress, her best. She combed and braided her hair as neatly as possible. She watched the clock. At ten minutes to four, she was ready to go. Then it was a quarter past. She rebraided her hair. Rory told herself there could be any number of reasons Ramon was late. By half past four, the large room felt like a jail cell. What if Ramon didn't come? She should have found a way to talk to Ramon at church. What if the Martinezes had decided that it would be easier for Vi to adjust to the family without Rory? What if . . .

Tap, tap.

Rory hurried to answer the door, a welcoming smile on her face. But instead of Ramon a small Chinese boy in hotel livery stood in the doorway. Her smile faded. With a small bow he handed her a note.

Unfolding the paper, she read, "Cheng will bring you to me. Ramon."

Rory nodded and carefully shut the door so as not to wake Sister Anna. Cheng led her down the uncarpeted back stairs into the kitchen.

"You're Chinese?" Rory asked.

Cheng seemed surprised that she was talking to him but what he didn't know was that Rory was friendly with the Chinese boys who delivered the linens to the Foundling.

"I'm American. My parents came here from China to build the railroad and I was born here," he said, holding the door open. Sitting at a table in the corner of the kitchen, a cup of coffee in his hand, was Ramon.

"Ramon!" Rory cried. He cocked an eyebrow at the relief in her voice. "I was worried you wouldn't come," she explained.

"I told you I would," he said.

"I was just being foolish, I guess." Rory hung her head.

"I understand," Ramon said. "I know what is at stake for you. Nothing less than your sister's happiness."

Rory gulped and nodded, unable to speak past the lump in her throat.

"Cat got your tongue?" Ramon teased.

"Why were you late?" Rory asked. Now that sounded more like her usual self.

"The hotel wouldn't let me come into the lobby and collect you properly."

"Why not?" Rory was puzzled. "Who would stop you?"

She glanced around the kitchen ready to take someone to task for making her worry.

"No Mexicanos allowed," he said simply. "This hotel is owned by the copper company. They built it for their own people, not us."

"But that's not fair," Rory cried. "Ramon, I don't like this town."

"Neither do I," he said with a cheerful grin. "But let them keep their hotel. They can't run their mines without us. Let's go." He stood up and drained his coffee cup in one gulp. "Oh, I almost forgot. Elena wants me to give you this." He held out a shapeless bundle wrapped in paper.

Rory hesitated, feeling the soft heft of it.

"Open it," Ramon said.

Rory carefully unwrapped the package. It was a dark green handmade shawl.

"It's beautiful," Rory said, stroking the wool.

Ramon looked pleased. "I told Elena you were cold last night."

"It's the first new thing I've ever had," Rory said. She held it to her cheek and used it to brush away a tear before Ramon could see. With his help, she wound the large shawl around her body and followed Ramon out to an alley that led to the street. The sky was dark with storm clouds and the streets were deserted.

Rory glanced back at the Clifton Hotel. Rory, a penniless Irish orphan, was permitted to stay there but Ramon couldn't enter by the front door. There was something she had to know, even if she offended Ramon by asking. "Ramon, what will it be like for Vi to have Mexicano parents?"

"Elena thinks love is enough, but I'm more realistic than she is. It won't be easy," Ramon finally answered. "But we're going to be good parents to Vi and William. They won't want for anything."

Ramon looked to the sky. "We should hurry before it rains," he said. "Our guests are already at the house to meet the children, and you of course. I wish the children's *padrinos* could be there, but it is impossible."

"*Padrinos?*"

"Godparents," he said. "We've chosen my brother and his wife, but they are still in Mexico."

Rory heard the longing in Ramon's voice. She considered everything she knew about Ramon: his problems with the company, his homesickness for Mexico and his family, and how hard it would be for a Mexican family to keep white children in Clifton. Her stomach tightly twisted like a knot, and she forced herself to ask, "Are you going to take Vi and William to Mexico?"

Matter-of-factly, as though it didn't change absolutely everything, Ramon nodded. "Since the strike, the company wants to get rid of me. We have no future in Clifton. We only stayed here this long because we were waiting for Violet and William." He walked on, not noticing that Rory could barely breathe.

Mexico! She had thought the Arizona Territory was far away from all they knew in New York, but Mexico was another country. What would it be like to always be a foreigner and have to talk in a language not your own? Would Violet even remember being American?

Violet would never know New York the way Rory did. She'd never have a chance to see the fireworks over the river. Or the balloons in Central Park. Vi would never have the fun of jumping onto the back of an omnibus. Maybe the best thing was to bring Violet back to the Foundling and they could try again. Sister Anna had offered Rory a permanent place at the Foundling. Rory could bargain with Sister Anna to keep Violet close to her a while longer. After the mess Sister Anna had made of the adoptions in Clifton, she owed Rory that much.

On the other hand, wasn't family the most important thing? Ever since Mama died, Rory had tried to be Violet's whole family, but now Elena and Ramon wanted to be Violet's parents. And they were good people.

First things first. She hadn't yet had the chance to ask the most important question of all. Hurrying to catch up with him, she began, "Ramon, I know you asked for two children—"

"Really only one—a boy. But Father Mandin is persuasive," Ramon answered with a wry chuckle.

She steeled her courage before she asked, "Ramon, would you consider taking a third? Would you take me?"

He watched her, his face saying nothing.

"I'm a hard worker and I'm an expert at taking care of children." The words tumbled out of her mouth. "I can write, read, and even do multiplication!"

Ramon ran his fingers through his thick hair. "Elena and I discussed this last night. Rory, we like you and it would be right to keep two sisters together . . ."

Rory knew there was a *but*.

"But we cannot afford three children," he went on. "I'm sorry, Rory. But that is my answer. Two children are all we can take."

"If Sister Anna finds out that you plan to take the children to Mexico, you won't have any children," Rory pointed out. "She'd never permit it."

"If she asks, I will tell her the truth," Ramon said. "I can convince her if I have to. It will be a decent life in Mexico for William and Violet. We will love them as if they were our own blood. And don't forget, they'll be raised in the Church."

"But if Sister Anna doesn't ask?"

He shrugged. "Then I don't feel I need to go out of my way to make trouble." His eyes crinkled when he smiled, inviting her to smile back. But the stakes were still too high.

"She would worry most about the children having no one American to look after them . . . but if I went too . . ." Rory let her voice trail off.

Ramon laughed. "You are the clever one. Do you ever give up?"

"No," Rory assured him.

He shook his head. Before he could say no again, Rory interrupted. "I'm old enough to work—what if I could pay my own way? Do people in Mexico want to learn English? I could teach them!"

"They do want to learn—but you are so young." He tugged gently on her braid. "You deserve to stay a child a little longer."

"Not if it means losing Violet." Rory spoke simply and she could see from Ramon's face he understood.

The rain began coming down in sheets and the wind picked up. "Quickly," Ramon urged, taking her hand.

"But we haven't decided anything!" Rory had to raise her voice to be heard against the rising wind.

"We'll talk later," he promised.

As they ran, she consoled herself that he hadn't said no. When they reached Ramon's house, Rory could hear the muffled sounds of a party. But she wasn't prepared for the din when Ramon opened the door. There were so many people that Rory wondered how they fit in the room. The conversation stopped abruptly, then started up again when they saw Ramon. Greetings were called in Spanish, and Rory wondered how hard it would be to learn the language. If she didn't, she would never be able to speak to anyone if they went to Mexico.

She noticed that almost everyone had the same dark skin as Ramon. Rory held out her hand and compared the difference between her skin and theirs. Even freshly scrubbed, the men still smelled of sulfur, from the mines. All the women wore white dresses with colorful embroidery on the bottoms of their skirts. Their shawls were a rainbow of bright colors. Some of them had paper flowers in their buns. Others had ribbons braided into their dark hair. Near the back door, an elderly man played a cheerful tune on his fiddle while a group of people sang and clapped. The tune was unfamiliar and she couldn't understand a word of the song. Feeling suddenly alone in the crowded room, Rory searched for Violet.

Ramon took her new shawl and hung it on a hook on the door as he joked with his guests. Elena hurried across the crowded room to embrace Rory, who didn't flinch this time. She was getting used to Elena's hugs.

"Rory, at last you are here!" Elena said. "Are you hungry?"

"No, thank you," Rory said. "Where's Violet?"

"Where else but at the table with all the desserts." Elena laughed.

"May I go to her?"

"Of course." Elena hurried away to greet a new arrival.

Rory saw William first. He had found a friend, a boy who was as dark as William was fair. The two of them were running around being petted by the women. She saw Violet across the room, sitting on the lap of an elderly woman, and headed for them. Violet was taking tiny bites from a piece of cake in her hand. She saw Rory and waved. When Rory came within speaking distance, Violet said to the elderly woman, "This is my sister, Rory."

The woman replied in Spanish, but her broad smile was welcoming. She set Violet on her feet and moved away to talk to another older woman watching the fiddler.

There was a gust of rain against the window. Rory hugged herself, glad to be inside.

Violet leaned her head against her sister. "Rory, I don't feel so good."

"No wonder," Rory said with exasperation. "How many cakes have you eaten? Vi, these cakes aren't like the cakes back home. They might upset your tummy."

Violet started to count on her fingers. Suddenly she put her hands to her mouth, her throat convulsing.

"No, Vi. You can't be sick in the middle of the party," Rory said. She swept Violet up in her arms and headed for the back door. She tried to catch Elena's attention, but she was busy refreshing the cakes on the other end of the table.

"Hold it just a little more," Rory ordered. Outside the door, the day's light had gone, swallowed by the storm. Heedless of the drenching rain, Violet began throwing up what seemed like dozens of partially chewed cakes. Rory held her sister's hair away from her face until the retching was over. Then Violet held up her arms and Rory obediently picked her up.

"I'm sleepy," Violet said, her face pale, as she leaned her head on her sister's shoulder.

"Let's take a little nap," Rory said. She knew from past experience that a nap was the best thing to settle Vi's sensitive stomach.

The two wet girls slipped back into the noisy room. Rory carried her limp sister into the children's sleeping alcove, and placed her on the neatly made bed. She arranged the colorful folded shawl around Violet so snugly that only the tip of her snub nose showed.

"Now I lay me down to sleep," Rory began. Violet dutifully recited the familiar prayer.

Violet's eyes grew heavier until she fell fast asleep. Rory thought, no matter how vexing Violet might be awake, she looked like an angel when she slept.

Rory waited a few moments to be sure her sister was truly napping before she rose from the small bed. Then she stood watching the party from the shelter of the curtains at the doorway to the children's room. They were all strangers to her, even Ramon and Elena. What did she really know about them? Their language, clothes, and food were alien to her. What kind of sister would she be to send Violet away from everything she knew to a foreign country? How would Violet cope?

Violet stirred in her sleep and Rory moved to her side and leaned over her. Vi's eyes, so much like Rory's own, half-opened and she whispered, "*Buenas noches*, Rory, that means good night." With a little sigh, she rolled over and burrowed into the blankets. Rory bit her lip to keep from crying. She'd forgotten how strong Violet really was. Vi would be just fine.

Rory returned to watching the party. Despite the joyful music and the festive clothes, Rory detected the same uneasiness she had seen at the church. The men were speaking quietly together in the corners and nervously glancing at the door.

And the women tried to be cheerful for Elena's sake; Rory could see strain in their faces and hear tension in their voices. When the door opened—no one knocked, it seemed—all conversation stopped. As the partygoers recognized the new arrival, the noise level would rise—until the next time.

A thundering knock on the door plunged the room into silence. Flung open, the door crashed against the wall. A gust of wind extinguished the candles on the table and tossed the lantern so shadows danced ominously. A single discordant twang from the musician's fiddle sounded loud in the sudden quiet.

Two men strode out of the rain through the open door. Behind them, other men crowded into the opening. The leader had a badge and a sodden list. He read out loud, "Ramon and Elena Martinez."

"Sheriff Simpson, we're right here!" Ramon snapped.

His hand on the gun at his hip, the sheriff said, "We're here for the children."

CHAPTER Thirty

ALL EYES TURNED TO ELENA. HER FACE WHITE AGAINST HER DARK hair, Elena stepped in front of William. Her eyes met Rory's. Rory jerked her head behind her to let Elena know Violet was in bed. Who was Simpson and who said he could take the children? No one would steal Violet away if Rory could prevent it.

"My children are not for you to take," Ramon said. His voice was quiet but its anger chilled Rory. Couldn't the sheriff see how mad Ramon was?

"Martinez, be sensible," Simpson said. Rory could hear his fingers tapping nervously on his gun. "A mistake's been made. These children don't belong with your people."

"They belonged to the Foundling Hospital in New York," Ramon said. There was a rumble of agreement from the crowd. "They gave the children to me. You have no authority over them."

A rumpled man, smelling of rain and alcohol, burst

through the door brandishing a pistol at Elena. Ramon stepped in front of his wife.

"*Señora*, just hand the kids over."

Ramon didn't hesitate. He leapt onto a stool, grabbed his rifle from the top of the wardrobe, and pointed it at Simpson's chest. "You broke into my house, disturbed my guests, and pointed a gun at my wife. Even in Clifton, I'm within my rights to shoot you where you stand. You'll take the children over my dead body." He stepped lightly off the stool.

"Ramon, no!" Elena cried. "You mustn't fight them."

"Stay back, Elena," he ordered. "I'll handle this."

Simpson eased his gun halfway out of the holster. "Ramon, put the rifle away. There doesn't have to be any violence. We've sent for Judge Little to come from Solomonville. He'll settle this, legal-like. In the meantime, it's better if all the children stay together."

Ramon kept his gun trained on Simpson. Rory knew in her heart that he wasn't going to give in.

Elena stepped between Ramon and the sheriff, her hands outstretched like a saint. "We don't want any trouble, Sheriff."

"Elena!" Ramon ordered. "Step away."

She touched his arm, but he wouldn't take his eyes off Sheriff Simpson. "Ramon, please. We can't let the children be hurt." She turned to the sheriff. "Where will you take them?"

"To the hotel."

"They'll be returned to the Sisters?" she pressed.

"Yes," he said. To Rory this sheriff looked shifty. She wanted to shout, "He's lying! Can't you see?" But Elena was too trusting and Ramon couldn't refuse Elena's pleading look.

"Now that that's settled," the sheriff said with a wary eye on Ramon, "where are the children the priest gave you?"

Slowly Elena moved to one side, revealing William playing with his toy horse.

Simpson consulted his list. "This says you have two." He paused. "Now where's the other one?"

Rory didn't believe Sheriff Simpson for one moment. They might bring Violet and William to Gatti's meat market and not even Sister Anna would be able to get the children out of Mrs. Gatti's greedy clutches. Everything had turned topsy-turvy since they had arrived in Clifton. Rory wasn't sure of anything anymore except one thing. No matter what, Mrs. Gatti was not getting her hands on Violet. Her legs shaky, as though she was about to step onto a high wire, Rory tiptoed out of the alcove.

"I'm right here," Rory said.

Simpson gaped. He looked her up and down. "You're no baby."

"I'm an orphan," Rory said. "I'm the second child."

"But—" Elena protested.

"Elena, these men are going to take two kids from your house, no matter what you do," Rory said, briefly casting her eyes toward the alcove. Elena understood.

Simpson was holding the list up to the light. "It says, 'Fitzpatrick, girl, red hair.'"

Rory held up her braid. "And if you need further proof," she said, "look." She pulled her collar away from her neck and let him see the ribbon with her name.

"Fitzpatrick," Simpson said with a shrug. "All right, let's go."

"At least let us say goodbye," Ramon said.

"There's no time," Simpson said. "Look at the weather. The streets are already flooding."

"There's time," said Ramon flatly, fingering his rifle.

"Hurry, then," said Simpson. He and the other man waited by the door. While Elena fussed over William's coat, Ramon brought Rory her new shawl and draped it around her shoulders.

"You don't have to do this," he said quietly.

She nodded. "Better me than Violet."

Elena hugged her. "Rory, you are very brave. But it won't work. They'll come looking for Violet," she whispered.

"It's the best I can do," Rory whispered. "Keep Vi hidden."

"We'll get word to you somehow," Ramon promised.

The sheriff bellowed, "Time's up. Let's go."

CHAPTER Thirty-One

ORY PULLED THE SHAWL MORE TIGHTLY AROUND HER SHOULDERS. Through the sheets of rain, she made out the shapes of two other children, Josephine and Colin. At three years old, they were too little to be out in such weather.

"Rory!" They rushed toward her, clinging to her skirt as though they were afraid of being swept away by the storm.

"I'm here now," Rory said, giving them quick hugs. "Hey, Mr. Sheriff," she called. "It's too cold out for these little kids! Who said you should scoop us up in the night? Not the Sisters, that's for sure."

Sheriff Simpson ignored her. He held his lantern high and gestured toward the center of town. "Let's go," he said.

Simpson moved along the slick sidewalk. The man who had waved the gun at Elena slipped off the sidewalk into the mud. He tried to catch himself but needed both hands to stop his fall. When his rifle fell into a puddle, he cursed freely.

"Hey, mister, not in front of the kids," Rory scolded. She

giggled but the little kids were too scared to find anything funny.

"Where are they taking us?" Josephine asked.

"Back to Sister Anna, I hope," Rory said.

"Where's Vi?" William asked, looking back toward the house.

Rory glanced apprehensively at the men, but they weren't paying any attention to the children. "Shhh, Vi's all right."

Rory then asked the sheriff, "Where are the others? There should be thirteen of us." She was proud she remembered to say "us." If Rory could buy them some time, Ramon and Elena would find a way to hide Violet. After that? Rory didn't know what would come next for her and Violet, but right now this was the best she could do for her sister.

"They're already at the hotel. I saved the Martinezes for last. I knew there'd be trouble there," Sheriff Simpson called back over his shoulder.

"You brought the trouble, Mr. Sheriff," Rory pointed out.

"Just be quiet. I've never known a kid to talk so much."

The children slipped and slid in the greasy mud. Rory tried to keep them upright, but the fierce wind threatened to blow her into the street. Finally they reached a main street with safer wooden sidewalks. Rory kept her head down against the driving rain. The cold and sodden group was relieved when they finally arrived at the Clifton Hotel, its first floor ablaze with light. Mrs. Abraham was keeping watch at the entrance and she held the door wide to let them in. "Hurry," she called, "it's too cold for the little ones."

She ushered them upstairs to a parlor that had been transformed into a makeshift dormitory. Rory's eyes scanned the room for the Sisters but they weren't there. Five or six women, Anglos all, were taking care of a dozen children. Some of the little ones were sopping wet like Rory, but most were bundled in warm blankets in front of a roaring fire. Every child given to the Mexican families the day before was here. Sheriff Simpson had been busy. The only good news was that Mrs. Gatti was nowhere to be seen.

"Where's Sister Anna?" Rory asked. "She should be here."

"Don't worry now," hushed Mrs. Abraham. "Just come and get warm. Plenty of time for questions later."

"You've no right . . . ," Rory began.

Mrs. Abraham's mask of kindness disappeared. "I said, be quiet!" Her eyes narrowed as she took a closer look. "Who are you? You're too old to be an orphan."

"And you're too respectable to be kidnapping children," Rory shot back.

Mrs. Abraham raised her hand as if to strike Rory, but she stood tall, ready for the blow.

"Mrs. Abraham!" said the sheriff. "We're protecting the children, remember?"

Her hand slowly fell to her side. "Of course, Sheriff Simpson." To Rory, she said, "You, just be quiet."

Mrs. Abraham turned away. Rory slumped against the wall. Her hair felt heavy with the rain and her neck and back ached. Maybe it was time to stop making trouble. So long as the children were in the hotel, they were safe. She just had to get to Sister Anna and tell her that they were here.

A heavy-set woman offered William hot chocolate and he followed her willingly. Another lady hovered near Rory. She couldn't stop staring at Josephine, who refused to leave Rory's side. "Tom," the lady said to Sheriff Simpson. "This little girl is soaked through. Let me warm her up."

"All right, May, but don't get too attached," Simpson said as he yawned. "We don't know if we can keep her."

Rory rolled her eyes. Now she knew why the sheriff was so eager to confiscate the kids. Was everyone in this town so desperate for children? Rory shivered and she wouldn't have taken bets on whether it was from fear or cold.

"Tom, I heard that there were twenty more children on that train who got sick. The Sisters gave them to the Indians to get them out of the way before they died."

Rory stared at Mrs. Simpson. "That's a barefaced lie."

"Don't listen to her, May," Sheriff Simpson said. "That one's been nothing but trouble."

"Doesn't mean I'm not right," Rory declared. "There *were* other children but the Sisters placed them with good Catholic families. The same as they did here."

Mrs. Simpson scowled at Rory. "That's what they want us to believe. But these families were not suitable in any way," she said. Then to Josephine, "You must be hungry, honey. Let me get you a treat."

"I want to stay with Rory," Josephine said, her voice muffled by Rory's skirt.

Rory knelt down and looked her in the eye. "Josephine,

this lady will get you warm and give you something good to eat. It will be all right, I promise."

"They're frozen," said another woman who wore her hair piled up on top of her head. She carried a tray with mugs of hot soup. "Only those Mexicans would send them out in such weather." She handed Rory a cup.

"We were safe and warm," Rory muttered, "until you people snatched us up and brought us out in the cold."

"For your own good," the woman said defensively. "And aren't you a little old to be one of the orphans?"

Rory sank down on a velvet armchair and sipped her soup without answering. Sister Anna would want to know everything, so Rory kept her eyes open. Two women came through an archway at the rear of the room. They were carrying stacks of towels. The only one Rory recognized was Mrs. Gatti, looking smugly satisfied as she bustled into the room.

Mrs. Gatti spied William. She dropped the towels on a cot and rushed over and scooped him up in her arms. He started to howl in protest, but Mrs. Gatti was wise to the ways of greedy little boys. She pulled a sweet out of her pocket and popped it in his mouth.

"Poor little one," she said to William. "Would you like to come home with me and eat meat every day?"

"Roast chicken?" William asked. He beamed when Mrs. Gatti nodded.

"He's starving," Mrs. Gatti announced. "Those people don't know how to feed children properly."

"Because we were kidnapped at gunpoint before we could

eat," Rory called out. Mrs. Gatti scowled in Rory's direction.

Sheriff Simpson approached Mrs. Abraham and Mrs. Gatti to make his report. "That's all of them." He sighed wearily. "And if you don't mind, I have to go watch over the priest and that agent."

"Wait . . ." Mrs. Gatti's eyes swept the room and she counted on her pudgy fingers. "We're missing one."

"I was told to get thirteen, I got thirteen," Simpson snapped.

"Where's the adorable little girl with red hair? Her name was Fitzpatrick," Mrs. Gatti said. "I particularly wanted that one."

"That's her." He pointed at Rory. "And watch her sharp tongue." Tipping his hat, he said, "Good night, ladies."

"But . . ." Mrs. Gatti was too late; Simpson was gone. Although Mrs. Gatti was not a big woman, there was strength in her arms. Rory was sure she could butcher beef with the best of them. Carrying William on her hip, she strode over to Rory and stared down at her. "You! I remember you. You took away my girl at the station. Where is she?"

Rory met her gaze, sipped her soup, and did not say a word.

"Where is the Fitzpatrick girl?" Mrs. Gatti's voice rose. "What did you do with her?"

"I am the Fitzpatrick girl," Rory said. She put the mug down and stood up, her eyes level with Mrs. Gatti's. "If you don't believe me, why don't you ask the Sisters? I'm sure Sister Anna would be happy to discuss it."

Mrs. Gatti didn't have time to argue, interrupted by the arrival of her bear of a husband.

"There you are, Louisa! Stirring up trouble as usual."

"Thank goodness you are here, Jacques. They made a mistake. The sheriff was supposed to bring back the little girl I chose. Instead he brought this one. And I don't like her at all."

"Girl?" Mr. Gatti gave Rory a disdainful look. "I agreed to a boy."

"A boy for you and a girl for me," Mrs. Gatti said.

"And feed two mouths instead of one?" he shot back. "At least a boy can follow me in the business. What does a girl do that doesn't cost me money and good food?"

"But—"

"Enough. One boy, Louisa. That's it." He turned to go. "I'm going home and if you know what's good for you, you'll come with me."

"I'm just finishing up, Jacques." She turned to him and her tone became sweet as pie. "I'll be right home and I'll bring some extra soup. You need some warming up on a night like this."

"Don't be long—it's not a fit night to be out and about." He turned and left.

Mrs. Gatti beckoned to one of the ladies and asked her to watch William. "Take good care of him—he's going to be mine."

Rory blocked Mrs. Gatti's way. "William doesn't belong to you," Rory said, staring her down. "The Sisters won't let you take him."

"Take that smirk off your face. Your precious Sisters won't

have a choice," Mrs. Gatti snapped. "They aren't fit to choose parents for white children."

Mrs. Abraham came up next to Mrs. Gatti. "One of the sheriff's men told me that there was alcohol at the house where these last children were picked up. The man was too drunk to stand and he threatened the sheriff with a gun."

The two of them loomed over Rory like two desperadoes. Rory wanted to shrink away but there was too much at stake. She straightened up and met the leaders of this gang of kidnappers head on.

"That's nonsense!" Rory snapped. "It was a welcoming party for the children and no one was drinking. And as for threatening the sheriff, Ramon was only defending his home."

"Ramon Martinez?" Mrs. Gatti said. "He's a troublemaker. If he had his way the town would have burned to the ground in the riots last year!"

Rory deliberately turned her back on Mrs. Gatti and addressed Mrs. Abraham. "Where are Sister Anna and the others?"

"They're sleeping," Mrs. Abraham said. "I won't let you disturb them."

"Do they even know you've taken the children?" Rory asked. "Wait till I tell them—they'll have the courts on you."

Mrs. Gatti and Mrs. Abraham turned away and conferred in worried whispers. Mrs. Abraham handed Mrs. Gatti a key, which she put in her apron pocket. Mrs. Abraham went to the doorway and looked out in the hallway, then beckoned to Mrs. Gatti, who grabbed Rory's elbow and marched her toward the door, past Mrs. Abraham. Rory started to cry out but Mrs. Gatti muttered in her ear, "Do you want to scare the little ones? They've already been through so much tonight."

Rory closed her mouth.

"I thought not." Mrs. Gatti hauled Rory down the stairs. She was as strong as Rory had feared.

"Where are you taking me?"

Instead of answering, Mrs. Gatti stopped in front of a closet door. She inserted the key, quickly opened it, and shoved Rory inside.

"Hey!" Rory fell to the floor with a thud.

Mrs. Gatti slammed the door shut and quickly locked it.

"You can't shut me in here!" Rory yelled. She couldn't see her hand in front of her face.

"I just did," said Mrs. Gatti, purring with satisfaction.

Rory pounded on the door. "Let me out!" she cried.

"Scream all you want, little girl," said Mrs. Gatti. "No one will hear you." She paused. "The judge comes in the morning and he'll tell your Sister Anna what's what."

Mrs. Gatti's footsteps moved away.

The darkness was thick and Rory felt it press on her skin, smothering her. Closing her eyes so the lack of light mattered less, she forced herself to inhale and exhale slowly until her heartbeat quieted and she could think again. First things first. She had to warn Sister Anna. She had to save the children, no matter what.

But first Rory had to rescue herself. She'd done it before.

CHAPTER Thirty-Two

How could Rory warn Sister Anna if no one could hear her poundings or her screams? The closet reminded her of the paddy wagon in New York. At least she wasn't sharing this cell with a hardened criminal.

Rory turned her back on the door and held out her hands to explore every inch of the pitch-dark closet. Not even a tiny line of light appeared under the door.

There had to be a way out.

A high stack of what felt like folded curtains lay on the floor by the back wall. She shifted them to one side, then stepped back. Was she just imagining it or was that a glimmer of light where that pile of fabric had been?

She reached and felt . . . glass!

Behind that pile was a narrow window. Pressing her face against the glass, Rory could make out an alley with a blank wall on the other side—the same alley she had passed through with Ramon. The light must be from the hotel windows above her.

She tugged at the window but it wouldn't open. Her fingers felt layers of paint over the wooden sill. Grabbing a handful of fabric, she covered her fist and forearm and broke the window. She gulped in the fresh air as though she had been suffocating. She swept the fabric around the frame to knock the broken glass into the alley.

Quickly, she clambered through the window. Her sleeve caught on a jagged bit of window still left in the frame. Rory jerked herself free. Her arm burned but she kept going and landed in a crouch in the alley. The throbbing in her arm was more pain than she'd ever felt before. Gingerly she touched her arm and felt wetness. Crimson blood stained her fingers. Rory wasn't fond of blood, and she leaned against the building waiting until the dizziness passed.

The rain had ended but the air was bitter cold and she could see her breath hanging in the air. The bleeding had nearly stopped, and she considered her next move. She desperately wanted to go to Sister Anna. It would be a huge relief to hand her worries over to her. But if she snuck back into the hotel, would Mrs. Gatti and Mrs. Abraham catch her? Those women wanted only one thing and if Rory got in their way, she wasn't sure how much further they would go. Maybe she should find Ramon and make sure Violet was all right.

But she would never find them in the dark. And if Ramon had done as Rory asked, they might be hiding for Violet's sake.

She made her way to where the alley met the road. It was late on a Sunday night after a storm and she didn't expect to meet anyone on the street. She was wrong. Two men were carrying a large vat covered with a piece of wood. She jumped back into the shadows and they passed by without seeing her.

"Careful with that," one said to the other. "You nearly spilled it."

"My hands are burning!" the other said.

The vat had a foul smell of pine that made Rory's eyes water.

"I don't know about this," the second man said. "Could we go to hell for tarring and feathering a priest?"

Even though Rory wasn't quite sure what tarring and feathering was, it sounded bad. Father Mandin wasn't her favorite person, but torturing him was beyond the pale.

"Nah," the other man answered. "It's not like it'll kill him. We're just going to teach the priest and that agent a lesson. They can't get away with giving kids to those people."

Her breath coming fast and shallow, Rory felt light in her head. They were going after Mr. Swayne too. She crept out into the street to watch where they went. They wrestled the steaming vat over the cable bridge spanning the creek to a large white building standing alone on the other side. One of them pounded on the door. When it opened, light spilled into the darkness. Rory heard a crowd of angry people inside.

Rory glanced up at the hotel to the third floor. Every aching, tired bone in her body told her to go to Sister Anna. But what about the priest and Mr. Swayne? Rory had to help if she could. Making sure that the street was empty, she darted across the road and onto the cable bridge. She stopped, spinning her arms for balance. The bridge swayed over the creek. Earlier today the creek bed had been almost empty, but now it was full of rushing water. Her feet slipped and slid as she crossed and she tried not to look down at the fast-moving water.

The building loomed in the dark and rain. Rory didn't dare go to the door. She headed to the nearest square of light, a window open just a crack. She could distinguish individual voices, including Mr. Swayne's.

She pulled herself up to sit on the windowsill and lifted the window. It was steamy from the warm breaths of fifty or so people. Inside, Mr. Swayne stood on a platform at one end of the room. Father Mandin hovered nervously behind him. "The children belong to the Foundling Hospital," Mr. Swayne shouted hoarsely.

The room was filled with men. There wasn't a woman in sight. Rory wasn't sure if that was good or bad after everything she'd seen today. Were the women more dangerous than the men?

The sheriff and his men stood between the crowd and Mr. Swayne. The lawmen had their hands on the butts of their guns. She quickly scanned the room and counted at least a dozen guns and a few rifles.

"The Foundling would never place them in harm's way!" Swayne yelled over the crowd's jeers.

"Too late for that!" one man called out. "You put white children with dirty Mexicans."

"That's not true!" Swayne cried. "Every family was selected and vouched for by Father Mandin. We turned down families who looked too dark."

The crowd roared, "Tar the priest!" and parted like the

Red Sea, letting the two men with the vat through. A third man trailed behind, easily balancing a large sack on his shoulder. A shower of feathers floated in his wake. The soup in Rory's stomach came back up to her mouth with a sour taste. They were going to cover Father Mandin in hot tar and roll him in feathers. Humiliating and painful too, she bet. And Mr. Swayne would be next. Nothing in *Wild West Weekly* had ever prepared her for this.

On the platform, Mr. Swayne stared at the vat and staggered back a few steps. Rory didn't blame him for being afraid; this wasn't hectoring a group of desperate womenfolk. He and Father Mandin were in real danger.

The sheriff pushed the crowd back, saying loudly, "The priest and the Foundling agent are under our protection." But anyone could see that if the crowd rushed the platform, the priest and Mr. Swayne were done for.

"Sheriff, they can't come here from New York and sell the babies to the Mexicans!" Another accuser had stepped forward. It was one of the men from the posse that had collected Rory. He still carried his mud-covered rifle.

"The Foundling is wealthy," Swayne insisted. "We don't need to sell children. We find them homes."

"Money was exchanged." It was Mr. Gatti, the butcher. "My wife witnessed it." Rory thought back. It was true; Elena had offered Sister Anna money. Mrs. Gatti, obsessed with her heart's desire, had misunderstood.

When Father Mandin saw Gatti he began babbling in French. The crowd demanded that Gatti translate.

"He says the money was just a few dollars. It was to pay for the children's transport," Gatti said. "He didn't know there was any difference between Americans and Mexicans." He paused. "But I don't believe him."

The men answered with shouts and swears. Rory couldn't distinguish what they were saying until a rowdy group in the back began chanting, "Tar 'em! Tar 'em!"

The color drained from Father Mandin's face. He groaned and fainted to the floor like a sack of flour. Rory winced as his head hit the ground with a thud. Mr. Swayne barely spared him a glance as he addressed the crowd again. "Citizens of Clifton," he said, his voice cracking. He cleared his throat and tried again. "You've already removed thirteen children from their foster homes. We haven't placed the remaining orphans. We'll take them all back to New York. There's no harm done!"

Rory nearly fell off the windowsill. Mr. Swayne was a blockhead. This crowd wasn't going to let him sweet-talk his way out of this. How did he not see that?

"You're a liar!" shouted one of the men. "We'd better keep all the kids just to be safe." The crowd of men surged toward the platform, fists raised in the air.

Swayne stuck his chest out and glowered, seeming more angry than afraid. "You just want the children for yourselves! This has nothing to do with the Mexicans!" He made a dismissive gesture that caused another rush of men. One threw a bottle at him. Swayne ducked just in time and the bottle shattered on the wall behind him.

The sheriff leapt onto the platform and pushed Mr.

Swayne down. "Jack Foley and Bill Morse, you put that tar and those feathers away right now."

"No!"

The sheriff shot his rifle into the air. Rory started, banging her head on the windowsill. A large chuck of white plaster came down from the ceiling with a crash and a cloud of white dust. The crowd stood in shocked silence.

"That's enough," the sheriff said. "I'm declaring a curfew. Go home peacefully now or I'll throw you all into jail."

One man in the crowd, braver than the rest, called out, "What about the children? I can't go home unless I have something to tell my wife!" There was a shout of laughter. Rory nodded to herself. Yep, the women were the ones driving this wagon train. They were the real threat.

Simpson shouted over the noise. "The judge will be here tomorrow. He'll decide what to do. Tell your wives that!"

The crowd started leaving, in groups of twos and threes, but a few men stayed, staring down the sheriff. He patted his rifle and said, "Don't make me do it, boys."

Reluctantly the men turned and headed for the door. One of them caught sight of Rory and headed to the window. With a yelp, Rory dropped to the ground. She heard someone shouting after her, spurring her to race across the bridge back to the hotel. Then she ran down the alley, raced through the kitchen and up the back stairs, and pounded on Sister Anna's door.

"Who's there?" Sister Anna's tired voice asked.

"It's Rory! It's an emergency!"

Rory yearned to throw herself into Sister Anna's arms

and be comforted but when the door opened, Rory stared, dumbstruck. Sister Anna was still fully dressed in her habit but her bonnet was crooked and there were smudges of mud on her wide skirt. It was as if the Virgin Mary had dirt under her fingernails.

"Rory, what are you doing out at this time of night?" Sister Anna yawned, too tired to cover her mouth. "I assumed you were spending the night with Violet."

"Sister, the kids are in trouble!" Rory cried.

"The children are asleep in the next room," Sister Anna said.

"Not those children. The ones you already placed." Rory couldn't stand still as she tried to explain.

"What are you talking about?" Sister Anna noticed the bloodstained cut on Rory's arm. "You're hurt."

"It's nothing, Sister." Rory slipped inside, shut the door, and quickly told her everything that had happened. The only information she left out was that Violet was not with the other children.

Sister Anna stood up straight, adjusted her bonnet, and after noticing Rory's surreptitious glance at her skirt, brushed away the mud. "Those children belong to the Foundling and they won't go to any family that I do not personally approve. Bring me to Mrs. Abraham."

Relieved to see the old Sister Anna back, Rory led the way down the hall to the main stairs. Rory started to take the stairs two at a time, but Sister Anna said, "With dignity, my dear."

When they reached the landing outside the room where

the twelve children were, Rory got a bad feeling in her stomach. It was too quiet. Even if the children were all asleep in their makeshift beds, there should be some noise. They opened the door. Sister Anna's eyes raked the empty room.

"They're gone!" Rory cried. The cots and used dishes were still there, but the children were missing. Rory ran to the window and looked in the street. Empty.

"Rory, are you sure you didn't imagine . . ."

Rory held up her bloody arm. "Like I imagined this, Sister?"

"No, of course not," Sister Anna said. She prowled about the room looking for any signs of the children. She reached under a sofa and picked up a bit of ribbon with embroidered lettering. "This is Josephine's and it has no business being here. The children *were* in this room." She turned to Rory. "But where did they go?"

Rory thought she saw Sister Anna's hand tremble, but that was impossible; Sister Anna was never scared. "I'm sorry, Sister, this is my fault," Rory cried. "I told Mrs. Gatti you would never let them have the kids. They must have decided to take them away so you wouldn't interfere."

"My child, you're not to blame," Sister Anna said wearily. "If anyone deserves blame, it is I. I should have sent Mr. Swayne ahead to see the town and the parents. We would have known then not to come."

"Sister, we'll find them," Rory said. Sister Anna did not make mistakes. In the world of the Foundling, that didn't happen. "We have to."

"Of course we will," Sister Anna said. "I promised you

that I would take care of Violet and the rest. I'm going to call the police and demand they get the children back."

"Sister, there's no police here except the sheriff. And he's the one who collected them," Rory said. "They won't give the children back just for the asking." Thank goodness that Violet was safe with Elena and Ramon.

Sister Anna's hand went to the crucifix around her neck. "We need help. Rory, can you find Mr. Swayne? Or Father Mandin?"

"They won't be any help at all." Rory grimaced. "Mr. Swayne was in fear for his life tonight. And Father Mandin passed out."

Sister Anna placed her hand on Rory's shoulder. At first she thought Sister Anna was steadying herself, but then she realized that Sister Anna was trying to reassure Rory. "Rory, I'm sorry you had to see that dreadful scene. But I'm sure it wasn't as bad as you say. You're young and didn't understand what you saw."

"Really, Sister?" Rory forgot to watch her words. "Then where are your children? And what about the rest? How are we going to protect them?"

Sister Anna swept her hand across her forehead and Rory saw that she was sweating under the bonnet.

Rory went on, "If the town wants those babies, they'll just take them. They don't care if anyone else gets hurt."

"Well, we'll have to convince the judge when he comes in the morning." Sister Anna adjusted her habit. "He'll set everything right."

Sister Anna went into the other room to warn Sister Eileen and the nurses, leaving Rory alone.

It was warm in the room and the plush sofa was soft and inviting. Rory let her head rest on the sofa arm and closed her eyes. Even if Sister Anna was wrong, Rory couldn't do any more tonight. But exhausted as she was, she couldn't fall asleep. The image of Violet sound asleep at Elena's house wouldn't leave her mind. Had Rory done the right thing by leaving Vi there? And where would they hide?

Rory sat bolt upright, her heart beating loud enough to echo in her ears. Why would Ramon bother to hide when he could just run to Mexico? There was nothing to stop him and every reason to go. What would that mob do to Ramon if they found him and Elena with a white daughter?

Rory rushed to the window. The street seemed deserted, lit only by a few lamps on the porch of the hotel. If Ramon had left for Mexico, there was nothing Rory could do. She didn't know where his family lived. And even if she went looking for them, she didn't speak the language. She'd never find Violet. Knowing the Foundling wouldn't approve of Vi being taken out of the country, Ramon would have no reason to write. She should have never left Violet alone. At least Violet still had Ma's necklace.

Tears rolled down her cheeks but Rory barely noticed. She hadn't even said goodbye.

CHAPTER Thirty-Three

RORY SPENT A RESTLESS NIGHT AND WAS AWAKENED BY A KNOCK at the door. She bolted from the sofa. Sister Anna hurried in from the other room.

"I've got the door, Sister," Rory said.

"Be careful," Sister Anna said.

Rory pulled the door open slowly, ready to slam it shut if need be. It was the servant, Cheng.

"It's all right, Sister," Rory said. She turned toward Cheng, hoping for news. "Did Ramon send you again?" she asked.

"He gave me this for you," Cheng said, reaching into his vest pocket and pulling out a chain with a saint's medal dangling from it.

"My mother's necklace," Rory cried, grabbing it from his hand. She tried to understand what it meant. Had Ramon sent it? An apology for stealing Violet away and leaving Rory behind? Or did it mean something entirely different?

"Where is Violet?" she asked, dreading the answer.

"Come with me." Cheng turned and walked away.

"I'll be right back," Rory yelled to Sister Anna, stuffing the necklace in the pocket of her dress.

"Rory!" The sound of Sister Anna's voice faded as Rory followed Cheng down three flights of back stairs—not to the kitchen but to the hotel's lobby. Rory wanted to ask many questions, but she held her tongue. Soon enough she would know if Violet was still in Clifton. Cheng pointed to the barbershop with its gaily striped pole.

Rory pulled open the unlocked door slowly. The room was empty. Two barber chairs reclined as though expecting customers for a haircut and shave. There was a window high in the outside wall and white smocks on hooks next to the entrance. She followed the faint murmur of voices to a velvet curtain spread across the back of the shop. "Let Vi be all right. Please," she prayed. As she reached for the curtain she saw her hand was trembling. She swept the curtain aside to reveal Ramon and Elena.

Ramon's hand moved instinctively to the tied-down holster on his hip, and Elena placed a restraining hand on his arm.

"Thank God you're still here," cried Rory. Her knees buckled and she held onto the curtain to steady herself. "I was so afraid . . ."

"Of course we're still here," Elena said, puzzled.

"Where's Violet?" Rory said, her voice cracking.

"Here I am," Violet said, scooting out from behind Elena's legs, a mischievous grin on her face. "Did you know it was us?" she asked. "Ramon said we couldn't let anyone see us, or we'd ruin the surprise."

Rory hugged her with all her might. "It's the very best surprise!"

"Ow, Rory, that hurts."

Over Vi's head, Rory said, "This is the last place I expected to see you." Then she spoke to Ramon and Elena in a voice she hardly recognized as her own. "Is it safe? What if Mrs. Gatti sees her? Or that mob?"

Ramon said, "Who would look for her in the hotel?" His sly smile invited her to smile back. Maybe another day Rory would find it funny, but not today.

"Where's Mama's necklace?" Violet asked.

"Right here, Vi," Rory said, pointing to her pocket. To Ramon, she asked, "Did you hear what happened last night?"

Ramon's smile faded. "Swayne and the priest are lucky to be alive."

Elena said, "The parish is hiding Father Mandin. We'll keep him safe."

"And Mr. Swayne is lying low in his hotel room," Ramon added. "What happened when the sheriff took you? Did the Anglos notice that Violet was missing?"

"Mrs. Gatti definitely knew I was the wrong Fitzpatrick girl, but the sheriff wouldn't listen," Rory answered. "She would have made a fuss, but then her husband told her he only wants one child, and a boy at that." With a quick glance at Elena, Rory finished, "They took William."

Rory could see from Elena's face that this wasn't unexpected. "The good news is that she won't make trouble about Violet for fear she'd lose William," Elena said heavily.

"A judge is coming today," Rory said. "Sister Anna is counting on him to tell Sheriff Simpson to bring the children back."

Ramon shook his head. "Do you know where Sheriff Simpson is right now?"

"No," Rory said.

"Reporting to Mr. Mills, who manages the mine and smelters for Arizona Copper. He lives in the hotel. The law reports to him first, then the courts. And most of those children were taken by the managers' wives. The judge will do very little and the sheriff will do less."

"But what about the law?" Rory protested. Ramon was only confirming her worst fears.

"Copper is king in Clifton, not the law," he said. "Your Sisters don't know it yet, but they have already lost. The children will not be returned."

"What's going to happen to Vi?" Rory asked.

"If we're going to keep her, we need to leave right away," he said. "Before anyone realizes that a Mexicano family still has a white child."

Rory seized on the most important word. "If?"

"It depends on you," Elena said in her gentle voice. "The Foundling Hospital gave her to us, but you are her family." Elena glanced down at Violet then back to Rory. "We couldn't leave without talking to you."

A hundred images of the Foundling floated through

Rory's mind—a nicely run orphanage with kind Sisters and a beautiful chapel. But it was an orphanage nonetheless. Ramon and Elena were offering Violet a home. A family.

"In Mexico?" Rory asked, just to be sure she understood the offer.

Ramon nodded. "It's the safest place we can go."

In a small voice, Rory asked, "What about me?"

The moment it took Ramon to answer felt like hours to Rory. Everything depended on what happened next.

"If you will come," Ramon said, "we'd like you to be our daughter too."

Rory felt joy she hadn't felt since her mother was alive. She was floating and her only tether to the ground was Violet's hand. "You want me?" she asked, fighting for breath.

"We want both of you," Ramon said.

For years Rory had dreamed of hearing those words. Now that they were spoken she was almost afraid to believe in them.

"Both of us?" she whispered.

"You were so brave last night, taking Violet's place; how could we leave you behind?" Elena said.

Rory looked at Violet. Her sister was sneaking her hand into Rory's pocket, searching for the necklace. "Can I speak with Vi alone?"

Ramon nodded and Rory guided Vi back into the alcove and drew the velvet curtain. She sat on the floor and put Violet on her lap.

"Rory, you have dark circles," Vi said, tracing her finger around Rory's eyes.

"I didn't sleep much," Rory said.

"I did," Vi chirped. "Then I had eggs for breakfast, except that Elena called them *huevos*." She rubbed her stomach. "Yummy."

"Do you like Ramon and Elena?" Rory asked, praying for the right answer.

"Silly!" Violet laughed—a happy, carefree five-year-old laugh. "Of course I like them. They're nice."

"They want us all to be a family," Rory said.

Violet nodded. "Me too. Rory, you kept your promise." Violet held up her hand. The chain of the necklace was looped around her finger. "I'll give this back now."

Solemnly Rory took it and fastened it around her neck. "The thing is, we'll have to leave this town and go to Mexico."

Violet shrugged. "I don't like this place anyway."

Rory thought how simple it was to be five years old. "We'll never see the Foundling again—or Sister Anna or the other kids," she warned. "We'll have to learn a new language too, Vi. And there won't be any American kids to play with. We'll always be different."

"Special?" Vi asked, her blue eyes shining with pleasure.

"I guess so," Rory said ruefully.

She put her fingers to her lips and thought harder than she ever had in her life. Clearly Vi would be all right in Mexico. Better than all right. Elena and Ramon would cherish her and teach her everything she needed to know. But what about Violet's older sister? Rory didn't like Mexican food and the language was gibberish to her. She was a New Yorker, born and bred. If Rory stayed with Violet she would probably never return to New York.

Suddenly she heard Sister Anna's voice in her head, offering her a job with the Foundling. Rory hadn't given the matter a second thought before. But now she thought: who could possibly do this work better than she? Finding new families for orphans was an important job—one she had been training for her whole life. Was Rory willing to give up her own future for Vi's sake?

Violet tugged on Rory's sleeve. "Rory, you promised we would always be together."

Rory nodded wordlessly.

"Then that's all that matters." Violet gave a sharp nod as if that decided everything. *Well, why not*, Rory thought. *We've made our choice.*

They hurried back to Elena and Ramon. Rory didn't waste a second. "We want to go with you," she said. "We want you to be our parents!"

Elena held out her arms and enveloped Violet and Rory in an enormous hug. She smelled of waxy candles, chili, and cookies. Rory had never experienced a perfume so delicious.

"Good," Ramon said, rubbing his hands. "We must go at once. Can you get your things without the Sisters seeing?"

"Now?" Rory asked, dismayed. "But the Sisters are neck-deep in trouble. We can't leave them."

Elena touched Rory's arm gently. "Rory, Mrs. Gatti may be distracted for now, but we cannot hide two red-haired daughters for long."

Ramon said, "Rory, there is nothing you can do to help.

The most important thing is to get you and Violet to safety."

"Is it?" Rory asked.

"Of course," Ramon said. "That is what parents do. They protect their children."

"The Sisters do too." Rory nodded slowly. "They've protected me for three years. I didn't always agree with them. I broke their rules. I did anything to trick them into letting me stay with Violet. But they never gave up on me."

Ramon leaned toward Rory. "That's all very well, but it is not your job to protect them."

"Maybe not, but I can't abandon them." She faced Ramon. "I won't leave Sister Anna and the others in danger."

"It is more dangerous for you to stay!" Ramon said loudly, staring down at her. "We could lose both of you."

"Just until the Sisters are safe," Rory pleaded. "The judge—"

"Won't do anything, Rory," Ramon finished.

Outside the barbershop Ramon and Rory heard a sudden crash and shouting, but they couldn't make out the words. "Elena, stay here with Violet," Ramon said as he ran out of the barbershop, Rory less than a step behind him.

Men poured into the hotel lobby. Others crowded the wooden sidewalk in front of the hotel's big double doors or climbed in through the broken front window. It was the start of a brawl. Rory had seen it before in Hell's Kitchen.

"People, you have no business here!" the sheriff roared.

"Where's the priest?" someone shouted.

A person in the mob called out, "And that agent! They're

selling white babies and we're going to stop them!"

He was answered by another angry voice. "There are more kids, my wife told me so. We'll take them too!"

Sheriff Simpson held up his hands. "We went through this last night. The children aren't going anywhere. Now turn around and go home!"

"They gave the babies to the Mexicans and the Indians— they'd do anything! We can't trust those big-city folks."

Another man shouted, "We're not budging without the priest and the agent! I'd like to see the nuns try and stop us."

Ramon stepped back into the barbershop, pulling Rory with him. "Your Sisters are out of time." He paused. "And so are we."

CHAPTER Thirty-Four

VIOLET PERCHED IN ONE OF THE BARBER CHAIRS WHILE ELENA braided her hair. Elena's hands shook as she folded one length of hair across the other. She looked up when they returned. "What's happening?"

"Another Anglo mob—they want the priest and the agent," Ramon said, his ear to the door.

"And the kids. All of them," Rory added.

Elena went pale and stumbled. Ramon hurried to Elena's side to steady her. She let him help her to one of the barber chairs. "Ramon," she implored. "You can't let them take Father Mandin!"

"Elena, it's not safe for us either," Ramon reasoned. "We have to go now."

"No!" Rory cried. "The Sisters need our help."

"Ramon, it's our duty to watch over the Father," Elena added.

"There's nothing we can do," Ramon pleaded with both of them.

Rory looked from one to the other. There was one thing that she knew would make Ramon help them, but it was desperate and unfair. Did she have a choice? She lifted Vi out of the chair and clutched her sister to her chest. "Then Violet and I have to go back to Sister Anna."

"Rory!" Elena gasped. "You can't do that!"

"I don't want to leave Elena," Violet whimpered. "Rory, you said we could stay with them."

Rory kept her attention on Ramon. "I'll do it if I have to," she said.

"It's not safe," he repeated.

"Help me help the Sisters," Rory cried. "Once they are all right, we can leave for Mexico."

Ramon scowled. "Rory, you're as stubborn as—"

"You, Ramon," Elena finished. "She's as stubborn as you. We don't have a choice. We must do the right thing and help them."

Ramon held his hands up in surrender. "What do you two ladies want me to do?" he asked.

"If the judge can't tell the townspeople what to do, who can?" Rory asked.

"Mr. Mills is the only one," Ramon said.

"Yes, Ramon, go to Mr. Mills!" Elena turned to Rory and said proudly, "He's powerful. But when the workers were on strike, he listened to Ramon bargain for the miners."

"Can we tell him what's happened?" Rory asked.

"I'm sure he knows everything already," Ramon said. "He has spies everywhere."

"Is he a good man? Will he help the Sisters?" Rory wanted to know.

Ramon lifted his shoulders. "If we make it worth his while."

Rory wasn't sure she liked the sound of that.

Before they knocked on Mr. Mills's door, Rory turned to Ramon and touched his arm. "Thank you, Ramon. I know you didn't want to get involved."

"You and Elena were right. Someone has to protect the foolish priest and your Sisters. I only hesitated because I wanted to protect my family."

Mouthing the word "family," Rory banged on the door.

A tall man with dark hair, graying at the temples, opened the door. He wore a suit but his black cowboy boots made him look like a Westerner. "Ramon Martinez!" he said, with a tight smile that seemed painted on his face.

"*Señor.*" Ramon was polite but not friendly. He gestured to Rory. "This is Rory. She's with the Sisters from New York."

Mr. Mills smiled and nodded. "What can I do for you?"

"We're here about the orphans," Ramon said.

"That's none of my concern," Mr. Mills said, starting to close the door.

Ramon's grin showed all his teeth; it was as false as Mr. Mills's smile. "Keeping peace in Clifton is your concern. Men who are rioting are not mining copper."

Mr. Mills reluctantly waved Ramon and Rory into the

room. "But I hear a judge has been sent for."

"The judge will be useless. We both know that," Ramon said. "The priest arranged it all, but it is the Mexicanos who will be blamed."

"Then let the priest work this out with the judge—" Mr. Mills said.

"You know he cannot. The priest is completely discredited," Ramon interrupted. "I hear that there was talk of lynching him last night."

"That bad?" Mr. Mills sounded surprised, but Rory couldn't believe he didn't already know.

Ramon nodded. "And also talk of tarring Father Mandin and the agent. Worse, the children were seized by armed men."

Mr. Mills stared out the window. His face was like granite, impossible to read. Rory figured it was time for her to make the most of being an orphan and a girl. She let her voice tremble, "They pointed their guns at me too."

His head jerked to look at her. "That's not right," Mr. Mills said. "You're just a kid."

"It's true. Sheriff Simpson led the posse." Ramon paused. "We are devout, you know. That is why the Sisters gave us the babies. If the Catholic nuns or the priest are harmed, I guarantee the Mexicano community will explode. Have you forgotten the violence last year?"

"The situation is already out of my control," Mr. Mills said irritably. "I can hear the crowd in the lobby from here. What do you expect me to do about it?"

Ramon raised an eyebrow. "It is the Anglo women who have caused all the trouble," he said meaningfully. "They wanted the children so they took them. They've pushed their men to go after the priest and agent. If the priest and Mr. Swayne leave town, the mob will lose interest and go back to work."

Mr. Mills went to a side table and poured himself a cup of coffee. Without offering any to Ramon and Rory he drained his cup in one gulp. "I can't just snap my fingers and send a mob on its way."

"*Señor,*" Ramon said silkily. "You can get the men out of town. It will have the same effect."

"I don't think I should get involved," Mr. Mills said, shaking his head. "Sorry, Ramon."

"Ramon, did I tell you how many powerful friends the Sisters have?" Rory asked.

As if they had practiced it, Ramon replied on cue. "No, Rory, you didn't."

"Governors and Senators and editors at newspapers," Rory added casually. "The papers love stories about orphans."

"How embarrassing for the Arizona Copper Company," Ramon said. "And for their representative in Clifton."

Mr. Mills carefully placed his cup on the table and paced around the room. Finally he turned to them and said, "Maybe I can help the priest and this Swayne man. But I draw the line at the children who were taken. It's more than my life is worth to tackle those women."

Ramon shrugged. "*Señor,* we mere men must be practical.

Let the Foundling fight for the children in their own courts."

Mr. Mills sat down in a large upholstered armchair next to the stove and stretched out his feet to enjoy the warmth. "The Sisters won't kick up a fuss?" Mills asked.

"It's the only way. They'll see reason."

"Ramon!" Rory said leaning in so only he could hear her. "We can't leave the kids here."

"I'll have to think about it," Mr. Mills said. He got up and held the door. "Good afternoon, Ramon, Miss Rory."

"It wasn't enough, Ramon," Rory whispered. "Do something, please."

"I have an idea, but you won't like it," he replied.

Rory gulped. "Do whatever you have to."

Ramon took a deep breath. "*Señor* Thompson is your superior, is he not?"

Mr. Mills watched Ramon carefully. "That's not a secret."

"His wife lost a second child last year."

Mr. Mills frowned. "I didn't know that. How did you?"

"My wife's friend is *Señora* Thompson's seamstress. We all pitied her. We know what it is like to want a baby and not be able to have one."

Mr. Mills checked to see if the hall was empty. "What exactly are you suggesting?"

"*Señora* Thompson is light-skinned with yellow hair. Rory, are there any such children with the Sisters?"

Rory stared at Ramon with horror. "Ramon—you can't!"

"Rory, is there such a child?" Ramon insisted.

Rory faced the fact that he was only doing what she

asked. Reluctantly, she nodded. "There are two, a brother and a sister. Both are fair and blond."

"That would do very well." Mr. Mills looked pleased. "I'd be willing to arrange safe passage for Father Mandin and the agent in exchange for two children."

Rory closed her eyes and prayed for the strength to face Sister Anna when she found out about this unholy bargain.

But Mr. Mills wasn't finished trading yet. "Tell me," he said. "Are there any boys with dark brown hair and eyes?"

"Why?" Rory asked suspiciously.

"I have a friend, a doctor, visiting from San Francisco. His wife can't have children. I could get him a baby too."

Rory jabbed her finger in the direction of both men. "You're both treating these children like livestock that you can buy and sell."

"Your Sisters are in the adoption business, aren't they?" Mr. Mills said reasonably.

"Yes," she admitted reluctantly.

"My friend is well-to-do. The boy will have a fine life and a good education."

"And in exchange?" Rory said weakly.

"I'll get your Sisters and the kids they have left out of Clifton and back to New York." Mr. Mills rubbed his hands. "You can't ask for anything fairer than that!"

"Rory, it's the best chance to get them home," Ramon said.

Mr. Mills and Ramon stared at her, until she nodded slowly.

Ramon clapped her on the shoulder. "Good." Turning to Mr. Mills, he said, "So, *Señor*, we have a deal?"

"Yes," Mr. Mills said. "Two children to get Mandin and the agent out of town. And another kid for putting the Sisters and the orphans who are left safely on their train."

"Agreed," Ramon said, pulling an unwilling Rory out of the room. "We'll need to convince them. Come to the Sisters' room in one hour."

In the hallway, Rory turned on Ramon. "You can't just give away children like that!" she said accusingly.

Ramon put his hands on Rory's shoulders. "Rory, the children will be well taken care of. These aren't bad people, just desperate. They'll cherish the babies as much as Elena and I will cherish you and Violet."

"But they won't be raised Catholic," Rory reminded him. "And that's what Sister Anna cares about."

"But the rest will be saved and your Sister Anna can place them wherever she likes." He sighed loudly. "I've done my part. Now it is up to you. *You* must explain to your Sister Anna what has happened."

Rory felt ill. "What about you? I thought you would come with me." Her voice faltered. "I can't face her alone."

Ramon shook his head. "I have to take Elena and Violet somewhere safe."

"What about me?" Rory asked in a panic, clutching his sleeve. "You said we're a family now. You can't leave without me!"

His chuckle put her fears to rest. "Stay with the Sisters

until the last minute. I have a bad feeling they may need you. Collect your and Violet's belongings. I'll fetch you at the train. I promise."

She looked deep into his brown eyes and knew she could trust him. "All right," she said.

In exact detail, he told her where he would be waiting, out of sight. "Can you get away without being seen?"

Rory nodded.

"Don't look so worried," he said. "It's almost over. This time tomorrow we'll be on our way to Mexico." He held out his arms and she stepped into his embrace.

Against his rough coat, Rory muttered, "All I have to do is convince Sister Anna to sacrifice sixteen children. Easy as pie."

CHAPTER Thirty-Five

R ORY TOOK THE STAIRS TWO STEPS AT A TIME. AFTER EVERYTHING that had happened today, the stairs seemed steeper and Rory couldn't catch her breath at first. Panting, she knocked at the Sisters' door. Sister Eileen opened the door a crack then wide open when she saw Rory.

Mr. Swayne had turned up. He was slumped on the sofa. Rory spared him a glance. Although he had shaved and changed his clothes, his face was haggard and his eyes were bloodshot.

"There's a crowd down on the street." Sister Anna stood at the window.

"They're here for Father Mandin . . . and you, Mr. Swayne," Rory said in a hurry. She didn't have much time. "Sister, we need to talk. There's someone who can help us."

"Yes, the judge. The sheriff has to listen to him." Sister Anna spoke as if it were a rote fact, like the way Rory had learned her multiplication tables.

"But Sister . . ."

"Rory, sit down and have some tea," Sister Anna ordered. "Have you eaten anything this morning?"

All at once, Rory realized how hungry she was. Even though precious time was passing, she sat obediently and accepted a piece of buttered bread and a cup of tea.

Casually, Sister Anna asked, "How is Violet?"

Sister Anna's words floored her. "How did you know?" Rory asked.

"Aha!" Sister Anna's eyes gleamed like the old Sister Anna who always knew when the children were up to something. "I knew she wasn't taken with the others!"

"How did you guess?"

"If Violet had been kidnapped, you wouldn't be here. You'd be out there searching for her." After a moment, Sister Anna added, "Where I should be. Those children were in my care."

"But it's different for me. I'm only responsible for me and Vi," Rory protested. "You're responsible for everyone. You have to take care of the children we still have."

Sister Anna's face went blank for a moment before she recovered herself. "So where is Violet?"

"Elena and Ramon have her. I took her place when the posse came to collect her and William."

"A good thing you did or else we might have lost her, like the others." Sister Anna made a brave attempt to act like her usual decisive self. "When this is over, we'll collect Violet and bring the two of you back to New York. I won't make a mistake like this again."

Rory hesitated. She had to tell Sister Anna that she wasn't returning to the Foundling but there was a more urgent matter first. She slurped her tea. A soft tap at the door saved her from having to decide what to say next.

"I hope that's the judge now," Sister Anna said, standing to answer the door. Mr. Swayne sat up and made a futile attempt to straighten his tie and jacket.

Mr. Mills filled the doorway. "Sister Anna Michaella Bowen?" he asked.

Sister Anna nodded warily.

Rory glared at him. They had agreed she would have an hour to talk to Sister Anna, but Mr. Mills had come after only a few minutes.

Mr. Mills introduced himself in a voice as slick as his manners. Sister Anna was impressed with him, treating him the same way she did the patrons of the Foundling. Rory rolled her eyes; she knew better. Mr. Mills was a snake in a nice suit.

"Are you getting enough food?" he asked. "I can arrange for some to be sent up."

"Thank you, we would appreciate that." Sister Anna gestured to Mr. Swayne. "This is the Foundling Hospital's agent, Mr. Swayne."

"We met yesterday in Mr. Swayne's room," Mr. Mills said, his voice flat.

Mr. Swayne nodded brusquely. There was no love lost between these two.

"And this is one of my charges, Rory Fitzpatrick."

Mr. Mills didn't spare Rory a glance; he went straight to business. "I'm sorry that your visit to Clifton has been so troubled," Mr. Mills said. "My employers are appalled."

"As are we, Mr. Mills," Sister Anna said wearily. "Thank goodness a judge is on his way. We need some law and order."

Mr. Mills hitched his thumbs in his belt loops. "Ah, Sister, the judge arrived an hour ago. He's already ruled."

Rory had to restrain herself from going over to Mr. Mills and kicking him in the shins. He had known about the judge all along but hadn't told them. Well, on further thought, what difference did it make now?

Sister Anna straightened. "Without hearing our side?"

"The town got to him first," Mr. Mills said, shrugging.

Mr. Swayne leaned back in his chair and put his head in his hands. "What did he say?"

"He refused to issue adoption papers for the children who were . . . shall we say reclaimed?"

"Of course he did," Sister Anna said triumphantly. "Those people kidnapped our children at gunpoint. They can't be legally adopted, not without my permission."

"Which you wouldn't consider giving by any chance?" Mr. Mills leaned back against the mantel.

"Absolutely not!" Sister Anna raised her voice. "I won't leave Clifton until we've retrieved each and every child. Did the judge order the town to bring the children back?"

"I'm afraid not. He wasn't willing to stand up to a roomful of angry mothers."

"That's not a judgment at all," Sister Anna exclaimed in frustration. "I still don't have the children, but they can't legally keep them."

"We are at an impasse," Mr. Swayne said, his voice muffled by his palms.

Mr. Mills shook his head. "A dangerous impasse. The crowd downstairs is in an ornery mood." He glanced at Swayne. "Sister, we should continue our discussion without Mr. Swayne here."

"I won't leave Sister Anna," Mr. Swayne protested.

At Sister Anna's shoulder, Rory whispered, "Listen to him, Sister. Mr. Swayne shouldn't hear this next part."

Sister Anna considered Rory, then Mr. Mills. "Mr. Swayne," she said. "Please excuse us for a moment."

"But . . ."

"I insist," Sister Anna said in her no-nonsense tone.

"If you say so," Mr. Swayne muttered as he went into the other room and shut the door with a bang.

"Now, Mr. Mills, what do you have to say that you cannot say in front of Mr. Swayne?"

"Sister, that crowd is out for Swayne's and the priest's blood. If they don't leave soon, and I mean today, they're dead men," Mr. Mills said. "I can get them out, so long as my price is met."

"Your price?" Sister Anna asked, suspicious. "What do you want in return for helping us?"

Mr. Mills lifted his eyebrows at Rory. "You haven't told her?"

"You didn't give me a chance—you were supposed to wait an hour," Rory said sourly.

Sister Anna looked at Rory, slowly shaking her head.

Rory hurried to say, "Sister, you don't understand. Mr. Mills's plan can save Mr. Swayne and Father Mandin."

Mr. Mills nodded. "I get your men to El Paso tonight and you give me the two kids—Rory, what are their names?"

"Frank and Lynn," Rory said faintly, afraid to meet Sister Anna's eyes.

"Absolutely not," Sister Anna said. "Rory, I'm ashamed that you would even consider it. Mr. Mills, regardless of what that crowd has accused us of, we do not barter children!"

"But what about Mr. Swayne? He has a family. Are you going to make them orphans?" Rory entreated. "And don't nuns have to protect priests?" At least the incompetent ones, she added under her breath. She hadn't forgotten that this was all Father Mandin's fault.

Sister Anna's fingernails dug into her palms. "We are sworn to protect the children, not trade them away."

"The kids will have a good home—you don't need to worry about that," Mr. Mills said. "The couple I have in mind is educated and well-to-do." With a glance at his pocket watch, he said, "Sister, I don't want to rush you. But the train to El Paso leaves soon and I've got a powerful lot of arranging to do."

Sister Anna held up her hand and said, "Give me a moment." She took out her rosary and closed her eyes. Her mouth moved in a silent prayer.

Rory tapped her foot. Was this really the time to pray? Did Sister Anna think God would suddenly appear with a better option? Mr. Mills walked to the window and drew back the curtains to look at the street. Finally Sister Anna took a deep breath and turned back to Mr. Mills. "If I should agree, what happens?"

"My men will escort Swayne and the priest to the train."

"And the crowd?"

"Everyone in that crowd depends on me for their livelihood. They'll do as I say. And if they get a mite excited, my men are armed."

"Oh my." Sister Anna fanned her face.

"Tell Swayne to get the priest and meet me in room 220 in a quarter of an hour." Mr. Mills walked to the door. "Afterwards I'll come back and we'll discuss getting you and the other children out of town."

"We won't leave without the missing children," Sister Anna said flatly.

Mr. Mills shook his head. "Your dedication does you credit, Sister. But you aren't ever going to see those thirteen children again. Do you want to lose the rest?"

"Of course not. But . . ."

"There are no buts, ma'am. You can save the kids you've got left or lose them all." He opened the door. Looking back, he eyed Rory meaningfully. "Explain it to her."

Sister Anna and Rory were alone. Rory opened her mouth, but Sister Anna held up a hand. "Not one word, Rory Fitzpatrick."

Sister Anna went to the adjoining room. Rory heard Mr. Swayne's voice protesting, woven in with Sister Anna's best "nun voice" telling him what to do. He didn't want to leave the Sisters. But Sister Anna was firm. After a few minutes, he hurried out without any farewells.

"So, Rory, you've been busy, haven't you?" Sister Anna asked bitterly once they were alone. "Was this exchange your idea?"

"No, it was Ramon's," Rory admitted. "But I finally agreed because it was the only way to keep you all safe. And the children will have a good home. Isn't that why we're here?"

"A good *Catholic* home, Rory," Sister Anna said.

"Sometimes we can't have both. We have to accept what we can get," Rory whispered then fell silent. What else was there to say?

Sister Anna fell into her armchair. "Those children were already abandoned by their parents," she cried. "I can't desert them too."

"You have to," said Rory. "At least for now. But when you get to New York, you can fight for them. You have to be sensible, not proud, Sister."

Sister Anna ran her rosary through her hands, thinking hard. "Do you think Mr. Mills can get us safely to our train?" she asked, and Rory knew she had accepted the inevitable.

Rory nodded. "Mr. Mills is the most important man in town. He can deliver what he promises."

"And what payment will he expect?"

Rory didn't like the bitterness in her voice. "Just one child. Mr. Mills wants a boy for a doctor friend. I thought Johnnie would do."

"May God have mercy on my soul," Sister Anna said faintly.

Rory was quick to reassure her. "I'm sure He will," she said.

CHAPTER Thirty-Six

RORY AND SISTER ANNA SAT IN AN UNCOMFORTABLE SILENCE. Before Rory could work up the nerve to tell Sister Anna that she and Violet were going to Mexico, a rumble of voices echoed in the hallway. Without a word, they both went to the door and peeped out. The corridor was filled with half a dozen white women speaking in very loud voices. They were all familiar from the train station, but to Rory's relief, Mrs. Gatti was not there.

They saw Sister Anna. "Where are the children?" they demanded.

"Close the door, Rory," Sister Anna ordered.

Rory slammed it shut, but before she could adjust the bolt, the door crashed open and the women rushed in. "Where are you hiding the children?" asked the first woman through the doorway. Without hesitating, Rory leapt in front of Sister Anna, her fists raised the way she had learned long ago in Hell's Kitchen.

Sister Anna shouted, "Get out of my room this instant!" But for once, her authority failed her. The women paid her no attention except to pepper her with more questions.

"Where are the babies?" shouted one of the women.

Another pushed forward, her hands on her hips, saying, "We won't be leaving without the children."

The leader of the group said, "It's our duty to save all of them." Three other women flanked her, waiting for orders.

"You tell them, Mrs. Johnson," said the first woman through the door.

"You can't have them," Sister Anna declared. "These children are in my care and I decide where they are placed."

"If you care about the children, you'll let us take them," Mrs. Johnson said loudly.

"I don't care how much you shout." Sister Anna stood firm. "My responsibility is to God and these children. I'll not jeopardize their immortal souls by placing them with heathens."

"Heathens are we?" Mrs. Johnson screeched. "I'll show you heathens." She advanced with her fingers out like claws.

Before her nails could reach Sister Anna's eyes, Rory dropped her shoulder and rammed Mrs. Johnson in the stomach. They both tumbled to the floor. Rory was quicker to her feet. "Sister Anna," Rory said in a voice meant to be heard. "Send word to Sister Eileen to lock the church doors."

"The church?" For a moment Sister Anna was confused, then she quickly understood. "That's not necessary. These women wouldn't dare violate a church!"

"The kids aren't here?" asked Mrs. Johnson.

"Do you see them?" challenged Rory.

"Ladies, to the church!" Mrs. Johnson stormed out.

As the women started to leave, Sister Anna said, "Rory, go tell Mr. Mills about this." She paused. "Let him know I agree to his terms but the deal is off if anything like this happens again."

———·———

When Rory returned to the Sisters' rooms the intruders were gone. She slipped inside and found Sister Anna packing her small traveling case.

"Your Mr. Mills is very effective," Sister Anna said. "He must be an excellent manager. I can't help but wonder if he sent those women here to convince me."

Rory was silent; she had the same suspicions.

"Did Mr. Swayne and Father Mandin get on the train?" Sister Anna asked.

Rory nodded.

"Good," Sister Anna said with satisfaction.

"So you're going back to New York?"

"What choice do I have?" Sister Anna asked bitterly. "I have to answer to the Foundling. And I can't justify losing all the children because I wanted to stay for the ones who were kidnapped."

"Once you're in New York . . ."

"Then I'll bring all the legal and moral weight of the Foundling Hospital against this godless, immoral town."

Sister Anna straightened to her full height—she looked unstoppable. Rory grinned. The town of Clifton didn't stand a chance once Sister Anna got back to her home ground. Rory wandered about the room, picking up small personal items and bringing them to Sister Anna.

"Shouldn't you be packing your own luggage?" Sister Anna asked, with a sidelong glance at Rory.

This was it. Rory took a deep breath and said deliberately, "I'm staying here with Violet."

Sister Anna stretched her stiff back. "I thought you might be."

"You did? How?" Rory exclaimed. "I didn't know until this morning!"

"It was your plan to go with Violet all along. Wherever she went."

"Sister!" Rory was dismayed and admiring at the same time.

"The Martinezes are good people," mused Sister Anna. "I could see that at our first meeting. Devout, kind, and hardworking. I couldn't choose better. Elena Martinez was the woman who wanted red-haired children, you know."

Rory remembered that day back in Sister Anna's office. It felt like a hundred years ago.

"It almost seems as though God intended you to go with them." Sister Anna reached up and tucked a stray red hair of her own back under the bonnet. She closed the case and buckled it shut. "But will the town let her keep you and Violet?"

"Ramon is going to take us to live with his family in

Mexico." Rory crossed her fingers and waited for Sister Anna to explode.

"Mexico?" Sister Anna's voice shook. "That's too far."

"Not so much farther than Arizona," Rory pointed out. "And it's very Catholic."

"The Foundling has no authority in Mexico," Sister Anna said.

"Begging your pardon, but the Foundling's authority hasn't counted for much in Clifton. And that's still in the United States."

Sister Anna frowned, and she suddenly seemed older and more discouraged. Rory dropped her eyes to the floor. After a moment, Sister Anna tilted Rory's chin up so she could see Rory's face. "Do you want to go to Mexico?"

Rory nodded. "Ramon put himself in harm's way to protect us. And he has a sense of duty too. Even though he wanted us to go to Mexico this morning, he stayed to help you and the others." Rory fingered her mother's necklace. "We're already a family."

"Yes, I can see that." Sister Anna hesitated. "But I saw such a bright future for you in New York."

"I appreciated the offer, truly I did, Sister," Rory said. "But it went out the window when I thought of leaving Violet."

"Since the day I met you, everything you've done has been about Violet."

Rory lifted her shoulders. "She's my sister."

Sister Anna nodded. "I worried at first. Your attachment

was almost too strong. I knew from experience we might have to separate you and I wondered how you would survive. But you were so clever—and worked so hard to stay with her. We laughed at all your little tricks to be useful. Indispensable even."

Rory stared. "You knew?"

"Of course. But Rory, what you don't understand is that you can't fake goodness. You *are* a good girl. And you proved it today. You stayed to help us even though it would have been safer for you and Violet to just go." Sister Anna turned her head away to look out the window. "I want you to know how proud I am of you. You are a true daughter of the Foundling and you will always have a place there."

"But I'm still going to Mexico with Ramon and Elena," Rory said stubbornly.

Sister Anna burst out laughing. "You'll go whether I give you permission or not, won't you?"

"I'd rather have it," Rory said solemnly.

"Before I give my blessing, I want to speak to Mr. Martinez," Sister Anna said.

"But . . ."

"Rory, I insist. For once, you are going to let the adults who love you make decisions for you. You can trust us."

Rory stared down at her hands, rather than meet Sister Anna's watchful gaze. Did Sister Anna know that a warmth in her belly was spreading throughout her whole body? It would be grand to be taken care of! In her most respectful voice, Rory asked, "May I know what you will say to Ramon?"

"I'm going to insist that I always know how to find you." Rory started to protest but Sister Anna silenced her with a steely glance. "For my personal records only. I'll send you news of the Foundling so you won't forget us. And more importantly, I'll send books so you can continue your education." She paused. "There's one more thing . . ."

"Yes?"

"I'll make sure Mr. Martinez knows that you and Violet can return to the Foundling at any time. And perhaps, if you wish, when you are eighteen, you can come back and work for me."

Rory did the sums quickly. She would be eighteen in six years. By then Violet would be almost twelve, the same age Rory was now. By then her little sister would be able to take care of herself.

"I can still have the job?" she asked breathlessly. "Really?"

"Really," Sister Anna said. "Now, promise me you will write."

"Sister, you're my other family. I promise."

"There might be questions about Violet," Sister Anna mused. "We'll have to adjust our paperwork so no one, either in New York or Clifton, questions where Violet is. You were never listed in our documents, so that's no problem."

Rory stared at Sister Anna with new admiration. "You'd fib in your official record for me?"

"I will have to—otherwise, someone might come looking for you and Violet." With a tired smile, Sister Anna said, "Luckily, Mrs. Chacon has already confused my records beyond all recognition. That will be an excellent excuse."

Rory looked up at this woman who had been her touchstone ever since her mother died. Never had she loved or respected Sister Anna more than in this moment. On an overwhelming impulse, she threw her arms around Sister Anna and hugged her tightly. Sister Anna stiffened.

"I love you, Sister Anna," Rory whispered.

Slowly Sister Anna hugged her back. "I love you, too, Rory."

Rory felt a dampness against her cheek but she dismissed it as her imagination. Sister Anna never cried.

Early the next morning, before the sun rose, the children ate their breakfast quietly in their rooms. A few asked about their missing friends, but most responded to the Sisters' mood and were quiet.

Sister Anna managed to meet with Ramon in the barbershop. When she returned, she seemed content. Rory was satisfied.

Their bags were packed and the children were dressed in their playclothes. A knock on the door revealed Sheriff Simpson and two men.

"It's time, Sister," he said.

The Sisters and nurses brought the children downstairs to the empty lobby. Mr. Mills's men waited outside to escort them to the train a block away. Rory wondered why they bothered since the streets were empty. After everything they had seen in Clifton, Rory found the silence unnerving. Sister

Anna didn't seem to notice as she marshaled the adults and their charges like a general moving troops on a battlefield.

At the station, their car was hitched to an engine puffing smoke. Not a moment was wasted getting the children on board. Rory helped until only a few children remained. Poised on the steps into the car, she met Sister Anna's eyes. Sister Anna nodded.

Rory slung the sack with Violet's and her clothes over her back. She hopped off the steps on the side of the train away from the station platform. She ducked down low and ran to a shed on the far side of the tracks. Ramon was waiting out of sight.

Nothing needed to be said. He led Rory through a maze of alleys and back streets until they reached a narrow track that went into the hills above town. They met no one, which was exactly what Ramon and Rory wanted. Elena and Violet were waiting. In a few minutes Rory was seated on a horse behind Ramon. Elena and Violet were perched on a donkey, except that Elena called it a burro. Vi was in heaven; she loved any kind of animal. Behind them were two more burros loaded with household goods and clothing.

The track was narrow and there was a sheer drop to the rocks below. A part of Rory thought she should be afraid of the steep cliff. But for the first time in a very long while, Rory decided to trust someone else to look after them. She leaned forward, her arms wrapped around Ramon's middle, and let him take care of the family. At the top of the valley,

Ramon reined in his horse to look back and down.

The sun was rising higher in the sky, outshining the glow from the smelters. From here the odor of the sulfur was not as strong as it had been as they climbed the canyon. They could see the train station far below them. The Foundling car that had seemed so luxurious and secure on the trip west looked small and vulnerable. There was a faint sound of a train whistle. The train slipped away slowly, carrying Rory's old life with it.

Looking south toward Mexico the sky was clear and there was a golden haze in the distance. The only green was from trees along the banks of a far-off river, but in the distance a hawk was floating on the breeze. From Rory's perspective at the top of the canyon, Mexico looked a lot better than Clifton.

She touched Ramon's arm. "Let's go," she said.

"Where're we going, Rory?" Violet called.

"Home."

A NOTE TO THE READER

RORY'S PROMISE is based on a true story.

Between 1853 and 1929, 250,000 orphaned, abandoned, or homeless children were placed on Orphan Trains from eastern cities to go west. The majority of children were sponsored by the Children's Aid Society of New York (CAS). The children would arrive in town and a local charitable organization would organize an event where anyone with a good reputation who wanted a child could have one.

The Foundling, a Catholic institution, designed their orphan program very differently. Their most important concern was to keep the children with Catholic families. The CAS did not place children with families of the same faith. In our story, you can see how Brigid's placement was very different from Violet's.

None of the orphan organizations had ever placed children in Arizona prior to the time of our story. But when a priest assigned to the towns of Clifton and Morenci offered homes for forty children in response to a letter from the Foundling's agent, George Swayne, the Sisters were convinced to go to Clifton without any firsthand knowledge. The Foundling had to rely on letters and expensive telegrams for their information.

Father Constant Mandin was a young French priest newly appointed to temporarily serve the Catholic population of

Clifton and Morenci. He did not speak English or Spanish and was unaware of the tensions between the Mexicans and Anglos in town. To many Anglos, the Mexicans were a lower, and despised, class of persons. Father Mandin was not prepared for the reaction of the Anglos to the placement of Irish Catholic children with Hispanic Catholics.

Many of the events in *Rory's Promise* occurred. The scene with the angry white women on the station platform was based on eyewitness reports. The Anglo women assumed they could have a child for the asking. They did not understand that the Foundling had already selected families from among Father Mandin's Mexican Catholic parishioners. So not only were they disappointed to find there were no children available; they were furious that the beautiful fair-haired children had been promised to Mexican working-class families.

Their eagerness to adopt was driven by the high rate of infant mortality in the copper mining towns. The 1900 census shows an Anglo woman had a 24 percent chance of losing one child and a 10.5 percent chance of losing two or more. The statistics were even more tragic for the Mexicans. A young woman like Elena had a 48 percent chance of losing her first child and a 28.5 percent chance of losing two or more. Not surprisingly, emotions ran high when the Foundling brought forty children to town.

The scene where the posse takes the children from their home in a driving rainstorm is based on eyewitness accounts. One adoptive father resisted the posse's demands with a rifle.

Also true to life is the scene in which Rory overhears the

crowd threatening Agent Swayne and Father Mandin with lynching. The Sisters were also in danger. Sister Anna's room was overrun with angry Anglo women just as it happened in *Rory's Promise*. Of course, in real life, there was no quick-witted Rory to trick the women into leaving.

To the Foundling officials, their charges had been kidnapped. Sister Anna did not want to leave Clifton without them, but it became clear the Foundling representatives were not safe. To ensure the safety of the remaining children, she took them back for placement elsewhere. Just as she did in *Rory's Promise*, Sister Anna was forced to agree to the adoptions of three children to ensure safe passage for the priest, Mr. Swayne, and the other children. She assumed she was only abandoning the sixteen children temporarily; as soon as she returned to New York she would enlist the courts to get them back.

In January 1905, the Foundling Sisters, nurses, and Swayne went to the Territorial Supreme Court in Phoenix, Arizona. They fully expected the court to restore the orphans to their lawful guardian, the Foundling. To the Sisters' dismay, the judge decided that since the business of the Foundling was to get homes for the children and this had been accomplished, he chose not to disturb the ones already in Arizona. Swayne complained the judge never considered the children were taken from the Foundling by force. No mention was made of the loss of the children's Catholic heritage. From a modern perspective, it seems the court was saying implicitly that despite how the Anglo families got the children, they would be better parents than the Mexicans.

The Foundling's attorneys objected to the Arizona court verdict at once. The case was taken to the United States Supreme Court in Washington, which dismissed the Foundling appeal on a technicality. The case attracted national attention. In newspapers across the country there were pictures of the orphans looking extremely well dressed, implying they were happy with their new families. Other newspapers had very negative opinions about the orphan abductions in Arizona.

Of the eight Anglo women who organized the kidnappings, seven took and kept orphans. It is unknown what happened to the rest. All their names were changed. However, one Mexican family may have kept their orphan. A persistent rumor circulated in Clifton that many years after the 1904 incident a Mexican family returned to the area with their red-haired daughter. The truth of the rumor cannot be confirmed. In 1914, the Clifton postmaster, E. J. Lehman, decided to find out more about the orphans. He wasn't able to learn much but he discovered a discrepancy in the lists of names. There was one orphan not accounted for. Her name was Violet. This was the germ of the idea that led to Rory and Violet's story.

For the sake of the plot, we increased the time it took to travel from Exchange Place in New Jersey to Philadelphia. Also, the actual events that inspired *Rory's Promise* took place in two towns, Clifton and Morenci. For simplicity, we combined all the action and set the story in Clifton. For example, the Clifton Hotel is based on the Morenci Hotel. We also changed the location of the smelter so Rory could see it when she travels between the train station and the church.

Despite the liberties we took with some of the details, we feel we have the essential history correct.

Sister Anna Michaella Bowen is as true to her life as we can make her from the distance of more than one hundred years. She was forty-one in 1904, spent much of her career supervising the orphan placement program for the Foundling, and in 1917 became the Foundling's director. Sister Eileen is invented. We wanted Rory to have a companion close to her age. The two nuns who actually traveled with Sister Anna to Clifton in 1904 were both over fifty.

Mrs. Gatti was based on eyewitness accounts and her testimony in court. Mrs. Chacon was indispensable to Father Mandin, acting as his translator and assistant.

Ramon and Elena Martinez are fictional characters we created to be the parents Rory and Violet deserved.

Rory is an invented character, as is Violet and all the other children and staff at the Foundling and on the orphan trains. Rory's arrival at the Foundling, baby sister in tow, was not the norm for the Foundling. Most of the children were dropped off by abandoning parents or found on the street. Almost certainly in history Rory would not have been permitted to stay with Violet in the Foundling nursery as long as she did in our story. But then, few siblings were as determined as Rory.

A NOTE ABOUT OUR SOURCES/FURTHER READING*
ABOUT THE ORPHAN TRAINS

There is an excellent website devoted to the history of the Orphan Trains. It is orphantraindepot.org, managed by the National Orphan Train Complex. The site is "dedicated to the preservation of the stories and artifacts of those who were part of the Orphan Train Movement from 1854–1929."

Andrea Warren, author of *We Rode the Orphan Trains* (HMH Books for Young Readers, 2001), focuses on one child who rode a train in 1926. The child's story is interwoven with general history about the Children's Aid Society orphan train program.

Elizabeth Raum, author of *Orphan Trains: An Interactive History Adventure* (Capstone Press, 2011), lets you sample a variety of outcomes for an orphan train trip. Some of them are really sad.

Marilyn Irvin Holt's *Children of the Western Plains: The Nineteenth-Century Experience* (Ivan R. Dee, American Childhoods Series, 2003) has wonderful photographs and a good narrative on what it was like to be a child on the American frontier. Although the book focuses on the nineteenth century, Arizona Territory was still the frontier well into the twentieth century. Another Holt book, *The Orphan Trains: Placing Out in America* (Bison Books, 1992), has commentary from orphans on what it was like to ride the trains.

ABOUT THE FOUNDLING HOSPITAL AND
NEW YORK CITY IN 1904

Primary records about the Foundling are available online at nyhistory.org/library/research. Most moving are the notes that parents left with their orphans on placement with the Foundling.

Martin Gottlieb's *The Foundling: The Story of the New York Foundling Hospital* (Lantern Books, 2001) covers parts of our story. If you want to learn how the Sisters of Charity created the Foundling in the nineteenth century, there is Maureen Fitzgerald's *Habits of Compassion: Irish Catholic Nuns and the Origins of New York's Welfare System, 1830–1920* (University of Illinois Press, Women in American History, 2006). For the Foundling's current activities see its website: nyfoundling.org.

*Websites active at time of publication

If you want more information on life in New York City in the very early days of the twentieth century, look at Raymond Bial's *Tenement: Immigrant Life on the Lower East Side* (HMH Books for Young Readers, 2002) and Deborah Hopkinson's *Shutting Out the Sky: Life in the Tenements of New York, 1880–1924* (Orchard Books, Jane Addams Honor Book Awards, 2003). An older book, John Grafton's *New York in the Nineteenth Century: 321 Engravings from "Harper's Weekly" and Other Contemporary Sources* (Dover Publications, 1977), has images of many of the places we describe. Jacob A. Riis, a famed New York photographer, in *Children of the Tenements* (1897; republished Cornell University Library, 2010), tells the story of life for children on these very mean streets during Rory's time.

ABOUT THE KIDNAPPING IN CLIFTON AND MORENCI

There are two books about the 1904 events in Clifton and Morenci, Arizona Territory: Linda Gordon's *The Great Arizona Orphan Abduction* (Harvard University Press, 1999) and Anthony Blake Brophy's *Foundlings on the Frontier: Racial and Religious Conflict in Arizona Territory, 1904–1905* (University of Arizona Press, 1972).

Gordon divided her book into chapters on what happened in Arizona and what the orphan incident meant for the region. The book also delves into race relations between Anglos and Hispanics, the role of copper in developing Arizona, and labor disputes in mining camps, and tells a great story to boot.

Brophy relies on papers presented before the Arizona Territorial Court, local newspaper coverage, and personal recollections of one of his ancestors. William H. Brophy, a banker and the general manager of the Copper Queen Consolidated Mercantile Company in Bisbee, Arizona, interviewed many of the participants. Unfortunately, Anthony Brophy's gracefully written, brief book is not easily available. You can get it through interlibrary loan.

Primary material about the Foundling is in the Patricia D. Klingenstein Library of the New-York Historical Society. Beyond what is available online, there is a clipping file of every newspaper article in the country on the orphan incident. Brophy's primary material is in the Arizona Historical Society: arizonahistoricalsociety.org.

CLOSE SOFTLY THE DOORS

BY RONALD CLAIR ROAT

STORY LINE PRESS

1991

Library of Congress Catalog Card Number:
90-52849

ISBN: 0-934257-48-5

Book design by Lysa McDowell

Published by Story Press, Inc.
d.b.a. Story Line Press
Three Oaks Farm
Brownsville, OR
97327-9718

Men at forty
Learn to close softly
The doors to rooms they will not be
Coming back to.

—Donald Justice

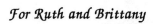

For Ruth and Brittany

ONE

I was half listening to the Detroit Tigers lose the first game of a "twi-night" doubleheader as I watched the five o'clock traffic thin out below my office window when he finally arrived.

I turned off the radio and set to work cleaning a 35mm lens. Busily engaged and professional. He knocked three times on the office door, opened it far enough to shove his head through, and then came in. He didn't shut the door.

"Where the hell do you park around here?" he said.

"According to the landlord, there is ample parking in the rear," I said. "Says so on a little sign in the lobby."

"Jesus Christ."

"No," I said. " The landlord. His name is Timinski, Herbert Timinski."

"What?"

"The landlord."

"Oh, Jes—" He entered the office and glanced around, probably taking in its compactness, neatness, and aura of professionalism. He stopped at my photo collection on the east wall.

"I assume you're Stuart Mallory, the detective."

I nodded.

"May I see some ID?" he said.

I thought about it, then reached into my jacket pocket for the identification folder issued by the Michigan Secretary of State. I put it on the desk. "The license is on the wall." I pointed at it.

The man glanced at the ID and tossed it on the desk. He wore a much wrinkled seersucker suit over a white shirt and yellow tie. Power stuff. He looked at the license on the wall and appeared satisfied. He then read the little typed note framed below it which said, *If men define situations as real, they are real in their consequences.* W.I. Thomas.

1

"I'm George S. Ackfield," he said. "I'm the attorney who called earlier." Ackfield sat in the client chair in front of the desk.

"Okay."

"It's rather simple," he said, and leaned back.

"Good." I leaned back, too.

"Got a letter today containing a postal money order telling me to contact you and see if you would drive to Hamlin to take a bodyguard case. You're to meet the client, a woman, at one tomorrow afternoon at a place called First Pier. I'm to take my fee out of the money order and give the rest to you." He reached into his suit pocket to get something.

"Who's the woman?"

"That's the mystery," he said, pulling some papers and folding money out of an envelope. "No signature on anything, but the instructions are very specific." He handed the papers to me. The top one, the letter, instructed Ackfield to do what he had said. If I refused the case, he was to hold the money until further instructed. She would call, the letter said, to verify my employment. The letter was typed. There was no signature.

I looked over the flip sides of all sheets. Nothing. I thought about smelling them, and I wondered what Ackfield would think. I smelled the pages anyway.

Ackfield said, " She's already called once. I was in court—corporate tax case—and my secretary explained that I would have to contact you later in the day. Anyway, this is on my way home, and it was convenient to come by."

"Except for the parking."

He nodded. "Except for that."

I handed the letter to him. The next paper was an unsigned receipt for eight hundred dollars, the retainer remaining from the nine hundred. Must be rugged making a living in the legal circles. I signed it.

"Guarding bodies isn't very much in my line," I

said.

Ackfield counted the bills and handed them to me. "You don't look much like a bodyguard," he said.

"I'm quick," I said. "I shoot straight, too." The eight hundred was all there.

Ackfield stood up. "Now, you know as much about this as I do." He turned to go, but changed his mind. "My curiosity begs me to query, but my ethics discourage it."

"To query?"

He sat down. "I assume, as dangerous as it is to assume, that this woman knows both of us. Otherwise, why write to me out of maybe five hundred attorneys in Lansing? Why hire you? Initially, I was going to let the letter sit, but I'm curious. Do you know who she is?"

"Nope," I said. "But if she wanted you to know, you would already know."

He stood and offered his hand. We shook. "Enough," he said. "A pleasure." He stepped toward the door and stopped. "I'll send you a copy of this letter and the receipt."

"Thanks."

"One more thing," he said. "Thomas... W something or other Thomas." He pointed at the wall with the license and the typed note on it. "Who is he?"

I shrugged a little. "Philosopher, sociologist, student of mankind."

He shrugged. The sounds of his wingtips carried back to my office as he went down the hall. He descended the stairs with a clickity click. George S. Ackfield, attorney at law.

My fingers began to tap on the desk again, finally tapping over to the radio and switching it on. Tiger announcer Ernie Harwell was explaining the Tigers' loss by harping at the bullpen. The pitchers had tired during the team's extensive road trip.

I attached the now clean 200 mm lens to my Nikon

and focused it on the fading image of George S. Ackfield. He stepped briskly toward the traffic light. Since
he was back-lit, I opened it another f-stop and waited.
Just before he stepped from the curb, he turned in
my direction. The shutter clattered.

"Your suit needs to be pressed," I said.

I had a client. A mystery client. I had things to do
if I was going to drive to the Western Michigan shoreline to meet a woman at the First Pier the next day. I
propped my feet on the window ledge, eased my chair
into a better position, and made mental notes. I would
have to leave a message for my lawyer neighbor, Patty
Bonicelli, with whom I shared an outer office, a steady
in-house respect, and an after hours friendship that
was somewhere beyond occasional, but we didn't share
closets yet. I would have to visit the laundromat tonight instead of tomorrow. Detectives need clean
underwear too. A couple of bills needed attending
now rather than later. Later might be miles away from
Lansing.

I reached for a cigarette and found an empty pocket.
Again. It had been a month since I quit. I hoped the
involuntary gesture would soon go away. It was a
nuisance.

The traffic below began to ease. The city permitted
parking only on the south side of the narrow street.
That was usually full. So was the small lot at the
building's rear. Such inconveniences kept my rent low.

Ackfield was wrong about the First Pier, but he
couldn't know it. First Pier was an old name of a
restaurant near the harbor, but it had been renamed.
Like most residents and former residents of Hamlin,
I had forgotten the restaurant's real name. But this
meant she was serious about concealing her contact
with me. It also meant she knew me.

I pulled my feet from the window and put the cam-
era back in the desk and locked it. Once the desk's
paperwork was arranged in three orderly piles—de-

tective stuff, graduate student stuff, other stuff—I locked the filing cabinets and selected two books from the shelf, typed Patty a note, and turned off the radio. The Tigers were still looking bad. The third pitcher was not holding the ground, such as it was. I locked up the office and knocked on Patty's door. As expected, no answer. I opened it with my key and put the note on her desk.

She came in behind me.

"Oh, good," she said. "You're still here." Patty carried a bulging satchel and leaned away from the burden. She stood slightly taller than the average woman and had dark brown hair cropped neatly at the shoulder. She took long, purposeful strides.

"That's the best compliment I've had in a week," I said, and meant it.

"Poor knight-errant," she said, dropping her baggage on the desk, covering my note. "Let me buy you a drink." She patted me on the head.

"I'll buy you a drink," I said. "I have a client. I'm to guard someone's body. A woman's body."

Patty took off her coat and threw it across her desk. The note was truly buried now. "I hope you don't get beat up again," she said, dashing around me to a shelf of paperwork behind me.

"Such faith," I said. "I won the fight."

"In a manner of speaking," she said. "The last one still conscious is hardly a criterion for winning. How're the ribs?" She punched me lightly in the rib cage on her way past.

I winced, but it didn't count. Her back was turned.

"Okay, you can buy me the drink," she said, sitting down with a thump. "But we have to use your car. I just left mine at the garage. Again." I sat in her client chair. It was softer than mine. And lower.

I said, "You look tired."

"Exhausted." Her eyes were closed and her chair full back against the partition between the windows.

"Some days I think you're right: justice is not what the courts are about."

I said nothing. We had discussed this. I wanted to make notice of the near agreement, but that would cause a recital of law school lectures.

"There's this place, the Bowman Center, for wayward people—everyone from runaway kids to gray-haired bums," Patty said. I nodded, but she didn't notice. "They get a place to sleep, something to eat, counseling, clothing, travel help for runaways. They all work together, too. Neat idea, neat place. Fills the gap between community charities — the illusionary safety net — and death in the gutter. But, the city's housing inspectors declared the building a hazard. The IRS wants Bowman to file for charitable organization status, which I've done for him. The city wants a new furnace in the building. The state is investigating the licenses of the counselors. The god- damned court, Mallory, wants a hearing to determine some stupid issue."

"Good thing Bowman has a good lawyer."

"Yeah," she said. "Maybe that's why no one's worried."

I began to tap my fingers on the chair arms. "This is going to sound self-centered. I've got to drive across the state tomorrow and there are things to do tonight, such as laundry. Let's get something to eat."

She opened her eyes and leaned forward. "Screw you, Mallory," she said. "People have been rushing me all day."

"There's a note under your barrister bag," I said. She slowly shifted her weight forward and with a squeak moved the bundle aside, picked up the note, and read it to me.

"Gone detecting out of town. If you water my plant, I'll cancel the personal ad saying you have the softest heart and the finest legs of any lawyer in town. Mallory."

Patty came around the desk and kissed me lightly on the lips. With her right hand she ran a finger lightly down my cheek. I stirred.

"Thank you, big fella," she said. "Run the ad."

"Golly," I said, and I meant that, too.

She swung the shoulder bag over her arm with a flourish and grabbed my left arm. "Let's be off," she said, letting me guide her to the door. "I'm hungry."

I said, "I'll try not to burp in public."

"You do and I won't let you wash your duds at my place," Patty said. We walked noisily down the hall.

"Will you let me use your soap?"

"We'll see."

TWO

I left Patty's apartment about 6 a.m. with two loads of fresh laundry and drove to my farm house northeast of the airport. There I made a thermos of coffee, packed a small bag, fed my cat, Basil, and left. I stopped at Dawn Donuts on the way to the interstate and picked up a half dozen. Cinnamon.

Ready to travel.

The El Camino ran well, despite its age. I had purchased it from an Oregon man. No rust. Ziebart did its thing on it and I washed it frequently. I even gave the engine a valve job and new rings just to be sporting. I pushed it a little hard until I passed Grand Rapids, the first urban landmark, and in a way the last. Although not in a hurry, I intended to follow the old highway along the shoreline, a longer trip. I am at the age where one appreciates the scenery as much as the destination. Sometimes more. At Muskegon I nudged a Bob Seger tape into the deck.

North of Muskegon I selected a turn-off which would

take me to what is called "old U.S. 31." That highway would carry me past wooden service stations
with porches which reach out to cover the gasoline
pumps, past small restaurants with neon "Eat" signs,
and past dusty crushed limestone parking areas marked
by short, white, wooden posts at least a decade behind on paint and scarred by ambitious snow plows
and Chicago tourists.

Rolling along the oldest highway on the Lake Michigan coastline, I could smell the water not far beyond
the trees. There is a freshness in this land the senses
detect but the mind seldom understands. The shoreline land itself, such as it is, is not good for anything
except growing millions of pine and fruit trees. The
land is not much good because it is fresh. It is new,
in geologic time at least, and was shaped directly
and indirectly by the great Polar Glacier. It moved
slowly but deliberately out of Canada gouging out
what are now the Great Lakes and the plains as far
south as the Ohio Valley. As the wall of ice progressed
south, it lay smooth an entire mountain range stretching from northern Wisconsin across upper Michigan
to New York state. It deposited the rubble in various
parts south.

At Montague, I paralleled the expressway for a few
miles, passing through the small agricultural towns,
Rothbury and New Era. The land began to roll a little.
Flourishing orchards evidenced improvement in the
soil. The temperature also climbed slightly as the lake
effect was reduced by the distance from the water.
On the other side of Shelby I stopped to have the
gasoline tank topped and to visit the men's room, a
side effect of making coffee a travel ritual. The price
of gasoline had risen a nickel since Lansing, a sure
indication of outstate Michigan.

But, I did not need to prod the attendant. He checked
the oil, water, windshield washer fluid, and cleaned
the windshield, another sign of geography. Soon these

folks would catch on, though. Armed with television, the bigger cities had a way of spreading the gospel of consumption.

The attendant stepped out with my change. "Going fishing?" he asked. "Gary" was embroidered in script on his shirt pocket.

"No," I said. "Going north to check out someone who is baiting me, though."

"Just as well." Gary arranged the oil cans so the labels aligned. "I hear it's been slow lately, slacking off for the season."

"Maybe the fish finally figured out what's going on, saw the pattern."

"Probably the weather," he said. "Stop again." The attendant returned to the garage and leaned back under the hood of a late '50s Ford. Woe upon us when we finally understand weather.

I adjusted two oil cans so their labels failed to align.

Across the street at a fruit stand I parked so as not to block the sun from the wares. I ignored the corn, potatoes, and assorted vegetables piled in the sun. I selected a quart of strawberries and a quart of sweet cherries. I moved the fruit on top to check that below. A young woman slipped out of the shadows at the rear of the hut and bagged the fruit. Her long blond ponytail swayed effortlessly with her every move, sensually accenting everything she did.

"Will that be all, sir? Can I interest you in anything else? Potatoes? Corn?"

"Nope. Need the fruit to balance six cinnamon donuts."

She took my five dollar bill and stepped to the back of the hut to make change. In her turn she showed she had performed that movement often enough to know the reaction she would get. She knew without having to peek to know. They always know.

She had to turn slightly sideways and squint to see me when she returned with my money. But she did squint. Maybe it was my blue eyes. They always complement a sunny day.

"Thank you," I said.

"Sure thing."

I stood at the makeshift counter with the bag of fruit in my hand and studied the light freckles summer had already nourished. I hoped the summer would be good for her.

She said, "Is there anything else?"

I shook my head. "I'm just waiting to watch you turn and walk back there again."

She bowed her head just a little, stifling a grin. She turned and walked back into the shadows. The act was not as good on command. There was something genuine under the act, something which could be embarrassed.

"Thank *you*," I said. I put the strawberries in the back of the El Camino and shut the canopy. I got in.

"Thank you," said a voice from the hut's shadows.

I U-turned in the street and slowly gained speed up the highway. Already I missed Shelby. Within a mile I was spitting cherry pits out the window at a rate of about one every two hundred yards. One of them hit the grill of a southbound Michigan State Police cruiser. Just south of the next little town, Hart, I stopped at a roadside rest area and unpacked my pistol and clipped it to the rear of my belt. I covered that with a summer weight light blue blazer and got back in. Within twenty minutes I approached the outskirts of Hamlin.

There is a difference between being laid-back and being back. Laid-back implies that a choice was made. It is an active decision. On the other hand, being back simply implies being back and not necessarily ever having been anywhere else or having decided to be elsewhere. That description fits Hamlin.

Hamlin had once been my home, and to return home after having been away for a great spell is to see home through eyes conditioned by experience and ideas acquired elsewhere. It is to see it partly for what it is, partly for what the mind remembers it to be, and party as something new and unfamiliar.

I saw it as a place where people thoroughly believe in respecting and loving their neighbors as long as the blacks stay in Detroit, the Mexican farm workers go home in the fall, and the Indians remain on the reservations. I saw Hamlin as a place where people frequently thank a divinity for what is on the dinner table and, as often, curse the very existence which requires them to work to exhaustion to put it there.

I also saw Hamlin as a place where people hold an honest appreciation for the environment, being closer to soil than to concrete. The people here only reluctantly climb the ladder of success, shifting their definition of the good life from gathering a pile of consumer booty to feeling a lake breeze and enjoying a water-enhanced sunset. Hamlin is a town which makes as much money from soothing the aching psyches of travelers from the big southern cities as it does from agriculture. It was indeed a place where a man could decide to lay back.

I also knew it to be a place where it is prudent to check in with the local sheriff. I parked in the shade of a maple tree, twisted to make the pistol inconspicuous, and strolled into the combined sheriff's office and jail.

The deputy in his early twenties sat in a far corner of the outer office and scribbled numbers on a form. Since my appearance made a conspicuous shadow, I assumed he knew I was there. But as George S. Ackfield says, it is dangerous to assume.

"Excuse me, deputy."

"Just a moment, please, sir," he said. He squinted at the form and put another number on it. I was glad I was not bleeding.

He stood and approached the counter. "I'm sorry,

sir," he said. "I was filling out an FBI crime statistics report, another new one. Damned forms. What can I do for you?" A plastic nameplate indicated his name was McLaughlin.

I slid my private detective identification folder across the counter. "I'll be in the area for a while."

"Okay," McLaughlin said. "Hold on a minute." He picked up the telephone, dialed once, and told someone there was a Stuart Mallory, private detective, outside. He hung up. "The sheriff wants to talk with you a minute," he said. He sat down at his desk and copied the information from my identification, looked it over, and then returned to the counter.

"Those FBI forms can be bummers," I said. Nice, friendly talk.

"Oh, that," he said. "It is some sort of follow-up to the quarterly foul-up. It takes two hours to figure out the directions, ten minutes to complete." He handed me the folder. "Sheriff wants to see all private dicks coming through here."

"Must be a lot of them, crime up here being what is is."

He shrugged and sat down. "It's the man's policy," he said. "He's the boss."

McLaughlin returned to his deskman duties. I looked through the brochures on the counter for tips for the detecting business.

"You Stuart Mallory?" said a man who had appeared from the hall to the right.

"Yes."

"Follow me," he said, and I did.

The man, in his early fifties and dressed tightly in khakis, led me down the hall, turned to his right and disappeared into an office. I followed, entering as he dropped into the desk chair and swung it around with a squeak. I handed him the identification and sat down, too. A sign on his desk said: Emery D. Frost, Sheriff.

Nametags, nameplates, signs, artifacts of our times. Perhaps thousands of years after the next war, a lost alien will visit this planet. Jutting from the still smoldering ooze will be venerable plastic messages, such as, "No smoking," "Please Wait for Hostess," "Ring Bell for Service," and "This Window Closed."

Frost opened the folder and turned it over in his fingers a couple of times. He then leaned across his desk and gave it to me.

"You're from here," Frost said.

"You have a good memory."

"Dahh," Frost said, waving his hand. He smiled. "I looked it up while you waited outside. I remember your father."

"He's in Florida. Fishing."

Frost leaned back and glanced at the big clock on the wall. Noon. "What brings you up here? Don't suppose you're just visiting if you came to see me."

"Got a case. I don't know how long I'll be here, but I'll try to stay out of your way while I'm here." Mallory, the diplomat, deliverer of reassurance.

"I'd like that," he said. "Who's your client?"

"Can't say, sheriff," I said. "That would be telling."

"Suppose it would," he said. "Been over to Fred's office yet?"

I raised an eyebrow and said, "Who?"

"Police," Frost said. "Chief of police."

"No," I said. "I'll get over there if necessary."

"Might be nice," he said. "They'd probably be upset if they heard of you the wrong way." He tapped his gathered fingers on the glass desktop. "Got a permit for the piece making you sit funny?"

I handed him the identification folder again. "Under the state license," I said. He looked it over and stuffed it back in place. He folded it with a snap.

A whistle blew somewhere in the distance. I had forgotten the sounds of the harbor. I considered smiling, but I knew the sheriff would not understand. He had been here so long he no longer heard the whistles and horns. The sheriff leaned over again and gave me the identification.

"We don't get many PIs here," Frost said. "We were crawling with them a few years back when we had some drug peddling problems. We arrested a lot of kids one summer, some of them the darling boys and girls of pillars of the community. You know the type. Families hired big city lawyers and PIs to prove their innocence."

"I heard," I said. I reached for a cigarette I did not have. Again. "Any of them do his job?"

Frost shrugged. "We did well. We busted one of them," he said. "Got too involved in the subject, both in drugs and in the under-aged daughter of his client."

I smiled. "I'll be careful, sheriff."

Frost smiled too. "That's just talk," he said. "I'm fishing. But, if there is something going on in this county that I should know about, I'd like to know about it. I'd hate to be the last to know. That's the purpose of this chit-chat. Do we understand one another?" His smile had disappeared.

I stood up. "We do, sheriff. If there is something you ought to know, you'll know."

"I'd like that," he said, and he rose to his feet too. "And if there is something we can help with..." Frost extended his hand as he rounded his desk. "Say hello to your father. Tell him the fishing's better in Michigan." He glanced at the clock again. I picked up the movement, too. Five minutes had passed.

"Late for lunch," he said, grabbing his uniform Eisenhower jacket. He waved as he walked toward the rear of the building. I heard a door open and close.

I let myself out.

I had a few minutes to kill, and I drove down to Lake Michigan to kill them there. My timing was good. One of the railroad carferries was just clearing the

lighthouse at the pier's end, picking up some speed,
its bulk aimed to the northwest. The bow began to
pierce the waves thrown by the wind. Gulls followed
the boat and looked for fish debris churned to the
surface. The notion that the gulls were having lunch
helped me remember the strawberries. I retrieved them
from the rear of the car and sat on a bench and tried
to eat. They still carried some of the sand which raised
hell with my dental work. I put them back into the
car and returned to the bench. The carferries do not
seem to move quickly when you watch them, but if
you take your eyes off one of them for a few minutes
you become surprised at how far it has traveled when
you again observe it.

Being near the water made me want to be in it. We
are breeding that desire out of us. Someday we'll reel
back in horror at the thought of water touching us.

My hunger and my curiosity about the client were
mounting. I had held myself in check long enough. I
drove over to the restaurant and found a good parking space just outside the door. People were leaving,
returning to work. I was arriving to begin to work. I
felt some kinship with their efforts.

I hitched up my belt a little, took a last look out
toward the carferry—which I could not see for the
buildings—and went inside. I stood dutifully by the
sign, "Wait here to be seated," and glanced around
the dining area. I recognized no one, although I saw
the backs of about a dozen heads. The hostess stepped
up and I told her a window seat would be nice and
that someone would be joining me. She directed me
to a table still covered with someone's dishes.

"I'll get someone to clean the table," she said, and
walked away. Within seconds someone did come and
clean the table and set it for two. I took a look at the
front of the heads I had already seen the backs of
and still did not recognize anyone. I glanced through
the menu and had considered the day's lunch spe-

cials stuffed under the plastic overlays when she walked into the dining room.

I knew that her hips would be about thirty-three and she would stand about five-four. She would have a funny little scar on the inside of her left elbow where she had fallen when she was a child. I knew these things what seemed to be a long time ago.

THREE

Kathy stood next to the table, her left hand gently touching the edge, and looked at me with a disarming familiarity.

"Hi, soldier," Kathy said.

"Hello, Kathy." I studied her for what I knew to be a long time, but I did it anyway. She wore something like a peasant's blouse with designer blue jeans. Although I could see she was about fifteen years older, I could not see where it made any difference. She shifted slightly, twisted her hip a few degrees and kept a growing smile under control. I cleared my throat because I had to and said, "Sit down before I faint."

She did. The controlled smile had forced her to compress her lips a little. Her eyes glimmered in the light, which they always did, and studied me with intensity. I became aware of the slight gray at my temples and the extra pounds I now carry, but I was also aware that the same fifteen years showed me how to conceal that awareness.

"You look good," Kathy said.

"You too."

Her eyes darted around my face and finally to my hands, now on the table.

"I have the advantage," she said. "I've been wondering what your reaction would be for a couple of days now. I could prepare. At least I thought so."

My high school girlfriend's hand came carefully across the table and I took it and squeezed it.

"It's good to see you," she said, her voice losing some of its strength. She winked and a tear fled her eye. "You're worth the wait."

"Long time."

"Yes," she said, catching the tear with her free hand. She smiled. "I'm being a child about this."

"The memories are strong," I said. "For me too."

She was regaining control. I suspect there was more to it. I don't have that kind of effect on women.

The waitress returned and stood at the table and held her pad in her hand. "Do you need more time?" She had a nametag. Her name was Sheila.

Kathy watched me.

"I'll have the day's special," I said. "And bring me a tall iced tea." I shoved the menu over to the waitress. "House dressing."

Kathy picked up her menu and glanced at it. She ordered a small salad with vinegar and oil and a cup of coffee. The waitress wrote it down on the pad, collected the menus, and left.

"Do you know what the special is today?" Kathy said.

I offered a small shrug.

"Corned beef hash, sauerkraut, and a small salad," she said.

"Sounds yummie."

She grinned. "Yummie," she said, considering the word.

"No more tears?"

"No," she said. "No more tears." She leaned back in her booth and looked at me, then out the window, then into her purse, and then out the window across the harbor entrance to the large, white cross marking the spot where the Jesuit priest, Pere Marquette, is said to have died. A gull flew by the window, banked into the wind, then climbed out of sight. I felt remiss.

"Kathy," I said. "You summoned me. I'm here. Tell me about it."

She took a deep breath and clasped her hands together. She looked at me. "Well, I'm in trouble. I'll tell you the details when we get out of here." She glanced around the restaurant. "It's not that I'm afraid someone will hear, it's just that, well, it will be easy to explain somewhere else. Anyway, a man who swore he would beat me within an inch of death or beyond— to quote him—is now hunting me down."

"Does he know you're here?"

"I doubt it, but he'll figure it out if he hasn't already."

"He'll come here then," I said.

"You're probably right."

"From where?"

"Indiana," she said. "That's where I live now. Carmel, a suburb of Indianapolis." She pronounced Carmel like the sticky stuff we pour on ice cream.

"Will he come alone?"

She looked up from her hands. "I hadn't thought of that. It's sort of personal, so I thought he would come after me alone. I hadn't considered he might have help."

"Who is he, what does he look like? I need to know these things."

She dug into her purse and removed a few folded newspaper clippings. She selected one and slid it across the table so that it faced me. "That's him," she said. "That's the first story."

The clipping had a one-column head shot of a man named Samuel D. Pendergrass indicted for fraud in connection with a vending machine business in Indiana. It was a week or so old. It was a nice photograph of a dark-haired fellow who looked to be about forty, a member of a Rotary Club, and an officer of the chamber of commerce.

"Pendergrass?"

She handed me a second clipping. The reporter had led it with a new charge, assaulting a U.S. marshal while Pendergrass was in court facing arraignment. It was four days old.

"Bad form," I said. "Assaulting a marshal in front of a judge."

"The marshal was trying to keep him from getting to me," Kathy said. "He had just learned that I testified against him."

"At the grand jury?"

She nodded.

"Surely, others testified too," I said. "Why you?"

Kathy shoved a snapshot across the table at me as a card dealer would. With her free hand she picked at something behind her ear.

The photo showed a man and a woman with arms around one another sitting in front of a statue somewhere. It was a picture of Kathy and Pendergrass. I looked at the statue again and realized it stood in Rome.

"Family dispute?"

Kathy shook her head. "Not exactly. There's some history to all this. We were once very close. He seemed like a fine man. Still is in some ways."

"You married to him?"

"No," she said. "I've never married."

The waitress brought the salads to the table and told us the lunch would be right along.

"Have you married, Stuart?"

"Nope."

"I heard that you had," she said.

"Perhaps he'll cool down, come to his senses," I said.

"Perhaps," she said as she got a bite of salad under control. "I thought he would too, but a few hours after that he was released and he called me. Told me he would come and beat me within an inch of death.

Kill me."

"Police offer protection?"

She shook her head. "I talked to the prosecutor. He said he couldn't do much for me until Sam tried to do something. Said he was powerless."

I nodded. "So you split."

"I split." She munched on more salad and then stopped eating and fell into tears. "Stuart, he killed my puppy." Her lower lip quivered and her chin dimpled. She covered her face with her hands, breathed deeply, and turned toward the window while she regained some control. "The next morning I got up and I couldn't find my puppy. I found him as I opened the back door. He was hanging to the doorknob..."

I put one of her hands in mine and held it. She bit her lip and winked tears from her eyes.

"He gave me the puppy," Kathy said, quietly sobbing. "And then he strangled him and hung him on the door." She watched a couple of gulls float by the window, then settle toward the water. "Oh, God," she said, clinging to my hands. "God damn him." She stood and paced quickly toward the women's room. I watched her dash through the door.

The waitress chugged over and placed the coffee and iced tea in front of the salads. She slid the day's special in front of me. Steam rose from it.

"Will there be anything else?"

"No. This is fine. Thanks."

Outside three gulls sat on a stout post and looked in three directions.

FOUR

When the waitress trotted by I ordered a piece of home baked blueberry pie and another iced tea. I kept one eye on the women's room door. If she went in, she had to come out. Says so in the detective manual under "surveillance."

Kathy came out. She came straight to the table, sat down, picked up her fork, and attacked the salad. I left her alone. We both had things to think about.

I hurried through my salad and finished the sauerkraut. I told Kathy not to leave for anything or anyone. She said okay. I picked up the two newspaper clippings and found a pay telephone near the entrance and within sight of Kathy. I called Patty's office and got the recording machine. I told the machine about Samuel D. Pendergrass and told it to find everything it could about the case, the status of the court proceedings, the mental condition of Pendergrass, and a summary of the case. I told Patty who I was protecting and the general nature of the threat and not to tell the righteous attorneys she would call for information where Kathy was. I said I would call back that evening. I got it all said before it beeped at me.

Patty and I have scratched one another's back at times when the situation required it. This was a job for an attorney who could charm the socks off Darth Vader. On the telephone. Long distance. Patty Bonicelli could handle it.

I went back and worked on the blueberry pie, which had arrived in my absence. On the fourth fork load Kathy looked up from her empty salad bowl and told me she had a plan. We would stay at her parents' cottage on the eastern shore of Hamlin Lake. The cottage had become her property seven years ago when her parents died. She rented the cottage each summer and hired neighbors to maintain it. Pendergrass knew of the cottage's existence, she said, but not where it was.

"He can find it," I said. "An old phone book in the library, old city directory, or even talking to some folks out there."

"I suppose you would know about these things."

"I know about these things."

Kathy paid the bill. She said she would pay all bills. I didn't argue. We went outside and climbed into the El Camino.

She pointed at a dark red late model Celebrity two-door parked half way down the block toward the marina. "That's mine," she said. "I don't want to leave it here long."

"We'll be back," I said. "If you're being followed already, we might discover it by driving away."

I drove out and turned into town.

"We going into town?"

"Some place else you want to go right now?"

She shook her head. We drove into town and stopped at the first traffic light. We glanced around some, remembering. If what Kathy told me held true, eventually Pendergrass would come to Hamlin and likely look for the cottage and find it within a few hours. Maybe he already knew she was there. Maybe I was the last to find out. It had happened before.

We drove around. Kathy mostly sat in silence. She tapped her fingers on the door, hummed, made attempts at conversation—"I wonder if Brady still owns that shop"—looked at a thin, expensive-looking watch on her tanned wrist, and sighed quietly. I turned on the radio and left it on low.

It was a fateful decision. I had forgotten the Seger tape. Seger launched into "Night Moves," the romantic remembrance of young lovers learning about one another in the backseat of a Chevy. After I failed to ignore it, I leaned over to switch to radio.

"Leave it alone," Kathy said.

Kathy put her hand on mine and I lifted it up and kissed the back of it. The song ended. She put her hand back in her lap. Neither of us said anything. I switched it to radio and Kathy picked up the three tape containers, including the empty one, and looked them over.

"The Pointer Sisters?" she said.

"They get me down the highway."

"I suppose."

We stopped at a grocery store. I followed her through the isles and let her be shopper. She told me to put in whatever I wanted to add. I dropped a six-pack of Bud Light into the cart. At the deli section I ordered three kinds of sliced meat and picked out two loafs of French bread.

"I like spur-of-the-moment sandwiches," I told Kathy.

We put five sacks of groceries into the back of the El Camino. Kathy said we needed staples because there was nothing at the cottage.

This Western Michigan tourist town's traffic gets interesting on summer afternoons. Hamlin is a small town, but in the summer the population increases five hundred percent. The streets aren't designed for it. It gets messy, especially when the tourists, who account for at least two-thirds of the traffic and who do not know the territory but who assume if you can drive on the Eisenhower Expressway in Chicago or the John C. Lodge Expressway in Detroit you can drive anywhere, join the locals, who have developed all sorts of local driving habits which clash with the ignorance of the out-of-towners.

We parked behind her Celebrity and looked around. I got out and walked around her car. Then she got in her car and drove off. I followed her out North Lakeshore Drive past big homes leftover from last century's lumber industry, past two busy golf courses and a small lake, and finally past the growing number of summer cabins along the southern shores of Hamlin Lake.

The cottage sat on a hill. Big oak trees would shade it from the morning sun. The road led to it from the rear while another road ran north and south on the west side. That road was out of sight down the hill. The big inland lake sat restlessly on the other side of the lower road. We pulled into the short driveway at the back.

Kathy pointed at the home next door. "Mrs Van-Johnson always looks after the place while I'm gone," she said.

"I'll go in and look around," I said. She gave me the key.

The door opened easily into the kitchen. It smelled fresh, like pine-scented soap. The bathroom led off to the left. No one hid in the shower. Two bedrooms were on the right and the beds were made with fresh linen. No one was concealed in the closets or under the beds. The living room was long and airy and led to a screened-in porch on the west side. The front door, separating the porch from the living room, was locked securely. A large window between the living room and porch was open but screened.

I could hear Kathy talking to someone and I returned to the back door in about four steps, skidding only once on a throw rug. She stood outside next to the car talking to an older woman who did not appear to be holding a gun or a blackjack. I opened the canopy and removed two heavy grocery sacks.

"This is Stuart Mallory," Kathy told the woman.

"Hi," the woman said, coming right over. "I'm Mrs. VanJohnson."

"Very glad to meet you," I said. "Kathy was just telling me about you."

I put one sack on the hood and shook her hand.

"Do you need help?" Kathy said.

"No," I said, silently thanking her for the cue. "But I should get the frozen things into the frig."

Kathy engaged the neighbor in conversation and I carried the groceries into the cabin. She came in after I had most of the food put away. She put the rest of the food away and checked through the cupboards and drawers saying, "Ah, ah."

I put my luggage into the smaller bedroom. Hers

was already in the larger. When I came out, she went into her bedroom and shut the door. I returned to the kitchen, put ice into a glass, and poured half a bottle of Hires rootbeer into it. It foamed over the kitchen counter. I cleaned it up with a hand sponge and carried it into the enclosed porch and sat in one of the cushioned wicker chairs and looked out over Hamlin Lake. I got up, took off my jacket and put my gun into one of its pockets, and sat down again.

Duty is not always rigorous.

Kathy came out in bare feet and sat in another chair. She wore a tank top and a pair of shorts. Those shoulders led upward along a very smooth neck and downward along rounded arms. The territory in between revealed that the advertiser's claim for a built-in bra did not match the reality perfectly. Her legs, tanned by the Indiana sun, were smooth and lively even in their stillness. The tree shadows spilled across her skin giving it an animated quality. Katherine Whitman, client. I turned my gaze upon Hamlin Lake.

"What do you want for supper?" she said.

"Corned beef hash would be nice," I said. "A little sauerkraut on the side perhaps."

She silently giggled. And wiggled.

"Seriously," she said.

I thought seriously about it. "Whatever you want," I said. I looked at the lake again. It was blue and it sparkled. A power boat seemed to be chasing another. "I'm not hungry enough to think about it much."

"I thought I'd get it started," she said. "You can sit out here and relax."

I stood up. "Whatever looks good. I'll go outside and look the place over." I looked down at her. The afternoon breeze, the playful shadows darting around, and the tank top. She stood up, too.

In her bare feet she came up to about the bottom of my chin, maybe less. Not my typical client.

"Thank you," she said.

I smiled. Always a good response.

Kathy reached up, put her hands behind my neck as a place to hang her weight, and pulled herself up and kissed me full and long. She was all woman and all mine for the asking.

I gently released her and set her down. My ribs hurt.

"Thank you for being there, for coming," she said. "Right from the beginning when the trouble started, I knew who I wanted to be with."

"I hope you feel safe."

"I do," she said. "And tired. I haven't been sleeping well these past few weeks." She strolled away and faced the screened windows toward the lake.

"I'm going to change into some cut-offs, and go outside and take a look around," I said. "Why don't you begin whatever you wanted to begin and then take a nap."

She looked at me for a moment, making a decision.

"Okay," she said, and strolled into the living room. "I'll put some pork chops and potatoes and stuff into the crockpot and we can eat in a few hours."

I collected my rootbeer and jacket and went into the bedroom. I felt a little funny closing the door, even after these many years, but I did. I emptied the two small suitcases into the empty chest. I changed into the cut-offs and sandals. The pistol fit a little snugly and conspicuously into one of the pockets, so I hung the blue "I LOVE OREGON" T-shirt outside the shorts.

Outside I circled the house to the north. The windows were nightmares for the security conscious. Wood-framed screens were tacked inside the window frames. An incompetent burglar would remove one in seconds. I tried the screen over my bedroom and the nails holding it in place fell out as I jiggled the screen. The one on Kathy's room was a bit more secure.

Bushes straddled the back door. They began at the ground and came up better than four feet, nestling against the house. The back door light worked and, if given a chance, would cover the area nicely. Mrs. VanJohnson watched me from her window. I waved and she pretended to be doing something else. She was better security.

Back in the kitchen I found my client peeling potatoes. "I need to nail the screens into the window frames," I said.

"There should be tools here." She wiped her hands on a towel and went to the front door closet. One was locked, but she moved a board on the wall and a key fell out and rang musically on the wooden floor. She opened the closet to reveal an assortment of carpentry and yard tools in a closet deeper than it appeared. A real find.

"A trimmer. You mind if I trim the bushes?"

"Why do you want to do all this?"

Cupping my hand around her chin and neck and giving her what I hoped was a wise look, I said, "So no one can hide and jump out at us." I felt silly saying it.

She put her arms around me and squeezed, then swayed back into the kitchen.

There were several little hardware store paper sacks of nails on a narrow shelf and I selected some common nails. With the hammer, trimmer, and a small pruning saw I worked my way around the house in reverse direction. I put two nails into each screen frame and left a bit of the nail out so they could be removed in the fall. However, they would discourage entry now. The idea in the less than ideal situation is to make entry a noisy, awkward affair.

The wind had shifted from the northwest to the west, suggesting warmer weather and eventually rain. One knows these things after living here a while. The memory momentarily pleased me.

The screens were no challenge. I thought about the real challenge. You can run from the pursuer if there is a chance the pursuer will tire and quit, or get distracted. Sometimes you can reason with the pursuer, but not often. If reasoning was possible, you wouldn't have to run.

The last option, of course, is to turn upon the hunter. It ends the game, and it is the only option in which the hunted can regain some control.

I put the hammer and nails back into the front closet, peeked in to see Kathy working on some carrots, and went back outside. I followed the same route around the house. I used the pruning saw on the thicker branches and the trimmer on the thinner stuff. I left a trail of trimmings. I began to sweat and wished my shirt was not serving as a cover for my thirty-eight. It was not easy work. I trimmed and sweated and cut my way around to the west. Kathy came out and handed me a Bud Light.

"I put it in the freezer," she said. "I hope it's cold enough." She waited and gave me eyes which hoped it was cold enough.

I sipped and then drank. "This is great," I said. "Perfect." It was. I drank half of it and set it aside and deliberately attacked the nearby bush. She hesitated, and went inside. I eased my attack on the bush and thought about her kiss and her legs and the jiggle, then drank the rest of the beer and went at the bushes again. Near the corner I glanced around, saw no one, and pulled the soaked shirt over my head and draped it across a trimmed bush.

"Half down and half to go," I said to the house. It said nothing. The sun beat on me as I worked my way back along the long side.

At the kitchen window I looked in and she was not there. I went back to the previous window which led to the bathroom and heard her stirring behind the plastic curtain. I worked at the bushes again. Kathy came to the kitchen window and scratched on the screen.

"Another beer?"

"Later, when I'm finished," I said. "Thank you, though."

I finished soon and raked the trimmed branches into piles at the building's four corners. There was a small brush pile at the lawn's southern edge, under an aged pine. I deposited the trimmings there.

When finished I went inside, locked and closed the back door, and went to the porch and sat in the breeze and sipped another Bud. I was drenched in my own sweat, but it felt good. I wondered whether the Tigers' pitching staff held true to the team's recent road fatigue. Probably tired of carrying all that money. I thought about calling Patty, but realized she did not yet have enough time to make any calls. The smell from the crockpot somehow made its way against the breeze to the porch and urged me to think about food, but I was not hungry. I eased the Bud down, locked the front door, and tip-toed quietly to the bathroom.

I tried the water and it came out hot almost immediately. I disrobed and adjusted the water to almost cold and got in. I sudsed up and let the rinse wash over me for a couple minutes. I had about finished washing my hair when Kathy stepped into the shower behind me.

"Stop being so god-damned bashful," she said.

Kathy yanked my lips down to her lips and kissed me while the water ran down our faces. My bruised ribs were in for a surprise.

FIVE

I awoke to find us cupped together like spoons in her bed. The evening's cooled breeze floated from the window and passed over us and out of the room. Kathy's head rested on my right arm. She slept. I kissed her shoulder and eased my arm from under her and stepped from the bed. She didn't stir.

Dressed in jeans and a shirt I sat on the porch and thought about a cigarette. The sun was low, spilling long shadows across the lawn. A squirrel carried his booty from somewhere north and bounded across the grass, disappearing in the trees. On the lake a color-ful sailboat tacked gently and slid along to the north-west. The sounds of playing children drifted from below the hill, brought by the gusty little breeze which went through the pines with a hush. It was good.

My feet were propped on another chair. The air passed by. The pistol made a bulge in my pocket. A reminder of roles. Somewhere out there was Samuel D. Pendergrass.

Duty beckoned.

The hour neared eight o'clock when I dialed Patty's home. She answered the third ring.

"You cause me a lot of grief, Mallory," she said. "I've got my own work, you know."

"I give you interesting things to teethe your legal mind on, and this is your appreciation."

"Screw you," she said. "I got the dope here. Take notes."

"Okay," I said.

"This guy Pendergrass was indicted on nine counts of loan fraud down there," Patty said. "They could have produced more, but nine was enough. They say. He is apparently the owner or chief executive officer in an outfit called Vendtronics. Vendtronics supplies vending machines—cigarettes, candies, and whatnot—to bars, along with things like pool tables and other goodies."

"Standard stuff."

"I thought so. Anyway, the outfit also has some sort of relationship with a beer distributor. The sys-tem works this way: Vendtronics loans money to bar owners who are just getting started, as well as some established types, for remodeling and updating of equipment, parking lots, signs, and whatever the bars need. The interest rate is low, lower than they'll get anywhere else. But the stickler is that part of the loan deal is that the bar owner must obtain his vending machines, pool tables, and beer from Vendtronics, or associated outfits, and—get this—must use the Vendtronics remodelers. It is a nice deal, all the way around. Am I boring you?"

I said, "Vendtronics works the way hundreds of operations work. Must be a catch."

"I think the catch is that the federal boys—these are federal indictments by the way—are on this get-the-mob kick. I wasn't told as much, but it makes sense."

"How?"

"The loan fraud charges are connected with some sort of restraint of trade law," she said. "I'd have to dig into the federal statutes to make sure, but apparently what happened was that Pendergrass started the business with some mob money and the feds are pressuring Pendergrass in order to put pressure on the mob. They contend that his loan procedure restrains interstate trade of goods."

"Hard to figure," I said. "Companies do that everywhere."

"Well, this federal attorney—he suggested I meet him in Detroit for a few drinks—mentioned the words 'test case' twice as he talked. Said the investigation began when Pendergrass started to foreclose on some delinquent loans. He's not done that before and apparently he has over-stepped the bounds of not only his contracts but also some other stuff. When a few bar owners got stiff-necked about it, someone busted up their establishments."

"Pendergrass."

"Or his friends," she said. "One owner ended up in intensive care talking to the feds who were anxious to listen. Things got rough."

"How rough?"

"Someone broke his legs. I didn't think they did that, really."

"So, the feds tighten the screws on Pendergrass who might be able to enlighten the feds on the mob," I said. "Nice justice system."

"I'm not defending it," she said. "Just reporting it."

"So, where's Pendergrass now?"

"Well, here's where it gets more interesting." She paused for effect. "He's got some background you might be interested in knowing. He is a former Green Beret instructor, spent four years in Vietnam, went to work in Los Angeles for an electronics company as a security expert—right up your alley—and then appeared in Indiana four years ago running this company. That's about all the feds would give me."

"Description?"

"In a minute, Mallory," she said. "That's across the room. About this client, Katherine Elizabeth Whitman. Wouldn't say much. Said she's a witness, more or less. Pretty tight-lipped about her. Did say she worked for Pendergrass at one time and had apparently been pretty chummy. Lived together for a while. But, he said little. He didn't ask where she was."

"Good, although a call from Michigan ought to tell him something."

"The description," she said, putting the phone down with a clunk. I could hear her walk across the floor, stop, rustle some papers, and return. "He's six-two, two hundred pounds, dark brown hair, traditional cut, brown eyes, sometimes has a mustache, one distinguishing feature. He has a bullet-wound scar on the outside of his right leg just above the knee. Vietnam."

"Big, handsome fella," I said.

"Two Bronze Stars," she said. "War hero. Born in

Edna Mills, Indiana. Farm boy. Hardly a dog-killer type."

"You could be right," I said.

"Graduate of Indiana University and got an MBA at USC following the war," she said. "Got all this from his former employer in LA. Told them I was a reporter and on a deadline and that he had been killed in an auto accident."

"Crafty."

"I get training in deceit," she said. "A detective works next door and gets information that way. I pick up a little here and there."

"The finer points."

"Those too. Listen, I've got to run. Going to see some clients tonight, possible class action suit. Might get Pendergrass' military record through a source in the morning. Maybe others will call me back. You might call me tomorrow to see if I have anything."

"Hope your clients have money."

"They don't."

"Of course."

"Does yours?"

"Yeah," I said. "Some."

"Good," Patty said. "She can pay for all those phone calls today."

"Give me a bill."

"You fool," she said. "I used your office phone."

"You learn quickly."

"I smart girl," she said.

There was silence.

"Be careful," Patty said. "Remember what Gene Pitney said about when two men go out to face each other."

"I'll be careful."

After the call, I rechecked both doors, closed a couple windows against the draft, pulled their curtains, and returned to both doors to turn on the outside lights. I checked the pistol now secured to my belt and made sure it was loaded.

Ready.

The smell from the crockpot filled the cottage. I got a little hungry. I peeked inside. The chops could wait.

There was a radio on the kitchen counter and I turned it on low, finding the Tiger broadcast. The Tigers were in Boston for a three-game series. Second inning.

The refrigerator seemed rather full. I pulled out a head of lettuce, carrot, green bell pepper, celery, green olives, several radishes, and scallions. Kathy had purchased brown mustard, and I put that on the counter, too, along with a lemon. Kathy had hustled around the produce department more than I had noticed.

Detroit first baseman Darrell Evans was at bat with two on. He fouled one deep to left. Just a long strike, they say. Intimidating.

I sorted through the pots, pans, and dishes in the cupboard and removed a big wooden salad bowl hollowed out from years of use. I cut the lettuce and began to add the other ingredients.

Evans swung at the next pitch and put it thirty feet beyond the right field fence. The Tigers were now ahead, six zip.

"Take that, Boston," I said.

The private detecting situation had begun to make more sense. Assuming the syndicate had seeded Pendergrass, the syndicate would want a healthy return unincumbered by legal entanglements. Meanwhile, Pendergrass gets a little low on money, falls behind on syndicate payments, and calls in a few marginal loans. Some politically ambitious U.S. attorney notices this while also looking for a test case. What better place to test this than in the comfort of the Bible Belt? The feds indict him and use, among others, a former employee and lover for evidence.

I thought about it. Like a Margerita without salt, the picture lacked something. A former Super Soldier, handsome lover, big shot in business circles attacks a woman in U.S. District Court and threatens her once he is released. Kills her dog.

A third-rate television plot.

Kathy had purchased a small jar of salad oil and it took me five minutes to find it. It was behind the small bottle of wine vinegar she bought. I measured out the oil, vinegar, and lemon juice into a bottle and added a smear of mustard. I shook it until the ingredients mixed. I tasted it. The salad dressing would do.

Galloping Gourmet, be warned.

I set the table at the edge of the living room and opened the wine Kathy bought. I went outside, locked the door behind me, and slowly circled the house. An occasional car passed by on the road below. The VanJohnson family, if there was one, watched television. The mosquitoes were out in mere scouting force due to the continuing breeze.

Back inside I went into the bedroom. Kathy was on her stomach, the sheet up to her waist, revealing a beautiful back with a tan hint of a two-piece. I kissed her between the shoulder blades. She stirred and settled again.

I ran my tongue down her spine. Then I blew on the trail. She had to roll over.

"Hummph," she said.

"Din-din."

She said, "Yummie."

She rolled out of bed and dressed. I felt a little embarrassment as I watched her, but watched anyway. She went into the bathroom and I hung around the table until she reappeared. She brought the crockpot over and we dished out what we wanted. The room echoed with the sounds of metal utensils colliding with stoneware. I longed for the sound of conversation, but could not think of anything appropriate to say. Kathy couldn't either.

Maybe this would have been the result if we had

gotten married. I thought about it. Perhaps she thought of the same thing. I considered talking about that.

Eventually Kathy put her fork down, looked across the table until I gave her my attention, and said, "I feel kind of out of place, out of sync." She reached across the table and touched my hand for emphasis.

"Me too."

"You are so much the same," she said. "So different."

"You too." The conversational wizard.

She tried a forkfull of carrots. I wanted a fork of pork chop, but it would be difficult to cut using one hand. I speared a chunk of lettuce and eyed the chop.

"I'm sorry I brought you into this," she said. She squeezed my hand and let it go. I cut the chop and made a couple of extra bite-sized pieces just in case the handicap returned.

"I'm not sorry," I said. "Always curious about where you went, what happened to you."

"I'll give you the history, if you want it," she said.

"No, it doesn't matter. Now that I know you're okay."

She seemed to have an inner laugh. "I guess I am okay," she said. She ate some salad. "Good dressing. The Grey Poupon people would be proud of you."

"Maybe they could put me in their next ad," I said. "I could be driving along, Smith and Wesson in one hand, and pull up to another car containing a private eye. He'd be preparing a salad. I'd tap his window with the gun barrel and say—"

"Please," she said, and shook her head. She said nothing more and went back to the salad.

"I'm a private investigator, Kathy," I said. "I carry a gun. People hire me because they are in trouble and need my help. It is what I am. Right now, that is what I am. You hired me."

"I know that."

"Yes, but it would be easier if you acted more like a client. Told me what the problem is. Put details into the sketch." I put some chop and some potato into my mouth. Perhaps before the evening ended I could wander next door and ruin the VanJohnson evening too.

"Be easier if you acted like a private eye instead of a man on the make," she said.

I said nothing. I ate the chop, salad, and potato and chewed it all carefully and thoroughly and wished I could go outside and take a walk.

She put her fork down and looked at me. "I'm sorry," she said. "That was uncalled for. Out of place. I think I am very, very tired."

SIX

She washed, I dried. The Detroit Tigers held Boston long enough to put one in the win column. The losing streak was over.

Kathy watched television, catching a late night movie from Green Bay. I read two chapters in a book Patty gave me about macho men in motion pictures and how that image was eroding the potential of both men and women. She told the graduate student in me to read it.

I was thinking about Patty and graduate school when Kathy switched off the television. She shrugged to show me her fatigue as she walked into her bedroom. The door shut quietly with a small click.

The next chapter addressed the private eye image in motion pictures. I tried to stay awake for it, but I grew tired. I put the book on the floor, pulled the chain on the light near the couch, and must have gone to sleep almost immediately.

I dreamed of being alone on a beach on a bright, still day. The water lay there like a pool of mercury. The silence was a little unnerving, so I welcomed the

sound of a screen being cut and torn to afford someone the opportunity to put a hand through the new
opening. It seemed out of place on the beach. The
nearest building was hundreds of yards inland. As I
searched for the sound's source, I began to awaken.

I was awake by the time I heard the thud of something small and heavy tumbling across the wood floor.

They say that if you place a sheet of paper to the
side of a stick of dynamite, you direct much of the
explosion's force in the other direction. Such is the
nature of explosions. While thinking of that, I used
my right hand to shove the wooden trunk across the
room toward whatever came through the window.
That action, coupled with my coiled feet against the
front of the couch, offered enough leverage to propel
me across the room. I landed on a throw rug, skidded past the bathroom door, and came to rest at Kathy's
bedroom door.

She opened it.

I yelled, "Get down."

I bent her at the knees with a right arm tackle. She
sank backward into the bedroom. I rolled so as to
protect her from the blast.

There was no blast. Within seconds I could smell
the tear gas, then I heard the hiss of the tear gas
grenade as it discharged into the living room.

"What's that smell?" Kathy said.

I crawled into the bedroom and shut the door. Kathy
was standing up and I guided her off another throw
rug and wedged the rug against the door.

"Tear gas," I said.

She was already rubbing her eyes. I grasped her
wrists, jerked her hand from her eyes, and towed her
to the bed.

"Breath through the blankets," I said. "Don't rub
your eyes."

"Let's get out—"

"DO IT." I shoved her onto the bed. She covered

her head.

My eyes began to feel the gas and there was nothing I could do about it. They would shut. I would cough. My sinuses would be a mess, and so would I. Pendergrass had arrived.

I shut the window, then thought better of it. He could as easily throw another grenade into the room with the window closed as he could with it open. Broken glass would only add to the mess.

I leaned against the wall opposite the window and waited. Before I lost control of my eyes, I pointed the pistol at the open window. I would fire at the first sound of screen tearing. I could also shoot at the door if I heard that moving.

I pulled the hammer back and waited for either sound. Soon a siren broke the silence. It was miles distant, but the still night air carried the approaching screech very well.

SEVEN

A small crowd of vacationers gathered along the road. They huddled against the night chill and mixed smells of tanning lotions, sun burn ointments, and cigarette smoke. Deputy McLaughlin, who had arrived first, kept the tourists at the proper distance and assured them war had not broken out in Vacationland. He knew his duty.

I was chatting with Deputy Pollak. Pollak had arrived moments after McLaughlin parked his cruiser behind my Chevy. McLaughlin then met me as I staggered out the back door. Pollak was demanding to talk with Kathy Whitman and I was telling him he would not be doing that tonight. I knew my duty, too.

"God damned PIs," Pollak said.

He marched back to his Ford cruiser parked on the lawn next to Kathy's car. He reached into the car and snatched the microphone and talked at it in very official tones. He watched me as if I might bolt into the darkness any second. Then he threw the mike on the front seat. Broderick Crawford.

Pollak returned.

"The sheriff'll be here in a few minutes," Pollak said. "He'll have your ass, that's for sure."

Dismissing me, Pollak walked halfway to McLaughlin and stopped. "Get those people's names," he said. "They're witnesses."

McLaughlin removed his notebook from his back pocket and found a pen in his shirt pocket. Several people strolled away into the dark. The rest began to look disinterested. Pollak came at me again.

"And I want to see the permit for that pistol, PI," he said.

"When I'm ready," I said.

We both heard the bathroom door open and feet step from there to another room. That would be Kathy going to her bedroom after taking the shower I suggested. Tear gas will itch, and the only solution is soap and water. I looked forward to it.

Pollak's eyes bored past me over my shoulder to the cottage's back door. He wanted to shove me aside and go in there, but he kept glancing at me. While tired and strained and probably looking it, I also probably did not look vulnerable. Pollak was unsure of his rights.

About the time I heard Kathy's bedroom door open again, Sheriff Frost drove silently in behind McLaughlin who, by virtue of height, had to look down at his boss, who never looked up. McLaughlin talked, pointed, and used his hands in explanation for about two minutes. Frost listened quietly. Finally, Frost said something, turned, and walked toward me.

McLaughlin urged the vacationers to return to their

cabins. The fun was over.

Frost had his hands in his pockets as he came up. He wore a pair of worn jeans and a sweatshirt.

"Morning, Emery," Pollak said. "We need to talk. This guy's uncooperative."

Frost looked at me. "Inside," Frost said.

I opened the door. Frost jerked his head to direct me ahead of him. "Make a careful circle of the house," Frost told Pollak. "See if you find anything."

I went in. Frost followed. We found Kathy sponging down the kitchen.

"Good morning, Miss Whitman," the sheriff said.

"Sheriff," she said.

Frost went into the living room, glanced around, and stopped at the discharged gas grenade. With his foot he nudged the trunk away to afford a better look. He removed his right hand from his pocket and examined the cut in the screen. From there he observed the cut screen on the porch door. Pollak went by outside, poking his flashlight beam here and there around the cottage.

Frost strolled back.

"As I understand it," he said, "someone cut the outside screen, unlocked the screen door, and entered the porch. From there he, or she, cut the screen here and dropped a tear gas grenade into the room. You were asleep on the couch here"—Frost gestured to the couch with his eyes—"and you thought it might be an explosive device. You fled the room, in a hurry, shoving the trunk over there. The two of you holed up in the bedroom until help arrived."

Kathy was going to say something and I held up a hand and she said nothing.

"Mrs. VanJohnson, who lives next door, heard someone run through the yard, someone heavy and moving quickly. She heard someone yell 'get down' and then she saw the front outside light suddenly go out. That's when she called us. Okay so far?"

I nodded.

Frost poked the tear gas canister with his right toe. "I don't suppose there's a fingerprint on it, do you Mallory?"

"I doubt it."

Kathy said, "Your deputy took a picture of it."

Frost looked at me.

"Pollak," I said.

Frost shrugged. "Just thorough police work," he said, leaning over and picking up the grenade. He examined it under the table lamp. "I doubt this will help much, but ATF might get all aflutter over it."

He showed it to me and with his thumb noted the small black number painted on the military green at the base.

Kathy looked at me. "Stuart, would you and the sheriff like some coffee?"

"I'd like that," Frost said. "But don't make it just for me. I should be getting along anyway."

"Coming right up," she said, disappearing into the kitchen. Frost nodded his head toward the porch and stepped out there. I followed.

When we were on the porch, he said, "Seems someone went to a lot of trouble to drive you out of the house and into the dark, perhaps with tears running from your eyes. Blind, defenseless."

I nodded.

"Mind telling me what this is about, Mallory? I'm just itching to know why tear gas is floating around Mason County."

"Katherine's life has been threatened by a man from Indiana, man by the name of Samuel Pendergrass," I said. "She hired me to protect her. I'm an old friend. Apparently he found her."

Frost set the grenade canister on a small end table and looked at it. "You're certainly brief," he said, bringing out a pen and a small notebook and sitting in one of the wicker chairs. "I need a few details."

"I'm a little short on details myself, sheriff." I sat in another wicker chair. "He's been indicted in Indianapolis on some federal charges in connection with some loans. He operates a company which puts vending machines in bars and apparently loans money for rehabilitation, modernizing, and whatnot, with typical strings attached. Feds charged him with restraint of trade or something in an attempt to put pressure on him because they believe he was seeded by the syndicate." I glanced toward the kitchen, the source of coffee-making sounds. "She testified against him, apparently without his permission."

Frost sucked his teeth and finished a few lines of notes. "The mob," he said. "Nice of you to bring it to me."

"Only the tear gas."

"So far."

A car horn beeped several times in the distance. A second car responded. I could see Frost wince in the dark.

"She told me very little of that, sheriff," I said. "I got it from elsewhere. She's said very little."

"Holding something back."

I nodded.

"You'll get to the bottom of this?"

"That's my job."

Frost completed another note and leaned toward me from the porch's shadows.

"It's important," he said. "I've got a felony or two here. I don't like to ignore them. If I don't think you'll look into this, I'll ease you both into my cruiser and we can go to my office and talk well into the morning there."

"I'll handle it."

The sheriff leaned back into the shadows. "I'd like that."

Kathy appeared and set three cups of coffee on the little table. Each took one. Kathy sat in a third chair.

The wicker squeaked. The coffee tasted good.

Frost slurped his coffee in the darkness. I wrapped my hands around my cup and looked at the cut screen. Kathy held her's near her lips and seemed to be looking at me.

"We're wondering what this is about, Kathy," I said.

She sipped her coffee, then put it on the table. She twisted her chair so that it almost faced Frost. Her fallen hair concealed her face from me.

"Sam Pendergrass and I were once lovers," she told Frost. "Sam is a big, strong man, and I needed one at the time. We eventually parted. I left him, but not before I went to work for his company, Vendtronics. My main job was simply a coordinator, office manager. I kept track of who did what, emergencies, work logs, work requests, and so forth. But I also kept the books. Two sets."

"One for taxes and one for in-house," I said.

"Yes," she said. "Vending machines take in a lot of cash. Easy to skim. I'm told it is common practice, although I don't really know. Anyway, we needed an accurate total to know who got what."

Kathy slipped from the wicker chair and leaned over me and closed the two screen windows at the porch's end. Her arm and breast brushed my cheek. Her scent coiled in the swirl of air she left me.

"Sam got drunk one night and hit me a few times," she said from her chair. "Things were not going well for him, so he took it out on me. Short on money again or something. There were other things worrying him, too. He was laundering money through Vendtronics for some crime bosses."

She looked at me.

"Of course," Frost said. "Who?"

She laughed. "Sam didn't talk to me about it much, so I just don't know, Sheriff," she told him. "And I'm glad I don't know."

We nodded in the dark. I was beginning to be able

to see Frost's eyes peering from a sketchy outline. He was watching me.

"Anyway, I copied the books. The books were in a word processing system, not in accountant's ledgers. Everything was stored on floppies. Inventory, employee records, cash flow, loan payments, even his personal finances. Sam fell in love with the computer at some conference and decided to put everything on it. He was probably right. It was convenient. Anyway, I made a copy of all his records and put it on two of the floppies. I also made a printout in case I couldn't find the right computer program when I needed it. That was my only protection. And then I quit."

I stirred. "When was that?"

"Three months ago, just before Easter."

"He know you copied the records?"

"Does now," she said.

"He wants the copies back, I suspect," Frost said.

"He wants me dead," Kathy said, standing and leaning against the closed screens between Frost and me. "That's why I ran to Stuart. I'm the key witness against Sam. If you use floppies and printouts in court, you need someone to testify about their authenticity."

"Makes sense," Frost said. "Never encountered using such records in a court case. Ought to be a precedent somewhere."

I squirmed in my wicker seat. "Let me do some guessing," I said. "The U.S. attorneys offered amnesty for your testimony. They threatened to charge you for being a part of the operation."

"Yes."

"So they pressure you in order to pressure Pendergrass in order to pressure the syndicate. If you don't fold, then Pendergrass is in trouble. If Pendergrass is vulnerable, then the mob stands to be threatened."

"That's how they explained it," she said.

Frost said nothing. He watched.

"Did you keep an extra copy of the records—a photocopy or something—for yourself?"

She grinned. "I kept the whole thing for myself. I gave them a photocopy. I have to produce the print-out and floppies for court."

"Odd," Frost said. "Why didn't they keep the records?"

"They wanted them, but I threatened to burn them if they gave me a bad time."

I said, "What if you gave the records back to Pendergrass?"

"I'm not sure I should hear this," Frost said. He finished his coffee in one gulp and stood. "I'm beginning not to be even sure I heard what you suggested at all. My hearing is not as good as it once was. Thanks for the coffee, Katherine."

"I'll see you out," I said.

"You're welcome, Sheriff."

"I know the way, Mallory."

"I need to lock the door behind you," I said.

Frost was moving away. "Mallory, the door has one of those cute little knobs on it so that I can lock it on the way out. But this will give me a chance to ask one more probing question."

I caught him at the door. He was looking at the night insects circling the light bulb.

"Mrs. VanJohnson said this light went out," Frost said. "It isn't."

"Whoever was out there turned it loose in the socket," I said. "I tightened it."

Frost stepped outside and took a deep breath and looked back at me through the screen door.

"I hope you know you've got your hands full," he said, turning the tear gas canister over in his hands. "Not much makes sense. I wish you'd take your show to another county."

"Good night, Sheriff."

He was on his way to his car and said something I could not hear. I probably didn't need to hear it.

I found Kathy in the same place we'd left her.

"Mind getting more coffee, Stuart?" she said.

I got the coffee pot and made sure the door was locked. Outside Frost was getting into his unmarked car. Pollak climbed into his cruiser. McLaughlin was talking to the sheriff. Pollak backed and left.

I brought the pot to the porch and filled both cups. She sat in the chair next to mine. Our knees touched.

"I won't give the records to Sam," she said.

"Okay," I said.

"Okay?"

"Sure."

"But you suggested it."

"Experimenting with possibilities."

"I didn't figure you'd be someone to back down," she said. "I need your help."

McLaughlin drove his cruiser out of sight.

"You seem to be awfully mad at Sam."

Kathy took her time responding. "He killed my dog."

And he beat her up.

EIGHT

Gusts of wind burst through the screened porch and elbowed their way past the wicker furniture and into the cottage. They came from a fine wind, as winds go, and I could smell the moisture. High in the sky, the sun slipped in and out of thick clouds, casting swift, deep blue shadows in the lake. I looked for my watch and found it on the floor next to the wicker couch where I woke up. Nearly noon. After a few seconds, I also found my gun where I had shoved it under the couch. Stuart Mallory, private detective, loser of guns.

The fresh, sensual air felt good. I was thinking about peeking into Kathy's bedroom when I spotted her in the corner of the porch. With her legs coiled under her, she sat with her arms folded, gazing toward Hamlin Lake, toward the Nordhouse Dunes to the north and probably well beyond them. I had to look to make sure she was breathing.

Coffee aroma engulfed me as I headed toward the bathroom. The breeze had robbed me of those odors when I was in the living room. I made a side trip to the kitchen and poured a cup. Since it was not hot, I gulped it down, hoping it would usher me into the church of the living. In the bathroom I showered again, although I showered the tear gas powder off about dawn.

This shower was a wake-up call to my psyche.

Carrying the second cup of coffee—which someone had warmed in the meanwhile—I returned to the porch through what was obviously a tidy living room and rearranged since last night. Kathy was in the same place, although in front of her were a cup of coffee and several donuts. I took two donuts and picked a seat with a view of Kathy's profile and Hamlin Lake.

There were no boats on the lake. The wind had begun to whip the waters into an unfriendly frenzy, a particularly dangerous condition for shallow water. Only an unwary tourist or a South Bend fisherman would venture upon the water on a day like that. I guessed one would wash up before dinner time.

"Good morning," I said.

She uncoiled and stood, covering the short distance between us with silent effort. She rested one hand on the back of my head and kissed me on the forehead.

"Be right back," she said, and she went into the cottage.

She left her scent behind again.

I ate a donut.

Kathy returned and handed me a large brown envelope thick with contents. She coiled back into the corner couch and faced me.

"The second set of books," I said.

She nodded.

"Explain."

Kathy looked into her lap and picked at her fingernail. It is an act of playing for time as good as lighting a cigarette. For Kathy, it was better.

Then she found a better one. She said, "Let me get the coffee. Be right back."

I put down the envelope and studied the other donut. Studying makes it last longer. Kathy returned and filled my cup and set an insulated pitcher of coffee on the aptly named table between us. She coiled again. The wind toyed with her hair. She examined her fingernail. I ate the other donut. A bird, probably a robin, sang in the background. I presume the electricity surged through the cottage.

She shrugged and looked at me. "I would rather you have those records," Kathy said. "Do with them as you see necessary. I trust you."

"Okay," I said. "I have a suggestion too." It was my turn to drag it out. I reached for another donut, this one a jelly-filled item, and pondered which edge to attack first.

"Yes?"

"It is difficult to be detecting when there is little detecting to do," I said. "There is now detecting to do. I can't do it while I'm protecting you."

"We could stay here," she said. "We have plenty of time. I can afford to keep you here, and I can't think of anyone I would rather spend money on."

I shook my head. "No. I need to get you out of harm's way for a while so I can work."

Kathy's gaze was over my shoulder. "So many years ago. Often I wish things had turned out different."

I reached out and squeezed her hand.

"So do I sometimes."

"There's still hope," she said. "We could pack up

and leave, go anywhere. Now. I'll pay you."

I shook my head again. "We'll talk about it later. But first, we have a problem to deal with. We'll stay the night and figure things out. We're very visible here. And vulnerable. I don't like that."

She smiled. "I remember. You don't like having to react to others."

"I don't. This is passive. I want to be active."

"A warrior, not a guard."

I nodded.

Her face darkened a little. "You and he have something in common, anyway," she said.

I let it go.

The third donut was crying out to me, but I felt dull, listless, and rock-like. It seemed too early in the morning—though it was around noon—to have three donuts. I left it on the plate.

"How does an omelet sound?" Kathy said.

"I don't know," I said. "I never heard one."

She jumped up and danced sideways across the porch. "Ya-ta, ta-ta, ta-ta..." The stage exit routine.

I smiled, but I continued to picture Pendergrass sitting out there somewhere enjoying another sort of joke.

"Well," said Kathy as she strutted back on stage. "You're getting an omelet, like it or not."

"I like it."

"With cheese?"

"And some green peppers too?"

"Okay."

"Maybe some onions?"

"You want a Denver omelet," she said.

I said, "In Denver they call it a Western omelet."

"In Brussels, what do they call Brussels sprouts?"

"Little cabbages," I said. "I'd prefer not having any little cabbages in my omelet."

"No, Brussels sprouts."

"None of those, either."

She was walking past me and I grabbed her arm and she bounced effortlessly into my lap. She coiled as before, except this time she coiled around me. I squeezed her and we held each other tightly, shifting our hands so we had direct contact with skin.

We stayed that way for a long time. I listened to the wind in the trees and brushed my lips across her shoulder which I had bared. She breathed into my neck and occasionally sifted the hair on the back of my head.

"I want to make love again," she said. Then she kissed my neck gently, uncoiled, and went into the cottage.

I followed.

NINE

The air cleared for a few minutes before the thunderstorms arrived. Approaching from Lake Michigan, the great, dark thickness of the storms seemed to hover a bit, then slide toward the east as they adjusted to the land.

The rains came. They came at us in wide, nasty sheets and pounded the cottage. It would have been a good time for someone to have broken in. No one would have noticed.

We took our clothes out of the dressers and put them into the suitcases. Kathy called the VanJohnsons and told them we would be gone about three days. She asked them to fix the screen and clean the building of tear gas.

Mrs. VanJohnson found the part about the tear gas very interesting. At my urging, Kathy did not elaborate. I wanted to leave the neighborhood something to talk about.

When the rain eased, I loaded the car. It went quickly.

I needed to get out of there and to work. A sense of unease had engulfed me. I scanned the trees and the neighboring homes to find the source of it, but it wasn't out there whatever it was.

I locked the front door and checked the windows. Kathy made the sandwiches and put them in the ice chest I always carried. I did not tell her I had to take a few boxes of ammunition and other trade tools from the chest in order to make room for cold beer, sandwiches, and ice.

"I hope this move works," she said as she hurried past me out of the kitchen. "I hate this moving around."

I stood in the living room and listened to the rain in the distance. The room had changed. The couch was in the same place. So was the television opposite it. But the old army trunk now served as a television stand. The table which held up the television now sat under a table lamp in the corner.

"It seemed so cluttered," Kathy said from behind me.

"Maybe you took your cue when I kicked the trunk over there," I said.

She stood beside me and held my arm. "Perhaps," she said.

I grabbed the ice chest on the way through the kitchen and put it into the back of my car. She checked the doors on her car and locked the driver's side lock. Then we left.

We circled the town on the way out to avoid the traffic and kept an eye in the rearview mirror.

"Bop, sha-bop, sha-bob," I said.

"What?" she said.

I said, "Sha-boom, sha-boom."

She shook her head a little at me, then sorted through my tapes, settling for the radio. We drove into more rain and then out again and I stopped at a gasoline station and went into a telephone booth and called Matthew Wiley. No answer. I called Patty's office.

No answer. Same with my office and Patty's home.

We headed along U.S. 10. We drove fast considering the wet conditions. I slowed down.

Kathy moved the FM dial through its paces. Every time she found a station, it faded and disappeared at the next turn. It reappeared only long enough to offer hope, then fade again.

"You won't get much here," I said.

She continued to play with the dial and I looked up and we were doing almost eighty again.

She turned the radio off and huddled in the corner. It is hard to huddle in the corner in the front of an El Camino and act as if there is no one else in the car and there is not a care in the world. She was trying, though, and I got the point.

"We are going to a little town northeast of here," I told her. "I am—"

"What's there?"

"I'm going to ask a friend if you can stay with him a while until I can straighten out this problem. His name is Matt Wiley. He's a good man, a smart man, and I think he will watch over you for a couple of days until I can do what I have to do."

Kathy huddled. She looked out the window and watched the Manistee National Forest whiz by. Her breath had fogged the glass a little.

"What's the hurry?"

We were still doing eighty. "I don't know," I said. I slowed to sixty-five. Seemed slow.

"I don't like being dumped somewhere, put in storage," she said.

"You could go back to Indianapolis," I suggested.

She huddled a bit smaller and coiled her legs under her. "You know what I mean," she said.

I eased it to seventy.

At the next little town I pulled into another station and had the attendant fill the tank, even though it would not take much. I made the same series of calls.

Same results. I got back into the car and headed east again, then turned south to Grand Rapids.

Ten miles up the highway Kathy took my Michigan road map out and asked if I would tell her where we were going. I used one hand to help her fold the map into a position to see the town. I pointed to it.

She looked at it, determining what highway we were on. She said, "Couldn't we have saved time going south directly from Hamlin?"

"Nope."

"Looks like it to me." She put the map back.

She said very little after that. I pushed a Randy Newman tape into the deck and tapped my fingers on the wheel and wished I had a cigarette. Maybe I would have to jog just to deal with nervous energy.

We took an aging road left off the highway and continued more or less south.

We made good time for the next half hour. People stay off the highway in a solid thunderstorm. There was a good one along that highway, one pushing the car from side to side. In the midst of that I remembered the coffee and poured myself a cup. After a few sips I began to feel normal.

I cleared my throat and said, "Maybe it was the experience last night and the odd sleeping hours this morning."

"Eh?"

"Our moods," I said. "Maybe it was the oddness of the night and morning that caused them."

She looked at me for a moment or two, then sighed.

"I'd like to be friends," I said.

She slid across the seat and sat next to me for a minute. She examined every pore in my face, then kissed me on the neck. "We are friends," she said. "We always have been friends. Always will be. That's why we are here together. That's why we make love so well together."

Didn't seem that simple to me.

"Stuart, we could be far better friends if you and I just split," she was saying. She ran a finger across my knuckles on the steering wheel. "I'd make it worth your while."

I drove a while. "Let's take care of this situation first, then we'll talk about it," I said.

"Promise?"

"Promise."

We turned west. The rain had eased considerably. In fact, the sky to the west looked almost tolerable. The sun would last at least another couple of hours.

Matthew Wiley was my friend in college, my comrade as a soldier, and my ally since. We had been there for one another when it was necessary and it had been necessary for both of us.

Wiley lived in a trailer along a small inland body of water called Potters Lake. He had some property at the western edge and was building a large A-frame cabin. He had been working on it two years. I had helped him through the initial steps of constructing the A-frame and I expected to be called on to do so again. I also helped Wiley carve his name into a large tree stump and then move it to within twenty feet of the gravel road he lived on.

I spotted the stump and pulled in and parked near the trailer. It seemed to be hiding among the tall pines. It needed paint. The A-frame cabin was enclosed and appeared inhabitable. I did not know which door to knock on until I got to the cabin. A sign said, "Check trailer." I did.

Signs again.

There was no one there either.

Kathy got out of the car and put her hands in her pockets and stretched with her elbows behind her. It did marvelous things for her chest.

Wiley kept a key under a loose step. I tried it in the door, but it opened without the key. Apparently rural crime was not Wiley's worry.

Kathy came up the steps and eased past me. "I need to find the bathroom," she said.

I returned the key to its hiding place and stretched. The place had not changed much. No surprise. It had only been nine months since Wiley and I had fished Potters Lake for Northern Pike and enclosed the A-frame for the winter. He intended to finish the inside during the cold months, while he was not fishing or writing.

His Bronco crouched on the south edge of the area of the forest clearing. I checked around the trailer and noticed that his boat was not tied at the ramp.

There was nothing to do but eat the sandwiches and wait. I unloaded the ice chest and brought it into the trailer. Kathy came out of the bathroom as I put the chest on the floor.

"Some place here," she said.

"I like it. I'd like to spend some real time here." I sorted through the sandwiches and selected a ham. I added a cold beer and sat at the table. I pulled the curtain back so I had a good view of the lake. I could see the driveway entrance out the other window.

The unease had not eased.

"What's that?" she said. She pointed to a stuffed fish hung on the wall over the couch.

"Northern Pike."

"Oh."

"Good ham sandwich."

"I'm not hungry."

"Okay."

Kathy stood in the middle of what passed for a living room and studied her surroundings. A trailer takes some getting used to, but Wiley's use of the available space had pretty much gone the way of a lonely bachelor. He needed a bulldozer.

Kathy studied the wall and the big desk. A crude gun rack displayed a shotgun, a military carbine, a .22 caliber plinking rifle, and two fishing rods. The desk was burdened with an array of books, papers, envelope boxes, magazines, and newspapers. Its centerpiece was a microcomputer terminal, two disk drives, a printer, and a modem. She seemed to be staring at the carbine.

I shrugged. Perhaps the rain was getting to me. Maybe the dampness. Maybe it was just worry.

Kathy ran her finger over a book on the desk and then rubbed her fingers together until something invisible escaped them.

"Matt Wiley is an old friend," I said. "We knew one another in college."

"He's a college man?"

"Graduate degrees in history, University of Michigan, and anthropology, University of Chicago," I said. "That computer isn't here to play games on."

She looked at the books some more.

"In the army, he zigged when he should have zagged. The bullet hit him near the spine. He doesn't walk real well now, but one hardly notices. He lives partly on a disabilty pension from the army, and he writes freelance articles for magazines. He's good. He writes an outdoor sports column, too, syndicated to many midwest newspapers."

"Where is he?"

"I don't know."

"Shouldn't we go somewhere and look for him?"

"Where?"

"I mean, just staying here..." She didn't finish. Instead, she subtly floated a hand through the air to indicate the trailer's interior.

"We've been here ten minutes, Kathy," I said. "Give it a little time."

"Time," she said. "Wish I had a lot of it."

"Look, Kathy," I said. "Stay here three or four days. Give me that much time to see what I can do to solve this for you. Then you can go wherever you want to go."

She sat down, then got up and looked at the chair. She sighed and sat back on the chair. For a moment she held her eyes very tightly shut and clenched her fists around the corners of the chair's arms until little white knuckles appeared.

I could hear a small outboard motor on the lake. It was not within sight, but the wind carried the sound to the trailer.

"Finish it in three days, Stuart," she said. "Please."

"I'll see what I can do."

It was Matt Wiley's motorboat and it was Wiley sitting in it, a lone figure against the little choppy waves. He eased the boat toward the dock, shut off the motor twenty feet out and stepped onto the dock unlike a man who had been shot near the lower spine.

"He's here," I said.

Tears glistened from both her cheeks. I reached down and gently rubbed the back of her neck with one hand.

"I lived in a trailer out west," she said. "I had nothing. Nothing. God, I hated it, and I swore I would never do it again. Never."

TEN

Wiley carried a string of six or seven fish. They looked like bluegill or bass and he carried the fish in one hand and his tackle box in the other as he came up the path. He noticed the El Camino but did not appear to notice. I think he saw me in the window because his eyes flashed as they moved rapidly across the trailer's length and then back to the muddy path in front of him.

He trudged up the path and, with one hand, opened a tall shed and put the box and rod into it, then continued to the trailer. Somewhere around the front of it he turned on the water and filled a bucket.

"I can't meet him like this," Kathy said, heading to the bathroom.

Wiley pounded on the side of the trailer. "Come on out," he said. "I want to show you something."

"I'll be right back," I told Kathy as she rounded the corner at the bathroom door.

Outside Wiley was heading toward the A-frame. I followed.

"I want to show you what I've done," Wiley said. "I've worked my ass off since you disappeared." He opened the door and was inside. I followed. Lights came on and his footsteps on the wooden floor echoed out of the structure. Inside I found him opening a small room on the left.

"Look in there," he said, nodding toward the hole in the floor. "Used heat pump system I got for $150 at a going out of business sale. Needed a gasket. Operates on ground heat. Had to dig a whole new basement for this damned thing to put the coil into the ground."

"Good to see you, too, Matt," I said.

Wiley stroked a carefully trimmed beard with a hand which jutted out of a rain jacket from the pages of the L.L. Bean catalog. He was thickly built and muscular.

"Well," he said, "I got my hellos all said out on the lake today because I thought you might show up. Patty called around noon."

"I've been trying to reach her this afternoon."

"You two ought to communicate more," Wiley said, closing the floor hatch.

"What did she say?"

"You know lawyers, even friendly ones," Wiley said. "Looking for you. If I see you I'm to tell you to call her and to tell you to be careful. Not much else." He was moving toward the back of the cabin. "So, be careful."

"Okay, I will."

"Use my phone."

"Matt."

"I have an extension in here," he added. He tapped the telephone with a bony finger.

"I need your help."

"Sure," he said. "Call Patty."

I walked to the telephone and dialed it. Wiley stood a few feet away with his back to me. He faced the lake through the triangular window. The view was excellent.

The phone rang at her office and at her home. No answer. Not even an answering machine as before.

"Strange," I said.

"There was something in her voice I didn't like," Wiley said. "Nervous, and she's not the nervous type."

"I have a woman with me," I said.

"Oh?"

"She's an old friend, now my client. I need someone to watch over her for two, three days so I can get her out of the mess she's in." I told him about the mess, the dog, the tear gas grenade, and Pendergrass. While I talked, Wiley lighted a cigarette and leaned against a partly constructed bookcase. The ashes made a little pile on the floor.

"Want company?" he said.

"I want to do this one myself."

"He's got to come looking for you. No choice."

"That's what I figure. I'll make it easy to find me."

"Unless he looks for you and finds Patty."

I had hoped that the fear creeping up from my stomach was unsubstantiated. Now it crawled from the stomach. Wiley understood.

There was silence. The wind blew outside and big drops of water fell from the towering pines onto the roof.

"Leave a trail," Wiley said. "It'll either make a good book or give me a way to find him if he finds you first. And I've got two books in the works already."

"I've got to go," I said. "Appreciate this."

"I'll keep the powder dry," he said.

I went outside and unlocked the back of the El Camino and removed Kathy's suitcase. I never knew what
to call the El Camino. Truck or car.

"Door locked?" Wiley said.

I was standing outside the trailer's door.

"No. Just thinking."

"Let me take that bag. You can think better if you
are not using all that energy holding the suitcase."

He opened the door and stepped inside. I followed.

"I'm Matthew Wiley," Wiley was saying somewhere
in the darkness of the trailer. "Please, call me Matt."

Wiley was bowing.

Wiley kissed her hand.

"My home is your home, what there is of it," Wiley
was saying. "I hope the next few days become memo-
rable, wondrous and loaded with palaver."

Palaver.

Kathy smiled. "Are you like this all the time?"

"Only when it rains. Under the sun I am as dull as
a raisin."

"What's the forecast?" she said.

"Rain," he said.

Wiley finally stood straight. "And, what's more, I
am an occasional decent cook. Tonight, trout almondine,
fresh from the nearby waters."

"Excuse me," I said.

"Sure," Wiley said. "I have chores outside."

Kathy moved to get her bag and I interrupted her
path.

"Questions," I said. "You typed the original note
on a typewriter. What typewriter?"

"I typed it at home, in Carmel," she said. "Before I
left. Why?"

"Just an unanswered question." She nudged me aside
and got her suitcase. I blocked her return path.

"Another question."

"Please," she said, pushing to get around.

"Why did you choose George Ackfield?"

"Why?"

"It matters."

"Who the hell is paying you, anyway?"

"Ackfield," I said.

"He was at a conference in Chicago a year ago or less," she said. "He represented some liquor service business in Michigan and was playing the trade. I met him, remembered his name. He probably doesn't remember me."

"Did Pendergrass meet him?"

"I don't know," she said. She sighed. "He could have. I see what you're driving at. No, it probably doesn't matter. Ackfield was just there like so many others trying to make contacts. He seemed new. If Sam met him, it wouldn't matter. There were so many young lawyers around it wouldn't make any difference."

"Okay."

"Okay?"

"Okay." I took her bag and carried it back to one of the bedrooms. When I returned she was still there looking at me. She looked very tired.

I kissed her on the forehead. "I'll be back," I said.

"You damned well better," she said. "We have some talking to do. You promised." She went past me to one of the rooms in the back and shut the door.

I went outside. The rain had returned, but gently. It would not dent my El Camino, whatever I might call it.

There was a whistle from the cabin and I went over. Wiley was holding the door open.

Inside Wiley pointed to the telephone. I called and got no answers.

"Where will you be if I need you?" Wiley said.

"Call my home or the office, but for no more than a few seconds. Long enough for me to understand who it is. No names."

Wiley nodded. He strolled over to the half-built

desk and extracted something from the top drawer. "One of these days I'll move everything over here," he said. He gave me a card.

In the upper left hand corner was a red symbol for the ten of Diamonds. His name was in the center. A Detroit telephone number and address sat in the corner.

"Cute," I said.

"Call it anytime, day or night," he said. "It's an answering service and a computer bulletin board all in one."

I put it into my wallet.

"I've got to go," I said, zipping my jacket against the wind and rain outside. I could hear it pelt the roof.

"I'll take good care of the lady," he said. "You take care of Patty."

"Three days," I said.

"Take your time," he said. "It doesn't look like difficult duty."

Outside I hurried to the El Camino. I backed toward the cabin, and pulled out the way I came in. In the rearview mirror I could see Wiley walking to the trailer and Kathy peering out a window.

By the time I got to the two-lane the weather had boiled down to scattered showers. A few miles more and the rain stopped entirely and, conveniently, there was a little rest area with several green picnic tables. I hit the brakes hard and skidded into the rest area, gravel scattering to the sides.

A dark brown windowless van sat at the far end. I stayed at the near end and parked so that the El Camino was pointed at the van. I got out and opened the canopy and went to work. I removed the M-1 carbine from its plastic, padded case and shoved a loaded standard five-round clip into it and jacked one round into the chamber. I put that to the side and covered it with a folded blanket. Next I unloaded my leather

boots and set them on the gate. I sat down and removed my loafers and socks.

The boots contained the thick socks I needed. I put
them on and then put the boots on. The right boot
contained a small .22 caliber automatic on the inside
calf. The left boot had a thin hunting knife. I felt a
little like Paladin when I pulled on the boots, and a
little silly.

And scared.

I closed the gate and got in and drove away. I hit
the expressway fairly soon. I found U.S. 27 and turned
south to Lansing.

ELEVEN

I took the Grand River Avenue exit and within a
block of Patty's apartment swung into a Seven-11 store
and went to the telephone booth at the side. The teen-
aged girl inside leaned into a corner and listened to
the telephone. I went inside the store and looked around.
No phone. I bought a candybar and returned to the
booth. She leaned in a second corner, still listening.

I tapped on the plexiglass window and she turned
her back to me. A veteran. I unzipped my jacket so
the pistol was visible, held up my wallet to expose
the important looking badge-type certificate and then
kicked the metal at the door's foot. She swung around.
I showed her the certificate. I frowned deeply. She
hung up and stepped out.

"Stick it," she said.

Patty answered on the second ring.

"Free this evening, lady?" I said.

"I've got news for you," she said.

"Later," I said. "Right now I have to see if your
place is being watched."

She was silent for a second. "Okay," she said.

"Hungry?"

"Just ate," she said. "But I can prepare something."

"Better yet, I'd like you to go downstairs, get into your car—your car is fixed, right?"

"Fixed is a poor description of that car."

"Okay, go down to your car, drive to the Roseville. Take Michigan Avenue. Take your time. Park in the rear. Go inside and wait. I shouldn't be long."

"I don't like this."

"I don't either, but it's the easiest way. It's possible someone's watching you to find me."

"They'll have to stand in line."

"Ready?"

"You buying?"

"Sure."

I circled the block and parked where I could see the small rear parking lot. Someone watching the house would be situated to see both sides in case she came out the front. But I knew where she would come out.

Patty stepped out of the back and walked to her car, looking damned good in jeans. She had a walk of long strides and purpose.

She swung out of the lot and drove past me. If she saw me, she didn't show it.

Five seconds after she drove by a second car fired up and pulled out of a street space and followed. It was a late model dark blue Chevy four-door with Indiana plates. I jotted the license plate down on the notepad in the console, then pulled behind the Chevy.

Some distance ahead the Chevy turned left on Michigan Avenue and headed toward downtown Lansing. I U-turned in the street and headed back to the parallel street. I needed to get to the Roseville first.

I did. I parked on a side street and hurried to the back of the Roseville. It was almost dark. I moved along the sidewalk to the dumpster at the restaurant's rear. I hoped no one would select this moment to empty the trash.

Patty pulled into the lot, hesitated, then swung toward the rear and pulled next to a white Cadillac. She got out. As she did, the blue Chevy slid into the lot and parked toward the front. A man inside seemed to be fiddling with his coat on the seat. Patty would have to walk by the Chevy on her way to the restaurant. I did not like the setup.

Patty walked past the Chevy and then around the building and out of sight to the side door.

The Chevy's engine stopped. The man leaned back and waited. I put the pistol away. A couple walked arm and arm from where Patty went and walked into the lot and got into a Datsun 300Z. The car's headlights flashed past the man in the Chevy just for a moment as it swung around and left on the side street.

The man looked young. He lit a cigarette and opened the window about halfway. He puffed three times before I put my pistol barrel through the window and nudged it firmly against the skin on his neck just behind his left ear.

"Wha—?" he said.

"Hand me the keys."

"What the hell?"

I jutted the cold barrel deep into the flesh of his neck. His head bobbed. His right arm reached for the keys.

"Toss 'em out the window," I said.

He did. The keys hit the side of a black Ford and fell to the ground. As he tossed I opened the back door and was inside with the door shut with the pistol back into his neck before the keys hit concrete.

"Hands on the steering wheel," I said. He put them there. I twisted the rear view mirror so he had a good view of the floor.

I patted him down with my free arm and took the automatic from his belt. I stuck it under my belt.

"You're going to be a sorry ass," he said.

I cocked the pistol. He heard the click.

"Now," I said. "I want your wallet. Which pocket?"

"Find it yourself."

With the ball of my left palm I popped him on the back of the skull. His head bobbed forward and then back.

"Left pocket, rear," he said.

I reached down and removed it. He helped by leaning forward.

His Indiana driver's license said he was Bernard Hackett. He was 27 and had brown eyes, brown hair, and about 220 pounds. I tossed the wallet on the front seat.

"Why you following the lady, Bernie?"

He knotted his hands into fists, but kept them on the wheel. Maybe he was relieved this was not just a robbery.

"Suck ass," he said.

He would be waiting for that little pop on the head again. I could feel his neck muscles brace for the blow. His right arm tensed. He was recovered enough now to make a stab at dealing with me.

"Bernie, remember I have a pistol," I said. "It is in your neck, hammer cocked. It won't take much effort—even accidental effort—to blow your face onto the dashboard. Remember that as you think about what you are thinking about. I'm just not worth dying for."

Then I hit him. I used a lot of strength. Sure enough, he had relaxed. His face hit the leading edge of the steering wheel and came back into position. He went, "Ahhh."

"Bernie?"

He breathed hard. He sniffled a little. I think his nose was bleeding.

"You Mallory?"

"I'm the man who wants to know why you are following the woman."

"I'm bleeding, for Christ's sake," Bernie said. "You've

got to know why we're here."

I did.

"That's right, Bernie," I said. I removed a handkerchief from my pocket and held it just over his left shoulder. "Slowly, with your left hand, take this." Bernie took it and held it under his nose.

"Ahhh," he said.

"Deliver a message to Pendergrass," I said. "Tell him he has to deal with me and with me only. Tell him I have what he wants. Got it so far?"

He nodded.

"Tell him he is to go to the Lansing airport tonight. Ten o'clock. I'll call there for him and have him paged. We'll arrange a meeting."

Bernie tossed the handkerchief back over his right shoulder. It fell against my chest. It looked bloody.

"Stick it," Bernie said.

"I'm going to keep your automatic, Bernie," I said. "You understand. I'm going to get out of the car. I want your hands to stay on the steering wheel for at least one minute. Then you can do what you wish." While he was thinking about it, I got out of the car. I left the right rear door open behind me. I walked to the restaurant while keeping an eye on the Chevy. Bernie didn't move.

It was a Friday night in the Roseville. A lot of people would be eating and dancing. The Roseville was unusual for the Friday night drinking crowd because it was patterned after the late 1930s. Michael Jackson posters did not cover the walls. The jukebox pumped something soft. Instead of a rock guitar, big bands filled the air. The dance room moved to "Skylark."

Trends being what they are today, it probably wouldn't last another six months before sliding into bankruptcy.

Patty sat near the front window and smoked a cigarette. Two of her cigarette butts peeked from the ashtray. She had a drink in front of her and two glasses of water. A photo of downtown Detroit in 1938 hung on the wall at the table's side, but the table itself had a good view of the front street. I sat down.

"Nice to have you back in town, Mallory," she said. "Pistol in your belt. Blood on your shirt. Dressy. A fashion plate."

I looked. Some of Bernie's blood from the hand-kerchief had soaked into the shirt. I closed the jacket and the blood disappeared. So did Bernie's automatic.

"Hi."

"Things were so dull," she said. "Now you're back, I get followed, you have one of your business sessions in the parking lot, and you dash in with such flashy colors splashed on your shirt." She sipped the drink.

"I'll tell you all about it," I said and picked up the menu.

"You needn't explain," Patty said. "I'll probably read about it in the State Journal tomorrow."

I checked my watch. It was nearly 8:30. The waitress came over and I ordered a BLT on whole wheat and coffee. She took the menu with her.

"You were being followed," I said.

"Blue Chevy," she said. "I saw him. The skills I learn from you make me so versatile."

"They want to find me," I said, trying to ignore the growing conversational tone. "They need to get Pendergrass' financial records."

"Ahhh," she said, raising a finger in the air.

"I let the fellow outside know where I can be found later," I said.

She indicated my chest with her finger. "I'll bet he got the message right."

I nodded.

"I'm trying to be light-hearted about this, Mallory," she said. "I'm real crazy about splattered blood on your shirt, and this macho display. I'm not pleased to hear you are in danger and I'm not even sure I have the right to be concerned."

"You do."

"So, tell me what has happened since you left," she said. "I've done what you asked tonight. Fill me in."

The BLT arrived. I took one bite and one sip of coffee and told Patty about Katherine Whitman, Emery Frost, and the tear gas grenade. I told her where I left Kathy and that Wiley was concerned about the tone of her call. I told her my thinking about Pendergrass' next move and that I had to know whether her apartment was being watched.

Patty signaled the waitress for another drink. I had finished my sandwich and I pointed to my almost empty coffee cup. The waitress seemed to understand.

"Bothers me about my apartment being watched," she said.

"It should," I said. "It means they got smart and figured the proximity of your office to mine would tie you to me or, more likely, the attorney or someone else you talked to in Indianapolis is loose-lipped and mentioned your name to someone else."

The waitress filled my cup and left another drink for Patty.

"Well," Patty said. "It's worse. Just before I went to lunch today, a man came to see me." She reached into her purse for a card and pushed it across the table toward me. Howard F. Benson, attorney at law. Detroit.

I shook my head. "Don't know him."

"He wants to know you," she said. "He had a three-piece suit that would cost $1,000. On sale. He didn't carry a briefcase, someone carried it for him. He oozed authority. The essence of self-confidence. He asked me nothing. He stayed only five minutes and he looked right through me as though I wasn't there." She shivered. "All he had to say was that he very much intends to see you on the matter of your current case.

That's what he called it, your 'current case.' He instructed me to get in touch with you immediately and see that you contacted him."

"Hummm."

"He ignored anything I had to say about not being your messenger or to leave a message next door," Patty said. "He acted as though I wasn't there."

"No threats?"

"His whole presence was a threat," she said. "He knew too damned much and he knew that I knew it. He was right, though. I scrambled to get in touch with you."

I reached across the table and tried to take her hand. She moved it just enough to skirt my attempt.

"I'm sorry about this, Patty," I said.

She looked through the window into the darkness of the street. A couple of cars went by. I ran my finger down the back of her left hand. She did not move it away.

"I'm sorry I got you in the middle of this," I said.

She looked at her drink and finally took a strong sip of it. "Oh, Mallory," she said.

She grabbed her drink with both hands and looked up at me. "Let me explain something to you."

"If I can—"

"Don't interrupt me," she said. "I've had some time to think today. Now I have more to think about, and more drink to help me speak."

The waitress returned and filled my cup and left.

Patty took a deep breath. "When that three-piece suit left my office today, I was unbalanced. Frightened. This is not what I am used to. Sure, I can joke and make fun and talk to you about your business, but it felt a lot different sitting there in my office with that suit."

"Please, Patty—"

"Don't," she said, holding up a hand. "What bothered me was that I wished you were there. I've come

to depend on you, lean on you, consider you something more important than a friend. I can trust you
with my feelings. And there I was—this macho, young,
go-getting bitch attorney—sitting and squirming,
wishing to God that this god-damned private detective next door would come back.

"Not only were you not there, but you were off in
danger or cavorting with a client who happens to be
your high school sweetheart. Both things bother me."

"Patty," I said.

"I'm not finished," she said. She thought some more.
"We are pretty flippant about our relationship. I don't
want to be as flippant about it anymore."

I waited. Sipped my coffee. Thought about what
she had said.

"Some speech, eh?" she said. "Don't get worried. I
can see it in your eyes. I need you to know how I
feel. When you're ready, you respond."

"Okay."

"Make it damn soon." The dance room music changed.
Gershwin's "Someone to Watch Over Me" began. I
stood and took Patty's hand. We led one another to
the dance floor and joined about a dozen other couples
in some of that cheek-to-cheek stuff.

"Bop, sha-bop, sha-bob," I said into her right ear.

"Ding dong," she said into mine.

TWELVE

Lansing is not a big city, as cities go. Congress, in
its wisdom, decided that the capital cities of the five
states composing the Northwest Territory would be
in the geographical center of the state to make the
trip to the capital more equal for most citizens. That
didn't mean those capital cities would prosper and

grow because they were capitals.

Lansing is such a city. It is no Detroit or Chicago. Its airport is no Detroit Metro or Chicago O'Hare. But Lansing is the home of Oldsmobile as well as the seat of state government. In East Lansing, Michigan State University draws about 40,000 students, plus those who run the place. Lansing's airport had plenty of passengers, especially on a Friday night. I arrived about 9:30.

I had one advantage. I knew where the four white paging telephones were, due to some work five months earlier. We had a job then: Identify and track an incoming passenger. He fell for the paging gimmick. We staked out the telephones with two men. One watched three of the telephones and the other watched the fourth. The third made the call.

I parked next to the airport security car in the "official cars only" side lot and entered the building through the side door. I walked directly to the one lone white paging telephone that I would not be able to see from the other position near the front door. I cut the wire and wrapped the cord and receiver wires around the phone in a very official manner. I took it back to the car and locked it up.

No one gave me attention. If you act like you know what you are doing, people will assume you are who you pretend to be.

At the front of the terminal building I took a quick look at the parking lot. No blue Chevy in the first two rows. Too many Olds company cars.

Fifteen minutes to kill.

A jet arrived. It came out of some low clouds to the northwest, its landing lights piercing the haze before it. It swung and approached from the southwest. Once on the ground, it disappeared behind the terminal building, leaving me with a sense of disappointment.

The wind was shifting from the southwest to the northeast. I assumed that meant the weather would dry up for a few days. The wind contained some chilling gusts.

At a few minutes before 10:00 I stepped into one of the phone booths at the building's edge and called the airport. I asked the woman to page Samuel Pendergrass. She did. I waited. Pendergrass didn't answer.

"Try him one more time, please," I said.

She did and I left the phone dangling and hurried to the front of the terminal. I could see the three telephones from there. No one made a move toward any of them. No one gave the phones any attention.

Back at the booth I hung up and returned to the El Camino. Bernie Hackett sat in the right front seat and waved a duplicate of the automatic I recovered from him less than two hours previous.

"Shut the door, asshole," he said.

I did.

"You have a nice, consistent taste in guns."

"Shut up," Bernie said. He pronounced shut like "shat." "Hands on the steering wheel." He cocked the automatic's hammer with deliberate effort.

Bernie was thinking he would pat me down as I had done with him, but from the right front seat it was not going to be easy. He was thinking about it.

"Bernie, this is where you take my gun away from me."

"Shut up." He waved the automatic at me. "Take it out very slowly an' hand it to me."

I slowly moved my right hand toward the pistol. "You impress me, Bernie," I said. "I didn't figure you were smart enough to pull this off alone."

"Shut up," he said.

I handed him the pistol. He put it into the right pocket of his light jacket.

"How's the nose, Bern?"

"Don't try to piss me off, asshole," he said. "Drive to your office. Piss me off there."

"You probably say that to all the guys," I said.

Bernie mumbled something.

"Can I get the keys out of my pocket?"

"Slowly, asshole."

I got the keys, started the car, and backed out. Bernie sat quietly. I wondered if he knew where the office was. I assumed he did. I drove quietly and went the direct route. There didn't seem to be much to gain in taking another.

"You and Sam old friends?"

Bernie said nothing. I turned off Grand River Avenue.

"He suck you into this mess easily or you just work cheap?"

Bernie still said nothing. I picked a side street and hurried south on it, whizzing by parked cars close enough to open Bernie's eyes a little. Any closer and I would remove side mirrors.

"You a dog killer, Bernie?"

He glanced at the car we nearly hit.

I swung my right fist at his nose as hard as I could. It hit him somewhere at the bridge.

The automatic roared. My ears began to ring.

I braked hard.

I swung at Bernie again and his head hit the door post hard and snapped back.

I gave him one more shot and his head hit the window with a "thunck" and he leaned heavily into the corner.

The car stopped. The engine had died.

Bernie's automatic fell to the floor mat. I reached over and removed my revolver from his coat pocket and got the automatic from the floor.

I put the revolver into the shoulder holster and removed the clip from the automatic.

I ejected the round in the chamber. It flew across the front seat and fell on Bernie's chest.

I got out of the car.

We had skidded to a stop in the middle of a narrow residential street. No one seemed to be around, although the darkness could be crawling with people. A large, 1940s style brick apartment building stood to the right. Several smaller apartment buildings composed a quad on the left. Some windows were lighted, but no faces peered from them.

My ears remembered the blast. I could hear nothing.

I was not bleeding. I could stand. The car took the blow. The exit hole was just in front of the door.

"Damn," I said.

I hoped the god of private detectives would arrange a second chance. My first mistake had been in going to the airport. Nope. The first mistake was telling Bernie Hackett that I would page Samuel Pendergrass. My second was being so confident about my territory. My third was in underestimating Pendergrass. I was working on adding to the list when a small group of teenagers came up the dark street. It was apparent this was their street. I got back in the car and drove away.

I had to get rid of Bernie, but I could not open the door and drop him somewhere. I could not take him to a hospital. He would not be rooming with me. As I was thinking about it, I found a closed discount drug store with a big parking lot and slipped between two cars. I removed some rope from the back of the El Camino and tied Bernie up. I stuffed a rag into his mouth and tied another around his face so he could not remove the rag. I checked his pulse and breathing. They were normal. His bleeding had stopped and I dabbed some of it up with an oily rag. I was running low on rags.

I drove away.

I got to my office's neighborhood and cruised the side streets looking for luck. I found it. The blue Chevy was parked under a big oak tree in front of a dark house. Maybe I was getting another chance. Maybe he was dangling another trap before me. I parked in front of the Chevy and got out. Bernie was heavy. His feet dragged across a puddle and one of his shoes came off. I propped him against the car and opened the Chevy and deposited him behind the wheel. I put his legs and feet in. I put his shoe on the front seat beside him. Bernie looked like a man catching a nap, except for the rag in his mouth.

I drove two blocks and parked the El Camino next to an all-night convenience store. I thought about putting Bernie's automatic with the first one. Instead, I put the clip back in and jacked one round into the chamber. I eased the hammer down and stuck it into my belt. In the back I disarmed the M-1 and put it back into its case.

Then I walked to the office. Pendergrass had to be there, somewhere, waiting. No more mistakes, Mallory. No more assumptions about the opponent's clumsiness. No more hitting people tonight with the right fist. It was beginning to hurt, as was my right shoulder. Every time my fist hit Bernie my right shoulder wanted to give in the other direction. The arm was shaking a little from the effort. I bet Bernie felt worse.

My hearing was returning. I could almost hear the Peterbilt truck which nearly crushed me as I crossed the street. The horn blast came through clearly. So did the driver's remark.

I approached the office building from the rear, coming up the alley to the small parking area the landlord considered adequate. Two cars sat in the lot. I stopped, watched, and tried to listen. The two people in the nearest car were engaged in mutual fondling. I kept my distance and moved around a small residential garage, stumbled through a garden, and scaled a fence. I stood in the bushes near the corner of the parking lot. The cars were on the opposite side.

I squatted and waited. The luminous dial on my

watch indicated 11:10.

It would be stupid to go into the building. Same with going home to get a good night's sleep. It would be stupid to go through the front door where a light flooded the entry.

So, I squatted in the bushes and waited. I did not know what I waited for, but I knew where to wait. Pendergrass had to be waiting inside. I wondered if he was sitting in my chair, feet propped on my desk. Sipping my booze. Perhaps he was crouched behind the door.

He was there. That was Bernie's last instruction. Pendergrass would not know when I would come, but he assumed that someone would come. Time was my ally. Time would work on him like an Arizona breeze on bread.

I waited some more. I finally sat on the dirt and spread my legs before me.

The lovers left at midnight. Thirty minutes later the wind came up in cool, dry gusts. The bushes waved in the breeze and I realized that I was in blooming lilac bushes. An owl cried. About one in the morning a raccoon stumbled around the garage and tried unsuccessfully to open a garbage pail on the other side of the lot. He finally moved off to other hunting grounds.

At 1:30 there was a roar of a big engine about two blocks away followed by the screech of tires. A few seconds later a police siren came from even further away.

At about two in the morning a gun went off three times inside the office building. I was on my knees with my pistol in my hand in about two seconds. I stayed in the bushes. Within seconds Pendergrass bolted from the back door and zigged and zagged his way through the parking lot. He headed for the row of lilac bushes where I crouched. In fact, his last zag was straight at me.

I don't think he saw me. He was planting his left

foot to get a jump on the bushes when I began to stand. Perhaps it was my stiff legs. Perhaps it was a product of bad lighting and long shadows. Perhaps it was pure chance.

But Pendergrass' left forearm caught me squarely in the forehead and I bounced back toward the metal fence I knew was right behind my head.

THIRTEEN

I was in the backseat. There were four or five of us back there. It was night. The car screamed through curves. I leaned forward—prying myself free of the others—to talk over the situation with the driver when the dream shifted focus and was replaced by a pounding pain in my head and a strong light in my eyes.

"He's coming around," a man said.

I opened my eyes and closed them almost instantly, but I saw someone leaning down at me. His face was deep in shadow, and the light seemed far away. I tried my eyes again.

"Well, Mallory," a man said. "Well, well, well."

Familiar and friendly, but under the tone lurked a message telling me to be still. I thought about that.

"Maddox," I said.

Maddox said, "Cancel the ambulance."

"Okay, lieutenant," said a man up and behind me who then continued a conversation on a telephone. Maddox stood up. I tried to focus on him. It hurt. Maddox crossed the room and sat in a chair, the client chair in my office.

I leaned on my side, then faced Maddox, a physically small and apparently frail man. His legs were spread a little. He looked down at me with unamused regard. As I leaned, blood trickled from my eyebrow into my eye.

"Tell me about it," Maddox said.

I creeped into a sitting position. My head followed about three seconds later and arrived with a vengance. Maddox watched me for a long time. The officer speaking on my telephone hung up and turned to Maddox. Maddox held up one hand to silence the uniformed officer, who said nothing. Maddox never took his eyes off me.

"Tell me, Mallory."

"I got hit by a man I tried to stop in the parking lot," I said. "I had been looking for him. I didn't think he hit me this hard."

Maddox's crisp, finger-length trench coat seemed to cover him like a tent. He looked tired. His rapidly graying hair looked very gray from the floor and his eyes looked a little red.

"Man?" he said.

I thought about leaning to get up, but my head vetoed the move. "I have a case, and for a moment there I thought I had it wrapped up." I looked at my watch, which read 2:30.

Maddox stood up. "Officer Schelter," he said, "read Mallory his rights."

Officer Schelter flicked a card from an inner pocket and without looking at it read me my rights. They offered no comfort.

I looked up at Maddox. He looked down at me.

"You are a sorry son of a bitch," Maddox said. "You ever hear or meet a man by the name of Phillip Waymire?"

I thought about it. There was a Waymire who was a professor at Michigan State, but Phillip was not his name. I shook my head slowly and looked up at Maddox.

"Yes or no," he said.

"No," I said.

"Remember your rights," Maddox said.

"Jesus Christ, Maddox, who's Waymire?"

Maddox let out a long breath and turned away from me and seemed to study my bookcase. "Officer Schelter," he said. "Help Stuart Mallory to his feet."

Schelter was a big policeman. Come next fall he would return to the Detroit Lions defensive line. He took me by the armpits and brought me quickly to my feet. I swayed a little and he held me until I stopped bobbling. The pain in my head crawled to its feet and caught up with me in a few seconds and made me bobble some more.

Maddox walked around the two of us and kept his eyes on me. As I turned I discovered the source of the drama. A man in a three-piece suit was sprawled against the wall. He lay on his left side, his right arm stuck across his body at an odd angle. He gave the room a continual examination as if he was conducting an experiment and wished to miss nothing. He would miss nothing ever again. His chest was wet with his blood and his neck was half blown away. He had bled very little on my floor.

"Phillip Waymire," Maddox said.

I said nothing.

Maddox looked down at the body and then strolled into the hall and spoke to someone. Four men came in. They moved Waymire to a litter and then picked him up and poured him into a body bag and zipped him out of sight. They carried him out of my office, down the hall, and probably out of the building. There was nothing left but an outline of tape on the floor and a dark stain.

It was not a way I wanted to go.

Schelter moved me toward the chair Maddox had taken earlier.

"No," Maddox said. "Take him to Sparrow. Mallory is in custody pending a murder charge."

"This way," Schelter said.

I could have told him I knew the way out of my office, but I left it.

"Mallory," Maddox said as I was ushered through the door.

I looked back.

He stuck his thumb up.

I nodded.

Schelter half carried me down the hall, down the stairs, and through the front door. Three men stood outside next to two unmarked detective cars. Two black and whites were nosed into the curb. About thirty people loitered just outside the immediate police limits and watched the officer dump me into the back of a black and white. A heavy screen separated me and the front seat. There were no handles on the doors. Schelter got into the passenger side of the front seat and the officer who had been sitting in the car started it up.

The car bolted to the corner, then circled the block. We passed my El Camino. Two uniformed officers stood at the side of my car. One smoked a cigarette and waved at my escort officers. One waved back.

I felt around in my pockets. My wallet was gone. I still had my comb. The knife and small pistol were not in my boots. In fact, I had nothing of value.

We went down Grand River Avenue to Saginaw Street, then east to Pennsylvania Avenue to get to Sparrow Hospital's emergency room.

The emergency room was quiet. We were ushered into a little screen cubical where a doctor went over me from head to foot, checked blood pressure, looked in my eyes, and then had me strip to my shorts so he could check for abrasions and broken bones.

"Gunshot wound back here?" he said, touching my lower back.

I nodded.

"Somebody did a nice job on you."

"The gunman or the doctor?"

He never answered.

He finally centered his interest on my head. He

pushed and jabbed and said that I should keep an icepack on it for a bit and try not to rub gravel into it again. He let me put my clothes on and sent me down the hall for an X-ray. Schelter went with me. The other cop read a magazine.

When we got back, Maddox was talking with the doctor. Maddox took notes. Schelter spoke with Maddox and then the two officers escorted me back to the cruiser and took me to the police headquarters in City Hall. Across the street the state capitol building frowned at me through the darkness and trees, much like I would imagine the weight of the society would frown at me if I were guilty.

I frowned back.

Inside the men took me to the detectives' quarters and put me into what today is called the "conference room." Thirty years ago they called them interrogation rooms and used hoses. Now they use guilt. I sat in one of the chairs. Schelter asked me to remove my shirt, and then he and the other officer went outside with my shirt and shut the door.

The room smelled like cheap cigarettes and tired sweat. I sat in one of the chairs and hung an arm on the edge of the battered and dented gray metal desk. Another chair waited at the other side of the desk. The chairs and the desk. We waited together.

The door opened and Schelter came in and handed me a folded towel. It was cold, wet, and apparently full of ice. He also brought a pack of cigarettes.

"Thanks," I said.

"If you want, I can light it for you," Schelter said.

"I cannot be trusted with matches," I said.

He shrugged.

I waved it off. "I quit a few weeks ago."

"No matter," he said. "Maddox's money."

He picked up the cigarettes and went out. Then he returned.

"Are you the guy in that Connors kidnapping last

year?" he said.

I nodded.

"Thought so," Schelter said. "I was at the academy then and read about it. Talked about it in class. Heard you did a fine job."

"Thanks."

I put the icepack on my head and winced.

"I'll be right outside," he said.

"Okay."

Schelter stepped into the room a little further and said, "Did you do this?"

I shook my head.

"Okay," he said and went outside and shut the door.

I held the icepack on my head until my arm cramped. Maddox came in. He took off his crisp overcoat and folded it neatly over the chair. He walked back to the door and opened it up and left it that way. The sound of a typewriter in use floated in, along with squad room cigarette smoke. Maddox sat and ran a hand through his hair, leaned back, and looked at me. I looked at him.

Another detective came in and put a folder in front of Maddox and left. Maddox opened it and read through it quickly, scanning the four or five pages. Before he could finish the detective came back and placed a tape recorder on the desk. He left again.

"You want an attorney?" Maddox said without much interest.

I changed the ice pack's position.

"Let's see how it goes," I said. "I'd prefer just telling you about it without the tape recorder. Then we'll go from there. I'll take the polygraph, if you want."

"Thought you might," he said. "We just sent for him." He leaned back on his coat and waited.

I told him what had happened in the previous thirty-six hours. I called my client "Kathy," figuring he could get the rest. I did not tell him where I left her, so I did not give them Wiley either. I included Bernie Hackett

and Samuel Pendergrass and ended the story in the
parking lot when Pendergrass came out and ran into
me.

Maddox listened to the story without interruption.
He watched me all the time. He ran his fingers lightly
along the edges of the report in front of him as he
watched me. He let about two minutes of silence follow my story.

"Okay," he said, and looked at his file. "Here's some
of what we have. We got a call from a neighbor who
lives somewhere behind the building. Said he heard
shots, looked around outside from his window and
didn't see anything. Then called us. Waymire was
shot with a .38 caliber special registered to you. At
least we think so."

"Probably from my desk."

"Probably," Maddox said. "The fingerprints on the
gun are your prints. Right hand."

"Paraffin test will settle that."

"You'd better hope so."

He shoved across the desk a hand-drawn diagram
and some polaroid photographs. The scene included
an unconscious private detective next to his supposed
victim. I looked at them and moved them back to his
side of the desk.

Maddox got up and left the room. He did not shut
the door. I could see Schelter's foot protruding from
a chair just to the door's side. Maddox returned in
five minutes.

"Okay," he said. "We'll check on this Samuel Pendergrass thing. Get the sheriff out of bed and call
the feds in Indianapolis."

I said nothing.

"This is the list of things on you when you were
taken into custody," Maddox said. "You know the
procedure."

I looked over the list and Maddox handed me a
pen. The police had my two pistols and the knife,

my wallet, and everything else in my pockets. My
wallet had almost $400 in it, the list said. I signed it.

"You always armed like that?"

"Sometimes I carry a bazooka. This was a light duty
operation."

"You also didn't mention the blood stain on your
shirt," Maddox said.

"Bernie Hackett's nose bleed," I said.

Maddox leaned back and carefully examined the
wall behind me.

"It's like this," he said. "You'll have to repeat your
story in a reasonably crisp fashion for the tape recorder. I'll have someone give you a paraffin test in
a few minutes and as soon as we find our polygraph
man we'll put you on the box. Somewhere in there
we'll type up your statement and you can sign it. By
then we'll have the ballistics done, but I doubt that
will change the situation any. And, because it would
look bad if I continue to handle this investigation
because you and I have been known to share a drink
now and then, I'll have to turn it over to the captain.
We confirmed the bullet hole in that heap of yours—
you know, if you had reported that, Waymire would
still be alive—and we found the other forty-five in
the back of the truck. We'll check on the blood stain
too. Everything you have said so far has checked,
including the wrapped up and stolen white paging
telephone. But, Stuart Mallory, I think you'll be charged
with murder sometime this morning and there isn't
a damned thing I can do—or will do—to prevent it."

I said, "Who's Waymire?"

"We ought to leave something for the polygraph,"
he said.

I nodded.

Then he reached over and switched on the tape
recorder. I repeated my story. Maddox questioned
me off and on, sometimes in not so friendly a fash-

ion. The tape would not hurt me. Then I took a paraffin test which produced the first evidence in my favor. Although it was positive, it indicated there was no way I would have held a gun and received that display of powder. The polygraph went well, too. I believed the results and so did the examiner. Maddox, too.

I thought things were looking up when Maddox had me escorted back to the detective section and into his office. The sun rose over his shoulder and slanted hard into my eyes. The lieutenant looked tired. He needed a shave and about eight hours sleep.

"You look like shit," Maddox told me.

I adjusted my chair a little so that the sun did not hit my face.

"Don't do that," Maddox said. "I rearrange my furniture weekly just to get that effect."

"Who's Waymire?"

Maddox gave me a long stare and then selected a sheet of paper from a loose stack at the corner of his desk. It looked like a teletype sheet.

"Age 29, such and such address, Detroit," Maddox said. "A lawyer, worked for Howard Benson, another lawyer. Specialized in taxes. Divorced, one child. Says he handled a lot of cases for the syndicate. Benson is, among other things, a top lawyer for syndicate cases. Detroit PD."

Maddox put the sheet back into the pile, leaned back and looked at one of his fingers. "You certainly could be in a better position, Mallory. Hope no one I know gets seriously splattered when they find you."

"Am I under arrest?"

"We can hold you a bit longer," he said. "You know that."

I started to get up. Maddox's intercom buzzed and he picked it up. He listened for about a minute, thanked someone and hung up. He pointed at my chair and I sat down.

"Well, you're lucky," he said. "We aren't going to file on you yet. Probably got the prosecutor up a bit too early and he isn't awake enough yet to understand what the captain told him about you. They both figure you did it, but don't think we have the evidence. Yet. We're going to keep your hardware for a while. Check it out, admire it some."

"Am I going to have chocolate smudges on my pistol grips again?"

Maddox almost grinned. "I thought you were studying social problems in graduate school, not country and western lyrics," he said. "Anyway, you can have your car back after we finish going through it. Maybe we'll find a Stinger missile taped under the dash."

He got up to leave. "I'm going home now, Mallory. You go home too. Work on that damned master's degree you keep avoiding. Get out of this line of work before someone blows you away."

The police released me an hour later. The car inventory was complete. Whoever searched it found an adjustable wrench I lost, so the evening hadn't been a total loss.

The state capitol building did not seem to be as gloomy as it had when I arrived. It also did not frown down at me. I drove to Dawn Donuts on Michigan Avenue and armed myself with eight glazed and a large coffee. Across the street I filled the tank and bought a *Detroit Free Press*, and then drove out Grand River Avenue.

Time to go home and get some sleep.

It took only eight minutes to get home from where I abandoned Grand River. The yuppies can have their dwellings within the conglomerate. They can have neighbors so close they can hear them whisper on hot, humid nights. If that is their haven, then they don't know what they are missing in the country. I won't tell them. Basil and I got along nicely knowing that suburbia was not within shouting distance.

I put the El Camino between the house and the barn and got out and stretched. Being in a police station half the night can be bad for muscles and nerves. Especially nerves. I stretched and felt something pop in the back. I added that stretch to the long list of things I would regret.

As I began to work on the first doughnut I heard the little clunk of Basil's upstairs door. Basil is an outdoor cat, but he is no fool. He wants the best of both worlds. So, after discovering he would climb the tree on the house's north side, jump from a branch to the roof, and then follow the roof extension to the window, I put a little door in the screen so both worlds were available.

Basil trotted around the house and stood between the El Camino and the porch. He looked at the car and me and sat. Cats are like that. When they observe, they render all they see as substandard.

"Come here," I said.

Basil hopped up the steps and approached the swing. He mounted the swing in one easy move and took notice of the doughnuts. I gave him a piece.

Exhaustion was creeping into every muscle. I was in a poor mood trying to get into a better one with a mind loaded with doubt. I selected a second doughnut and removed a chunk. Basil's eyes widened. Then he got a whiff of the doughnut bag and his attention began to slip. I gave him a piece of my doughnut and moved the bag.

I pulled the top off the coffee cup and took a long swallow. It had cooled to about the right temperature. It would not keep me awake. It would bring me to a point where I could comfortably go to sleep.

"If only you could converse," I said.

Basil jumped from the swing and moved along the wall to the edge of the steps where he sat down and checked his territory from there.

FOURTEEN

The porch swing squeaked and snagged my attention. It usually squeaked as irregularly as the wind blew, but this squeak had a rhythm to it, a steady, forceful, predictable rhythm. I looked at my watch. Two o'clock.

A piece of oiled steel prodded my neck, and a hand touched my shoulder.

"Don't be alarmed, Mr. Mallory," a voice said. "I don't intend to harm you. My boss is downstairs and he would like to talk."

"Who's your boss?"

"Do you have a pistol or other weapon within reach? I couldn't find one, and I don't want to hurt you if you reach for one."

I leaned to get out of bed and the pistol went deeper into the spinal bones.

"Not until you tell me about weapons," said the voice behind the pistol.

"There's nothing in this room," I said. "The cops' collection grew enormously this morning."

"So we hear," he said. "You may get up and get dressed, slowly. Please, no heroic gestures."

I put on my battered work jeans and a safari shirt. I stood in front of the full-length mirror and admired the appearance and took off the shirt and put on a red cotton job with short sleeves and again admired the effect.

"That's enough," said the man who was standing near the room entrance, and he reached to grab my shoulder.

I accepted his reach and pulled his arm forward past my chest. The man lost his balance and stumbled toward the bed as I worked to trip him. His right hand, which held the pistol, went up and tried to

reach back to aim at me. I grasped the wrist and dug
my fingers into the flesh and with both hands peeled
the revolver from his hand. He hit the bed and bounced
up and to my left like a professional. His right foot
rose and slammed into my abdomen, sending me
gasping toward the room's entrance.

He came at me as if he used the bed as a spring-
board, but just before he reached the door I fell to
the floor and came up in his abdomen with my shoulder. He hit the door frame hard. I hit him harder
with my fist containing the pistol, and he folded and
sagged.

I went down the stairs in two bounds, and as I
rounded the corner at the kitchen, an arm caught me
at the neck and flipped me upside down. I hit the
floor hard enough to make the dishes rattle and found
myself in a position to take a close look at a pair of
expensive gray deck shoes. One foot held my armed
wrist to the floor. Another hand put a shotgun into
my left eye.

Within seconds the man from upstairs arrived too.

"That your gun or his?" Shotgun said.

"Mine," said the man who removed the pistol from
my hand and pointed it at the side of my head. "We
really didn't come here to hurt you," he said to me.

Shotgun said, "No more."

They pulled me slowly to my feet and kept two
weapons attached to my body. We moved in unison
to the front door.

Outside sat a man in two pieces of an expensive
gray three-piece suit. The jacket was folded neatly
over the swing backrest and his tie was loose at the
neck. He swung gently in the swing and looked past
a light blue Cadillac to the cornfield. I knew who he
must be.

We slowly negotiated the doorway. The screen swung
shut noisely behind us.

"Your cat is a little standoffish," Benson said.

The three of us stood in the afternoon breeze. The two weapons held me in place.

"I'm Howard Benson. I assume you've heard of me. Certainly you've heard of me in the past few hours, Mr. Mallory. I take it by the nature of your arrival that you did not come down willingly."

The second man said, "He's not armed, Howard, but he's quick. You want him tied up or hobbled?"

"Well?" Benson said. "All I want to do is talk. It's up to you, Mallory."

"Tell your meathooks to back off," I said.

"Agree to settle down."

I shook my head as well as I could with a pistol in my ear. "Give me some room, or you will have wasted the effort."

Benson looked at Shotgun and nodded. They slowly backed away and I straightened up.

"It has been a long night for all of us," Benson said, and he got off the swing.

"You've figured out that I didn't kill him," I said.

Benson stood in the shade and looked at me. "If I thought you did, I wouldn't be here. I'm here because we have a mutual problem."

"Pendergrass."

"And since I could not find you yesterday when I was looking for you, I had Phillip go to your office and wait for you. He didn't want to go, but someone had to. He was a pleasant, patient man, not the sort to be riled by anyone, and I think your story is accurate and I have so told the police detectives this morning."

"You didn't come here to tell me that."

"Yes, actually I did, because I want you to know what kind of man Phillip was. What kind of man died in your office with your gun which carries your fingerprints. Phillip was a good man. He was our research man, good at contacting people. He worked quickly. His report on you indicated you are a reasonably competent private dick, as those sorts go. You are respected, although unknown. You don't work much, but you could. You are too selective and spend too much time working on a master's degree. As a pilot, you earned a bronze star in the military doing something, and refused to accept it. You are an interesting fellow, Mallory. Knowledgeable, independent, credible, experienced, broke. A loner. And, you'd be warming an interrogation room chair right now if I hadn't made some phone calls."

"Do I owe you a favor, or the pick of my large cat's eye marbles?"

"Don't be flippant, Mallory."

"Maybe I should wag my tail and pant."

Benson sucked his cheeks. Shotgun vanished behind me. I couldn't see him. The other man shuffled his feet on the porch.

"Tell Shotgun to get back where I can see him," I said.

Benson sighed. "You forget who's in charge of this conversation," he said. "You're in no position to worry about where Frank is."

I swung around and hit the shotgun with my left leg. It bounced against the screen door and tore half of it out of the frame. The man who rousted me from bed was slow and began to swing the pistol from his side toward my stomach but it was too late. I kicked him hard in the chest and he went off the porch into the bushes. The pistol bounced off the edge and into the bushes too.

Shotgun was a big man dressed for an afternoon of golf, and his well-tanned left forearm reached out to get a grip on my shoulder and I swung up below it and sent it high. My hands came down toward his nose but he saw it coming and broke my power with his right arm as he stepped away from me.

"Stop it," Benson said.

I slowly picked up the shotgun and pumped the

shells out the side. They rolled around the porch in wide arches. I tossed it into the bushes.

Benson hadn't moved an inch.

"There must be another man here," I said, and I looked around. "You're an awfully calm man, considering." Basil was sitting in the yard looking at the barn door.

"Come on out," Benson said.

The barn door cracked, then opened wide enough for a man to slip through. He was dressed in a light summer sport jacket and slacks and carried either an AR-15 or M-16 with a scope. He went to the back of their big Cadillac and waited. All I could see of him was his head. Just looking at him made me a little short of breath. How close had I come.

"I'm glad you were sure of my innocence," I said.

"You had nothing to do with it," Benson said. "Understand a few things, Mallory. Yesterday I wanted the records that your client has and will soon give to the federal autorities, and I wanted to talk to Pendergrass. Today I want Pendergrass."

"You have more resources than I do."

"They are not being wasted," Benson said, picking up his jacket and folding it over his arm. "But odds are good that Pendergrass will find you first. He already has. You deliver him to me, and you'll be paid. If it works any other way, you lose, Pendergrass loses, and the woman loses."

"I don't want your money."

Benson started to leave the porch. "You don't have to take the money, but you'll do the rest." He walked down the steps. "And I think you're able enough."

Benson was off the porch and walking to the car. Shotgun pointed at the bushes and the other man picked up the shotgun shells, then reached into the bushes to get the shotgun and the pistol. Shotgun removed a card from his pocket between his first two fingers, and he came over and stuck it into my shirt pocket.

"'Round the clock service," he said, and he left the porch too.

Benson got in the back and the two gunmen who were on the porch got in the front seat. Only then did the rifleman get in the back with Benson. They backed all the way to the road and pulled away.

The card had only a Detroit telephone number.

FIFTEEN

I made coffee and breakfast. I lifted off part of the kitchen counter I intended to fix someday and took out a forty-five automatic a cop guaranteed untraceable. I stuck it into my belt and checked inside the barn. Everything was still there, and there didn't seem to be anything new.

Then I went through the house. The old farm house is no fortress, but it is difficult to approach in the daylight. There are seventy-five yards of open lawn between the house and the road. There was a field full of knee-high corn to the south. The barn sat in the rear and behind that was 200 yards of tall grass. Same grass grew to the north. Good for sneaking around at night, but not thick enough for day.

No one was in the house.

I went back to the barn to get the only piece of equipment which worked. It came with the old house. The John Deere lawn tractor with two rotary blades fired up and I left the barn and mowed a strip on the north side, then angled back and did one on the south. If Sam Pendergrass waited nearby for a chance to sneak to the house, he would have to guess where I would mow next.

I mowed some strips along the front, the north

side, then back to the barn and around the barn, and
so on. A passerby would think me nuts, but Pendergrass would understand my pattern. I hoped he squatted in the ants and fleas and knew I knew he was
there.

It was not paranoia that made me think Pendergrass might come to the house. Over breakfast I considered the man's options. Pendergrass could quit the
chase, pack his bags, and leave the country. But he
was in too deep. Second, he could wait to see what
happened. He didn't have time for that. Time was
no longer his ally, and his enemies grew in number.

He could continue to pursue what he came to get,
and he had to come through me to get her. That was
the only Pendergrass option which I had to plan for,
and I had to assume he was out there somewhere
figuring a way to get me alone with a couple of hours
to chat.

I completed the lawn in front and north side of the
house, so I moved to the wide area to the south and
near the barn. I made a wide swipe next to a small
flower garden Patty planted about two weeks ago
and decided to water the flowers after I mowed. Some
commitments need to be nurtured.

I backed the John Deere tractor into the barn and
watered the flowers and went inside and poured a
Bud. I collected the Pendergrass papers and adjourned
to to an easy chair on the porch. I was reading the
Pendergrass records when a new Dodge Aries four-
door with thin white-wall stripes pulled in behind
the El Camino. Basil took up a position along the
cornfield.

Two men got out. One was Frank Wright, an FBI
agent from the Lansing substation office and no rela-
tion to the architect. As they came up the porch steps,
I put the Pendergrass papers into the thick envelope
and put that on the wire table.

"Stuart, this is Agent McWilliams of the Indianapolis office," Wright said. McWilliams flashed his identification folder. I lifted it from his hand and looked it over, then returned it. McWilliams frowned and looked at Wright. Wright peeked through the porch windows and around the yard. McWilliams sat down and pulled out a notebook.

"We're alone, Frank," I said.

"Sure," Frank said. "Mind if I look around?" He pointed inside my house.

I looked at McWilliams. "This chat going to be that serious?"

McWilliams took off his jacket. "Depends. I hope I haven't come a long way for nothing."

"I don't mind if you've come a long way for nothing. I mind if you snoop around my house."

"Anything to hide?" McWilliams said.

"We all have something to hide."

Wright hesitated at the door looking at the freshy torn screen, then went inside. Seemed I would not want for company as long as Kathy was my client.

"I'm getting a little tired of not being trusted," I said.

"So am I," McWilliams said.

"Stop working for Uncle Sam," I said.

Wright came outside and nodded to McWilliams.

"Can we get on with this?" I said. "You didn't come here to show me your new car."

Wright sighed and sat on the railing a few feet away and appeared to watch someone working in a cornfield a mile away. "Agent McWilliams figures maybe he can get something from you before the Lansing PD puts you away for murder."

I looked at McWilliams. He looked sturdy. Dark blue suit, silk tie, square jaw, and a little gray at the temples. He removed a gold-plated pen from his pocket and lifted a notebook. Then he looked at me.

"We want Pendergrass," he said.

"Seems to be popular."

"We want his testimony," he said. "If his testimony will be what we think it'll be, we're prepared to offer him immunity from prosecution on related charges to get it."

"How wonderful for him," I said. "Nice to have the FBI around to take the wrinkles out of your suit after you've roughed up some barowners, beat up a woman, tossed tear gas into her home, and shot a Detroit lawyer two or three times. Don't you feel squeamish taking a law enforcement paycheck?"

Wright walked to the end of the porch to near the steps and turned his back to us. He put his hands on his hips and looked at his feet and began to step from the porch.

"Those charges are not substantiated," McWilliams said. "When proven, he'll face them. The states will take care of that."

"Bullshit," I said. An airplane flew over and banked to the southeast.

"The way we see it," McWilliams said, "Pendergrass is getting pressure from the syndicate to eliminate the evidence against him. If he doesn't, he'll get the axe."

"That evidence is my client," I said. "When you say 'eliminate,' you mean kill. If Katherine Whitman is killed, then Pendergrass is off the hook with you anyway, government witness or not. Right?"

"Pendergrass is not that stupid." McWilliams stood up and walked a small circle and put his hands into his back pockets.

"You must know him well to be such a judge of his intelligence."

"We do offer him a way out of this mess," he said. "Once he's a federal witness, we shall do our best for him with the state charges. We hope you'll tell him that when— "

"Jesus Christ," I said. "Let me make sure I have this straight. Pendergrass has this business seeded by the mob which skims money off bar paraphernalia and gouges a few tavern owners. A few scream about the terrible spot they are in, and for their trouble someone breaks their bones and trashes their establishments. One of Pendergrass' employees decides to get out, copies his records, and leaves. Pendergrass kills her dog and threatens her life. You turn your back like Frank there. Then Pendergrass drives to Michigan and tosses some tear gas into her home. He chases her halfway across the state and while waiting for the private investigator she hired he puts three holes into a lawyer who happens to be in the PI's office."

McWilliams rolled his eyes.

"Then, the emissary from Indianapolis drops in and says the federal government is ready to forgive, that all is well, as long as he testifies about the seeding."

"Hearsay," McWilliams said. "Won't amount to much in court, if anything. You're able to protect your client, aren't you, hotshot?"

I walked off the porch and found Wright poking his foot into a gopher hole.

"You can come back," I said. "Everything you weren't to witness has been said."

Wright came back.

McWilliams stepped off the porch behind me.

"Cooperate with us, Mallory," McWilliams said. "If you bring Pendergrass to us, we'll help you, too."

Wright glanced at McWilliams and said, "Finished?"

"Depends on your friend here," McWilliams said and went to the car and got in the passenger side. He left the door open. Probably already getting warm under the sun.

Wright looked at me for a moment. "Later, Mallory," he said and he got into the car. I went back to the porch and sipped the Bud and looked at the envelope containing the records.

The two agents sat in the car and talked for a min-

ute. Basil came out of the corn and slinked over to
the barn. He sat there in the shadow of a bush and
watched something in the air. Wright got out of the
car and slowly mounted the steps and stood next to
the railing overlooking the yard. He would not look
at me.

"I told him it wouldn't do any good," Wright said.
"But he wants me to come up here and tell you that
this is the best deal for everyone. The feds get their
case, Pendergrass lives, your client goes free, you don't
get arrested. Says if you don't cooperate, he'll make
it rough on you."

I made a show of finishing the beer, then said, "You
know, even though I know different, I keep wanting
to believe in the system. Then someone like McWilliams steps up and reminds me."

"So, what'll I tell him?"

I blew air into my cheeks. "Tell him you were right
not to bother. Tell him to stick it. Tell him it seems
perfectly obvious to most people that Pendergrass isn't
likely to do as I suggest. But make sure you tell him
to stick it. I like that answer."

Wright nodded. "I just told him that I would tell
you. See you around, Mallory."

"Yeah."

The two agents talked in the car again, then Wright
backed it up and pulled out to the road.

I sipped at the almost empty Bud can.

SIXTEEN

I finished reading the papers shortly before sun-
down. Pendergrass had over three hundred and fifty
separate pieces of equipment in sixty or so bars. He
owed $120,000 to equipment wholesalers and about
the same to something called ZZX Enterprises in De-

troit. About a dozen bars were in serious debt to Pendergrass.

Pendergrass had side ventures. He had installed
"security equipment" in some of the bars, presumably with the owners' consent. The papers did not give
details about the security equipment, but another paper
inventoried devices ranging from wire tap equipment
to sophisticated burglar detectors.

Pendergrass also had what appeared to be a few
thugs on an occasional payroll. Bernie Hackett picked
up $200 a week now and then for "services," but
someone named "Parrish" received more money more
often. Both became major expenses in the later months
of the business.

I hoped Parrish had a full-time job in Indianapolis
and did not come to Lansing.

Vendtronics skimmed routinely and in an organized way. In a typical week, the machines alone would
bring Vendtronics about $18,000 in cash, mostly coins.
It was counted to the penny. Pendergrass would de-
duct fifteen percent from the top so the actual books
showed a little over $15,000. The fifteen percent cut
was then divided equally between himself and the
syndicate.

Almost as routinely Pendergrass laundered money.
Each amount was carefully recorded and divided among
the banks and employees so that it would start drib-
bling onto the streets and into the banking system at
the same time. By the time the authorities discovered the money, everyone would seem to have some
of it and not know where it came from.

The papers gave me a break. Pendergrass had worked
into another sideline, predictable since he handled
lots of coins. He had three contacts through which
he sold rare coins and apparently other items, such
as jewelry, "art objects," and trinkets, perhaps objects containing rare metals, like gold and silver. Pendergrass fenced them through these outlets. He would

buy them from thieves and sell them in turn to the outlets who could get them to men in the business of returning the metals to the market in their purest and least traceable form.

Not many people dabble in this, but Pendergrass found about a dozen. All were out of town where he could dump items with less chance of the local police picking up the trail. First on his list was a Detroit jeweler. The second was a pawn shop owner in Louisville. The third an antique dealer somewhere in Missouri, probably outside St. Louis. The fourth a small time coin dealer in Lansing.

He was my break. Norman Childs was a numismatic with a history not so clean, and visiting Childs was better than sitting around waiting for Pendergrass to come through the door.

I kept some notes from the Pendergrass papers but I put the Pendergrass papers into the envelope and that into a plastic bag. That I put into the bottom of the kitchen garbage. I tossed the coffee grounds on top to authenticate it. Then I showered.

Childs had been in an old downtown office building before it was razed and replaced with a modern office building which now stood half empty and in Chapter Eleven. He moved to a side street behind a West Side chain discount store. It was not a heavy traffic location, but his people knew where to find him.

I drove south on Logan Street. I took my time. No one seemed to follow. It didn't matter whether anyone was following, but it is good to know.

On West Saginaw Street I turned west and headed briefly away from the city. No one made the same turn behind me. Within half a mile I left Saginaw and drove to the discount store and pulled up in front of Childs' shop. It seemed isolated and alone, much like the roadside store in the beginning of the movie *Them.*

The small car lot was empty.

I went inside. A bell rang. Childs stepped from around the partition and stopped and studied me. His age and experience were beginning to show. A man in his mid- 50s, Childs had hair that had turned almost pure white. Attached to the right lens of his bifocals was a thick loop lens. A pair of overalls and a dark red button up sweater barely confined his stomach. He needed a shave.

"Stuart Mallory," he said, exhaling a long time. He swung the loop lens to the side. "Just like clock work."

"I'm expected?"

"More or less," he said, going around me to the door. Childs locked the outside door with two deadbolts and switched the "open" sign hanging in the window to a "closed" sign. "But I won't tell anyone," Childs added.

He made his way back around me to behind the counter again. "I'm supposed to call someone if you show up," Childs was saying as he walked back into the inner shop. I followed. "You probably know who he is. He thinks you might show up."

"But you won't tell him."

Childs was in his back room, coins and books stacked, catalogued, and piled on wall shelves, stacked boxes, and on a long counter. "No, I won't tell him. Not from loyalty, God knows. Seems like a lot of trouble when I can just say you've never been here, if I'm ever asked."

I went to the back to make sure everything was locked, but Childs had no back door or window.

"Paranoid?" Childs asked.

Childs was seating himself presumably where he had been. He began to clean some silver coins. I pulled a chair from the corner and arranged it so I faced the door. On my left Childs worked on coins.

"Made an interesting splash in the paper today, Mallory," he said. "Nice photo. Not every day a PI gets on the front page. Nice to see you there like that. Suspect a lot of people enjoyed reading about you being in trouble."

Using a blackened rag, Childs worked on one coin trying to get tarnish out of the crevaces.

"Tell me about Sam Pendergrass," I said.

Childs grinned.

"How much you want to know? You want to know where I met him, how long we've been doing business, what sort of things we've sold back and forth?"

"He operates out of Indianapolis. He fences through you, especially lately. What things? Tell me about them."

Childs finished with the coin and moved to another. He laid the previous one on the counter. It landed with a reassuring clink.

Childs was grinning again.

"It's funny," he said. "When I told him that I knew you, he wanted to know about you, too. I told him to be armed."

"When?"

"This morning. Late this morning."

"Tell me about him."

"I expect you can guess some," Childs said. "He runs into an item now and then—like a coin or two— and needs to market them somewhere, out of town, across a state line. I can handle some. He hasn't brought me anything special lately, if you are looking for something special."

"He gave you $50,000 two months ago," I said.

"He did?"

Childs continued to polish the big silver coin. He finished and set it aside, got up, and picked out a metal box on one shelf. He put it on the counter and removed a gold coin from it. He removed the coin from a thin plastic case and carefully placed it in my hand.

"Careful," he said. "That's uncirculated. Worth $500 or $600 on a good day, give or take."

It was a nice, hefty coin. Looked expensive.

Childs was back at work on his silver coins. "Pendergrass bought about one hundred of those through me, for various prices," he was saying. "He likely bought more through other dealers. I could not get my hands on enough of them for his tastes."

"Why this coin?"

He finished cleaning one coin, slipped it into a small plastic case, and moved to another.

"Gold," he said. "And taxes. Those are Saint-Gaudens series coins. Double Eagles. American. The sale of some bullion material is reportable to the IRS. These are not. People who invest these days—especially those inclined to invest in metals in the first place—are turning more to these coins. Or coins like them."

"For a tax break?"

"There's that," he said. "There are other reasons. Their price will fluctuate, but it's always higher than bullion. These coins are a damned good investment, too. The Double Eagle's been made since 1849, the Saint-Gaudens only this century. Stopped making them in 1934."

The coin in my hand felt sweaty. It glittered like only gold can glitter. It creates itches where you can't scratch. I gave the coin back to Childs, and he put it into the box.

Childs still lectured on investments. "People are buying the Saints these days because of politics. The Krugerrand, the South African gold coin—more of a traditional investment—is no longer the popular item. This'll change. A smart investor should buy up Krugerrands today because people will forget about South Africa's racism. But, today some people are even trading their Krugerrands for Saints."

"Why buy the coins?"

Childs shrugged, but his heart was not in the shrug. "He had the money," Childs finally said, working on his coins. "He wanted something without a lot of government paperwork." Another shrug. "I told him about the Double Eagles." He stopped working. "It would be nice to have money like that, wouldn't it Mallory? Enough to invest, to collect, the amount of money you need to make a clean cut and start somewhere else.

"Neither of us will have that kind of money, hey Mallory?"

It was my turn to smile. "You said you were supposed to let him know if I showed up. Where do you reach him?"

Childs kept working without looking up. "Said he has a recorder on his telephone back in Indianapolis. He checks it from here. The number's out on the counter where I wrote it down."

I found a number with "Pendergrass" written next to it. I copied it.

"Did he say where he could be reached here?"

"Nope, but he's somewhere around. When he showed up here, you could still smell the shower on him. His hair wasn't quite dry yet. Smelled of Old Spice and bleached underwear."

"You actually smell things that well?"

Childs looked up.

"Sure," he said. "And you smell like a shower too. No Old Spice, though. Something cheaper."

"Had a long night."

"Bet you did," he said. "Let me be straight with you here. I don't give much of a damn about you, Mallory. You know that. I'm just telling you all this because, well, you'll be around later and I'll need to get along with you. Sam's a man going out of business. But, please, try to keep me out of this. I'm an old man."

Another coin went clink in the growing pile of plastic-enclosed coins.

"How much money has he invested in these coins?"

Childs thought about it. "I don't really know since

I did not sell all of them to him," he said. "But, I suspect anywhere from $200,000 to $300,000. Maybe more. He did it pretty secretly and regularly and during what had become regular visits up here. He always did it himself. No messengers."

"What would all that weigh?"

"Weigh?"

I nodded.

Childs looked around the room, then pointed to one box. "About what that weighs," he said.

I picked it up. I figured 50 pounds or so.

"The problem, Mallory, is that I suspect Pendergrass no longer has the coins."

"Sold them?"

Childs shrugged. "He acted a little short of money. I offered to buy a few coins back and he said that was not among his options." Childs seemed to chuckle to himself. "'Not among my options' is exactly what he said."

I put the chair back where I got it.

"Did he make these trips alone?"

Childs looked at me. "As far as I know, he was alone most of the time. Only once did he show up with someone, a woman. Beautiful woman, the sort of woman that makes you think about things. Said they were going to escape."

"Her name is Katherine Whitman," I said.

"Sounds right."

"When was that?"

"Thanksgiving weekend," he said. "Easy to remember. He paid me extra just to be here that weekend. I was going to get a headstart on a meeting in Pittsburgh."

"She seem to know about the coins?"

"Oh, yes. Took sort of a personal interest."

"See her since?"

"Just that once."

"No one else ever came with him?"

"Not that he brought in here," he said, putting his work aside. "You through with me yet?"

"I think so."

"I have to call my wife," he said. "She picks me up. Don't drive anymore."

He dialed and made no attempt to hide the number. He told his wife to get him in twenty minutes and hung up.

"I'll let you out," Childs said.

He waddled to the front door and unlatched the deadbolts and waited at the door's side. He said nothing.

"I owe you one," I said.

"Can't collect from a man in prison," he said.

"Not to worry."

"Can't collect from a dead man, either."

SEVENTEEN

The air outside the coin shop smelled of pine trees and drying fields, not coin polish and tedium. I headed downtown. I might visit the office. At least I would drive past and think about visiting.

People who invest in gold are losing faith in the economic system, the monetary system, the established economic order. So says Wall Street. There are other reasons. Pendergrass simply had created a retirement fund, with the syndicate being an unknowing investor.

Kathy fit that picture too. Now I knew why the line of people looking for her had grown so long and so silent.

I drove east on Saginaw Street. I took my time. I turned on the radio and sorted through three FM stations and settled on the Lansing semi-rock station featuring old and new. Neil Young was singing "Cowgirl in the Sand" in concert with Crosby, Stills and Nash.

Katherine Whitman was sort of there at the start. I was thirteen and she was about eleven when Kathy started to phone me to giggle for a while. She never gave me a hint, but I knew who she was. We both knew not to mention it when we saw each other. Sometimes I peddled past her house, although I was careful not to glance in her direction.

Three years later it was safe for us to know one another and to talk like normal people. But this, too, assumed some of the distance and privacy of the friendship's origins. We talked, laughed, and chatted, and a year or so later we began to spend some serious time together. We'd stroll along the Lake Michigan beach in the evenings of hot summer days and feel the cool sand on our feet and the warmth of the other's hand. We said very little. I would study the softness and shape of her neck which rose gently from her shoulder and disappeared under her chestnut hair, hair which waved in unison with the breeze. Her knees seemed almost miraculous the way they moved, turned, and twisted. And each time I began to think about her neck, her hair, and her knees, she would squeeze my hand and somehow shift much of her weight to our joined hands, leaning on me.

"You're a keeper," she would say. "You're a keeper."

Sometime that summer, or the next, after an evening's expanding knowledge of one another at the drive-in theater, we drove to the Lake Michigan sand dunes. I parked my '56 Chevy at the foot of the tallest dune. She reached into the backseat and removed the blanket that was always there, and we plowed slowly and silently through the sand to the summit. There, lying on our backs on the blanket, we counted that night's August display of shooting stars. At about the tenth star I leaned on my side and watched her hair move with each gentle gust of warm air.

It was not long after that she too leaned on her

side and studied me in the semi-darkness, and not long after that we seized one another, pushing our mouths so close that there was only one mouth. We clawed at what little clothing summer required and shoved it into a heap with our feet, and on the blanket atop the sand overlooking Lake Michigan under the intermittent gathering of the summer's meteors, we made love for the first time.

"You're a keeper," she whispered into the lean lake breeze.

It ended too soon. My father managed the local radio station, and just before my senior year in high school he became the general manager of a station eighty miles to the south. We moved. I often drove up, but I was losing touch. Her father suggested she see no more of me. Kathy blamed the crumbling relationship on me and suggested I not return.

If it was a test of my desire, I failed it. I never returned. She called me when I was in college twice, but never urged that we get together. After I graduated a friend told me she had moved to Arizona or Southern California with a guy named Jim and they had married and soon had children. She became a welcome but infrequent memory.

At Logan I turned north, then angled east again to my office. I switched off the radio. It was almost 10 when I parked out front. The landlord had not yet changed the front door lock. The publicity about the dead attorney would upset him. A man of action, Herbert Timinski certainly would want to talk with me about my lease, after he collected the rent.

I considered being careful about going to my office, but this was my office and this was the scene of a very recent murder. Pendergrass could hardly be stupid enough to be there the next night. Maybe.

With reckless abandon, I went up the stairs and headed down the hall to my office. I liked the idea of reckless abandon. "Reckless abandon," I said in

the dark, vacant hall. "Not calculated, careful abandon."

I knocked on my door. No one answered. It wasn't
locked.

That day's mail was on the floor just inside the
door, as was Saturday's *Lansing State Journal*. I carried the pile to the desk. The pine cleaner scent hung
in the air. I left the lights off. The street lamp offered
enough light for the desk. I sat down and unlocked
the desk and looked for the rum in the bottom drawer.
The drawer was empty, and I hoped this was not a
sign.

I dialed Patty's sister in Ann Arbor. The line was
busy.

I tapped my fingers on the desk. Sometimes it helped.

The phone rang. I answered it.

"Mallory?"

"Patty?"

"What're you doing down there?"

"Answering the phone."

Patty spoke with someone else to the side before
she came back on the line. Sounded like who it should
be, her sister in Ann Arbor.

"I heard the news," she said. "Serious stuff."

"Yeah." Even in the dark I could see the three-col-
umn, two-line headline on the *State Journal's* front
page on my desk. Story like that certainly had to make
the wire services. That meant even TV might get the
story. Golly.

"Want to talk?"

"We shouldn't."

"Bugged?"

"Could be," I said. "Can't chance it."

"You okay?"

"Yeah, I'm okay."

She waited. "You don't sound okay."

I said, "I didn't say I was fine. I said I was okay.
And I'm okay."

I could picture her thinking about that. I thought about that picture.

"Not much that can be said when you suspect the phone is bugged," she said.

"You probably say that to all the guys."

"No, just when I'm paying for the call."

"I'll try to call you from a safer phone. Don't know when. I think things are about to get a little busy here."

"Be careful. Remember Liberty Valance."

"Why?"

She sighed. "Because he's a badass son of a bitch."

We both listened to the static on the line. Ann Arbor seemed a long way away just then.

"I'll be careful," I said.

"Okay."

We hung up and I sat in the darkness again. I swung the chair around so I could oversee the street where the El Camino was parked and where routine neighborhood traffic moved in and out of the city.

I looked at the mail. There was nothing in it that could not wait a week. Maybe longer. The newspaper, though, was interesting. It was not the sort of news story I would tack on my office wall or in my yellow page ad. If I had one.

I opened one of two filing cabinets and removed an electronic bug detection device a friend had built for me in exchange for some work I did for him. I put it on the desk and pulled out the yard-long antenna, then snapped it on. The little lighted meter and I scrutinized one another in the dark.

Walking around the small office, I wiggled the antenna here and there, keeping an eye on the meter. I worked slowly. I paid particular attention to the telephone and the wires near it. The device gave me no reason to hurry or to think the office was bugged, but I thought the procedure prudent. After all, in the past twenty-four hours my office contained a mob lawyer, a man who used to sell and now installs se-

curity equipment, and an unknown number of policemen. Don't trust any of them. Besides, the equipment is too cheap today.

No transmitter excited the device. I turned it off,
collapsed the antenna, and locked it back into the
cabinet. I would have to show that cute little thing
to the guys in the lodge.

Then I got down on my hands and knees and followed the telephone line into the wall. Nothing seemed
attached. That didn't say much about the line in the
basement or at the pole, but I didn't have good luck
working outside my office building at night.

I sat in the dark a little longer.

Outside a little breeze began to stir some life into
the leaves. Sounded nice. I tapped my fingers on the
desk and wondered what to do next. I could drive
up to Hamlin and break into Kathy's cottage and find
the gold, but that could probably wait. Maybe it was
somewhere else. I could drive down to Ann Arbor
and have a late dinner with Patty and hope something occurred to me while I was gone. I could drive
to Matt's place and have a late night drink with Matt
and Kathy and talk about retirement funds.

Or I could try to find Pendergrass.

I placed on the desk the one page of notes I took
of Pendergrass' paperwork. It contained enough information to find the paper trail to Pendergrass, if
he was stupid enough to leave one.

A man short enough on cash to ask a coin dealer
for some money was also a man who would take a
chance on a credit card.

I reached for the phone.

EIGHTEEN

Dutch Warren was a bank card company "security
analyst." His work gave him quick access to bank

card computer records so he could follow the paper trail of someone who stole or misused a bank card. Dutch would then turn that record over to the authorities and, meanwhile, get the card off the street.

Dutch worked in a predictable way. Using the purchases a fleeing thief made, Dutch traced the thief from, say, the United Airlines ticket counter to a lounge in Miami International to a Miami restaurant to a Holiday Inn near the coast there. From there he would follow the paper trail to Freeport in the Bahamas to an Avis dealer.

When Dutch worked fast—which meant the thief thought the computerized paperwork would be slow— he could trace someone in a matter of hours and predict, based on previous performances in similar circumstances, that person's intended destination. People leave paper trails behind them like mudprints in the spring. To find them you must learn to recognize the signs, like an Indian following the trail.

Dutch's prime objective was to quickly get the thief and the card off the street, thus saving the banking system heavy losses. Dutch wasn't always trying to save bank money. Occasionally he pursued a trail of a man suspected of fleeing after a heavy crime, such as murder.

Dutch and I met on such a case. We were pursuing the same man, a guy suspected of a massive confidence fraud. I found him and gave Dutch not only the man but the credit. I did this because I wasn't supposed to be there. Dutch said then that he owed me one anyway.

So, even though it was late Saturday night, I called Dutch in Detroit. The phone rang twice before an answering service took my number, told me Dutch would be paged, and suggested I wait.

I waited. It was a good bet. I was counting on an American to be an American. We are a people of numbers—account numbers, social security numbers, license plate numbers, credit card numbers, telephone numbers. It is a difficult world for a man who wants to hide his trail to do so by not leaving a number somewhere in that path that will tell his stalker that he is hunting the right path.

I made a pot of coffee. Unless I stumbled into some luck, this would be a late night. I sorted through a few selected files in the desk and came up with two more security people that also matched the credit card numbers and companies I sifted from the Pendergrass papers.

I was sipping the first cup when the phone rang.

"The *Detroit News* said you were in jail," Dutch said.

"Tell me about it."

I told him.

"So, you're in a hurry to find Pendergrass."

"Yep."

"Tonight?"

"If possible."

Dutch paused. "Okay, give me the numbers."

I did.

"Got gas card numbers too?"

"You trace those?"

"We are all brothers in the world of credit."

I gave him the numbers. "I apologize for screwing up your Saturday night."

"No problem. Just watching TV with a gorgeous lady. I can still watch TV as I set the wheels in motion. They'll call back. I need your word, though."

"I didn't call you."

"Right."

"I have not spoken to you since last year. September was it?"

"Better. You realize, of course, that we won't be able to do much for you unless, by some chance, he happened to use one of the cards at a location on security minimum or a call-in?"

"How's that?"

"Well, some merchants have a reputation for being fairly loose on how they verify the cards. When they end up losing too much of our money, we make them call us for a clearance and get our okay for any purchase above, say, $35. We'll do that until their act straightens up or we see that they won't straighten the act. Some are so sloppy we make them call EVERY sale for a few days."

"In other words, if I'm lucky, he stopped at one of those places."

"You got it."

"Otherwise, nothing."

"Pretty much. You get the sales receipts sent by mail, maybe two or three days old at best."

"I'll take what I can get."

"Cheer up. Gas receipts come through faster. I'll get back. Sit tight."

I called both people I knew in the gasoline credit card security business. The first, a woman, was on vacation. The number for the second got me another answering service. The woman took my number. I tried to make it sound like life or death.

"It isn't always?" she said.

I walked around the office, even though I knew the activity was just nervousness. Pacing's better than smoking cigarettes. There is no substitute for smoking. You just know that not doing it is better than doing it. Walking around my office waiting for the return call seemed to help.

I peeked outside. Nothing. Eyes were there, though. Pendergrass could be there. An FBI agent had to be sipping coffee somewhere out there, maybe sitting in that early '80s windowless van half a block down the street, focusing on my window with infrared equipment. The agency would not pass up an opportunity to get what it needed from me by just following me around for a couple of days. Lansing police had to be represented on the street, too. Maybe they had a

man in the late model Dodge parked in the small
parking lot on the other side of the street.

Maybe that was the syndicate car. It looked too
new to be a taxpayers' purchase. Howard Benson would
not be secure in my hint of cooperation. He wanted
Pendergrass, and he knew that Pendergrass would
be watching. Maybe they were all watching each other
down there and only pretending to watch me.

I raised my hand to wave, then changed my mind.
A thought did occur to me, though, that might be
fruitful at some point. The roof might be helpful tonight. Maybe I could spot one of them from up there.

I filled the coffee cup the second time and walked
around more. I thought about the roof. I wondered
why I did not think of it last night. Maybe Pendergrass watched me from up there. Maybe his leap was
no coincidence.

The telephone rang. It was Dutch.

"Pendergrass used his Shell oil card at a call-in
yesterday," Dutch said. "Last night, as a matter of
fact, couple of hours short of about this time."

"Where?" I grabbed a pen.

"Bud's Shell, Charlotte, on U.S. 27," he said. "Seventeen gallons of full-service gasoline—premium—and
a quart of anti-freeze. $22.45. That's it. I'd like more
to give, but I don't have it. There's a source we'll
try, but don't get your hopes up. I'll get back to you
if anything turns up there."

"Thanks. This gives me something to work on."

"There's more," Dutch said. "The feds are looking
too."

"Someone call?"

"One of the sources thought I was the FBI calling
back to check our progress. I played along. The feds
will check everything. Probably already have."

"Thanks again."

"Good luck."

I put the phone back and listened to the silence in
the building. It was reassuring.

NINETEEN

I didn't wait for the other phone call. That source just might tell the feds, since I was an unknown to them.

I locked things up and left. In the hall I checked the door to the roof and found it unlocked. The door led to a steep, narrow set of stairs which in turn delivered me to the unlocked door to the roof.

The roof was flat with a three-foot facade on all sides. It was difficult to see the actual roof in contrast to the lighted buildings and trees nearby. Staying out of the lights from the street, I looked over the edge to the neighboring building. It would be difficult—although not impossible—to jump to the carpet shop roof next door. Pendergrass could have gone to the roof for a better view and stayed out of my sight in the process.

I went to the lobby.

Knowing I probably had an audience, I tried to look sharp, brisk, and business-like, as if I left a chamber of commerce economic development committee meeting. One never knows where the next client will come from. I went out the front.

I started up the El Camino and U-turned. It approached midnight. I went two blocks and stopped for a traffic light. Behind me the van turned into the street as if the driver was indifferent about where he intended to go and how quickly he would get there.

I was right about the van. Police have fallen in love with the benefits of conducting stakeouts in comfort.

Behind the van a shiny, large car U-turned.

The light changed and I headed downtown. Another car coming from the north slipped in behind me. The van followed that car. The shiny car pulled up the rear. The car behind me was part of the surveillance team, but I was not supposed to notice.

The van turned on a side street to dash to a paral-

lel street where the guy behind me would radio him
of my next move. They would change off from time
to time to fool me.

Lansing PD or the FBI. Put money on the FBI. It's
a matter of resources.

It says in the book under "surveillance by automo-
bile" that night hours change some rules. It is easier
for the subject to detect the surveillance because the
headlights of the followers draw so much attention.
The later the hour, the harder it is to follow the person because there's less traffic to hide in.

On the other hand, it is often difficult for the subject to see differences among several cars at night
because he must determine those differences based
on headlight glare in rearview mirrors. At night you
can probably follow closer, especially when there is
at least a little traffic. In some cases, you must be
closer.

The traffic increased when I turned east on Saginaw Street. If I maintained the pace, the van might
not catch up. The only good parallel was Oakland
Street, but the van had to be too far south now to
efficiently backtrack to either Saginaw or Oakland.
The most important thing when following someone
loosely is to know the territory. If you lose him, you
might be able to pick up the trail quickly.

That left two cars.

I gently moved to the right lane and flipped on the
right turn signal. The car behind me slid into the right
lane. The other car, the one following from a distance, gathered a little speed so as not to lose me
and moved into the right lane three cars back.

A parade.

I eased on the brakes and checked the traffic.

I moved quickly, swinging abruptly left. I jammed
the transmission in low and dashed across six lanes
in front of traffic going in both directions, turning
onto a residential street. The car directly behind me

skidded and then tried to turn left and follow me. It was blocked by traffic. The car three back tried to cross the lanes and was hit by a car behind it.

Then they were out of my sight. I accelerated, skidded at Oakland, then entered the traffic going west. A block later I turned north again. It was a long residential block and came out on Grand River Avenue. I took that one block and found another residential street going north and got on it.

Four homes up I parked in front of a Ryder rental truck and turned out the lights. I waited five minutes before I left.

TWENTY

A man not running from the mob, local cops, and the FBI might notice that his car needs a quart of antifreeze. A man running from the mob, local cops, and the FBI isn't likely to notice that his car needs a quart of antifreeze because there are just too many other things on his mind.

If a gasoline station attendant sold it, that means the engine was probably cold because a hot engine tends to "push" antifreeze back into the plastic coolant reservoir bottle. Hard to sell antifreeze when the bottle is full.

A cold engine meant Samuel Pendergrass drove only a short distance, if any, before he bought that gasoline. A man taking the kind of risks he has been taking while trying to find a woman—and desperate enough to kill a man during the search for that woman—does not worry about how much antifreeze his auto engine contains. No. This was the work of a diligent gasoline station attendant who noticed an empty coolant reservoir bottle and sold a quart of antifreeze. I would bet on it.

I drove to Charlotte to see if I could find out.

The possibility had supporting evidence. U.S. 27 nicks Charlotte on its way south and eventually turns into an interstate highway, a direct route to Indianapolis. It would be the obvious route between Lansing and Indianapolis.

I considered the possibilities. Maybe Pendergrass returned to Indianapolis for a few hours, collected some equipment and some help, then drove to Lansing to follow the trail to Stuart Mallory, owner of the vehicle at the Hamlin cottage. Perhaps he stayed in Michigan and sent for Bernie, meeting him in Charlotte. Maybe Bernie arrived in Charlotte first and waited for Pendergrass.

Maybe I was wrong. But I bet on being right. The Charlotte connection awaited the detective willing to find it.

I kept a pretty good vigil on my rearview mirror, something I was getting used to. As the book says, it is difficult at night to know for sure what is behind you since all you can see are headlights. But the traffic thinned as I left Lansing and there were times that no one was back there.

If someone suspected I was going to Charlotte, then he would be waiting for me there anyway.

Bud's Shell was closed. I parked between the full service and the self-service pumps, turned off the lights, and examined the road. This short section of road was the old U.S. 27. It went through Charlotte and became I-69. The new highway separated from the old less than a quarter mile east and angled to the southeast around the small town.

Further into town there were two motels, one on each side of the town. There were two more motels back in Lansing's direction. Both were on the north side of the highway. A restaurant stood across the street from the Shell station.

I decided to start at the motel nearest town and

move toward Lansing. The first proprietor was asleep. I woke him. He looked at his records and at Pendergrass' picture and shook his head.

At the second a part-time woman and her boyfriend had been watching television in the inner office. Her boyfriend munched popcorn in the background as she let me thumb through the registration cards. She said all the guests were in now except the two men registered in the end unit. But, she had not been on duty the previous night and could not identify the men. The motel owners would return in the morning, she said.

The card for that room listed one name, R. K. Jones, Detroit. There was no notation about a vehicle or vehicles. I wrote it all down.

I drove to the remaining two motels near the place where the old U.S. 27 met the expressway which circled Charlotte. The first one was a fancy new motel with swimming pool, bar, sauna, weight room, and a 24-hour restaurant. The deskman was very helpful. He asked me to come around the desk and into the office where he showed me the registration records.

I jotted down one room number registered to an Indiana couple, but it did not look promising.

The fourth establishment was closed. It was a small, eight-room motel which was in the process of going out of business. There were eight vehicles in front of eight little doors. There was not an Indiana or Michigan plate among them.

I bet on the empty room at the place where the boy munched popcorn and hustled the clerk.

I returned to the restaurant and ordered two large coffees and two BLTs on whole wheat toast. Then I parked back in the Shell station, this time between two cars awaiting repair. I had a perfect view of the end room at the motel about a hundred yards away. If anyone drove a car to the door, drove one away, or turned on the bathroom light, I would know it.

I opened a coffee and a sandwich. I turned on the radio low and listened to a Jackson rock station. It was better than the sound I had enjoyed the previous night while waiting for Sam Pendergrass outside my own office.

In about fifteen minutes the motel's sign went out. The "no vacancy" sign remained lighted. The office's interior lights went dark.

The second BLT was cold when I reached for it. The second coffee still harbored a little warmth. I munched the sandwich and drank the coffee and was finishing the sandwich when Bernie drove the dark blue Chevy into the motel and parked in front of the vacant end room.

I sat up and smiled.

Bernie got out of the car. He still had spring in his movements. He opened his trunk and sorted through it, closed it, and went into the room and shut the door.

The lights went on and stayed on.

Bernie was in there about ten minutes before he came out carrying one small suitcase and one long duffle bag. Neither appeared heavy. He put the baggage in the trunk, sorted through the contents, and stuffed a few small items into an inside pocket of his jacket. He closed the trunk and went back in.

I thought about what I should do. I had an ice pick in my glove compartment for such situations. The idea is to poke a hole in the man's taillight, extinguishing it. I could then quickly see the difference between that car and others on the road. I looked in the glove compartment, but it was not there. It was probably among the "weapons" the Lansing Police Department had in its property room.

Maybe I just lost it.

Bernie came out and stood for a moment beside the Chevy. He got a cigarette out of his shirt pocket and lighted it. As he stood reasonably still in the motel's yard light, I could see that he had a small bandage on his head and another on his face.

He got into the car and backed up. He pulled out of the motel and turned back to Lansing. I let him get to where the old U.S. 27 separated from the divided highway where he stopped. As he pulled on the highway, I pulled onto U.S. 27.

I kept the quarter mile distance and we drove like that all the way to Logan where Bernie exited. I hung back as much as I could. I played him loosely because he was all I had. I found him through the only recorded credit card purchase Pendergrass recently made in the area. He did not appear to be returning to the motel, the only place I could pick him up again. He was probably the only link to Pendergrass I would find for the next few days, unless Pendergrass bumped into me again, and I wanted to avoid that.

Bernie turned north on Logan. I followed and picked up some of the ground as we entered more dense territory. We stayed on Logan and then turned east, apparently using a back route to my office or a fairly direct route to my home.

By the time we got to Grand River Avenue Bernie had passed the more direct route to my office. The odds improved for my home. I gave him more room. He went east on Grand River just a few blocks, then turned north. I was about to give him more room when he jammed on his brakes and swung into a 7-Eleven Store, parking at the side away from the gas pumps. He went inside.

I swung into the adjoining side street, grabbed my flashlight and tire iron, and ran back to the store. I reached inside the blue Chevy and pulled the hood release. I opened the hood and flashed the light around on the inside of the wheel wells.

I was looking for the gasoline line and found a likely suspect on the passenger side. One end angled around the front, then to the engine block, and finally under the air cleaner. The other went toward the back of the car. I wacked the nearest metal clamp until it flattened. I slammed the hood and ran to the street again.

Sometimes it pays to know something about cars.

Bernie came out in a couple of minutes. He had a fresh cigarette in his mouth, a carton under his arm, and a small brown bag. He got into the Chevy and continued in the same direction.

I followed.

TWENTY-ONE

Bernie's Chevy began to balk as we approached the city limits. He pulled to the side and turned off his lights.

He would be trying to start it. I let the El Camino coast for a bit and pulled far to the side, then saw a two-track entrance into a patch of what was once a roadside park and turned in there. I drove it out of sight of the road, locked it, and broke into a trot.

I had two worries. If a car approached from behind, I would be silhouetted in its headlights. Bernie would see me. The other worry was Bernie getting out of his car. I kept my eyes on Bernie's door as I ran. I had the automatic in one hand and my tire iron in the other.

I could still hear the grind of the starter motor as I approached the car, which would cough momentarily and then run out of fuel and die. In a crouch I went to the right front of the car and waited. He would have to get out eventually.

The hood release popped and Bernie got out and went to the front. I waited until he unlatched the hood and began to lift it into position. I stood.

"Need some help?" I said, then swung the tire iron

hard into his stomach and slipped my foot behind
him as he stepped back. He went down on the shoulder's
gravel. I dropped on top of him and stuck the thirty-
eight into his right nostril and pulled the hammer
back.

"Move, and you'll never get up."

He did not move. I went through his pockets and
removed another pistol, two loaded clips, a silencer,
and a knife. He still had not moved. He was breathing comfortably. I probably hit him too hard.

I rolled him until I could get his jacket off and then
ripped his shirt into pieces. I stuffed his handkerchief into his mouth and tied that securely with a
piece of shirt. I pulled him up and dragged him behind the car and then got the keys out of the ignition
and opened the trunk. I removed Bernie's bags and
tossed them into the passenger seat. I dragged Bernie
to the car's trunk, then hoisted him to the trunk's
edge and rolled him until he fell in.

He was heavy and I was out of shape. His feet still
hung from the trunk. I bound them with the last piece
of shirt, stuffed them into the trunk, and closed it.

I leaned against the door as a car approached. I
inhaled a large gulp of air and let it out in a long
sigh, then casually shielded my face. Using the tire
iron I pried the bent metal clamp from its mooring,
then twisted it from the rubber tube. I closed the hood,
put on Bernie's jacket, and got into the car.

It turned over three reluctant times and started.
Bernie had left enough in the battery. It ran rough
for a few seconds, then smoothed out.

I U-turned and drove back to the El Camino and
went through Bernie's bags. One contained clothing
and personal items. I tossed it into the back seat. The
other was a small arsenal, containing another automatic, two tear gas grenades, a box of three-eighty
ammunition, and an M-16 with two loaded clips.

Maybe I had misjudged the situation when I unloaded my rifle. I put everything but one tear gas grenade and his fresh pack of cigarettes into the El Camino and drove to the farm.

I hoped it would work. While some things might seem out of place, the illusion should be convincing long enough. Bernie might have planned to conceal the car and walk to the house. He might get a signal from Pendergrass, who would be staked somewhere, as to whether I had returned. Maybe Bernie was to hide the car on my property, maybe the barn. And what would be the arrangement if they detected a cop or FBI agent staking out the house?

Maybe they didn't have a plan.

The grenade went into Bernie's jacket pocket. It was a bulky arrangement, but Bernie's jacket was a size or so too large for me. I used the gun butt to smash the interior light.

I lit up one of Bernie's cigarettes and drove into my driveway. There were no lights at the house, no warning reflections from a vehicle or other machinery. I would be operating blind, but within the charade I drove back to the barn, then turned left and parked on the other side of it as if I was trying to get it out of sight. I turned off the lights as I neared the barn. Bernie might have done that because the barn could hide the car from the road. Pendergrass might think Bernie used good judgment hiding the car.

I got out and shut the door and moved to the barn's side, staying in front of the car. I had my pistol in my hand. Hammer cocked. I listened. There was no sound. No cricket chirped in the fields. No bird called. The wind no longer rustled leaves. The only sound was the car's engine, ticking occasionally and unpredictably.

Then there were shoes walking on the lawn, shoes hitting blades of grass and making "swish" sounds. Pendergrass approached from the house's north side. He stopped short of the worn spot where I usually parked my car and listened to the night sounds. Armed with a long-barrel weapon and listening for prey, he looked like anything but the secretary of the local Rotary Club. He looked more like Chuck Norris.

I circled the car and walked toward Pendergrass. There were many reasons he would simply assume I was Bernie returning from the motel. At least I hoped so.

"Put out that damn cigarette," he said.

I flicked it into the night sky and he turned to watch it.

"No problem," I said, and I leaped in front of him and put my right foot between his stomach and chest. Hard. As he buckled his weapon fell to his feet. He began to fall backward, but he twisted so that he fell away from where I was coming down.

I hit the ground and swung to my right and caught my right boot in his left armpit. He went "oooof" and rolled away from me. I kicked at what looked like his pistol with my foot and flipped it into the lawn from the direction he came at me. It was a big pistol, perhaps with a silencer.

Pendergrass was quick. Already he rolled away from my reach. Just before I could get to him I saw the glitter of something bright in his hand. He lunged at me and cut a wide arch through the air. The knife's tip hit the barrel of my forty-five and knocked it spinning toward the house.

Before Pendergrass could come at me again, I stepped inside his reach, took his knife hand by the wrist, and kept pushing him back until we crashed into the barn wall. As we hit, I tried to put a knee between his legs, but he was already twisting, taking advantage of his superior height, slamming his left fist into my skull.

My sight went blank for a second or two, and I knew I couldn't take much of his fist on last night's injuries. I dropped to my knees and rolled back, rid-

ing him up and over me on the soles of my feet. He
hit the ground with a crunch and rolled away.

In the roll, the knife caught the back of my left
hand. In the semi-darkness I couldn't see how badly
I had been cut. Pendergrass was scrambling to his
feet and going after his pistol.

I went into the barn and climbed the ladder and
rolled into the loft in what I hoped was a silent ma-
neuver in the dark. I knew the inside of the barn,
and knew there was only one way in or out.

I waited and watched and listened to the quiet.
Pendergrass circled the barn, his shadow slipping
through consecutive spaces between the slats. Then
the car door clicked quietly. Twice. Checking for Bernie.
I moved to a position just above the door and let my
legs dangle over the edge. I laid the tear gas grenade
in straw next to me where I could find it in the dark.
I waited some more.

At my office, Pendergrass had proven himself good
at waiting, but time was again my ally. He just could
not depend on waiting for developments. Just as I
was considering that, Pendergrass flashed through the
barn door and jumped into the dark to the right. I
heard him hit something made of metal and roll away.

I pulled the pin on the grenade and tossed it behind the John Deere. I heard it hit something metalic
and bounce deeper into the barn. I swung down into
the door opening and fell to my feet. I rolled forward and out of the barn.

Pendergrass fired twice with a silenced weapon. I
heard at least one bullet hit the house. The barn door
swung shut behind me, trapping him.

I rolled to the barn wall and searched around for
something to hold. I found the handle of an old, rusty
spade used as a barn door prop and stood up. Pendergrass would not be long. He would recognize the
trap and flee before I could get organized.

He stumbled against the John Deere on his way

out. I got ready for the fast ball. As I swung foward,
the door slammed open and Pendergrass came charg-
ing from the barn, pistol well in front to feel his way
forward.

The shovel blade hit his chest with a "swack" and
Pendergrass went down, the pistol toppling into the
dirt. I went after the weapon, falling to my hands
and knees. When I got it, I swung behind me to find
Pendergrass stunned but trying to get to his feet.

I crawled over to him, picked up the shovel, and
hit him on the back of his neck. He didn't move again.

TWENTY-TWO

Tear gas hung in the air near the barn as I crawled
to my feet. It was strange, out of place, without connection to the darkened farm.

I staggered into the tool shed and got a roll of
mechanic's tape and returned to Pendergrass and wound
it around his ankles. As I taped his wrists behind his
back, I discovered I was bleeding heavily from the
back of my left hand where his knife dug a four-inch
trench through the flesh.

I taped Pendergrass—which included a patch across
his mouth—and dragged him toward the barn, but I
made it only half way. I sat in the dirt and looked at
him in the dirt and felt sick and near sleep. I could
drag him no further.

I began the trip to the house on hands and knees
and finally rose to my feet. I fished my keys from
my pocket and opened the door and I sat beside the
telephone and switched on a light and tried to remember where I had put Howard Benson's card. It
wasn't near the phone. My eyes were filled with driveway dirt and tear gas and I forgave them for not
finding the card. There also seemed to be blood seep-

ing into my right eye from somewhere above it.

I found the card in my wallet. I got my blood all over the wallet, card, and telephone. I dialed. It rang twice.

"Yes?" said a man.

"Mallory."

"Yes?"

"At my house," I said. "As soon as you can."

"Two hours," said the voice.

"Sooner," I said.

There was a pause.

"Problem?"

I looked at my blood on the phone cradle and on the card.

"I'm bleeding," I said, and hung up.

I went to the bathroom and rinsed out the wound. It looked worse under the light. It was beginning to smart. I found some gauze and tried to hold it on the wound, but it was awkward and the position made sure I couldn't do anything else. The arm was beginning to feel like a stuffed chair armrest, and the wrist throbbed, so I got one of those elastic belts you get with some pairs of pants and twisted it around my arm above the elbow. I pulled it tight until the blood stopped oozing from the wound and then noticed a trickle of blood coming from the top of my head. That explained why my head throbbed. It still had a hangover from last night.

In the mirror I looked like Harrison Ford in *Blade Runner* after he and Leon chatted about it being time to die.

I turned out the lights and went outside. Pendergrass was where I left him. I found his pistol where he had dropped it and I picked it up, and for two or three minutes I didn't know what to do with it. I just held onto it until I found my forty-five in the lawn. Then I jacked one round into the forty-five's chamber and tossed Pendergrass's cannon in the flowers.

Bernie began to stir and moan and kick the side of the Chevy's trunk. Pendergrass just looked dead. I didn't want to go ask him if he was dead. Might be the last question I asked anyone. But as a couple cars went by on the road I realized I couldn't leave him tied up in the driveway where people could see him, especially if the FBI came by to visit or the Lansing Police Department stopped to pick up the trail again.

It was time I eased the tourniquet on my left arm anyway. I grabbed a handful of Pendergrass's jacket at the shoulder and dragged him another twenty feet to the barn. With a final effort I dragged him through the door, his shoes bumping over the threshold. I propped him up near the ladder, frisked him for more weapons, and I sat in the straw and dust opposite Pendergrass and tightened the tourniquet.

In the thin light from the doorway, his face was barely a sketch, but I could see he was a handsome man, as Kathy had said. Rugged. He looked a bit older now and a little tired. He did not look defeated, even with his head slumped on his chest, which rose and fell as he breathed deeply. As my eyes adjusted to the darkened barn, I still could not see him well.

I began to get cold. Without working up a sweat getting the life beat from me, I was vulnerable to the night's chill. I tried not to think about how much blood I had lost and instead squirmed to wrap myself tigher in Bernie's jacket, then fell asleep.

I dreamed of researching an almost forgotten topic in the social science stacks at the Michigan State University library. Surrounded by 10-foot piles of books, I took notes for hours. I needed food and began to get cold. When I packed to leave, the power failed. I sat in the darkness and listened to people elsewhere among the stacks curse the dark as they walked into things.

I awoke to find Pendergrass squirming in the dirt trying to break the mechanic's tape on his ankles. I wondered how long the tape would last, or how long

I would last.

"If it breaks, I'll kill you," I said.

He stopped and rolled so he could face me. He began to twist his ankles again. "You had your chance to kill me," he said. The tape on his mouth had come off.

He worked at his wrists behind his back and kept them hidden from me.

"Surprised you're still alive," he said, flashing his eyes to my arm. "Not for long, though."

He was right. I could see the open wound on the back of the hand. It had formed a sealant from the barn dirt and straw. I eased the tourniquet and began to feel something in my arm again. It was pain and it made me straighten and twist a little. It made me realize how cold I was.

"You can still bargain with me," Pendergrass said. "It's worth a lot of money to take me to Katherine Whitman."

I said, "How much?"

"I'll pay you ten thousand," he said.

He had rolled so he could work at the tape on his wrists better. The tape had rolled upon itself, turning into a dirty, gummy rope which cut a long, smooth groove into Pendergrass's wrists as he twisted back and forth. His blood lubricated the twisting. He would remove the adhesive, I figured, but it would tear off his skin. Maybe he would bleed to death before I did.

The light was improving in the barn. Dawn was not far away.

"Not enough," I said.

There was a sound outside and for a moment we both stopped and listened. It was Bernie in the trunk. At least I wouldn't serve time for killing him. "That worthless bastard," Pendergrass said. "Wondered where you left him." He had worked his way toward the far wall where several garden tools hung. His twisting and turning had churned up the dust in the barn, putting a light haze in the air.

"Fifty thousand," he said.

Bernie began to kick something in the trunk and start a good racket.

"Dollars or Double Eagles?"

Pendergrass twisted to face me.

"She told you?"

I said nothing. I looked at my arm. I wasn't sure it was my arm. Not a good feeling. I tightened the elastic belt again.

"The bitch," he said. "Knowing her, I thought she'd just hide it from everybody."

The first thin rays of light pierced the far barn slats and sliced through the dust hovering in the air. It was an erie sight, the dust circling through the light and disappearing, and then reappearing in the light.

"Waiting for the cavalry?" he said.

"Waiting."

He laughed. "You're dying, Mallory," he said. "Just sitting there bleeding to death, your butt sitting in a pool of muddy blood, your face as white as my teeth. Lips turning gray. You stupid bastard." He laughed again.

I could see that he was leaning against the wall and working on his wrists. Events were in slow motion. It took a long time to see he was rubbing the tape on his wrists on the edge of a sharp hoe hanging from the wall. He would be free soon. Maybe he was already free.

I began to feel like a dead man. It all seemed inevitable and perhaps ironic, although just. I would be unable to stop it. I looked for my pistol beside me and couldn't find it. I looked on the other side and saw the muddy blood. Must have drained a little while sleeping. I reached into the jacket with my one good hand and felt around for something metalic. My one good hand was less than perfect. I found the pistol and hoped I wouldn't shoot myself taking it out.

"Tell me about Rome," I said.

"What?"

"Rome," I said. "What you did in Rome. With Kathy."

He was quiet for a while. I could hear him working on the hoe. I hoped it was duller than I remember it being.

"I should have guessed," he said. "One of Katherine's priors. You're still in love with her. You think you two will disappear in the sunset with my money."

"Rome," I said.

Pendergrass laughed. "We screwed one another's eyes out." He laughed again and I heard the tape give and break behind him. Soon he would be free.

Maybe. I carefully pulled the forty-five from inside the jacket. It was very heavy. It shook, dancing in the early light in front of me like a Christmas tree ornament. I swung toward Pendergrass in what I hoped was a graceful, controlled motion. I found the hammer with my thumb and pressed on it with my thumb. It barely moved.

Pendergrass worked at his ankles. He tried to pull the tape off, but like the tape on his wrists it had rolled into a rope. In his position he could not see where his hands worked. He hobbled closer to the wall and pulled the hoe down and worked at the ankle with the same edge that freed his wrists.

"I'll find her, Mallory," he said. "And when I do, I'll own her, just like I own you."

I got the hammer cocked. I could hear Bernie kicking up a new storm in the Chevy. I hoped he would not get out of the car. I couldn't kill two of them.

Pendergrass' legs flew apart as the tape cut through. One of them hit something metallic and he cursed me from the shadowy dust. Pendergrass stood and blocked the dawn light, placing my entire end of the barn in shadow. I raised the heavy automatic and pointed it somewhere near the center of his chest.

That's when we both heard a car door shut. Pendergrass dropped almost into a crouch and I found myself aiming at a blank spot of barn wall and squinting into the sun. Almost as suddenly he towered over me with the bloodied hoe in hand. He pushed me aside so he could look out the door. As he squinted through the near edge of the door, I used what strength I had left. I braced my feet against a beam to my right and hurtled myself at the back of his knees. Pendergrass folded like a lawn chair and fell through the door and into the morning light.

"There," said a man who sounded like Shotgun.

Pendergrass scrambled to his feet, pivoted toward the open barn. I had my pistol pointing roughly in his direction, hammer still cocked. He slammed the door shut and it bounced open again.

Still carrying the hoe, Pendergrass headed for the cornfield to the south.

"Hey," said another voice.

I crawled out of the barn and into the open. Pendergrass was running in hobbled fashion across the lawn to the field. A man came from nowhere in his path and pointed a shotgun at his chest. Pendergrass slid to a stop and swung the hoe in the air at the man with the shotgun, then turned toward the barn again.

"It's no use," said another man near the car, who walked to Pendergrass from the car. He was the man who had concealed himself in the barn with a rifle.

Pendergrass spun and looked back at me where I lay in the dirt. Our eyes met and I knew he had begun to see the trap, and knew that I baited it. I could see him sag slightly as the awful truth of his situation began to wash over him.

Then Pendergrass the warrior came at me. He ran full tilt. Grabbing the hoe handle as one grabs a baseball bat, he hoisted the bloodied weapon over his head. He howled one continuous cry as he charged me where I crawled in the dirt.

I held the automatic with my right hand and propped that hand over what was left of my left wrist, and as the shiny, crimson edge of the hoe descended, I fired twice. Both rounds hit him in the upper chest. The impacts were beginning to spin him slightly as he disappeared over my head. Pendergrass hit hard and noisily and did not move.

Shotgun came over and looked at Pendergrass, then he bent down on one knee beside me.

"Is he dead?"

"Let's goddamned hope so," Shotgun said, and examined my left wrist.

"His car," I said. "His buddy's in the trunk." Bernie kicked the car a couple of times as confirmation.

Shotgun looked over his shoulder and motioned to someone to go to the Chevy. Two men went over.

"Leave me," I said. "Take them. I'll be fine."

"Sure," he said, and motioned again.

"Really," I said.

"You look like a dead man," he said, and eased the big automatic from my right fist.

TWENTY-THREE

I got to Hamlin about sunset and I went to sleep in the bed I didn't get to sleep in three days earlier. No one from the VanJohnson family or anyone else stopped to talk. There were no deputies outside. The smell of tear gas was gone and Kathy wasn't there either.

Once in the night I got up and sat on the porch and listened to the lake winds and thought about what I'd done to Sam Pendergrass and wished I had someone like Matt Wiley to talk with about it. I woke up shortly after dawn smelling the Western Michigan moisture in the air coming through the screens. Today would be a hot one in Detroit and Chicago, but not in Hamlin.

I was still exercising restraint when I looked at the somewhat beaten and soiled man in the bathroom mirror and decided that, though he deserved less, I would reward him with a shower. I did and held my left arm as much out of the spray as I could. The splint-bandage Sparrow Hospital had given me got wet, but it dried as quickly.

The emergency room people were not as convinced as Shotgun that Stuart Mallory's wound was caused by a lawn tractor and that he lay bleeding in the garage most of the night waiting for help. They weren't pleased that he declined to spend a night there. Said he had work to do. They were so displeased that someone called the Lansing police. A Lansing homicide detective showed up at the farm moments after Shotgun drove away in his rental with a package with coffee grounds on it. The detective got the same explanation Shotgun offered at the hospital and he wrote it down, looked at the John Deere, and drove away.

I continued to exercise restraint when I donned clean, dry clothes and brewed coffee.

Then I sat in the living room and thought about the gold. I was feeling weak and didn't want to make my search any longer than necessary, so I thought about where to look. First, I would search the concealed tool closet. Then, I would check the kitchen cupboards. Perhaps later I would pop open her Celebrity's trunk with a pry bar. Maybe, I thought as I sat in the living room, it would be worth looking in the old army trunk I pushed against the tear gas grenade that night and which no longer served as a coffee table.

I stood to begin the search and decided to try the trunk. Kathy had moved it the day we left for no apparent reason. Gold would be a good reason.

The television sat on the table, perhaps to hold it down. There's probably some symbolism in there, and I decided to think about it later if it amounted to anything. I moved the portable television to the floor and the effort caused me to breath hard and my knees to wobble. Sparrow was right about my loss of blood.

Then I opened the trunk and discovered I wouldn't

need to look in her car or the cottage cupboards. I squatted on the floor and looked into the pile of coins and wondered.

The coins were in mixed containers. Some were enclosed in plastic, mounted on fancy cardboard. Most were in some kind of plastic. Some were in boxes and some just lay in the bottom of the trunk.

That's when I called Matt Wiley's number. It was time Katherine Whitman came home.

TWENTY-FOUR

Matt and Kathy came through the back door about two that afternoon. They arrived at the end of my five-hour nap which left me feeling better, but stiff and useless.

Matt came in far enough to check things out and set down two suitcases.

"Hi," he said.

Then Kathy came in.

"Hi," she said.

I said, "Hi."

"Stopped at the deli on the way and got lunch," Matt said. "I'm starved."

"Me too," Kathy said, smiling and looking at me.

"Won't take ten minutes," Matt said. "After I find the bathroom."

Matt disappeared.

"He brought a boat," Kathy said. "He intends to fish out on Hamlin while he's here. Matt doesn't want to waste a trip anywhere. Says he'll write it off on taxes."

"That's Matt," I said, working my way into a standing position.

"Your wrist," she said.

I looked down at the bandage. I had almost forgotten it. For a moment, anyway.

"We'll talk later," I said.

She said, "Are we safe here?"

"Later," I said, and went after the sounds of Matt working in the kitchen. I found him making three big sandwiches from cold cuts, cheese, lettuce, and a package of large kaiser rolls.

I leaned on the counter and faced into the room.

"Don't suppose you brought anything to drink," I said.

"Actually, that ice chest is full. Same one you brought." He glanced at my hand and went back to work. "I'll get the ice chest in a minute. You can help with some of the other stuff."

"How'd it go?"

"Actually, I should ask you first," Matt said. "You don't look well."

"I'm alive," I said.

Matt put the tops on the sandwiches and moved each to a plate and tossed some potato chips into a bowl, then looked at me. "Is Pendergrass?"

I looked at Matt and shook my head slowly.

"Tell me later," he said. "Work on some napkins and stuff while I get the chest."

I put a couple of napkins on each plate and stood around in the kitchen wondering what else to do. I peeked around the corner and the television set was still on top of the trunk just like I left it.

Matt opened the door and swung into the kitchen with the ice chest. "Sorry," he said. "Drank your beer, but we got some wine coolers. Kathy said they go nice with the sandwiches."

"And I was right," she said, grabbing the plates and leaving the room again.

Matt emptied the chest into the refrigerator and said, "She's a beautiful woman."

I nodded.

"Once she stopped pacing all the time, she seemed to enjoy herself," he said. "Thought you would call now and then, though. I told her not to wait."

"Glad it went well," I said.

"I'll leave as soon as we eat," he said. "I'll be just down the road where we stayed two years ago. Find me there."

"I will."

And we took the chips and drinks out to the porch where Kathy had three chairs around a wicker table. We could see Hamlin Lake and beyond it the Nordhouse Dunes to the northwest, despite the air thickened with moisture. It would rain again in a day or two.

My sandwich was gone before I realized how hungry I was. I shoveled in potato chips until I said I had better make another sandwich and get some chips. Matt and Kathy rattled on about the history of the region, although only one of them seemed to know much about it.

I made more coffee, then constructed the second sandwich like Matt did the first and returned with a second bag of chips. Finally I leaned into the cushioned wicker chair and finished off my third wine cooler. I was beginning to feel human, though weak.

Matt and Kathy had finished eating and each was trying not to look at my wrist or my color or the fact that I represented an untold story that apparently I would keep to myself for a while.

Matt finally explained that he dragged along a john boat and gear and intended to fish Hamlin Lake as long as the weather held.

I nodded.

Kathy looked at me and then at Hamlin Lake.

Then Matt left. We both followed him to his truck where I thanked him and Kathy gave him a friendly kiss. Matt saluted and backed his truck and boat into the street and pulled away.

Kathy and I went in and got the coffee pot and went to the same wicker chairs and sipped coffee and stared through the screens at the lake.

"You lied to me," I said.

"I had to," she said, turning from the lake. "You wouldn't have helped me if I told you everything."

I said, "You don't know me very well."

She got up and moved her chair very close to mine.

"It doesn't matter, Stuart," she said. "It really doesn't matter anymore. It's over and we have what we need. We can finally have a life together. We can have almost anything we want together. We can live here or we can sell this place and move somewhere else."

"No."

"Sure we can," she said, sitting on an exposed corner of my chair cushion. "We can do any of those things. What the hell do you think all this was for, anyway?"

I pushed her off the cushion so she had to stand.

I stood up too.

"There is no future for us together," I said. "The Kathy I remember isn't here. Not anymore. The Kathy I remember would not have sent me to kill a man she once loved."

"I *didn't*," she said, and she tried to coil against my chest.

I looked down at the top of her head, and I controlled an urge to put my hand on it. Instead, I took her shoulders and looked at those eyes.

"I loved you for a very long time, Kathy. I still do. Let's just keep all that somewhere inside us, and go our separate ways. I want to remember the Kathy I left in Hamlin years ago, the one full of heart, the one who loved me so much I would sweat thinking about it."

"I still love you."

I said nothing.

"Where's Sam?" she said.

"Out of your life," I said, and pulled a shiny coin from my pocket. I dropped the coin on top of the wicker table. It rang as it spun in a small circle on the painted wood. Kathy watched in growing horror.

"Oh my god," she said, turning toward the coin.

"What have you done?"

I let her go.

"I kept you safe because I've loved you," I said. "The money is now where it'll do some good. If you go looking for it, they'll kill you."

She picked up the coin and rubbed it between finger and thumb.

"You can start again with what's left," I said. "They owe you that much. For me, let me go back where you found me. It's the only way this can end, Kathy."

I kissed her on the forehead holding the back of her head, then walked through the living room and headed to the door. Behind me I could hear Kathy's footsteps on the living room's wood floor. Then I heard the television hit the floor with a solid sound.

TWENTY-FIVE

Far down the street from my office a city work crew dug a trench across the street. The roar of the jack hammer echoed up the street and into my office through the open window. It was an unpleasant sound, but I couldn't shut it out. The weather had taken a serious turn for the warm and the open window was my only ventilation. Gusts of heavy, hot air barged into the office. The landlord had announced that the air conditioning was "on the fritz" and would be two or three days in repair. A little typed memo slipped under my door also told me he would appreciate it if I found another office. He offered to forego this month's rent if I did so.

It was Tuesday my first day in the office since the trip to Hamlin. I had spent much of the previous day sleeping and thinking at the farmhouse. I ran some errands, bought a few groceries, and located some books at the university library.

Mostly, though, I slept.

I did not wonder who watched the house or how many of them were watching. I also did not wonder who probably followed me from the house to the library and back. Or to the office. I didn't care if my phone was tapped.

On my desk was a note Patty had left me that morning. It said one of her clients had run into some money and she would like to take me to lunch. She would call me, the note said. I doubted I would accomplish much by lunch, so I sat behind my desk and thumbed through the books. It was time to devote some serious hours to the thesis research and this was as good a time as any. Better than some.

That's when Shotgun came into my office and looked quickly at my four walls. He wore a summer weight sport jacket with tie and khaki pants. Almost business-like.

"He would like to talk with you downstairs in the car," he said, looking past and through me, as if I was incidental to this task. "Figures this room's bugged."

I put the books down and followed him down the stairs to the Oldsmobile idling at the curb. The man who had tried to disarm me was at the wheel. Howard Benson sat in the back seat in a crisp three-piece suit. Shotgun opened the curb side back door and I got in and he shut me inside with all that air conditioning.

"Interesting story in this morning's *Detroit Free Press*," Benson said. "Apparently some charity, some sort of home for the wayward—"

"Bowman Center."

"That's the place."

"Read about it."

Benson looked at the driver and said, "Take a five-minute walk." The driver got out and stood on the curb with Shotgun. They began to saunter down the street, probably to the doughnut shop. The heat would get to them soon.

"Amazing story," Benson said. "This Bowman Center, which until just a couple of days ago not only was dead broke but was in the middle of a very costly and significant lawsuit, suddenly got well over $200,000 in gold coins—a conservative estimate no doubt. All from some anonymous donor."

"And they say newspapers only print bad news."

"It was not good news for some," Benson said. "We all have bosses, and mine weren't pleased."

"Odd," I said. "I thought it was good news. Maybe your clients should be more careful whose hands they entrust money to."

"Almost my words."

"These are tough times," I said. "Times to be particularly careful about investments. This one went sour."

Benson cleared his throat and looked directly at me for the first time. "If there'd been more money involved, they'd have to kill you, and probably your client too. They probably would have killed you if you took it for yourself. But this Bowman Center? Ridiculous investment, but I'll find a way to give others credit for it."

"Bowman Center helps the people your other investments destroy," I said. "So don't try to work on my guilt. It's got an awful lot of other things weighing on it that come first."

The heat was beginning to sound better than the air conditioning, so I started to open the door.

"Not yet," Benson said. "Just so both of our stories have the same ring ... a blue rental car from Indianapolis was abandoned in Windsor recently and contained some documents stolen from my departed and former junior law partner. He had those documents the night he was in your office, as a matter of fact. I explained the nature of those documents to two Lansing police detectives a few minutes ago." Benson tapped the mobile phone for emphasis. "They figure the documents were stolen from him by the man who murdered him, probably the same man who rented the car."

"Maybe the police and FBI will stop following me," I said.

"Perhaps. Said they will issue a warrant for the man's arrest, but they have not been able to find him. Indianapolis police will look for him too."

I looked outside the car and saw Benson's men coming. Very short five minutes.

"No one will find him," Benson said. "Or the man with him."

Shotgun and his sidekick strolled toward the Olds. Probably hot in the doughnut shop too.

"Like Jimmy Hoffa?"

"Don't talk about Hoffa," Benson said.

I opened the door and put one foot out.

"One more thing," Benson said. "See that neither you or Miss Bonicelli suddenly get richer than a crusading lawyer or a hack detective ought to get."

I shut the door. Shotgun's sidekick walked to the street side and got in. Shotgun slowly passed me and watched me. Neither of us said anything until he got into the front seat.

"We'll do lunch sometime," I said.

He shut his door.

TWENTY-SIX

Patty called a few minutes before noon and told me to meet her at a ritzy steak and seafood restaurant on the West Side at a quarter to one. Jacket and tie, she said. That's why she probably gave me the extra hour. She knew I had to go home for the coat and tie.

I went home and slipped into my seersucker suit and I got to the restaurant early.

Patty was early too. She swung through the parking lot until she spotted my dusty El Camino, then pulled beside it.

In her long strides, she looked good in the three-piece taupe cotton suit as she headed toward the door where I stood in my suit.

"When I see you come up here like that I know what a lucky man I am," I said.

"You don't look bad yourself," Patty said, kissing me and putting an arm around me. "Except for the bandage, and perhaps the rings under your eyes."

"I don't know, I thought they went with the suit."

"The bandage does," Patty said. "Not the rings."

She guided me inside and the hostess took us directly to our table. We ordered drinks and steaks and coffee later and waited for the waitress to go away.

"So, tell me about the bandage," she said.

"First, tell me about this Bowman Center thing."

"Oh, that," she said. "Well, it's just like you read in the *State Journal*, I guess. It's one of the reasons you're eating today. They can actually pay me now."

"You were working free?"

"Sort of. It's hard to charge a man who's devoting his entire life to such a project. But I get paid now, and it looks like the money will actually solve most of his bigger problems. At least for now."

"Good."

The drinks arrived and we sipped them.

"So, what about the god-damned bandage," she said. "Or are we keeping secrets? If so, I'll find some handsome guy without a bandage." She looked around. "Maybe that guy over there who looks like a rich accountant."

Probably an FBI agent following me.

"I'll tell you, but I'll tell you later," I said. "Can I barbecue something for you this evening at the farm?"

"Ribs?"

"Perfect."

"You going to ply me with liquor?"

"Ribs aren't enough?"

"Yes, but the liquor would be nice."

"I thought my ribs were pretty enticing," I said. "I'm slipping."

"You going to tell me about you and Liberty Valance?"

"Really want to know?"

She leaned back and looked at me. "I thought about that after our last conversation. Yeah, I want to know. No secrets."

"Could be dangerous."

"Worse for you if you don't tell me."